Paige Toon

POCKET
BOOKS

LONDON · SYDNEY · NEW YORK · TORONTO

First published in Great Britain by Pocket Books UK, 2007
An imprint of Simon & Schuster UK Ltd
A CBS COMPANY

Copyright © Paige Toon, 2007

1 3 5 7 9 10 8 6 4 2

Simon & Schuster UK Ltd
Africa House
64-78 Kingsway
London WC2B 6AH

Simon & Schuster Australia
Sydney

www.simonsays.co.uk

A CIP catalogue record for this book
is available from the British Library

ISBN-13: 978-1-8473-9043-1
ISBN-10: 1-8473-9043-9

Typeset by M Rules
Printed and bound in Great Britain by
Cox & Wyman Ltd, Reading, Berks

For my gorgeous husband, Greg.

And for my dad Vern, my mum Jenny, my brother Kerrin, and my two best friends from childhood, Bridie and Naomi.
I still miss you all, every day.

Prologue

London to Singapore

Friday: Depart London Heathrow at 2105
Saturday: Arrive Singapore at 1750
Duration: 12 hrs 45 mins

'Ladies and gentlemen, would you please fasten your seat belts, stow away your tray tables and put your seats in the upright position. All electronic equipment must be turned off during take-off and landing, and mobile phones must be switched off until you're safely inside the terminal at Singapore International Airport, as this can interfere with the aircraft navigation systems . . .'

Oh, bugger it, I think I've left my phone on. Bollocks! It's in the overhead locker. I weigh up my options: ask the fat bloke next to me to move or cause a possible plane crash? Fat bloke? Plane crash? Better not risk it.

'Excuse me, please.'

He looks confused.

'I've left my phone on.'

Grunting unhappily, he nudges at his skinny wife to move.

1

Then, huffing and puffing, he hauls himself from his seat. Now all he has to do is edge sideways and we'll be home and free. Argh, this is taking forever! Wonder if he'd be quicker in an emergency? I'm starting to regret my decision to have a window seat.

Path cleared at last, I quickly locate my phone in my bag and see that a text message has come in. My finger hovers over the off button, but that tiny blinking envelope is far too inviting. Nope, I can't resist. Aah, it's from James.

> HI LUCY! JUST SHAGGED JAMES IN UR BED. THOUGHT U
> SHOULD KNOW. 4 TIMES THIS MONTH. NICE SHEETS! XXX

It doesn't compute. I don't understand. It's from James. What does he mean, just shagged James . . . Oh, no. My stomach feels like it's plummeted 10,000 feet but the plane hasn't even taken off yet.

An air hostess hovers in the aisle. 'Miss, would you take your seat, please? The aircraft is about to depart.'

I can't. My feet are frozen to the spot. I look at her in alarm, my grip tight on the phone.

'You need to turn that off.' Her tone is steely as she nods towards the phone's glowing screen.

'Please. I just have to make—'

She shakes her head, slowly, adamantly, and Fatso heaves a heavy sigh. I feel the weight of dozens of pairs of eyes staring at me as I stagger, stunned, into my seat. The whole row quakes and judders as my hefty neighbour manoeuvres himself back in beside me.

'Miss. Your phone.'

I glance up at the unsmiling air hostess, then back down to my mobile. The message screams out at me.

`HI LUCY! JUST SHAGGED JAMES IN UR BED.`

But I have no choice. With her beady eyes watching me like a hawk, my finger slowly presses down on the little red button. There's no nuclear explosion. No one dies. The light on the phone merely dims and my heart sinks.

James has cheated on me.

And the slag had the gall to text me from his mobile phone.

The plane is taxiing to the runway. Outside the window it's a cold and windy English winter night. I'm on my way to Australia for the wedding of my two best friends, Molly and Sam. And some summer sunshine . . .

But right now I don't know how I'll ever be warm again. I feel like someone has ripped out my intestines and replaced them with shards of ice.

My gorgeous sandy-haired boyfriend has been having sex with another girl.

The image of him in bed with someone else slams into my mind. Someone else running her fingers through his hair. Someone else gazing into his blue, blue eyes. Someone else writhing up against him, their bodies bathed in sweat . . .

I think I'm going to throw up. I rummage around the seat pocket in front of me and manage to find a sick bag. But the feeling passes and I force myself to take a couple of deep breaths. Oh, God, this is a thirteen-hour flight! I don't know how I'm going to cope.

The plane lurches forward and forces me backwards into my

seat as it zooms off down the runway. Suddenly we're in the air, and we're climbing, climbing, climbing, and leaving the lights of London far behind us. Then abruptly there's cloud and it all goes dark outside.

My mind whirrs into action. Who is she? Have they been seeing each other long? How many times have they slept together? Is she better in bed than me? Is she slimmer? Taller? Sexier? Does he love her? Oh, God. Oh, God. How could he do this to me?

Nausea rockets back through me and this time I really do throw up.

'Urgh.' Fatso flinches in disgust, while his anorexic wife peeps at me nervously from behind his great hulk of a frame.

Ding. *'Ladies and gentlemen, the captain has switched off the fasten seat belt sign and you are now free to move around the cabin . . .'*

'Excuse me.'

It's uncanny how much quicker my neighbour moves when the stench of vomit is filling the air. Sick bag in one hand, phone in the other, I edge out and begin to walk uphill to the toilet as the aircraft continues to climb. As soon as I'm inside, I lock the door and empty the revolting contents of the bag down the pan, before rinsing my mouth out with water. The diamond earrings that James bought me for my twenty-fifth birthday last October glint back at me in the mirror.

'Hey, baby . . . Lucy, wake up . . .'

'Urgh.'

'Happy birthday.' James smiles, kissing my forehead. I wrestle myself awake and look at him, deep blue eyes peering eagerly into mine.

'I'm so tired. What time is it?'

'Six thirty.'

'James, six thirty? I don't have to get up for another hour!'

'I know, but I have to go into work early. I wanted to give you this.'

He places a silver gift box on my stomach, on top of the downy duvet. Looking at his expectant face, it's impossible not to forgive him for the early morning wake-up call. I sit up in bed and smile at him.

'I hope you like them.'

Them? I lift off the lid to find a black velvet box. Nestling inside is a pair of diamond solitaire earrings.

Now I'm awake.

'James, these are beautiful! They must've cost a fortune!'

He flashes me a mischievous grin and takes the box, carefully lifting the earrings out.

'Will you put them on? I want to see what they look like.' He hands them to me, one by one, while I fasten them to my earlobes. Then he leans back and nods his approval.

'Stunning. They suit you.'

I climb out of bed excitedly and go to the wardrobe mirror, while James flicks the bedroom halogens on. The earrings immediately sparkle, white diamonds perfectly set off against my dark hair. They're heavy, but I love them so much I don't think I'll ever take them off.

'Thank you.' I turn back to him, tears welling up in my eyes. He holds his hand out to me and I crawl back under the covers and into his warm arms.

'Do you really have to go into work early?' I ask, as he starts to kiss my neck.

'Nah. Well, not this early.'

'*You little sod . . .*'

He grins and undresses me until the only thing I'm left wearing are the diamonds on my ears . . .

I switch my phone back on, needing to read that message again, whatever the consequences. I look at the time it came in: 9 p.m. I tried to call him on my way to the departure gate at Heathrow. He didn't answer. Now I know why. I crouch over the pan and throw up again.

Fatso is sitting in the aisle seat when I get back, and grumbles about me being up and down all night.

I ignore him, while his wife smiles at me apologetically. 'Are you alright, love?' she asks, as soon as I'm seated. The small act of kindness breaks me. I answer 'No' in a small voice, and the floodgates open.

It's the worst flight of my life. I can't eat, I can't sleep, I can't concentrate on any of the films. I take a sleeping pill and as I curl my legs up underneath the window, and in between terrible dreams and recurring pins and needles, I manage to doze off. Every time I wake up, stark reality hits me and I check the time on the digital flight chart to see how much longer I have to wait before we arrive in Singapore and I can call him.

Ten hours and fifty-one minutes . . .

Seven hours and thirteen minutes . . .

Four hours and twenty minutes . . .

It's agony. What if he doesn't answer? No, I can't think about that right now.

James and I met at a party in London three years ago, introduced by a friend of a friend. He was already working as a corporate lawyer, while I was barely out of university. I didn't even fancy him at first. Fairly tall at six foot, well built with shortish, sandy blond hair, he was still wearing his dark grey work suit with a white shirt unbuttoned at the top. He'd taken his tie off so he didn't look *too* City Boy. But his cheeky smile reeled me in. That and his blue, blue eyes.

On our first date he took me to the Oxo Tower, where we drank champagne looking down over the city of London and the boats on the Thames. We made love four days later in a flat that he shared in Clapham with a South African bloke named Alyn. Two months after that, I moved in and Alyn moved out. Some people thought we'd moved too quickly. I couldn't move quickly enough.

James paid the lion's share of the rent while I pulled warm pints in a pub most evenings and did work experience at Mandy Nim PR, a public relations firm which promotes everything from vodka to lipgloss. After eleven weeks – one week short of the time I'd given myself to find a 'proper job' – I was lucky enough to be in the right place at the right time and landed a junior position there. Now I work as a senior PR and my friends tell me I've got the best job: taking home all the freebies I could ever dream of.

Thinking about it now, even in those early days James would often arrive home later than I did after my shifts down the pub. Were all those late nights at the office really necessary? Surely he wasn't cheating on me back then . . .

No. No. It's not possible. I just don't get it. He would *never* cheat! Would he?

Oh, Christ, I don't understand. Maybe there's been some mistake with that text. Maybe his friends sent it! That could be it. Maybe he was down the pub and they grabbed his phone when he went to the Gents. That's possible, isn't it?

But in my heart of hearts I know that's simply not true.

Fatso is guffawing at some joke on the TV screen. His wife whimpers in her sleep. I wonder if she's getting a better night's kip sitting upright in a chair than she would at home in bed where the gravity of his body weight must pull her in. She looks fairly peaceful.

I stretch my legs out under the seat in front of me and flex my feet. I'd like to go for a walk up and down the aisle but I can't be bothered going through the rigmarole of getting out past Fatso again.

Oh, bugger him! I ease myself up and over his sleeping wife. 'Don't get up!' I whisper loudly as he looks at me in surprise. I tread carefully, toes nudging aside his flabby flesh that was spilling over onto the armrests. Finally I'm free.

I pace the aisles for a couple of minutes before starting to feel self-conscious. Eventually I go and lock myself in one of the toilets. I look tired, drawn. My eyes are red and puffy.

Oh, James . . . I love you. I don't want to lose you. This flight is taking forever. I've never gone so long without being able to use my phone. I sit down on the toilet seat and start to weep with frustration.

What am I going to do? The thought of moving all my stuff out of our flat . . .

Our lovely, lovely flat. We bought it last summer. It's in Marylebone, just off the High Street. It's only a small one-bedroom, but I adore it.

For a short, sharp moment, anger surges through me. No. *He* should move. Bastard! If he's been shagging around . . .

But my rage soon dissolves back into despair. Where would I go? Would he move in with her? I couldn't even afford the mortgage on my own. If I moved out, would she move in? What would I do with all my stuff? How would we divide our CDs? DVDs? Who would get the sofa? The TV? The bed? Oh, no, the bed. Please don't let me think about it.

There was a night back in January, when I woke up at two o'clock in the morning to see James at the foot of the bed taking off his suit trousers, seemingly trying not to fall over. He'd told me he was working late, but the stench of cigarette smoke and alcohol filled the air. I pretended to be asleep because I didn't want to talk to him when he was drunk. The next morning he denied he had a hangover, even though his face was practically grey. He insisted he'd had only two drinks after getting his work done. I don't know why he lied. It was obvious that he went out and got hammered. But sometimes it simply isn't worth arguing with him.

Just the other evening I was searching through the kitchen cupboards for my box of chocolate cherry liqueurs. I knew James hadn't eaten them because he doesn't like them, but I asked if he knew where they were, anyway.

'No,' he'd replied.

'I can't find them anywhere.'

'Oh, shit, that's right, I gave them away.'

'You what? Who to? There were hardly any left!'

'A tramp.'

'A tramp?' I asked in disbelief.

'Yeah.'

'Oh, please.' I shook my head.

'It's true! He was rummaging around the black bin bags on the pavement downstairs and making a right mess. I ran back up and grabbed the first thing I could find to get him to bugger off.'

'James, cut it out. Where have you put them? Stop winding me up.'

'Lucy, I'm not joking. Why would I lie?'

'I don't bloody know. Anyway why would you give liqueurs to a tramp? He might've already had a drinking problem and there's you encouraging it.'

'Yeah, it probably wasn't very smart, was it?' he relented. 'But I wasn't really thinking.'

What a load of bullshit. There is no way he gave away my chocolate cherries to a tramp. I bet the bitch he's been shagging scoffed them.

I get back to my seat feeling nauseous, and the smell of the greasy food on the trolley coming through the cabin doesn't help. I won't be eating anything. I don't think I'll ever be able to eat chocolate cherry liqueurs again, either.

Which is just brilliant.

Who the hell is this slag? Someone he works with? A memory suddenly comes back to me of James's office Christmas party a couple of months ago. He left me chatting to one of the firm's secretaries as he went to get us something to drink. Ten minutes later he still hadn't returned so I set off to find him. He was standing by the bar talking a little too intimately, I thought at the time, to a tall, slim brunette. Their body language was close, and I remember feeling a white stab of jealousy. But when he glanced up and saw me he didn't look guilty. 'Lucy, there you are! I was just talking to, er, Zoe here.'

Later, when I asked him about her, he told me he was embarrassed because he almost hadn't remembered her name. She was new, he said, and didn't have many friends. He thought she seemed nice, but she wasn't his type. I asked, of course. I always ask.

I feel a shift in the atmosphere and look at the digital flight chart: only twenty-five minutes to go. A wave of nerves soars through me, followed by a quick throb of nausea. Seconds later the captain makes the announcement about landing. I fasten my seat belt, stow away my tray table and put my seat in the upright position. As other passengers switch off their electronic equipment, I clutch my mobile phone tightly – Singapore International Airport terminal is only minutes away . . .

Singapore

Singapore International Airport
Stopover time: 2 hrs 10 mins
My phone is in my hand as I walk through the gate towards the airport terminal. I can see that it's busy up ahead so I do a U-turn and push back through the throng towards the emptying gate. Then I'm dialling his number and it's ringing, ringing, ringing . . .

Voicemail.

I don't believe this! I've waited thirteen bloody hours to make this call. It's just after ten in the morning in England – where the hell is he? I'm not sure I want to know. I press cancel and try again, but then the sickness in the pit of my stomach engulfs me and I slump down into a seat and bury my head in my hands.

'I wish I could come with you. I'm going to miss you so much,' he *murmurs into my hair as he holds me tight.*

'I wish you could come too.'

'No Aussie blokes are allowed within a foot of my beautiful girlfriend. I'm issuing them all with a restraining order!'

'As if, you nutter.'

'I love you, Lucy. Call me as soon as you get there. And call me tonight before you board the plane.'

'I will do. I love you too.'

He kisses me tenderly, then opens the door before pausing and looking down at my suitcase.

'Baby, how are you going to manage that? Are you sure you'll be alright?' he asks anxiously.

I tell him that I'd planned to go to work as usual in Soho, then come back here later this afternoon to collect my suitcase and catch a cab to Paddington. I'm taking the Express to the airport.

'I've got a better idea,' he says, coming back inside and closing the door. 'Why don't you catch a cab to work and take your suitcase with you, then taxi it to Paddington later? That way I can carry it down the stairs for you now.'

'Oh, James, it's too expensive. Honestly, I'll be fine.'

'No, it's not. I'll pay, don't worry about that. Come on, are you ready?'

I waver, as he looks at me with concern. I haven't tidied up the flat after my panic packing but I don't suppose that matters.

'Well . . . okay.' I smile at him gratefully. 'Thank you.'

His face lights up as he takes my suitcase and leads me down the stairs.

I press redial.

'Hello?'

'James!'

'Lucy! Hey, where are you?' he asks me warmly.

'Where were you? I've been trying to call!'

'I was in the shower.' He sounds confused at the angst in my voice.

'With her?'

'Sorry?'

Suddenly rage swells up inside me.

'Were you in the shower with the bloody BITCH you were SCREWING last night who had the NERVE to text me from YOUR MOBILE PHONE?'

Silence.

'JAMES?'

'Lucy, what are you talking about?'

'You know what I'm talking about.'

'Lucy. I categorically do *not* know what you're talking about.'

'The girl, James, the girl you shagged last night. She texted me from YOUR MOBILE PHONE!' But my rage is losing momentum.

Now he's exasperated. 'Lucy, what the— I can *assure* you, I did NOT shag anyone last night. I had a couple of Friday-night drinks with the boys from work and then I went home to bed.'

'But—'

'ALONE.'

'So who sent—'

'I still don't know what you're going on about! *What* text?'

'I got it at nine o'clock, before take-off. It said, "Hi Lucy! Just shagged James in your bed. Thought you should know . . . Four times this month—"'

'Those fuckers!' James angrily interrupts.

'What?'

'It must've been the lads, trying to wind you up. They'll have nabbed my phone when I went to the bar.'

Tears spike my eyes and I take a few deep breaths as I realise he could be telling the truth.

'Lucy?' he asks gently. 'Are you alright?'

'No! I'm not! I threw up on the plane!'

13

'Oh, God. Lucy, I'm so sorry.'

'It's okay,' I sniff. 'It's not your fault.'

After a moment he speaks softly. 'Baby, you should have known. I would *never* cheat on you. I missed you so much when I came home last night and you weren't there. I can't believe you think I'd do that. It makes me pretty sad, actually.'

'James, I'm sorry. I didn't understand. I didn't know *what* was going on!'

'Hey, it's okay. It's okay. I love you.'

There are people heading down towards the gate next to me now so I dry my eyes and speak quietly into the receiver. 'I love you too. I'm sorry for doubting you. I was just really confused.'

'Don't worry. If one of your friends did that to me, I'd hit the bloody roof! But look, Lucy, promise me you won't let this spoil your holiday. You're going to have such an incredible time.'

When we finally hang up, the relief is so overpowering I actually laugh out loud. A few passengers queuing by the gate turn to stare. I realise I must look a right state, so I head off in search of the nearest ladies' loos.

It's a hot and humid Saturday evening in Singapore and when I packed my hand luggage, I had the intention of making the most of every warm minute. In the cramped toilet cubicle, I change out of my jeans into an emerald-green summer dress and swap my trainers for cork-soled, black strappy wedges. Back out in front of the mirror I tie my just-below-shoulder-length chestnut curls into a high ponytail and splash my face with cold water. I'm not wearing any make-up, but I do apply some moisturiser and cherry-flavoured lip balm.

Feeling much more normal, I set off looking for Singapore Airport's outdoor swimming pool. One of my work colleagues,

Gemma, told me about it. I don't want to swim, but there's an outdoor bar area and I sure as hell need a drink. I've got an hour and a half to kill before the flight to Sydney.

The humidity hits me the second I walk through the electric doors at the end of Terminal One. I decide on a bar-side seat and order myself a cocktail, trying to ignore the terrible Singaporean pop music blasting out of the stereo. Excitement suddenly surges through me. I'm going back to Australia!

The last time I saw Molly and Sam we were all sixteen and still at high school. I can hardly believe that was nine years ago. Molly and Sam were on-again-off-again back then – something which caused me a lot of heartbreak. I had the most overwhelming unrequited crush on Sam, and every time he got together with Molly or cooled it down, my heart would sink or soar accordingly.

I'm so relieved neither of them ever found out how I felt. But life goes on, and now I can honestly say I'm thrilled that my two friends are tying the knot.

At least I think I am, although that could all change when I see Sam again. I sincerely hope not. What is it with first loves that you supposedly never get over?

As soon as Molly called me with the news of their engagement, I knew I'd have to go back. I left Australia when my English mum married for the second time. It seemed a bit silly, her walking out on my drunkard dad in Ireland and taking me to Australia when I was four years old, only to meet an Englishman and move back to England again twelve years later. I cried and cried at the time. It felt like leaving was the most soul-destroying thing in the world. But it's amazing how you adapt. I love England now. I love the city where I live and work and I love going home to Mum and Terry's house in Somerset. I also love having two brothers – well,

15

two stepbrothers – Tom, who is twenty-one, and Nick, who is eighteen. It was lonely growing up with just Mum and me.

There are kids with armbands splashing in the pool. A young couple appear at the top of the stairs. They're both wearing jeans and carrying backpacks and they almost immediately wipe their brows. I'm glad I packed my dress.

I think I'll have another cocktail. 'Excuse me. Could you tell me what this is again?'

'Singapore Sling, madam.'

That figures. 'Another one, please.' The bartender nods and gets to work. What's in them, I wonder, grabbing a menu from further down the bar. Grenadine, gin, sweet and sour mix and cherry brandy . . . Mmm.

This Singaporean pop music is actually quite catchy. James would laugh if he could see me now, drinking cocktails and tapping my feet.

Maybe he did hide my chocolate cherry liqueurs as a joke. I still don't accept his story that he gave them to a tramp.

Okay, here's the thing about my boyfriend. He is prone to the occasional crazy white lie. But I genuinely believe he doesn't mean any harm. For example, at the party on the night we met, he told me his mum was once offered £10,000 to sell her chocolate cake recipe to the boss at Mr Kipling. He no doubt assumed I'd forget, but a few months later I went for afternoon tea at his parents' house and his mum, a tiny little sparrow of a thing, happened to be serving chocolate cake.

'Is this the infamous recipe?' I asked her knowingly, and she replied, 'Oh, no, dear, this is from M&S. I burn everything I bake!'

When I questioned James about it later, he cracked up and asked me where on earth I'd got that idea. I told him and he denied it, laughingly insisting I must've dreamt it. I don't know, maybe I did.

There have been other lies, which I know I didn't dream – some of them quite inventive. Like the one about his grandpa snogging Marilyn Monroe when she sang for the troops in Korea. I found out from James's dad later that the old guy didn't even fight in the Korean War, and anyway Marilyn had just married Joe DiMaggio at the time. I Googled it and everything.

But his mum selling her chocolate cake recipe to Mr Kipling . . . That's my personal favourite. Little ratbag. Sometimes I think James could be an actor. But no, he's far too good as a lawyer.

And he really is. He was promoted six months ago and got a massive pay rise. That's how he could afford to buy me those earrings for my birthday. Knowing James, though, even without the promotion he would have saved up for six months to get them for me. He spoils me rotten. I get flowers at least once – sometimes twice – a month and he's always taking me out to dinner and buying me presents. My friends think I'm ludicrously lucky.

There's a high-pitched buzzing and I can hear a plane taxiing by. It's noisy, as if we're going through a car wash. I watch as a balding forty-something man makes his way down the steps into the swimming pool, his pot-bellied stomach shuddering with every step. Three young guys are sitting at a table on the other side of the bar, drinking beers. One of them looks over at me and then turns back to his mates and says something. All three turn round and grin.

I feel so much happier now. Damn it, I'm going to have another one.

'Singapore Sling?'

'Yes, please.'

I'm feeling a little tipsy. I know you shouldn't really drink on your own but, bugger it, I'm on holiday. And I've been through a lot in the last, how long has it been? Fifteen hours or so? I wonder if I'll laugh about this in years to come. It's starting to seem pretty funny now – but I imagine the three Singapore Slings help.

The thought of poor James going home to an empty flat, sleeping in an empty bed and missing me . . . I wish he could've come to Australia as well. If he hadn't received that promotion he would have asked for the time off, but at the time I was booking my flights, he felt it was too soon. I really wish Molly and Sam could meet him.

There's a couple in the spa and they're kissing. The balding forty-something is doing breaststroke and he keeps copping an eyeful every time he swims past. You don't very often see guys do breaststroke, do you? I kind of wish I had my swimming costume with me now, but then I wouldn't be here, swinging my wedge-clad feet on this lovely high bar stool.

'Would you like another, madam?'

Is he *flirting* with me? That was definitely a twinkly grin. Can you have twinkly grins or is it just twinkly eyes and cheesy grins? I mean cheeky grins. God, I'm pissed.

This is definitely, definitely my last one. Whoa! Almost slipped off my stool. What time is my flight again? There's a TV screen with the flight times behind the bar and I struggle to make out the numbers. No, I'm not looking at you, pal. Where's my flight? Sydney, Sydney, Sydney – ah, there it is. Last Call.

Shit, does that say Last Call?

Bollocks! I slide, almost fall, from the stool and, practically tripping over my wedge sandals, make for the exit. Then I realise I haven't paid. I rush back, see the relief on Twinkly Grin's face after he must've figured I was doing a runner, throw down my credit card, will him to get a wriggle on and then turn and run. Where the hell is Gate C22?

Singapore to Sydney

Saturday: Depart Singapore at 2000
Sunday: Arrive Sydney at 0650
Duration: 7 hrs 50 mins

Oh dear, those air hostesses do not look happy. They've called for Lucy McCarthy twice over the tannoy in the last ten minutes as I've zigzagged my way here. I try to apologise for being late but 'sorry' comes out like 'shorry' and it doesn't help that I'm unable to walk down the plank in a straight line.

Did I just say plank? I meant aisle, of course.

The other passengers are looking at me. Yes, yes, I've had a couple of drinks, but what am I, a total freak? Ah, here's my seat. Window again, fab. Yep, you'll have to move. And I'm not so drunk that I can't see you raising your eyebrows at each other, either. Bet you thought you had a nice empty seat next to you – too bad! I think I'll take my carry-on bag with me to my seat this time.

I plonk myself down and try to locate the seat belt from under my bum. Blanket . . . No. Pillow . . . No. Where is the bloomin' thing? Ah, seat belt. I tug, tug, tug at it. Why won't it budge? Oh, okay, that seat belt belongs to the man next to me. Sorry, mate. I've found mine. Click. I do feel woozy.

'*Ladies and gentlemen, would you please fasten your seat belts, stow away your tray tables and put your seats in the upright position . . .*'

Yeah, yeah, heard it all before. Blahdeblahdeblah.

'. . . *mobile phones must be switched off until you're safely inside Sydney International Airport* . . .'

Yep, I know that bit too. Been there, done that. Oops, I haven't switched it off yet actually.

Can't . . . quite . . . reach . . . bag . . .

Seat belt . . . too . . . tight . . .

I eventually unclick myself and grab my bag, finding my phone. No messages, thank goodness. I switch it off and chuck it back into my bag. Then I buckle myself up again and breathe a nice big Singapore Sling sigh of relief.

My tanned legs are peeking out from underneath my sundress and I admire them happily. I do like this fake tan – it's a nice, natural-looking one. But it is *such* a pain in the arse having to use old sheets on the first night that you apply it. And then you have to wash them and put your good ones back on again . . . So it's two loads of laundry in two days. Well, I had to leave James to deal with the washing this time as he hurried me out of the flat.

NICE SHEETS!

The memory barely registers before my stomach freefalls and I ask myself: how the hell did James's blokey friends know about my shitty fake-tan sheets?

Oh, no . . . They didn't know. Because they didn't send that text.

I hurriedly unbuckle my seat belt and reach for my bag, giving the seat back and the person in front of me a big, solid head-butt. I fumble around for my phone and switch it on.

HI LUCY! JUST SHAGGED JAMES IN UR BED. THOUGHT U
SHOULD KNOW. 4 TIMES THIS MONTH. NICE SHEETS! XXX

'Miss – you need to turn that off.'

What, do they have eyes in the back of their bloody heads?

'I can't! I have to make a phone call!'

'Miss, the other passengers on this flight have already been held up enough, don't you think?' She looks at me meaningfully. 'So you'd better turn that off, right now.'

'Is there a problem?' Another bitchy air hostess arrives to join the party.

'No, Franny, we're alright here. This young lady was just about to turn off her phone.'

With a deep fury bubbling away in my very core, I comply. Power trip over, they smugly sashay off down the aisle. I'm tempted to hurl my phone at the back of Franny's frickin' head.

That lying, cheating son of a bitch. I'm going to kill him.

The plane takes off and I'm so full of rage that I barely notice. The forty-something man and his wife/girlfriend/mistress (most likely) next to me shift uncomfortably in their seats. And while I'd like to think I have a certain amount of self-control, at the moment I'm not entirely sure I do. It's just as well I've been given a window seat – I'd probably be rampaging down the aisle, screaming like a banshee, if I could get out. I can't handle another eight hours of this.

The sun is setting as we start our journey through another night. It calms my mood somewhat and it occurs to me that I haven't actually eaten anything since leaving London yesterday evening. Four cocktails on an empty stomach – oh, dear. I suddenly have an urgent need to go to the toilet. The people next to me are only too eager to oblige, standing up and eyeing me warily as I squeeze past them.

The nasty fluorescent light in the bathroom flickers on. I clock my diamond earrings in my reflection and seriously consider tearing them from my ears and flushing them down the toilet. Ha! Knowing how the bastard lied through his teeth to me, they're probably not even real. Lucy in the sky with cubic fucking zirconia. That'd be about right.

The air hostesses have started to serve drinks at the top of the aisle. I figure they can back up into Business Class and let me take my seat so I walk up towards them. The older one, Franny, nods at the younger one, who swivels round and spots me before turning back to Franny with an almost imperceptible shake of her immaculately groomed head. Then the bitches make me wait back by the toilets while they carry on serving the entire cabin with their frosty, false little smiles until finally they reach me and I'm able to pass. I am livid, but I won't let them see they've got to me. I get back to my seat and realise I haven't even been given a drink.

Franny and her evil counterpart are serving food now. The chicken stir-fry is slimy and unappetising, but I'm famished so I eat it all. Even the fake-cream sponge goes down nicely. The alcohol is starting to wear off and I find I'm exhausted, although I'm still so mad at James I can barely breathe.

So he lied about cheating. I can't believe I actually apologised for suspecting him! How dare he? The image of him in bed with another girl comes to me once more, but I channel my anger back fast and strong. I can't deal with those sick nerves again – anger is much easier to handle.

I need to go to the loo again. The air hostesses have already cleared our dinner trays, but they're still working on the seats behind us. The curtain that divides Economy and Business Class is tied back and the Business Class toilets are tantalisingly close. What the hell, I think, and walk up the aisle.

It's much nicer in here. They've even got hand cream and flowers.

There's a knock at the door. What now? I wee as quickly as I can while the knocking increases in urgency and volume, and then unlock the door. Surprise, surprise, it's Franny's frosty friend. She must have seen me come in here. I haven't even had time to use the hand cream yet – damn.

'Miss, these are *Business* Class toilets – the Economy Class toilets are at the other end,' she tells me condescendingly.

I motion to the passengers in Business Class and say, 'I don't think anyone here really mi— Wait. Are those *telephones?*'

An Asian businessman has a phone to his ear and this phone is attached by a cord to the back of the seat in front of him.

'That's certainly what they look like, don't they?'

I look at her desperately. 'I need to make a phone call.'

'I'm afraid you can't. They're for Business Class passengers only.'

'No, you don't understand. I *have* to make an urgent call.'

'I'm sorry, but there is nothing I can do. You need to take your seat now.'

I should've known better than to piss off an air hostess.

She determinedly guides me back to my seat as I look over my shoulder in desperation at the phones. I don't care that there's only a few hours left of this flight. I want to call the son of a bitch and scream at him NOW. I *will* use that phone.

An hour later, when all the other passengers are either sleeping or watching the in-flight entertainment, I hoist myself up in my seat and climb over my dozing neighbours, carefully treading on their armrests so as not to wake them. I lift back the curtain dividing us and Business Class and step through. The Asian businessman is sleeping, so I creep over to him. Carefully taking the phone from its mount, I scrutinise it. No! It looks like it needs a credit card.

'Miss! What *are* you doing?'

The businessman jolts wide awake at the sound of the air hostess's shrill voice and stares at me, startled. He shouts something I can't understand and, before I know it, the phone has been wrestled out of my grip by Franny and I'm being frogmarched up towards the front of the plane.

In the kitchenette area she turns to me and says with icy-cold hardness: 'You'd better listen to me long and hard. First, you rocked up late and drunk. You were lucky that we didn't refuse you passage on this aircraft—'

'I wasn't that drunk,' I interrupt.

'Enough! This is the one and only time I am going to tell you. If you don't go back to your seat and calmly stay there for the duration of this flight, you will be banned from ever flying with this airline again. DO YOU UNDERSTAND ME?'

A red flush has crept across my face and I nod my assent. Mortified, I make my way back to my seat. Again I climb up and over the sleeping passengers, all the time watched closely by Franny. When she's satisfied that I've been put firmly and literally back in my place, she turns and leaves, shaking her head in disgust.

After a few minutes of sitting there with my face burning, I decide I'd better watch a film or something – anything to try to take my mind off my situation. I won't be moving again.

An hour later, when they're bringing the breakfast trolley through, I barely look up, and when we finally land I can't meet their eyes as I walk out through the door. They don't say anything which may cause a scene in front of the other passengers, but I know they're delighted to see the back of me. I just hope they're not on my return flight. But right now, of course, there are other concerns on my mind.

Sydney

Chapter 1

I have to clear Immigration before I can call the wanker but as soon as I'm through and walking towards the luggage conveyor belt I'm dialling his number.

He picks up, laughing. 'Hello?'

'James.'

'Lucy! How are you? How was your flight?'

'You lying, cheating, son of a bitch.'

'Lucy?'

'You heard me, you bastard.'

'Hey?' Confusion reigns.

'The sheets, James, the sheets. How did your friends know about the shitty sheets I use when I'm doing my fake tan? They don't know, you arsehole—'

'Lucy!' he interrupts, but I'm on a roll.

'They don't know because they weren't there. Whoever it was that you were shagging knows – oh, she knows alright.'

'Lucy!'

'Shut the hell up, James, I don't want to hear! You have really blown it this time – I will never, *ever* forgive you!'

'Lucy!'

'No! Shut up!'

'EGYPTIAN COTTON!'

'What?'

'Egyptian cotton!'

'What are you talking about?'

He sounds panicked. 'I told them about the ludicrously expensive Egyptian cotton sheets you bought from Selfridges a few weeks ago. I was complaining about it to a bunch of people at work just the other day.'

'Why, James, *why* would you be talking about our sheets at work? I don't believe you.' My voice is flat.

'Well, you're going to have to because I was. Jeremy said something about how I must be enjoying my promotion and living the high life now and I said we won't be living the high life if you keep spending money on stupid Egyptian cotton sheets!' He barely pauses for breath.

'Oh.'

'Yes, *oh*. This is crazy!'

'I thought "nice sheets" was sarcasm.'

'Well, you thought wrong. Again.'

Neither of us can speak. The wind has been ripped out of my sails and I picture James all worked up, on the other side of the world, breathing hard and fast into his chest. I genuinely don't know what to say. I'm still so angry. It's like when you have a dream that your boyfriend has cheated on you and you wake up and look at him and still feel pissed off. He doesn't understand, of course, because he's done nothing wrong. But you still want him to apologise. I really don't feel capable of saying sorry again.

'Lucy?'

Nothing.

'Speak to me!'

'I don't know what to say.'

'Well, sorry would be something.'

'Sorry.'

'Doesn't sound like you mean it.'

'James, I have just had the worst twenty-four hours of my life! I thought you'd cheated on me. I thought I was going to lose you, have to move out of our flat, divide up our CDs, *everything*. I had to go through all that TWICE! All because of your sodding mates and a sodding text. Do you understand?'

This time he doesn't answer.

'You'd better find out who sent that text. I want names, James.'

'A poet and you didn't even know it.' He laughs.

'I am *not* joking. Names!'

'No, I'm not going to find out who sent that text, don't be ridiculous.' He's suddenly serious. 'If they knew how much trouble they'd caused they'd probably be over the moon. By not mentioning it, they'll never have that satisfaction.'

I'm not convinced by any stretch of the imagination – I want their heads strung up so I can throw stones at them – but I know what he means. Immature little twats.

'Are we alright, Lucy?'

'No, we're bloody not.' But his tone softens me.

My phone beeps and I realise my battery must be low. Good timing, as I see my bag making its way around to me on the conveyor belt. 'I'd better go – my battery's running low and my bag's here.'

'Baby, please. Give me a call when you've charged up your phone. I love you, okay? I would never, ever cheat on you.'

31

A thought occurs to me. 'Why were you laughing?'

'What do you mean?'

'When you answered the phone. You were laughing.'

'Oh! I was watching something on telly.'

'What was it?'

'Lucy, stop this! I haven't done anything wrong.'

'What was it, James?'

He hesitates, then says, 'If you can't trust me—'

'Tell me.'

My phone battery beeps again.

'I was watching a repeat of *Little Britain* on UK Gold.'

'I didn't even know we could get UK Gold on our TV.'

'Well, we can.'

I say nothing.

'Lucy?'

'I've got to go. I'll speak to you later.' I hang up on him.

I grab my bag and haul it off the conveyor belt, then, still feeling unsettled, I pull up the handle and wheel my way out through Customs.

As soon as I see them my heart swells with joy and forces out all the negativity from the last twenty-four hours. Molly and Sam are standing there at the end of the walkway. I rush towards them, tears brimming in my eyes.

'I can't believe you're here!'

Suddenly I'm being smothered in a three-way hug. It's so good to see them. Molly's slimmed down and is this tall, skinny pale thing towering over me with a shock of red hair blasting out from the top of her head. She always hated her 'mop-head', as she called it – but I can't imagine her without it. Sam looks different too. In contrast to Molly, he's filled out and is now, well, a *man*.

32

His face is a little rounder and his brown hair is shorter. He looks elated to see me and I check my emotions. Nope, nothing. Thank goodness for small mercies.

'We brought you something.' Molly beams and pulls a packet out of her bag.

'TimTams!' They were my favourite snack in high school: chocolate biscuit things – a bit like Penguin bars in England. You dip one end in your tea, bite it off and then dip the other end in, before sucking out the insides as quickly as you can, trying not to spill it all over you. 'Now we just need a cuppa,' I laugh.

Sam takes my suitcase from me and we head outside to the car park. It's still only about eight in the morning so it's not quite warm yet, but I'm anticipating a glorious, sunny day. Happiness washes over me.

'How was your flight?' Sam asks.

I groan. 'Not great. I'll tell you later.'

'I can't believe your English accent!' Molly squeals suddenly. 'You sound like a Pom!'

'I do not.'

'Yes, you do. Doesn't she, Sam?'

'She does indeed.' Sam smiles across at me fondly. 'Here we are,' he says, hauling my suitcase up into the back tray of an open-topped white truck, lying it flat next to half a dozen baby palm trees.

'Are you working today?' I ask him.

'Nah, I'm just doing a favour for a mate. I'm going to drop you girls off home and have a quick cuppa with you and then I've got to get off and do some gardening.'

Sam works as a horticulturalist in Sydney's Royal Botanic Gardens, which is where he proposed to Molly, high on a platform within the walls of the great pyramid-shaped glasshouse. He uses the truck for work and I'm lucky it's not raining, otherwise my clothes would get drenched.

We hit the Expressway, Sam zipping in and out of traffic, honking his horn like a madman. 'It's so weird seeing you driving,' I say. 'I never thought you'd end up being such a nutcase behind the wheel.'

'It's not me, it's everyone else that's the problem.' He grins.

I glance at Molly and bare my teeth in fake horror.

She rolls her eyes at me. 'This is nothing. You should see him in rush hour.'

We enter a tunnel and when we come out the other side the city is upon us, jagged skyline stretching up into the clear blue sky. The golden top of Sydney Tower glints in the morning sunlight.

'Do you want to go over the bridge, Lucy? Or shall we tunnel it?' Sam asks after a minute.

'Bridge! Bridge!' I bleat excitedly.

Sam and Molly live in Manly, one of Sydney's northern suburbs. You can access it by ferry from Circular Quay, but we're doing the journey by car across the Sydney Harbour Bridge.

Moments later the huge steel arch of the bridge looms in front of us. Two Australian flags fly high atop it and I can just make out little figures not so much scarpering like ants as straining to complete the bridge's strenuous climb. I look back over Sam's shoulder and glimpse a view of the ocean. The Sydney Opera House shines like a white beacon and the water in the harbour sparkles and glimmers like billions of tiny crystals.

Across the bridge we take a right towards Mosman and Manly. Car dealerships, shops, chemists, delis, newsagents, funeral homes and coffee shops whizz past and soon we're approaching the Spit where hundreds of different-coloured apartment blocks and houses step down the cliff face overlooking the bay. Palm trees and pines line the waterfront and the grass is yellow and dry.

'Hot summer?' I enquire.

'Very,' Sam answers. 'Terrible for the garden.'

Terrible for the garden, good for me, I think. I hope it stays that way for the next couple of weeks, and for the wedding of course.

Molly winds down her window and I breathe in the ocean air. I'm beginning to feel more like myself with every minute.

'So how's James?' Molly asks, as Sam drives right up the back-side of a silver Suzuki.

'Urgh.' I tell them a condensed version of my sorry story.

'Blimey,' Molly says when I finish. 'Do you believe him?'

'I don't know. I think so. I just don't know.'

At that moment I make a decision not to let what happened with James bring me down. I've saved up for months for this holiday; it's the first time I've been back to Australia in almost a decade, and I absolutely, resolutely, will *not* let him spoil it. I'll regret it for the rest of my life if I do.

'Get a move on, woman!' Sam breaks the silence by honking his horn.

After a few minutes we take a left down a pretty tree-lined street full of houses with red-tiled roofs. Before I know it we're pulling up in front of a two-storey wood-panelled green and cream house. A hammock hangs out on the porch and a fragrant frangipani tree is in full bloom in the front garden.

I've been to Sam and Molly's house plenty of times, back when it was Sam's family home. Shortly after I left Australia, Sam's parents, Joan and Michael, died in a boating accident. Their bodies were never found. Sam and his younger brother, Nathan, alerted the authorities when their parents still hadn't returned late at night after a whole day sailing. The boat was eventually discovered empty a couple of days later, drifting way out in the Pacific Ocean. The most popular theory was that Joan had fallen overboard and Michael had jumped in trying to rescue her, forgetting to put the anchor down. The boat had drifted and they'd both drowned or had been taken by sharks. Some speculated that they'd done a runner or been kidnapped. And there were even terrible whisperings that maybe Michael had murdered his wife and then killed himself. But anyone who'd ever met them knew that wasn't true. They were a wonderful, warm couple, their house always filled with Joan's infectious laughter. I was devastated when I found out. They'd always joined in with us 'kids' and we felt comfortable around them. Michael was a good-looking man with slightly-too-long-for-his-age dark hair and rough stubble, while Joan was tall, slim and elegant with short blonde hair. I always wanted to be like her when I grew up. But at five foot six, curvy and brunette, the most I can hope for now is having Joan's sense of humour.

After their parents' disappearance the boys moved in with their aunt, Katherine, in the city. When it was eventually accepted that Joan and Michael were never coming back, Katherine – Joan's sister – agreed to take them on permanently, rather than unsettle them even more by forcing them to move all the way to Perth in Western Australia to live with their grandparents. At almost eighteen, Sam would soon be old enough to move out and go to university, so it didn't seem worthwhile uprooting him and his brother. Neither of the boys could bear to sell the family home and as Michael had been a successful architect and, together with Joan, had run his own property development business, Sam and Nathan found they could afford to keep the house and rent it out.

Eighteen months ago, Sam and Molly finally moved back in and turned it into a B&B. They now run the place together and are kindly letting me stay in one of their two guest bedrooms for the next fortnight. There's a sign out at the front saying NO VACANCIES and Molly explains that they're not taking on any-more visitors in the lead-up to the wedding. I'm secretly overjoyed that we'll have the house to ourselves, although I feel bad that I'm not a paying guest. I hope they don't mind but the cost of the flight has almost wiped me out as it is.

Sam unlocks the front door and stands back to let Molly and me pass. The house smells familiar – sort of woody and even a little damp, but not in an unpleasant way. The kitchen, which I soon see has been newly modernised, has been moved to the front of the house off the hall, and the brand-new light, airy living room is straight ahead, opening onto the garden. Sam leads the way through to the kitchen and then carries on down the corridor where the downstairs bedrooms always were, lugging my suitcase with him. 'I'm just going to plonk this in your room, Lucy,' he calls back to me cheerfully. 'You're in my old room!'

Sleeping in Sam's room at last after all these years. How ironic.

'So how's the wedding planning going?' I turn to Molly.

'There's just so much to do,' she groans.

'I'll be able to help now I'm here.'

'You're going to regret saying that, you know,' she warns, as Sam reappears.

'No, I'm not. I can't wait.'

'Well, in that case, Lucy, would you mind grabbing those place cards there? The guests' names need writing out. You still remember how to use a calligraphy pen, don't you?'

I peer over at the pile of silver cards on the sideboard, then Molly laughs. 'I'm joking, you idiot. Sam, put the kettle on, let's have a brew.'

It's great to be back. I thought it would feel strange being here inside their house without Sam's parents around but it doesn't. It feels like home. Sam and Molly's home. I look at them laughing in the kitchen as they tussle with teabags and milk, both fighting to make me a cuppa. They look so perfect together. I picture Molly walking down the aisle to Sam, all suited up and waiting for her. It's going to be emotional.

Chapter 2

The next couple of days pass by in a jet-lag-induced blur. I have a short nap on the day I arrive and as a result manage to stay up until nine o'clock that night before crashing out. But early the next morning a fruit bat outside my window wakes me by squeaking and noisily munching on figs. I bash on the glass, but he ignores me and carries on as he was, bony little hook-like hands jutting out of his spooky black bat wings.

A batty bat expert on a school excursion once told my classmates and me that bats are four times more intelligent than dogs – 'Their brains are more advanced!' she'd cried. I beg to differ, judging by the way this one is failing to respond to my knocking. Then again, maybe he's made an informed decision to pay no heed to the wild-eyed madwoman on the other side of the glass. 'Just ignore her and she'll go away,' he's probably thinking.

I consider calling James – it would be Sunday evening at home – but in the end I really can't get my head around another conversation with him. I'm still feeling unsettled, and he just seems so very far away.

Eventually I accept that I won't be going back to sleep and get up. I make myself a coffee and take it through to the new living room, which looks like it's been recently refurbished in neutral shades of cream and grey. Very stylish. I sit there for an hour or so, reading Molly's old copies of NW and looking out through the new French windows at the pink and grey galahs in the fig tree.

'There you are.' Molly eventually appears in the doorway. 'Still jet-lagged?'

'Yes. And the bloody bat outside the window didn't help.'

'Aah, you've met Bert.'

'Bert?'

'Bert the bat. Or it might be Bertina, we're really not sure. Cute, isn't he?'

'Er, not at five o'clock in the morning.'

Molly just laughs. 'Lucy, come here. I want to show you something before I go to work.' She leads me up the stairs and into a large room.

Aside from running the B&B, Molly is also a clothes designer and she works part-time in a shop in Manly where her boss lets her sell some of her own designs.

Multicoloured patterned fabric spills and drapes over almost every surface, a large sewing machine takes up a good portion of the desk and ribbons and pins and scissors are scattered across the rest of the workspace.

'This is my workshop,' she exclaims proudly. 'And this,' she says, going to a large wooden wardrobe and pulling out a plastic-encased garment, 'is for you.'

I take it from her, intrigued and also, if I'm being honest, a little apprehensive.

I feel embarrassed that I don't own any of Molly's designs. I could order items from her website, but our styles are so completely different. She's more wacky and funky whereas my look is more high street. I hate to think of her being offended, but I just wouldn't look right in her clothes. I hope she understands.

So, with a certain amount of trepidation, I lift up the plastic and see a long, silver satin gown.

'This is *stunning*!'

'Will you be my bridesmaid?' Molly smiles.

I squeal with excitement and proceed to jump up and down on the spot for a few seconds while she laughs at me.

'Is that a yes, then?'

'Are you kidding? I would *love* to!' I lean across and give her a hug before turning my attention back to the dress.

'I hope it fits. I had to call James for your measurements.'

'You called James?' I ask, surprised.

'Yes – he was so sweet and helpful.'

'Really?'

'Yes, honestly. Lucy, I'm sure things will work out between you two,' she reassures me.

'I hope so,' I reply quietly.

'They will. You make such an ideal couple. That photo you emailed me of you two drinking through straws from the same cocktail – where were you again?'

'Florida, a year ago.'

'It was *so* cute.'

I smile at her gratefully. I don't want my personal dramas to take anything away from Molly and Sam's Big Day and the lead-up to it, so I hope she doesn't mind when I ask, 'Do you want to see the text?' I'm suddenly desperate to hear her verdict on that too.

'Sure.' She takes the dress from me while I run downstairs to grab my phone. When I get back, I hold the phone in front of her and scroll down slowly, so she can read the message.

'And he reckons his friends sent it?'

'When they were in the pub and he went to the bar, yes.'

'Nice friends,' she says sarcastically.

'Well, they're not really his friends, more his colleagues. So I don't have to see them that often.'

'Just as well,' Molly says. 'Lucy, I think you should delete it.'

I look at her, unsure.

'You must. It's only going to make you feel like shit every time you look at it, and if he's telling the truth, which I'm sure he is,' she adds pointedly, 'then why would you want to keep it?'

I don't know why, but I don't want to delete it yet.

She sees my hesitancy. 'You are *such* a glutton for punishment. Just like when we were at school,' she teases.

'What do you mean?' I laugh.

'Oh, you know, always looking up the answers to questions, straight after maths tests, just to torture yourself when you knew you'd got some of them wrong . . . Reading the last page of novels because you can't contain your curiosity, even though you know it's going to spoil the rest of the book . . . Rummaging through sales racks for ages, just to see if you can find the skirt you'd splashed out on months before at a reduced price . . .'

Falling for my lovely, brown-eyed schoolmate, even though I knew he was hopelessly devoted to my best friend in the whole world . . . I don't say that one out loud.

'Alright, alright!'

'Go on, then.'

'Oh, what the hell.' I press the delete button, confirm yes, and watch the message disappear. It's an uplifting feeling. I should clear out my inbox more often.

'Happy now?' I ask her.

'Yes, actually. I think that's a good start. So,' Molly holds up the dress, 'do you want to try it on?'

'Absolutely.'

We remove the plastic completely and take the dress off its padded hanger. Molly's seen me in my undies loads of times – although I'm sure my body has changed somewhat since we were both sixteen. With her help, I pull the dress over my head and she zips me up. For an awful moment I pray that James didn't take my measurements from the jeans I bought last summer because, with Christmas, I've put on a couple of pounds since then. But if he did, Molly must have been kind: the dress fits with an inch or two to spare.

'I can take that in,' Molly says. She opens the cupboard door to display a full-length mirror.

'It's beautiful.' I'm in awe.

'What's going on?' Sam asks sleepily from the doorway. Then he spots me in my silvery array. 'Hey, Lucy. Do you like it?'

'I love it.' I beam.

'Thank Christ for that. Molly's been fretting about it for weeks.'

Sam and Molly are both at work this week so I have to entertain myself during the day. Contrary to most visitors' expectations, the sun doesn't always shine in Australia. Sydney is actually prone to some serious rainfall, especially in March, which is fast approaching. But for now it appears I'm lucky, so I spend my first two days lazing around on one of the sunloungers in the back garden.

By Wednesday the skies have clouded over. Molly walked to work this morning, leaving me the car keys for her little red Peugeot and instructions on where to collect her from this afternoon. In Australia you insure cars not drivers so, brilliantly, anyone with a licence can drive, and as I was getting sick of reapplying Factor 30 suncream for the umpteenth time, I'm quite happy to take a trip down memory lane instead.

After an initial shaky start as I get used to the clutch, I cruise down the hill into Manly, passing Ivanhoe Park on my right, followed by the cricket ground. The ocean up ahead looks rough and choppy. Then I'm climbing again. Down below, the green stillness of the coves amazes me. It's incredible how calm the water is here in complete contrast to the open ocean on the other side of Manly, and I watch as a lone man kayaks in amongst the moored white sailboats. I keep driving and soon I'm heading back into town, past the primary school where Sam, Molly and I first met all those many years ago. Little girls in their blue and white checked uniforms play out in the front with the boys in white shirts and blue shorts.

At Manly beach the water is even choppier than I first thought and I see the beach is closed to swimmers. The rules don't apply to surfers, so I pull up in one of the parking bays overlooking the sea and pause for a minute, watching them.

A group of about fifteen guys sit bobbing on their boards, facing out into the vast ocean, looking like seals with their black wetsuits and dark wet hair. Suddenly one of them turns around and starts to paddle, then he's up on the board, crouching as he slices up and down through the curl of the water. One by one other surfers join in, boards moving like jet skis in the surf before the waves engulf them. Then they paddle back out and resume their bobbing, waiting for the next set to come in.

Off in the distance a lone pelican flaps and flies into the wind parallel to the horizon. I watch it for a while and almost lose it as it glides close to the surf, its wings camouflaged against the dark water and frothy white foam.

Ominous clouds hover overhead and it starts to rain. The surfers don't care – they're wet anyway. I wonder how long they've been there. I turn on my windscreen wipers and pull out, then drive back along the shorefront, past the surf shop where dozens of surfboards and wetsuits for rent are lined up. At the end I turn right and drive up the street where we lived for the three years before we went back to England. Stopping for a moment, I look up at the ugly four-storey red-brick building with its grey stone balconies.

Mum and I moved around, renting apartments for anything from one to four years before the landlord wanted their place back, so I wouldn't say anywhere ever felt truly like home. But I still feel a pang of homesickness when I look up to the second-floor flat and see the small balcony where we occasionally sat out for dinner. I picture Mum at home now in her picturesque English garden and smile. Who would've thought she'd go from working as a struggling secretary at an accountancy firm to owning and running a quaint little tea shop in Somerset? I'm genuinely happy for her. Terry was one of the senior managers at the firm and, even though he bored me silly when I first met him, he's a kind man and he's good for Mum. God knows how he put up with my tantrums when they made the decision to move back to England – because naturally I blamed him for taking me away from my friends. But now that house in Somerset feels more like home to me than any of these two-bedroom units ever did.

I suddenly wish James was here. I would have liked to show

him where I used to live. I spoke to him last night to tell him about being Molly's bridesmaid and the dress – just briefly because he was on his way out of the door for an early morning meeting, and I was feeling pretty exhausted anyway. But it was good to hear his voice, even if I still feel slightly anxious about what he could be getting up to back in London.

It's stopped raining now and I look at my watch. I don't have to pick up Molly for a few hours and I wouldn't mind having a coffee and seeing where she works, so I drive back into town.

Molly works in a funky little design store, which sells everything from candles and crockery to jewellery, cushions and clothes. She's serving a customer as I walk in but she looks delighted to see me, mouthing 'Hey, you' as she rings a purchase through the till. We sit chatting for the last couple of quiet hours of her day, planning the hen night on Saturday. As bridesmaid I know it's really my duty to organise it, but Molly kind of sprung that one on me and she already knew what she wanted to do. We're planning Circular Quay for drinks at a swanky bar overlooking the harbour, then dinner at an Italian restaurant nearby before going on to a club in King's Cross. We even manage to book a bright pink limo to take us from the restaurant to the club. Neither of us can wait.

'Do you fancy going for a quick drink on the jetty?' Molly suggests eventually.

'Sure.'

She calls out goodbye to her boss, Sandra, who's busy out at the back stretching fabric over wooden frames to make pretty prints.

The clouds have started to clear and the wind has settled right down. Blue sky stretches out ahead. 'You're so lucky with the weather,' Molly tells me.

Manly Wharf has had a revamp since I was last here, and the white art deco wood-panelled wharf front looks fresh and clean. The clock tower reveals it's 6.15 p.m. We walk around to the Jetty Bar and take a seat at one of the wooden benches. Vast white umbrellas hover overhead to protect us from the now quite warm sunshine.

'That guy is *really* cute,' Molly says of the barman as she returns to the table with two glasses of fizzing, berry liqueur-laced champagne.

'Molly,' I laugh, 'you're almost a married woman.'

Sam and Molly are getting married in the Botanic Gardens, in full view of the Opera House, Harbour Bridge and the city's crystalline skyline. Normally it would cost a fortune to have a marquee with such a spectacular view, but as Sam is an employee at the gardens he's getting a great discount.

'Are things all sorted with the venue?'

'I think so. Marquee's set to go up in, well, little over a week now.'

'What have we still got left to do?'

'Just get you some shoes. And Andie too. I don't think Mum's had any luck with hers yet. We can do that on Tuesday when I'm off work.'

Andie – Andrea – is Molly's little sister. She's eight and I haven't even met her yet. She was born the year after I left Australia. The year Sam's parents died.

'It still freaks me out that you've got a sister.'

'You're telling me! It freaks me out too. Especially when she's being a brat and Mum lets her get away with it. She's spoilt rotten.'

Andie and I are Molly's only bridesmaids. I still can't get over the fact that she asked me.

'Hey, I've been wondering,' I say. 'Are you changing your name to Wilson?'

'Yes,' Molly replies, 'I've decided I will. Well, it would mean a lot to Sam and I do really want to be part of his family, especially seeing as there's not much of it left anymore,' she adds sadly. 'But I will miss being Molly Thomas. Would you change your name to Smithson if you married James?'

'Um, I don't know,' I answer. 'It would be weird not being Lucy McCarthy anymore. But my mum changed her name to Brown when she married Terry so that link to her has already gone.'

Half an hour later, we drive up the hill to home and find an old battered green station wagon parked outside with a surfboard strapped to the top. 'Nathan's here!' Molly exclaims.

The last time I saw Nathan, he was a skinny fourteen-year-old who would lock himself up in his bedroom and play his guitar. Back then he would do anything to get away from his older brother and his annoying female friends, but I'm guessing from Molly's enthusiasm that's no longer the case.

Molly opens the door and leads the way into the kitchen where, there at the table with Sam, is someone who most definitely does not look like his skinny little twerp of a brother.

A jolt goes through me as a tall, dark, messy-haired surfer in faded jeans and a T-shirt stands up and smiles at me. He's even taller than Sam. 'Lucy, hi. Wow – it's been a while?'

'About nine years,' I reply, and I'm thinking what a difference almost a decade makes.

'I can't believe how much you've changed,' he says, as he stands there and surveys me.

I suddenly feel shy. 'You too.' I calculate his age quickly in my head. He's two years younger than Sam, Molly and me, which makes him twenty-three.

'Lucy, what are you drinking?' Sam asks, and I'm glad of the interruption. 'We've got rosé, white or beer. Oh, and red too.'

Molly and I opt for the rosé and we go out onto the back porch.

Nathan's presence right behind me is distracting.

We pull up black-painted wrought-iron chairs and sit around the matching table, Nathan to my left and Sam to my right with Molly seated opposite. Stone steps lead down to the neatly mown lawn, which slopes away from the house. The faithful sunloungers that I've spent the last couple of days getting to know intimately pepper the garden.

Sam starts to tell a story about his day at work but it's barely registering with me. Nathan's leg is jigging up and down at the edge of my vision, and the muscles on his bare arms tighten every time he reaches for his beer. It's the strangest sensation. I know people talk about chemistry and all that, but I've honestly never felt it before. When I met James at that party it was a gradual attraction, liking him more and more over the course of an evening and, at the end of the night, agreeing to go on a date with him. With Nathan I feel like I'm tuned into every movement he makes. I've got to get a handle on this. I take a large gulp of rosé and will myself to relax. I wish I'd put more make-up on.

Stop it! I have a boyfriend, for crying out loud. Who might be cheating on me. Oh, who gives a shit right now?

'Lucy, what are you smiling about?' At Sam's voice I realise that everyone around the table is looking at me. Nathan seems amused.

'Nothing!' I answer gaily and top up my glass with rosé.

We sit there, in the warm night air, and after a while Sam lights some coils and a couple of citronella candles to keep away mosquitoes. 'Do you mind if I smoke?' Nathan directs his question at me. I'm not really that keen but I'm hardly going to tell him that, so he lights up. I glance at him furtively out of the corner of my eye as he puts the cigarette to his lips. I wish I was that cigarette. Lucy! This is crazy.

Nathan shifts in his seat and turns to face me, being careful not to blow the smoke in anyone's direction. 'So what do you do now, Lucy?' he asks. Dark stubble grazes his jaw and I notice his eyes are bluey grey.

I tell him about my job at Mandy Nim.

'So that means you get shed-loads of free stuff?'

'Yep.'

'CDs?'

'Yep.'

'DVDs?'

'Yep.'

'Make-up?' That was Molly asking.

'Yep.'

'You lucky cow.' She shakes her head in amazement.

'And sometimes I have to go on trips abroad.' I tell them about how a few months ago I went to Amsterdam where we were taking on the PR for a plush hotel chain. 'It's pretty jammy, isn't it?' I don't deny it – it is brilliant.

'So what was the last free thing you got?' Nathan asks.

'These sunnies, actually.'

'I was just admiring them,' Molly exclaims. 'Can I see?' She puts them on and looks at Sam, who nods his approval.

'I might be able to get you some.'

'There's your birthday present sewn up, Mol.' Sam smiles.

'Actually, that's the only infuriating thing about this job,' I say. 'It makes finding Christmas and birthday presents for people a nightmare. You almost have to give them a receipt to prove you bought it.'

'Oh, our hearts bleed!' Molly laughs.

Nathan stubs out his cigarette; the hairs on his arms have been highlighted by the sun, even though he's naturally dark. He picks up the ashtray and places it at the other end of the porch, away from the table.

'What about you, Nathan? What do you do now?'

'Oh, this and that,' he replies, as he sits back down.

'Nathan doesn't really work,' Sam explains.

'He's too busy surfing.' Molly laughs fondly.

'I do enough to get by.' Nathan leans back in his chair and puts one tanned foot up on the opposite knee. He's not wearing any shoes and I imagine that if he were, his choice of footwear wouldn't extend further than flip-flops – or thongs, as they call them here.

'What's the time?' he asks.

'Eight o'clock,' Molly and I answer simultaneously.

'I should probably be getting off.'

No! Don't leave!

'Why don't you stay for something to eat?' Molly asks.

Yes! Stay!

'Yeah, go on, mate, we'll just order in a pizza or something,' his brother says.

Nathan seems to be wavering.

'Go on,' I bravely encourage. 'You can keep me company around these two lovebirds,' I add lamely.

51

'Oh, alright, then.' He grins. He has the most lovely smile.

Pizza, a few beers and a couple of glasses of rosé later, the sun sets and the mosquitoes zoom around more fervently so we move inside. Nathan looks out of the front window down to his beat-up car.

'You can't drive home now,' Molly says. 'Crash here and get up early in the morning. Are you surfing tomorrow?'

'I was going to.' He seems undecided and my stomach flips.

'Do you want to borrow the phone and call Amy?'

Now my stomach flops. Who's Amy? I don't need to ask out loud because Molly turns to me and explains. 'Amy's his girl-friend.'

'She's not my girlfriend,' Nathan protests.

'Well, she should be! Honestly, Lucy, she's beautiful. They live together and I swear they're perfect for each other.'

'Yep, you're nuts, mate,' Sam interjects. 'You oughtta snap that one up before somebody else does.'

'Mind your own business.'

'He's getting aggravated now.' Sam laughs and ruffles Nathan's hair.

'Gettoff!' Nathan waves his big brother's hand away and grabs another beer from the fridge before heading back into the living room.

'I guess that means he's staying, then,' Molly says.

Nathan's at the stereo when I walk into the room, flicking through Molly and Sam's CDs.

'Do you still play the guitar?' I ask.

'I do. I'm surprised you remember.'

'How could I forget? All you ever seemed to do was lock your-self away in your room playing that thing. You were pretty good.'

'Why thank you, miss.' He glances at me, smiling.

'What are you putting on?' Molly comes into the room. 'Can we have Kylie?'

'No, we bloody can't.' Nathan rolls his eyes at me theatrically. 'What do you want to listen to, Lucy?'

'I don't know if I dare say . . .'

'Go on, we've got The Killers, The Dandy Warhols, Jet, Beck . . .'

'No Mariah Carey?' His head shoots up and he looks at me in alarm. I laugh. 'I'm joking, you idiot – let's have The Killers.'

Molly and Sam go for the sofa and Nathan and I take a single-seater each. I slip off my shoes and curl my feet up underneath myself to get cosy.

The pizza has done a good job of soaking up the booze so I feel nicely tipsy, but nothing like during the dreaded flight on Singapore Slings. I push that memory right out of my mind and concentrate on the present. It's not difficult when you have the view I have.

'So, Lucy,' Sam says, 'are things all sorted with James now?' Nothing like a mention of your delightful boyfriend to bring you back to your senses. Nathan looks over at me but doesn't say anything.

'Um, I'm not entirely sure, to be honest.'

Molly turns to Nathan. 'Lucy had a bit of a rough journey over here. You don't mind me telling him, do you, Lucy?' I shake my head, and that recurring – if now much duller – feeling of nerv-ousness wafts through me as she starts to tell a short version of my story. I try to laugh it off when she gets to the part about the air hostesses, but Nathan just listens and nods, taking it all in. His quietness unsettles me.

'On that jolly note, I think I'll hit the sack,' Sam says.

'We can't go to bed now – Lucy won't be able to fall asleep with all that on her mind,' Molly counters.

'Don't be silly; I'm fine!' I insist.

Nathan smiles. 'I don't know about you, Luce, but I could do with another drink.'

So we stay seated, Nathan and I, while Sam and Molly head upstairs. I finish the last mouthful of wine and place my empty glass on the coffee table.

'Right, what are we having next?' Nathan jumps up to go to the kitchen. A second later he stage-whispers, 'Oi! Come here!' so I get up and join him. He's peering in the fridge. Wine, beer, soft drinks. 'I'm bored with beer,' he says, slamming the fridge door. 'Why don't we crack open the vodka?'

I groan. 'That is a bad idea.'

'Why, what are your plans for tomorrow?'

I picture another day sprawled out on a sunlounger. What the hell, I decide. By then he's already got a couple of glasses out. They chink together noisily and I tell him to '*Shh*'. I feel like we're two teenagers sneaking into Mum and Dad's booze cabinet.

We carry glasses, a carton of cranberry juice and the bottle of vodka through to the next room and settle ourselves back into our comfy armchairs.

'Why didn't your boyfriend come here with you?' Nathan asks. I tell him about James's promotion, and can't help comparing the two of them in my mind. Lawyer, surfer. Two years older, two years younger. Job, no job. London, Sydney.

I realise I don't like this game very much.

'So what's it like being back? Does it still feel like home?'

I answer yes, and feel depressed all of a sudden. In ten days I'll be leaving again.

'It doesn't seem like nine years ago that you left,' he muses. 'Even though a lot has changed since then. You do look different, but still the same.' He pauses. 'I like your hair long.'

'Thanks.' I smile. 'You look completely different. Are you really only twenty-three?'

He chuckles and climbs to his feet. 'I think I need a smoke.' He goes outside, leaving me still smiling. A minute later he calls to me, so I head out onto the porch with the vodka and cranberry to find that he's forgone the wrought-iron chairs and is instead sitting on the stone paving, leaning up against the wood-panelled house.

'What's up?' I ask.

He silently motions at the sky with his cigarette. Above our heads the Milky Way shines coolly like billions of flecks of silver glitter.

'Wow.' I look up in awe for a few moments. 'Where's the southern cross?'

'I wouldn't have the foggiest,' he responds, 'but there's the saucepan over there . . .'

I laugh and go to sit down. He moves his ashtray to his other side to make room for me.

We sit there in silence for a minute, looking up at the sky. 'I'd forgotten how bright the southern hemisphere stars are,' I finally say.

'They're even brighter from Manly beach.'

'Is that where you surf?' He nods. I like the thought of him surfing.

'I was there only this afternoon,' I tell him.

'Were you?' He glances sideways at me in the darkness. 'You might've seen me; I was out for a couple of hours.'

'Really? Those waves were enormous!'

He laughs. 'Not really. Good surfing conditions actually.' He tops up our glasses. 'Can you surf?' he asks after a second.

'No. I stick to boogie boarding.'

'You should come with me sometime. It's better early in the morning, though.'

'I'd love to. When?' My heart skips a beat.

'Whenever you like. I'm going tomorrow.'

'Sounds good!'

Too eager?

His face lights up with a warm glow as he takes another drag. I can feel the warmth of his body heat combining with mine as we sit side by side, and I have to force myself to concentrate.

'So what's the deal with Amy?' Where did that question come from?

He exhales deeply. 'She's my flatmate.' He pauses, then explains. 'She'd like us to be more than friends but . . . I don't know.'

'Has anything happened between you?' I hold my breath as I wait for his answer.

'Yeah.'

Those nerves come creeping back and I don't know what to say. He doesn't seem to know what to say either, so we sit there silently for a short while.

'Molly and Sam like her,' I prompt, and immediately regret it. What am I trying to do – force her on him?

He sighs. 'Maybe that's why I'm confused. She's a nice girl. But I don't know . . . I think Molly just loves a love story. And Sam just wants me to be happy like him.' He flicks his cigarette ash into the ashtray and his arm brushes against mine, giving me goosebumps.

I wonder what Molly would think if she knew what was going through my mind about her fiancé's younger brother. I get the distinct feeling she might find it funny. Or disapprove. Neither thought makes me feel very comfortable.

'What about your boyfriend? Do you believe him?' Nathan asks quietly.

'I don't know,' I answer truthfully.

'How long have you two been together?'

'Three years. But sometimes it feels like only weeks. Sometimes I feel like I don't know him at all.'

He nods his head in the darkness.

'He tells . . . *stories*,' I say cautiously. I've never really spoken to anyone about this before. I don't know why I feel compelled to tell Nathan now. 'They're not serious – just a bit bonkers,' I explain.

'Give me an example.'

So I tell him about the Big Feet.

When we first started going out James came on holiday with my family to Spain. On the first day, by the pool, he told my stepbrothers Tom, who at the time was eighteen, and Nick, fifteen, that he really wanted to buy some Big Feet.

'What are Big Feet?' we all asked, and James told us about these cool giant, inflatable feet-shaped shoes which literally allowed you to walk on water. He'd had a go with some in the South of France the summer before and he'd never had so much fun.

That night, Tom, a hard-up student, refused to buy a third pint of beer because he wanted to save his money for the Big Feet he was hoping to buy the next day. Every day for the rest of the holiday the four of us were on a mission to track some down. We'd drag my mum and Terry on trips via places that we thought might stock them. We scoured store upon beachfront store, department stores and sports shops. In pigeon Spanish we'd ask: 'Los Big Feetos! Grandes Feetos!' We'd mime gigantic webbed shoes, while Nick pretended to walk on water in big, astronaut-style steps.

The fact that we couldn't find them, and the fact that nobody else on the beach had them, only made us want them more. We imagined with glee the looks on other beach-goers' faces as we stepped onto the waves and strode out to the open ocean.

We never did manage to find those Big Feet.

Six months later when Tom, who'd just started university in London, joined us for a few pints at our local, James told him he had the original Darth Vader mask at home, which his uncle had bought for him after winning a small fortune on the lottery. I'd never heard this story before so we went back to our flat, Tom brimming with excitement. When James opened the cupboard under the stairs and pulled out a box containing a thin, vacuum-formed plastic mask that very obviously did not belong to Mr Vader, Tom accused him of telling porkies. And while James, perfectly straight-faced, continued to insist, Tom just laughed it off.

A couple of months later, it occurred to my stepbrother, still bitter about the time he'd wasted on holiday traipsing around looking for Big Feet, that maybe James had lied about that also. Were they real?

'No,' said James, he'd made them up.

Tom and Nick have never quite forgiven him.

Nathan shakes his head. 'That's mad.'

'Yeah, but it's not that big a deal, is it? I mean, we're just talking white lies.'

He doesn't answer.

'You know, it's pretty darn funny when you think about it,' I persist. 'There he was, leading us around the Costa del Sol in search of these great big inflatable feet, knowing all the while that they didn't exist.' I laugh. 'It's quite imaginative.'

'It certainly is that.'

I sigh. 'No, I know it's weird. I keep trying to kid myself that it's not. But it's hardly on a par with cheating, is it?'

'Don't you suspect he's been doing that too?'

'No! He would never, ever cheat on me. I really don't think he has. I don't know why I . . . Oh, I don't know.'

Nathan doesn't press the issue. Instead he moves on to a lighter subject of discussion: Molly, Sam and the wedding. We sit there and chat to each other for ages until eventually I stifle a yawn.

'What's the time?' he asks.

'Bloody hell, it's four o'clock!'

'In three hours from now I'd usually be getting up to go surfing.'

'In three hours from now I'd usually be getting home from work.'

'You must be knackered. Still jet-lagged?'

'I should be. I have no idea how I'm still awake and talking to you.'

But of course I have every idea. There's nowhere else in the world I'd rather be right now. Must be the vodka talking. But Nathan is already getting to his feet. He holds his hand down to me and I take it. His hands are rough, I notice, as I hang on for a second longer than is necessary. We make eye contact in the darkness. I can't see the expression on his face; I'm just glad he can't see me blushing.

Chapter 3

I'm hung-over, I've barely slept and my eyes feel like they've been doused in vinegar. But regardless of all that, I'm walking on air. I can't stop thinking about Nathan. James barely registers in my thoughts. I don't care if he's shagging a planeful of air hostesses – I just want to think about that sexy, messy-haired surfer.

The disappointment was crushing when I woke up this morning, expecting to see him at the breakfast table.

'Where's Nathan?' I asked Molly.

'He would've gone at the crack of dawn,' she answered casually.

But we were sitting outside under the stars only a couple of short hours before that, so I was sure he'd still be around.

'What time did you get to bed?' she enquired.

'Oh, I'm not sure. Not too long after you guys went.'

I don't know why I couldn't tell her we stayed up talking until 4 a.m. That's something I want to share with Nathan and Nathan alone.

I keep my phone close in case he calls about going surfing, although I'm pretty sure he wouldn't have sought out my number. I wish we'd made definite plans about meeting up again. We said we'd go today, but now the thought of us heading off to the beach together and alone seems surreal. I wonder if he even remembers. We did have a lot to drink, after all.

I go to the shop with Molly in the afternoon for a couple of hours. Every time the bell rings to announce the arrival of another customer my head hurts, and the whiney R&B music doesn't help either. Luckily Molly's boss isn't in this afternoon; I'm not sure how much she'd appreciate her customers seeing the green-faced girl sitting to the left of the cash register.

'You're quiet today,' Molly says. 'You're not still worried about James, are you?'

'Oh, no, I'm not worried about him.' I brush her off, perhaps a little too hastily. A flicker of something passes over her features and I'm not quite sure what it means. 'I mean, I do miss him. I'm just really hung-over,' I moan, and she smiles at me strangely but lets it be.

The truth is, I don't want to chat because I'm too busy replaying my conversation with Nathan over and over again in my head. I could have easily stayed out on the porch talking to him until the sun came up.

I heard him sigh when he went into his bedroom last night to sleep and it was heartbreaking. What used to be his cosy teenage retreat is now neatly made up for B&B customers. I can't begin to imagine what it must've been like for him to lose his parents at the age of fifteen. I still regret not being here for Sam when the accident happened. But at least he had Molly. I was selfishly jealous of that fact at the time, but that was probably when he and Molly finally realised how precious their relationship was.

In the early evening, when tiredness finally gets the better of me, I tell Molly and Sam I've got a bad case of jet lag and head to bed. I might not see Nathan now until the wedding in nine days' time and I don't know how I'm going to wait. I wonder if this bizarre crush will have passed when I wake up in the morning.

Soon after I fall asleep my phone beeps and I come to and grab it, imagining it could be him. But it's a text from James and I feel foolish and disappointed. He asks me to call, but I don't want to. That conversation with Nathan last night about his 'stories' troubled me. My unease is growing, not shrinking, and I can't help but doubt him again.

I try to go back to sleep, but ten minutes later my phone starts to ring. Is it Nathan? My heart hopes.

No, it'll be James. And it is.

'Lucy! How are you?'

'Sleeping.'

'Oh, sorry, baby. I should've known. Hang on, isn't it only about nine thirty there?'

'Yeah, but I'm tired. Still jet-lagged.'

'Oh, okay.' A pause. 'Sorry.'

I feel bad but I don't know what to say.

'What's wrong? You sound different.'

'Well, I'm a long way away. Sorry,' I say, forcing myself to perk up. 'Where are you? Shouldn't you be at work?'

'I am at work, Lucy.'

'Oh. Are you calling from your work phone?'

'Yes.'

'Won't that get you into trouble?'

'I don't think anyone in the company is going to notice.' He's sounding a tad frustrated now with my questions. 'I bought something for you yesterday,' he says, cheering up.

'Really? What?'

'I'm not telling you,' he replies, with a jovial note of secrecy.

I don't really know what to say to that.

'James, are you coming to this meeting or not?' I hear a woman's voice speak in the background.

'I'll be right there.' James's voice sounds muffled. He's obviously covering the receiver.

'Sorry,' he says to me. 'I should let you sleep. Love you.'

'You too,' I answer mechanically.

I can't get back to sleep afterwards. I feel naughty but when thoughts of James sift softly out of my mind and Nathan floats back in, I don't fight it.

In what feels like the early hours of the morning, I jerk awake, feeling hot and feverish. I was dreaming about Nathan kissing my lips and scuffing my skin with his dark stubble. For a moment I blame Bert the bat for interrupting my fantasy, but then I realise my phone is buzzing. Oh, *James* . . . I think crossly, and press the green button.

'Hello?'

'Lucy.'

'Yes?' I ask sleepily.

'It's Nathan.'

I sit bolt upright. 'Nathan! What time is it?'

'It's just after six in the morning,' he answers brightly. 'We said we'd go surfing tomorrow, right? Well, it is tomorrow. Just over twenty-four hours. Sorry, I'm a bit late.'

I'm a little lost for words.

'Too early?' he continues. 'Would you rather go back to sleep?'

'No!' I practically shout. 'I'm awake; let's get going.'

'Cool. Do you have a wetsuit?'

'No. Do I need one?'

'Yeah, you'll be freezing. Don't worry, you can borrow Amy's.'

I don't like that thought. At all. Are we even the same size? 'I'll be alright without one, won't I?'

'No, honestly, you'll need it. She won't mind.'

If she knew the dirty thoughts I'd been having about her boyfriend, or whatever he is, I think she might.

'Right, I'll see you in ten.'

Ten minutes? Ten bloody minutes? That gets me out of bed. I'm out of the shower within three, feeling surprisingly awake (thank you, jet lag). I put on my green bikini – I don't have a more suitable one-piece – followed by a skirt and T-shirt and then I have a dilemma about make-up. I smear on some lipgloss and immediately wipe it off because it looks like I'm trying too hard. I toy with the idea of waterproof mascara but in the end I go without. I'm lucky because my lashes are long and dark anyway and frame my hazel-coloured eyes quite nicely. I decide to plait my hair so at least I won't look too much like a drowned rat in the surf.

I scribble a note for Sam and Molly, wondering what they'll make of all this, and then go outside, quietly closing the front door behind me. I perch on the hammock on the porch and gently swing back and forth while I wait.

Nathan's beat-up station wagon turns up right on cue, headlights still on in the darkness. I pause for a second and watch him get out. He looks different to the image I had of him in my mind. But in that image he was barely dressed and doing things to me that right now are making me blush. I compose myself and stand up.

For a split second it's awkward because we don't know how to greet each other. He smiles and says hello before opening the car door for me. I climb in and hope the butterflies swarming around inside me will settle down.

The floor of his car is sandy and my Birkenstocks grate over it. 'Sorry about the mess,' he apologises when he's safely settled in the driver's seat.

'Don't be silly,' I tell him. He's wearing a faded brown T-shirt with a pink emblem on the front and long dark swimming trunks. I glimpse down to see if I was right about his footwear: yep, flip-flops.

He turns the key in the ignition and The Kaiser Chiefs' 'Oh My God' blares out of the stereo. Apologising again, he turns the volume down.

'It's okay, I like it,' I say, and turn it back up. After a minute or so, the stirring strains of The Verve's 'Bittersweet Symphony' fill the car. '*Great* song . . . What is this album?'

Nathan reaches across me and opens the glovebox. Several cassettes tumble down and almost fall out. He grabs for one, looking back up to keep an eye on the road and slams the glovebox shut, grazing my bare knee with his hand and making me feel light-headed. He passes me the cassette case. It's still quite dark outside and I can barely see so I switch on the overhead light.

'Do you mind?' I ask.

'Course not.' Messy handwritten scrawl lists about twenty band names and songs, some of which I recognise, and one or two which I don't. Rolling Stones, Radiohead, Powderfinger, Blur . . .

He's got my taste in music, which makes a nice change from James, who usually has house beats blasting out of the stereo.

'I'd love a copy of this,' I say. 'Don't suppose you have it on CD?'

'Nah.' He grins.

'iPod?'

'Nope,' he replies cheerfully.

Oh, well, never mind.

'How did you get my number?' I ask after a moment.

'Molly keeps her address book by the phone in the kitchen. I checked before I left yesterday morning.'

So, he was still thinking of me when he woke up.

'What time did you leave?'

'I think it must've been about seven. I felt like shit all day,' he replies.

'I told you the vodka was a bad idea but you wouldn't have it!'

'Good night, though, hey?'

I nod my agreement. 'Good night.'

Soon we're at the beach. It's 6.30, the air is cool and it's getting lighter with every minute that passes. We climb out and Nathan unstraps his red and white surfboard from the station wagon roof and props it up against the car before getting a large blue boogie board out of the boot. I wonder if that belongs to Amy too. I don't want to ask. He hands me her wetsuit. It looks tiny but they're supposed to stretch, aren't they?

Across the other side of the road there's a small wind shelter and I tell him I'm going over there to change. I don't really welcome the idea of him watching me try to squeeze into Amy's wetsuit.

It's tight, but it fits. Just. Nathan appears after a few minutes, already kitted out.

Apart from a few surfers I can just make out down the other end, the beach is deserted. We pad across the cool, damp sand towards the surf. The ocean looks calmer and the waves aren't nearly as big as they were the other day.

'Thanks for bringing this for me.' I motion to the boogie board under my arm.

'I came by the beach earlier and the conditions aren't ideal but you'll be alright on that,' he replies.

'I don't think I'd be very good at surfing properly.'

'Yeah, you would,' he tells me. 'But it takes time and I just thought, as you're not here for long . . .'

I suddenly feel downcast. If you were going to teach me to surf, I wouldn't mind using the rest of my holiday to do just that. But of course Nathan's got better things to do. It occurs to me for a horrible moment that he might just see me as a big-sister type. There's a very real and distinct possibility that he'd be appalled if he knew what I've been thinking about him.

'You ready?' he asks, snapping me out of my nasty thought as we reach the water's edge and he attaches his ankle strap. His surfboard stands tall – taller than him.

I squeal as a wave crashes against my feet. 'It's freezing!'

Nathan laughs. 'Do you want to sit this one out?'

'Yeah, I think I might, actually.'

I back up a little and watch as he strides into the water, pushing away from the beach on his surfboard before lying flat and paddling overarm. A wave comes and he ducks down, manoeuvring his board right through it before coming out the other side and paddling further out.

Soon he lifts himself easily up onto his board and straddles it, sitting there bobbing for a while until a decent wave comes and he flips his board around and starts paddling fiercely towards the shore. Then he's up and riding it, surfboard whizzing up almost vertically for a split second before it cuts back down, slicing through the crest of the wave. He rides it in towards the shore and then stands fully upright for a second before slowly sinking down into the water.

'You ready?' he calls, flicking his just-below-jaw-length wet hair back out of his eyes. God, he's gorgeous.

I nod.

'Right, we won't go out too far. The waves aren't that big at this end of the beach, but you won't need to go far to catch a half-decent one.'

It's still crazily cold at first but soon the water trapped inside my wetsuit heats up to body temperature and I feel warmer. We paddle out side by side, Nathan obviously going a lot slower than he's used to. This seems far enough out to me, and he must be thinking the same thing. He raises himself up so he's straddling his board. I stay lying flat on mine, as I'm not about to try to balance myself on this thing, and we both turn around to face the shoreline.

'Right, you first; I'll follow,' he says.

'Don't watch me,' I whine like a teenager.

'Why not?' He laughs.

'I might split Amy's wetsuit with my big bum.'

'You don't have a big bum.' He grins. 'It's a perfect fit.'

Hmm, if we're the same size I wonder how else he might be comparing us.

'Did she ask where you were the other night?' I query.

'Yeah.' Pause. 'I got a bit of stick for it.'

'Really?' I try to laugh, make light of it. 'Did you tell her you were up until the early hours talking to me?'

'Nah. She would have only got jealous.' Aha! Excellent, I think. Then immediately feel mean. 'She's not my girlfriend, remember,' he reminds me and holds my gaze. I tear my eyes away.

'Right, shall I go?'

He looks back at the waves. 'Not this one; wait for the next.'

The wave gathers momentum and I catch it just as it breaks and pushes me forward fast and furious towards the beach. I ride it all the way up onto the sand and suddenly find I can't stop laughing. I'd forgotten how much fun boogie boarding was. I push my drenched fringe out of my eyes and look for him. He's way out there, watching me. I wave and he waves back and then glances behind, ready to catch the next one.

There are many more surfers at the other end of the beach now as the sun climbs higher in the sky. We stay out for a while, sometimes meeting in the middle, sometimes not. I hope I don't look too horrendous with my wet, salty hair.

My arms are getting tired so we agree to have just one more go. I wonder how deep the water is out here. I'm glad I'm a half-decent swimmer, although I'm sure as hell no David Walliams, swimming the English Channel. I turn around and face Nathan on the beach. He just caught the last wave in and is standing on the sand watching me. He's stripped his wetsuit down to his waist and a towel drapes casually around his shoulders. There's a big wave coming and I commit to it. At the same time I see a movement out of the corner of my eye. A black fin. Oh, my God! I start to kick and paddle, all the while imagining the dark creature behind me, snapping at my heels. Or my knees . . . Or my thighs . . . Or my right arm . . . Oh, God. Oh, God. Oh, God! The wave picks me up and carries me hard and fast but the panic has well and truly set in and as soon as I reach shallow water and put my feet down I start to scream and run towards dry sand and Nathan. The blood has rushed out of my face. Nathan looks horrified and full of concern as he steadies me with his hands. 'I saw . . . I saw . . . Shark! A shark!' I'm pointing at the ocean and can barely get the words out as I start to hyperventilate. His body is tense as he looks in alarm down towards the other surfers and then out to the ocean. A few of them are peering up our way. It all happens very quickly because before he has time to warn them, I hear him laugh with relief. Tears streaming down my white cheeks, I look out to the ocean and see a pod of four dolphins dive up and out of the waves.

'Dolphins,' I stutter.

'Yeah, dolphins, you nutter. Christ, you scared me.'

I'm still breathing heavily and feeling really quite traumatised, thank you very much. Nathan must sense it because he pulls me down onto the sand in front of him and puts his hands on my arms. 'You okay?' he asks, his bluey-grey eyes looking steadily into mine.

I feel humiliated. 'I've always wanted to swim with dolphins,' I reply, to which he starts falling about, beside himself with the hilarity of it all. 'Stop it!' I snap jokily, and slap him on his arm. 'I'm embarrassed!'

He's still laughing. 'Oh, Luce, you crack me up. Don't be embarrassed. Look, this'll cheer you up. Two sausages in a frying pan. One of them says, "Blimey, it's hot in here!" And the other one says, "Shit! A talking sausage!"'

My laugh turns into a snort – very attractive. 'That's really funny!' I squeal. 'Okay, okay, I've got one for you . . . What do you call a fly once you pull its wings off?'

He shakes his head.

'A walk,' I answer.

Now he's snorting. Not unattractively, I might add.

'Why is it no one seems to tell jokes anymore?' I muse. 'When I was a kid growing up we used to all the time.'

'Yeah, that's so true,' he says. 'My mum used to make me tell jokes to her friends when we went out for dinner.' He smiles fondly. 'I'd feel like I was her "show and tell".' It's obvious he didn't mind. 'I used to have this elephant joke book,' he remembers suddenly. 'It was terrible. How did they go again?' he ponders. 'That's right, where do you find elephants?'

I shake my head, unsure.

'Depends on where you leave them.'

I giggle.

'How do you make an elephant float?'

Nope, I don't know.

'Two scoops of ice cream, soda and some elephant.'

'That's awful!' I cry, but he's on a roll.

'Okay, okay, wait. What does an elephant have that no other animal has?'

Pause.

'Baby elephants.'

I snort again. 'That one's funny. Hang on, I think I've got one for you,' I say. 'How do you fit six elephants in a car?'

'Go on, the suspense is killing me.' He grins.

'Three in the back, three in the front.'

'That's crap.' He laughs.

'What, and yours are comedy genius? I've got a better one for you.'

'Go on.'

'Let me see if I can remember how it goes.' I pause for a moment, trying to get the facts right in my head. 'Right, late one night, a burglar breaks into a house he thinks is empty. He tiptoes through the living room but freezes when he hears a loud voice say, "Jesus is watching you." It all goes quiet, so the burglar continues to creep forward. "Jesus is watching you," the voice booms again. The burglar stops dead. In a dark corner, he spots a parrot in a cage. "Did you just say Jesus is watching me?" he asks the parrot. "Yes," the parrot replies. The burglar breathes a sigh of relief then asks, "Is your name Jesus?" "No. It's Clarence," the bird says. "That's a dumb name for a parrot," sneers the burglar. "What idiot named you Clarence?" "The same idiot who named the Rottweiler Jesus."'

We both fall about laughing. Nathan collapses back onto the sand and I sneak a peek at his six-pack. A faded pink scar stretches jaggedly across his stomach, just below his ribs.

'How did you get that?' I ask.

'Surfing. Hit some rocks,' he replies, sitting back up.

'Oh, nasty!' I exclaim. 'What if that had been your head?'

'Sam would probably be an orphan right about now.'

The thought makes me shudder.

'I'm sorry about your parents,' I say quietly.

'Thank you. Me too.' We sit side by side and gaze out towards the open ocean. 'Sam won't go in the water anymore.'

'After the accident?' I prompt, but I know that's what he means.

'Yeah. He's fine on big boats, but anything smaller or

73

swimming . . . He hates it. For a while there I wasn't sure if I'd ever want to go surfing again. But I can't imagine a life without it.'

I glance up at him and the look on his face makes my heart want to break in two.

'Molly and Sam miss you, you know,' he says after a moment, looking across at me and brushing my fringe away from my forehead with his rough hand.

'I miss them too.'

'Have you ever thought about moving back here?'

'Right now I can't bear to think of ever leaving Australia again. I know that sounds dramatic, but my life in England seems so far away.'

'It doesn't sound dramatic.'

I realise I'm shivering.

'You're cold; you should take this off,' he says, and starts to unzip my wetsuit, before stopping abruptly and turning to look for a dry beach towel. I wriggle out of it down to my waist. He drapes the towel over my shoulders, and puts his arm around me, rubbing my cold arm vigorously with his hand. After a little while he stops and pulls me in tight to his warm body. We sit there for a few minutes longer watching the other surfers ride the waves. The way they keep their balance as their boards kick up and cut back down again reminds me of the skateboarders on the South Bank at home.

Finally Nathan speaks again. 'I guess we should get going. I promised a mate I'd help him on his house this morning. Do you fancy coming back to mine for some breakfast first?'

We pick up our boards and walk back towards his car. Nathan straps his surfboard to the roof rack while I change fully out of the wetsuit and pull on my skirt and T-shirt. My bikini isn't quite dry but it'll do.

He joins me in the front seat, looks down at me and smiles. 'It's good to see you again, Luce.' Then he starts up the engine and pulls away.

Chapter 4

Nathan lives in an apartment block just around the corner from the beach. Wetsuits hang out on a few of the balconies. So this is where the surfers live.

I follow him as we carry our boards and wetsuits over the prickly seaside grass to the main entrance. He lives on the top floor and bounds up the concrete stairs in front of me. I've no chance of keeping up but he waits at the top of the stairs in front of Number 7.

His key is in the lock and then we're inside. It's dark, the curtains still drawn. It's only about 8 a.m. – it appears Amy's not up yet. As Nathan opens the curtains, morning light spills across the small living room, presenting seventies-style carpets and matching brown and orange swirly curtains. Anyone else would probably make excuses for the decor, but Nathan says nothing and his confidence makes him seem so much older than his twenty-three years. I look around the flat and see a corridor leading away to what I'm guessing are the bedrooms.

'Can I see your room?' I hear myself asking.

'Sure.' He leads the way past another door which is shut. I wonder if Amy is sleeping behind it. His door is ajar. 'It's a bit of a mess,' he says and he's not lying. Jeans, cords, T-shirts and hooded jumpers spill out of open wooden drawers; a guitar is propped up against the unmade double bed. Books and magazines pile up precariously on one side of a wooden dressing table and an old TV set stands on the other. A portable CD/cassette player is on the floor next to his bed. A pile of CDs and cassettes lies messily next to it. Apart from those few things, he doesn't seem to have many other belongings.

As if reading my mind, he explains, 'I gave a lot of stuff away when I went travelling and it hasn't seemed worth buying much else.'

'When did you go travelling?'

'I've been a few times. I came back from my last trip early last year.'

'Where did you go?'

'Well, I've been to Indonesia and Thailand in the past, and have also spent some time backpacking around Australia, but most recently I just spent some months working up the coast on a few building sites, surfing and doing a bit of fruit picking, that sort of thing.'

I sit down on his unmade bed and pick up his guitar. 'Do you play?' he asks.

'No, not me.' But I give it a couple of strums anyway.

'Stop, you're shit.' He laughs.

'Go on, then; play me something.'

He sits down next to me, taking the guitar and tucking one long, lean leg underneath him. His dark hair is still damp from the surf.

'I'll get my own place, one of these days,' he says, resting his arm lazily across the guitar. He doesn't play it.

I pull my leg up underneath myself, mimicking his body language, and turn to face him.

'But I still haven't decided if or when I'll go travelling again.'

'Have you ever thought about coming to England?' I ask hopefully.

'Not really, but you never know.'

'You should!'

'Bit cold, though, isn't it?'

'It's not that bad,' I protest. 'The summers can be beautiful. And in winter there's nothing nicer than cosying up in front of a log fire with a pint. Well, actually I don't drink beer,' I correct myself. 'But you know, red wine—'

'Vodka . . .' he interrupts, smiling.

'Not anytime again soon, thank you. That hangover was a killer.'

He grins.

I can see now that many of the books next to the television are related to design and property.

'Dad's,' he says, clocking my stare. 'They're the only things of his that I really wanted to keep.'

'What happened to the boat?' I ask and instantly regret it.

'We sold it,' he answers curtly.

'Sorry, I didn't mean . . . I can't seem to keep my mouth shut.'

'It's okay.' He smiles.

'So what do you want to do? With your life, I mean.' I hope I'm not pushing my luck with all these personal questions, but he doesn't seem to mind.

'I don't really know yet. Sam was always so sure about what he wanted to do. He always liked being outside in the garden with Mum. I think I probably take more after Dad.'

'What, architecture?'

'No, not architecture. I've left it too late for that.'

'You've never left it too late.'

'No, I have. It's years and years of uni and I barely even finished high school.'

Suddenly the door bursts open and a slim, blonde, mussy-haired beauty is standing there in a skimpy T-shirt-and-short set.

'Hi!' I say a little too enthusiastically and leap to my feet.

Nathan calmly props his guitar against the bed and stands up. 'Amy, meet Lucy. Lucy, meet Amy.'

'Hi!' she exclaims, matching me for enthusiasm. 'I was wondering who was in here, chatting away.'

'I was just going to make some breakfast,' Nathan says. 'Want some?'

'Ooh, what are we having?' she coos.

'Depends. What do you fancy, Lucy?' He leads the way into a small kitchen and opens the rusty, pockmarked fridge door. 'Want a fry-up?' he asks. 'Or an omelette or something?'

'An omelette would be nice.' I realise I'm famished, having eaten hardly anything in my hung-over state the day before.

'Omelette, hey?' Amy chuckles. 'Your speciality, Nathan.' I don't like the way she says 'speciality'.

'So do you want some or not?' he asks her.

'No, I can't handle a stodgy meal at this hour. I'll stick to fruit.'

I'll stick to fruit, I echo bitchily inside my head. I don't know how I squeezed into her wetsuit. She seems to be having the same thought.

'Wetsuit fit okay?' she asks.

'Yes, perfectly,' I answer.

'Good!' She looks pleased. Or surprised. I can't tell.

'Orange juice?' Nathan interrupts.

'Yes, please.'

This is very domesticated. I can't see James doing the shopping while I'm away. It'll be takeaway all the way. Mind you, Amy may well have stocked up the fridge. I wonder if those are her eggs he's getting out. He cracks two into a chipped mug. Amy walks over to him and puts a hand on his back. It could be my imagination, but I swear I see him stiffen.

She then makes herself comfortable next to me at the kitchen table and asks me all about my trip. How long I'm here, how long since I was last here . . . Meanwhile Nathan brings our omelettes to the table and I attempt to eat, while answering her many questions. Blimey, she's an inquisitive little thing. A subtle shift seems to have taken place and I don't like it. The closeness Nathan and I felt on the beach has gone. He doesn't seem as relaxed with me, nor I around him.

'Are you going to Molly's hen night on Saturday?' Amy asks finally.

'I am. Are you?'

'Of course!'

I'm surprised. Why 'of course'? I didn't realise she and Molly knew each other that well.

'I'm glad she decided to have her hen night this Saturday instead of next Friday. Fancy considering having your hen night on the night before your wedding,' I say, shaking my head.

'Oh, she would've been fine. She just wouldn't have been able to drink much.'

'Exactly!' Nathan and I exclaim in unison before looking at each other and grinning, our familiarity temporarily restored.

A flicker of annoyance crosses Amy's face. 'I don't know why people need alcohol to have a good time.' Nathan looks at me and subtly raises his eyes to the ceiling. 'I don't really drink,' she explains. 'Seeing Nathan wake up after a night on the town is enough to put me off. Urgh!'

Seeing Nathan wake up. I wonder if she means seeing him from the other side of the same bed or just from the moment he walks out of his bedroom.

She glances over at the kitchen clock. 'It's almost nine, Nathan. Weren't you going to help Barry this morning?'

'Shit, yes.' He starts to clear the table.

'Don't worry, I'll do that later,' Amy offers, before I have a chance even to get out of my seat. 'Why don't I drop Lucy back?'

Oh, no.

'No, no, it's okay. I'll take her now.'

Thank you, Nathan!

'Don't be silly, I don't mind,' she persists.

I do!

'I have to go and see Molly anyway,' she explains.

'Is that okay?' Nathan looks at me.

'Of course,' I brightly reply. As if I'm going to say anything else.

'Go on, you, off you go,' Amy tells him impatiently. Is she waiting for him to leave first?

'Alright, Luce, I'll see you later,' he says.

When?

'Bye!' I force myself to sound merry. 'Thanks for, you know, taking me surfing and breakfast and everything . . .'

'No worries.' Nathan picks up his car keys from the counter

and heads out of the front door. As soon as he's gone, Amy tells me she'll be back in a minute and she returns wearing a short denim miniskirt and black T-shirt with a white Rip Curl logo. Her long blonde hair floats down her back. 'Right, then, let's go. You ready?'

Amy's car is a blue hatchback, the back window crammed full of cuddly toys. As I slam the door shut a small sleeping bunny in a hammock swings back and hits me in the eye. Amy laughs. 'Watch out for Snoozy!'

I know from self-defence classes in high school that you shouldn't have fluffy animals in your car because you could be targeted by rapists and murderers who think that you're a young, defenceless woman. I tell her this, a touch condescendingly.

She laughs derisively. 'I don't think there are too many of them around here. Anyway most of the time Nathan's with me.'

I manage to refrain from biting Snoozy's ears off with my bare teeth and spitting them out of the window.

'I like your earrings,' she says suddenly.

'Thanks.'

'Did you wear them to go surfing?' she asks, eyes widening.

'Er, yes,' I admit. 'I never take them off.'

'Are they from your boyfriend?' I nod. 'You're very, very lucky. I wish Nathan could afford to buy me diamond earrings.'

'I wouldn't worry. They're probably not even real.'

'Oh, *really*? Why do you think that?'

'I'm only joking.' I laugh, but even to myself it sounds hollow. Why did I say that?

'No, Nathan can't afford expensive gifts. He has to use his imagination instead.' I bet he does, I think, feeling slightly sick. 'For my last birthday he took me for a picnic on Shelly beach . . .' I don't want to hear this. 'It was so romantic. He packed everything himself.' Shut up! 'Yes, we ate lobster his mate had caught and drank sparkling wine. Not French champagne, of course, but it tastes the same to us.' I know I shouldn't be jealous because I have James, but the way she says 'us' makes me want to open the door and leap out of the moving vehicle. A minute later we pull up outside Sam and Molly's home.

'Amy,' Sam calls out warmly as we walk through the door. 'How are you?' He gives her a peck on the cheek and I suddenly feel like an outsider. He turns to me. 'Hi, you. Surfing, hey? That was a surprise. Molly and I could barely believe it when we woke up this morning and saw your note. When did you two arrange that little get-together?'

'Oh, he promised he'd take her the other night when he got so drunk he could barely speak the next morning,' Amy interrupts. She's smiling but I detect a hardness behind her eyes. Or maybe I'm just imagining it.

'Did you go too, Amy?' Sam asks, oblivious to whatever may or may not be going on between her and me.

'Oh, no, I find it too hard to get up these days.'

'Need your beauty sleep?' Sam chuckles. For the first time I notice he and Nathan have got the same laugh.

Molly comes into the room. 'Amy! Hello, love.' Another peck on the cheek.

'Hi, you! How's it all going? Only another week to go . . .' As Molly starts to fill her in on the latest wedding minutiae, Amy heads into the kitchen and puts the kettle on. 'Tea, Lucy?' I shake my head and make my excuses about needing a shower.

I'm taken aback by how comfortably Amy fits into my friends' home. Nathan seems adamant she isn't his girlfriend but she's sure acting like one. It's odd.

In the bathroom I catch sight of myself in the mirror and almost reel back in horror. In comparison to that pretty blonde thing out there, I look like a 'roo who's been pulled out of the bush backwards. Again I'm struck by the thought that Nathan might just see me like a big sister. How humiliating. Then my heart flutters as I remember his eyes looking searchingly into mine. Hang on, he had his arm around me! He brushed my fringe away from my face! That's quite an intimate thing to do, isn't it? Not the way you'd behave towards a big sister.

Is it?

I don't know. I really don't know. I have a horrible feeling I might be making more out of this than there really is, just to take myself away from my own sorry situation. Huh, I knew I should have been a psychologist.

The conversation I had with James last night comes back to me. I was very abrupt. I wonder what it is he's bought me. I should call him, I think miserably.

I'm not at all thrilled that Amy, let alone Nathan, saw me looking in such a state so I'm determined to scrub up nicely and get back out to the kitchen and chat to her. I'm ashamed about feeling bitchy towards her earlier. I wash and blow-dry my hair quickly and smooth on some hair serum. My hair is naturally wavy and thankfully it doesn't often frizz up, but the serum is my insurance policy against the sea air. I put on some of the Laura Mercier tinted moisturiser that Mum got me for Christmas, then apply lipgloss and a little mascara. Wrapping my towel back around me I duck outside and make a dash for my bedroom.

It looks like it's going to be another scorcher so I pull on a red and white dress from Warehouse and tie the straps of my favourite wedges around my ankles. Not half bad, I think as I look in the mirror; then I head out to the kitchen.

Oh, for pity's sake. She's gone, of course.

Chapter 5

'You look nice,' Molly gushes, as I walk into the recently Amy-evacuated kitchen. 'I like your dress.'

Sam's nowhere to be seen. 'Has Sam already left for work?' I ask.

'Yes, Amy's giving him a lift to the ferry. What did you think of her? She's lovely, isn't she?' Molly beams. Her eagerness is most definitely not contagious.

'Yeah, she seems really nice.' I know my voice is lacking conviction, but Molly doesn't seem to notice.

'Honestly, I can't believe she and Nathan aren't all loved up. They make *such* a fab couple.'

'From the way she was talking it seems like they're definitely an item.' I'm fishing.

'I don't think so. Well, I don't know. Maybe they are.'

'Well, like what he did for her on her birthday . . .'

Molly looks puzzled.

'You know, the fancy picnic with lobster and sparkling wine on the beach and everything.'

'Oh, that! The way Nathan described it to us made it sound like a bit of a beach party.'

A spark of hope . . .

'Really? I thought it sounded like he'd put it all on just for her.'

Molly snorts. 'You've got to be joking, haven't you? Nathan couldn't organise a piss-up in a brewery. He's hopeless. Nah, I reckon you must've got that slightly wrong.'

I'm confused. Amy made it sound romantic, just the two of them. Could she be jealous? Surely not with the way I was looking this morning.

I sit with Molly at the breakfast table while she munches on toast. My stomach still feels full from Nathan's omelette.

'He made you an omelette?' Molly squeals when I tell her. She really doesn't have a very high opinion of her soon-to-be brother-in-law, I must say. But I laugh along with her for fear of her getting suspicious. 'Seriously, Sam was quite concerned when he read your note this morning. I was relieved to see you walk back through the door.'

'Why?' I ask, irritated now.

'Just that Nathan's not very responsible. Something could have happened to you.'

'I can swim, you know.' I try not to sound too snappy. 'And actually he really looked after me.'

Molly raises her eyebrows, but doesn't push it further. Whereas I can't let it lie. 'I know Sam doesn't like the water anymore so I understand he might feel nervous.'

'Who told you that?' she asks, taken aback. 'Amy?'

'No, Nathan,' I answer, then quickly explain. 'He was just saying how he still loved to surf, despite his parents being killed.'

'He spoke to you about that?'

87

'Yes.' I can't help feeling smug.

'Nathan never, *ever* talks about their parents. I'm surprised. What time did you say you two stayed up talking the other night?' she pries.

'I don't know.'

'Huh,' is all she responds with.

'Want another cuppa?' I ask brightly, determined to change the subject.

The next day is Saturday and Molly and Sam's hen and stag nights are finally upon us. I don't know about the boys, but the plan is that all the girls will meet in Circular Quay later this afternoon. There are nine of us going in total, including Molly's boss, Sandra, and another friend of hers from work, Bea, two of Molly's university pals who I've never met and even a couple of girls from our school days.

Amy is coming to collect Molly, Sam and me at four o'clock to drive us to the ferry terminal so we don't have to walk down the hill in our heels. The boys are going bungee jumping this afternoon, God help them, and then on to a club or bar or something.

I'm aiming for simplicity tonight and have chosen a little black dress and kitten heels. I'm keeping my hair down and it's curling softly around my shoulders. Nathan hasn't seen me yet with my make-up on, so tonight I'm going for the full works. I'm assuming he'll be coming with us on the ferry.

I opt for a glimmer of gold eyeshadow, which brings out the amber flecks in my eyes, and I line my eyes with black kohl before slicking on two coats of lash-enhancing mascara. Rosy blusher highlights my cheekbones and then I apply lipliner and lipstick, before blotting my lips and dabbing on some shiny lipgloss. I stand back and survey myself. Yep, that'll do. I've got a nice tan now so don't need to vamp up my look too much. Quick spritz of perfume and I grab my clutch bag.

Sam wolf-whistles, wide-eyed, and I smile at him appreciatively. He's wearing a chocolate-brown shirt hanging loose over casual black khaki pants.

'Lucy, hi!' Amy appears from the living room wearing a short black miniskirt and charcoal-grey T-shirt with BABE emblazoned across it in pink diamanté. Her blonde hair is long and straight, and it falls halfway down her back. I suddenly feel overdressed, but then Molly materialises at the bottom of the stairs and I immediately feel better.

'Has the party started without me?' she asks. She's wearing a striking low-cut clingy red dress.

'You'd better not be going out looking like that,' Sam warns, 'or I'm going to have to cancel the stag night and be your bodyguard instead.' He puts his arms around her.

'You dag.' She giggles.

'You look beautiful!' Amy gushes, and I think: *I* was going to say that. 'Are we ready, then?' she asks.

Where's Nathan?

We pile into the car, Sam locking the front door behind us. Unable to contain my curiosity, I ask about Nathan. Amy explains he's meeting us at the ferry terminal because it would have been a bit of a squash in her car. Phew.

The next ferry is scheduled to leave in five minutes and I look around, distracted. I still can't see him.

We buy our tickets and go through the barriers as the ferry chugs into the wharf. Men in uniform lay the platforms down and incoming passengers stream onto the quay.

'Going without me?' a deep voice says in my ear and I turn around, elated.

'Hi, buddy!' Sam exclaims. 'Thought we were going to have to meet you over there.'

He looks sexy, more casually dressed than Sam in beige-coloured cord jeans and a slim-fit black T-shirt encasing his toned chest.

We file onto the big green and cream ferry and make our way to the top deck where there are four rows of wooden benches. Nathan sits facing backwards, next to Amy and opposite me. He leans back casually on the bench, knees almost reaching mine. 'You look nice,' he says.

'Thanks,' I respond, feeling shy suddenly. 'You too.'

The ferry chugs out of the terminal and we leave Manly behind us. As I look over to my right I see the Oceanworld aquarium on the shorefront. Nathan follows my gaze. 'Have you ever been?' I ask.

'Nup.'

'Me neither.'

'It's really good,' Molly says. 'You should try to go while you're here.'

'Sydney Aquarium is much better,' Amy interrupts.

'Have you been to both, then?' Molly queries.

'No, only Sydney Aquarium.'

'So how would you know which is better?' Nathan asks the question that we're all thinking.

'I just know,' Amy says tetchily, and I'm reminded she's only about twenty years old.

'I'll take you next week if you like?' Nathan leans in towards me.

'Okay.' I grin.

Amy shuffles uncomfortably in her seat. 'I'm going to sit inside,' she says. 'It's too windy out here.' She gets up and steps between Nathan and me, forcing him backwards in his seat. He leans back and watches her go.

'You should go and talk to her,' Molly urges.

'Why?' Nathan asks a little petulantly. 'I keep telling you she's not my girlfriend.'

'Well, she obviously feels something for you,' Molly responds sternly.

Sam stays quiet, keeping out of it.

Nathan just looks out to his left at the mainland.

'Well, I'll check on her, then,' Molly says brusquely, getting up.

'Do you want me to come?' I make as if to join her.

'No, it's okay. Probably better for me to chat to her alone. And anyway I don't want the wind to mess up my hair. I spent enough time with the straighteners this morning.'

'Been a long time since you were on this ferry, hey, Lucy?' Sam says, after she's left.

'Yeah,' I murmur, and as an afterthought get a hair tie out of my bag and pull my hair back into a ponytail. I remember how knotty it used to get on this crossing.

The last time I caught this ferry I was with Molly and Sam. The three of us hung over that very railing, Molly and I both flanking Sam in the middle. It was just before I left Australia and they were on one of their on-again times. I remember feeling terribly left out. On the whole they never made me feel like three was a crowd, but at that age and at that time, especially considering the feelings I had for Sam, it was quite painful. Sam kept putting his hand up to stroke Molly's mop-head and they

91

were laughing as our hair blew all over the place. I still recall the comb bringing tears to my eyes as I tried to untangle my hair that night.

Sam's mobile phone rings and he makes his way to the other side of the ferry to take the call, leaving Nathan and me alone and facing each other.

There are no buildings on this part of the mainland and it's green, full of trees. The tops of the city's business towers start to appear above the cliffs. I can just make out concrete structures on the cliff face.

'Look.' I get up and go over to the railings. 'I've never noticed those before.' Nathan joins me and we stand side by side. 'Are they left over from the war, do you think?' I ask, nodding towards the small, grey buildings.

He leans over, resting his elbows on the railings.

'That's right,' I continue. 'Didn't the Japanese manage to get submarines into Sydney Harbour?'

'That rings a bell. But I left school at sixteen, remember?' he answers.

I don't really know what to say to that.

'Sam would know for sure,' he says after a moment. 'Ask him when he gets back.'

I see some movement in the ocean and spot seals ducking and diving in the surf alongside the boat, their small black bodies slick with the water. The white foam from the ferry's wake is almost blinding in the sunlight.

I'm glad of the distraction.

'That reminds me of our dolphins.' I look across at him.

'That was a classic,' he responds. 'Actually, I've got a joke for you.'

'Not another elephant joke . . .' I groan.

'No. I found my old joke book last night and they really are crap. Well, unless you want to know why elephants have trunks?'

'Since you're asking . . .'

'Because they can't afford suitcases.'

'That's shit!' I squeal.

'I did warn you.'

'Was that the worst?'

'Of the elephant jokes?'

I nod.

'Hell no, I can top that.'

'Go on, then.'

'Okay, but this is definitely my last one, because the others really are appalling. What's the similarity between a plum and an elephant?'

Pause.

'They're both purple. Except for the elephant.'

I laugh, then snort and he grins down at me.

'So do you want to hear my properly funny joke?' he asks, after a while.

'Are you sure it's *properly* funny?'

'Yes.'

'I think I need to after that.'

'Okay. Brace yourself,' he says. 'A man is stopped by the police for driving a van full of penguins. Even though the man argues that the penguins are all his friends, the policeman orders him to take the penguins to the zoo. The very next day, the same man, the same van and the same penguins are stopped by the same policeman, except this day all of the penguins are wearing shades. "I thought I told you to take these penguins to the zoo," the policeman says. "I did," the man replies, "and today we're going to the beach."'

'What are you laughing at?' Molly and Amy appear through the cabin doorway.

'Oh, just telling silly jokes,' I giggle.

Sam returns, putting his mobile phone back into his pocket. 'Ben and Adam are running a bit late.'

Nathan looks at his watch. 'No worries. We've got an hour to kill. Beer down by the harbour?'

'Sounds good,' Sam agrees.

'Amy's going to pop in and see her mum when we get there,' Molly tells me. 'She'll meet us in an hour at the Ocean Room.'

I forget to ask Sam about the Japanese submarines in the harbour.

As the ferry turns the corner, the Sydney Opera House looms into view. There are dozens of sailboats out, all leaning in exactly the same direction. The ferry honks its horn as a small group of them veer dangerously close. One cuts in front of us and the three teenage kids on board laugh. Molly rubs Sam's lower back gently as he looks away from the sailboat, back to the Opera House. I peek at Nathan, but his face gives nothing away.

We pass Fort Denison on our left – the old penal colony where prisoners were once kept, as I definitely remember learning at high school. Surely even Nathan would know that one. I'm not about to ask, though.

'There's the Botanic Gardens.' Molly nudges me and points. 'Look, Sam, there's another function going on.' We can see a white marquee on the lawn. 'That's where we'll be having ours,' she says as she turns to me.

'It's going to be incredible,' I gasp in amazement.

'Isn't it?' Molly beams.

We pull past the Opera House and clearly see the two structures. It actually comprises three separate buildings; the small one is around the other side. Many people think the Opera House is made of one big structure.

I glance up and see a white jumbo jet flying above the city. That's where I'll be next week, I think, and my heart sinks as the plane soars higher into the cloudless sky.

The ferry pulls into Circular Quay and we follow the hoards of passengers as we walk through the terminal.

'See you later, then,' Amy says to Molly.

'Okay, love.' Molly gives her a quick hug, before Amy hurries off, shouting bye to the rest of us over her shoulder.

'What's up with her?' Sam asks.

'The usual.' Molly smiles sardonically. 'Boys!' She looks at Nathan. He just shrugs.

Outside again in the warm sunshine Molly looks at her watch and turns to the guys. 'We're early too. Do you fancy grabbing a quick drink together first?'

'I don't know if that would be allowed, would it, Nathan?' Sam teases. 'Drinking with the missus on my last proper night of freedom, and scaring all those single girls off?'

Molly kicks him up the backside and he laughs, pulling her in for a hug. It's lovely seeing how well they get on these days, compared to when we were younger and jokey comments like that would incite the other's insecurities. I wonder if I would find it quite so lovely if Nathan wasn't around. Would I feel a little left out, resentful even? I shouldn't do, knowing I have a boyfriend back in London. But that's hardly the most soothing thought right now, is it?

'Shall we just go round to the Opera Bar or somewhere?' Sam suggests.

The bars are already heaving. It's a warm late afternoon.

'What's that up there?' I ask, looking up at a first-floor window. We can just make out people wearing big puffa jackets and hoods behind what looks like a window made of thick, solid ice.

'minus5°,' Sam says. 'It's an ice bar. Literally. Everything's made out of ice.'

'Can we go there for a drink?' I turn to the others excitedly.

'You are such a tourist.' Sam laughs.

'Yeah, and?'

'Oh, come on,' Molly urges. 'It'll be memorable if nothing else.'

We make our way through the busy downstairs bar and head up the stairs. It's $30 to go in for half an hour – about £12 – and for that you get a cocktail. Or you can pay an extra $10 and get two cocktails.

'Thirty bucks!' Nathan scoffs. 'What a rip-off.'

'Do you not want to go in?' I feel myself losing enthusiasm.

'Oh, come on, what else do you spend your money on?' Molly laughs.

We look at the cocktail list and see they're all vodka based. Nathan and I grin naughtily at each other.

We pay up and the receptionist hands each of us long furry coats and pagers which we hang around our necks. 'When the first beep goes, you have five minutes. When the next beep goes, you have to come out,' she explains, then ushers us forward to the next door.

We stand behind a rope while a short bleached-blonde girl

hands us each two sets of gloves. 'These ones are for warmth and these ones are waterproof,' she says. 'The glasses are made of ice and they're your glasses for the duration, so if you choose to buy another drink, make sure you hang on to them. There's a water sculpture inside but it's made with antifreeze, so *don't* drink it,' she cautions.

Sam rolls his eyes good-humouredly. 'What a rigmarole,' he whispers as we're ushered through into another room where a man gives Molly and me sheepskin boots to put on in place of our heels. I'm beginning to think this is a bad idea. I'm looking less like a hen and more like an Eskimo every minute. Finally we're told by the blonde girl to go through to another room and close the door behind us before opening the door to the ice room itself. By this stage we're all sniggering.

'This'd better be good,' Nathan says.

The cold air hits us as we walk through the door and we're immediately greeted with an ice sculpture of a kangaroo. The whole room is made of ice – tables, chairs, the bar, decorations, everything. Giant ice chandeliers hang down from the ceiling. It's breathtaking and I'm already wishing I had an ice room in my flat.

Our flat, I mean. I'm feeling more and more single with every day that passes. I haven't spoken to James since he woke me up the other night. Every time he or that sodding text pops into my mind I force them back out again. One minute my heart is telling me one thing and my head is telling me another and the next it's the other way around. I don't know whether I'm coming or going. I'm just going to enjoy the here and now. Considering what could be waiting for me when I get home, I think I owe that to myself.

Is he cheating on me? No, no, he can't be. But maybe he is. Oh, give it a rest, Lucy!

The barman immediately whacks out four solid-ice glasses and starts pouring vanilla vodka into them. We look around the room. There are only about six other people in here.

I turn around and see a replica of Michelangelo's *David* behind us. 'Looks like the cold is affecting him too.' Nathan grins, observing the statue's not-very-ample genital region.

It's a surreal experience. Looking down out of the ice window we can see people walking by on the busy pavement, dressed in their summer clothes. 'It's freezing in here!' Molly laughs.

'That's the point, my darling,' Sam tells her.

Five minutes later the six people already in the bar when we came in make their way out, their pagers bleeping. The bartender collects up their ice glasses.

'Where are you all from?' he asks us. I notice his English accent for the first time.

'Manly,' the others tell him, but he's looking at me.

'Manly originally but I've been living in London for about ten years.'

'Which part?' he asks.

'Marylebone,' I tell him and he nods.

'If you're originally from Sydney, why on earth are you living in London?'

'I like it.'

'She's dating an Englishman,' Molly chips in.

'What about you?' I ask him quickly. 'Where are you from?'

'Essex, I'm afraid. I've been here since April last year. Almost time to go home again.'

Ten minutes and two free shots later, the barman points at the earpiece he's wearing. 'They've been telling me your half an hour is up for eight minutes now. Your pagers must be broken.'

We say our goodbyes and head outside onto the warm, bright pavement. I literally feel like I'm thawing out after the cold air in the ice room. The alcohol coursing through my veins probably helps too.

'Right, then,' says Sam, rubbing his hands together. 'This is where the fun starts.'

He pecks me on the cheek. 'See ya, Lucy. Look after her for me.'

Molly kisses Nathan and then grabs his arms, shaking him affectionately. 'And *you* look after *him*!'

'I will, don't worry. Bye, Luce, have a good night.' Nathan bends down and gives me a kiss, daringly close to my lips.

'Bye!' I immediately feel my face heat up.

'We wouldn't have wanted to stay in there for much longer – I was freezing my tits off!' Molly laughs as we walk away. For all of ten seconds I resist the urge to glance over my shoulder, but when I finally give in and look back I can't see them anymore.

Molly and I make our way around the other side of Circular Quay to the International Passenger Terminal. It may not sound glamorous but the bars gracing the downstairs decks certainly are, with their funky interiors, cool laid-back exteriors and perfect views of the Harbour Bridge and Opera House.

'There you are.' Molly smiles. Amy is already seated in one of the chocolate-brown outdoor sofas next to a couple of girls who look vaguely familiar.

'Lucy!' one of them exclaims when she sees me.

'Oh, my God! Amanda! Jenny!' I hardly recognise my friends from school. They jump up and hug me and drag me down to sit between them, whereupon they want to know anything and everything that's happened to me in the last nine years. After a few minutes Bea, Molly's work friend, arrives to join us, then Sandra, and then Molly's friends from university until eventually there are nine of us squeezed around the table, drinking champagne cocktails.

She might've booked a tacky stretch limo, but apart from that Molly was hoping to avoid drawing too much attention to us tonight, so she's not very impressed when Jenny pulls out a whistle shaped like a penis and starts to blow on it. That opens it right up for the other hens and soon poor Molly is being showered with a bright pink feather boa, handcuffs and L-plates, among other delightful little trinkets like glow-in-the-dark penis earrings. Nice. I notice Amy is rather quiet amid all the mayhem so I lean across to her and ask her how her mum was. 'She's fine, thanks.' She picks up her Diet Coke and takes a sip, looking away from me. I feel like I've been dismissed.

The sun sets over the harbour, casting an apricot glow across the Opera House. It's time for dinner so we make our way further around the Quay to where we've booked a table at an Italian restaurant. As we sit down, a jolly Italian waiter with an impressive moustache starts to serenade us.

Several bottles of red wine later I feel stuffed to the brim and can't believe I'm even *considering* dessert. Am I mad? The waiter comes around to top up my glass. The bottle's almost empty so I wave my hand vigorously and direct him to Molly's glass. 'She's getting married.' I'm feeling more than a little tipsy now.

'Aah, married!' he says, looking heartbroken. 'Shame. So beautiful . . .' And then he starts to sing again: 'Happy marriage to you, happy marriage to you . . .'

Forty-five minutes and lots of laughter later we've paid the bill and Molly and I lead the way, arms linked through each other's as we practically stumble down the stairs to the street where our bright pink limo awaits. The other hens squeal with delight. When our limo driver gets out of the car, I notice with glee that he looks a bit like a cross between Eric Bana and Mark Ruffalo.

'I'm getting in the front . . .'

Molly drags me back in fits of laughter. Poor guy has no idea what he's in for. We start to pile into the back of the car. It's a little shabby, which you wouldn't know from the outside, but we're not really in the habit of giving a jot right now. Amanda cracks open the champagne.

'Molly, what are you *doing?*' I look out to see her standing on the pavement, swaying slightly. Amy is talking to her. I almost fall over as I exit the vehicle and join them.

'Are you alright?' I try to pronounce my words properly. Amy looks at me brightly. Whoops, I forgot she wasn't a drinker. What was that she said yesterday morning?

'*Seeing Nathan wake up after a night on the town is enough to put me off . . .*'

Nasty thought, nasty thought . . . Go away.

'Amy's going to her mum's!' Molly exclaims, as though it's the most disappointing news she's ever heard.

'No!' I protest. 'It's only eleven o'clock. You have to come dancing!'

'No, really, girls, I'm going to go. I promised my mum. Sorry,' she says, perfectly sober.

'Do you want a lift?' Molly slurs.

'No, it's okay.' She smiles tightly. 'My parents live only up the road.'

'Are you *rich?*' I ask, drunkenly, surprised. You'd have to be wealthy to live in this area.

'Come on!' the other hens squeal.

Molly drags me away and we stumble back into the car. Jenny passes us a couple of full champagne glasses.

'I don't think I need any more,' Molly says. 'I'm feeling a little bit peeeesssed.'

We cruise out of the Rocks area and into the city, winding our way through the streets towards King's Cross. Our next stop is a nightclub.

Jenny's blowing Molly's penis whistle. I start to giggle and find I can't stop.

James seems so far away, so separate from everything that I'm going through now. I feel happy, free. I could stay here, I think. I could not go back.

We arrive in King's Cross, Sydney's red-light district. Molly and I called the club the other day and arranged a guest list, so we don't have to queue for ages to get in. The doorman lifts up the rope, leering at Jenny's penis whistle and paying extra-special attention to Molly's low-cut dress. But she doesn't mind; it's her night.

Inside, the music is pumping and the room is teeming with guys looking trim in tight T-shirts.

Is this a *gay* bar, I wonder.

'Is this a *gay* bar?' I yell.

'Lucy!' Molly screams, outraged. 'No, it bloody isn't. I want to be flirted with on my last single Saturday!'

'Humph,' I say. The guys here look pretty gay to me.

We split up and half of the hens head to the bar while Molly and I and a couple of others make our way to the dance floor.

Immediately a group of guys gyrate up against us, disgustingly. I've had too much to drink and I'm feeling a bit too out of it for this. Plus I'm missing Nathan – no, James it should be – so I excuse myself and go and sit in the corner. Minutes later Molly appears with a couple of waters and slumps down next to me.

'Fanks,' I say glumly, and take a sip. We sit for a few minutes watching the mayhem on the dance floor.

'Is this hard for you?' Molly turns to me suddenly, struggling to be serious.

'Why, because my own relationship's so shit?' I sink down further in my seat.

'No, because of how you feel for Sam.'

'What do you mean?' I sit up, immediately alert.

'Sorry, I mean how you *felt* for Sam. Back in high school,' she corrects herself.

'You *knew* about that?'

'Of *course* I did,' she says. 'You were – you *are* – my besht friend. How could I not?'

'Did Sam know?' How mortifying.

'Nah.' Molly shakes her head. 'He's a man. They're oblivious to everything.'

'Well, I can tell you now that I am well and truly over him,' I say, passionately over-pronouncing every word of my statement.

'I know you are.' She looks back to the dance floor.

'No, I *am*. I really am.' This is excruciating.

'I know, Lucy. You're with James now, and you guys will work things out.'

'Of course we will,' I insist, overenthusiastically.

The truth is I don't at this precise moment think we will. James seems part of another world. A world which I'm no longer a part of. My world feels like it's right here, right now, with Molly's fiancé's twenty-three-year-old surfer brother. But I'm hardly going to tell her that. Even drunk as a skunk, I know how ridiculous it sounds.

Jenny appears, blowing that goddamn penis whistle, and I feel bizarrely thankful for the rude interruption. We drag Molly back up onto the dance floor.

Two hours later, when we are all well and truly past it, we stumble out of the nightclub and back into the waiting limo. Hot Mark Ruffalo glances at us in the rear-view mirror. 'Manly?' he asks.

'Yes, please,' I manage to tell him.

Molly's boss and a couple of the other girls have already left, but we drop Amanda, Jenny and Bea at various points along the way and eventually approach the Harbour Bridge. There are seagulls or bats – I'm not sure which – flying above it, looking like hundreds of flecks of ash floating around in the light of the uplit buildings.

Molly and I lean back sleepily in our seats. 'I don't feel well,' she murmurs.

The house is dark when we get home; the boys aren't back yet. For the first time it occurs to me that Nathan *might* come back to the house with Sam. I hope he does. I hope so much that it hurts.

Molly stumbles upstairs towards the bedroom and plonks herself down on the bed, dragging me with her. 'That was the besht night,' she tells me.

'Hey?' Sam's voice is bleary in the darkness.

'Sorry!' I whisper loudly, startled that he's there.

It's only the last couple of steps that are bothersome. But fortunately I don't tumble down the whole flight. The door to

'Nathan's' bedroom is closed. I lie in my own bed, willing myself to sober up, still wondering if he's next door. Sleep eventually takes me and the next thing I know I'm dying of thirst and daylight is spilling down from underneath my blinds.

Chapter 6

BANG BANG BANG BANG BANG!

Huh? I think sleepily.

BANG BANG BANG BANG BANG!

Bert the bat?

The door flings open and Molly is standing there in the doorway, pretending to be furious.

'What the hell is THIS?' She lifts up the pink fluffy handcuffs which are attached to her arm. 'Call yourself my best friend and you don't even *uncuff* me?'

I try to sit up but someone whacks me on the back of the head with a hammer. Or at least, that's what it feels like.

'Ow!' I slouch back onto the pillow, holding my hand to my forehead.

'Yes, *ow*,' she says. 'How do you think I feel? I've been bloody arrested!'

'Stop it, you're making me laugh.'

Molly looks down at me sternly. 'I hope you've got a key, missy.'

Shit, a key! Where is it?

'Um . . .'

'Oh, for goodness sake, Lucy.' She laughs.

'I'm sure I must do. It should be in my handbag. Let me check.'

She leaves in a fake huff and I get up, S-L-O-W-L-Y, so as not to do any more damage to my hammer-head.

I pause for a moment, listening. I can't hear the boys. I'm sure Nathan won't be here, but I'm buggered if I'm going to risk it. I pull open the cupboard door and eye my reflection. Good job, Lucy, I think sarcastically as I spot my panda bear right eye next to my clean left eye. Didn't quite pull that off, then, when I attempted to remove my make-up last night.

I search my handbag for a key, without any luck, and drag on my jeans and a T-shirt. I try to ignore the attractive bruises on my legs, courtesy of those inconvenient stairs last night. I attempt to smooth down my hair, then pad barefoot down the corridor in the direction of the bathroom and my make-up remover. Nathan's bedroom door opens suddenly and I reel backwards in surprise. The smell of cigarettes, alcohol and sleep wafts out of the room.

'Morning,' he says groggily.

'Hello!' I reply a little too brightly and start to hurry past him, resisting the urge to cover up my right eye with my hand.

'Have you been in a *fight*?' he asks.

'No, no, just a make-up incident.'

'A what?'

'I'll be with you in a minute!' I nip into the bathroom.

Oh, God. Oh, God. Oh, God, he's here! My stomach backflips in quick succession like an Olympic gymnast on a bench. Quickly I brush my teeth, while at the same time doing a rush job on my right eye.

Sam, Molly and Nathan are in the kitchen when I re-emerge, Nathan studying the handcuff attached to Molly's right arm.

'No key?' he asks. I shake my head remorsefully. 'One of those little hairclips should do it,' he tells me.

Two minutes later, there's a click and Molly is set free. 'Yay!' we all yell.

'You're pretty nifty, mate. Where did you learn to do that?' Sam turns to his brother suspiciously.

'Read about it in *The Famous Five*,' is his dry response.

Nathan, I notice, is still wearing the same outfit he had on last night. He looks rough.

Phwoar.

'Did you have a good night?' I ask him, when Molly and Sam have gone back up to their bedroom.

'Yeah.' He scratches the stubble on his jaw.

'How was the bungee jumping?'

'A massive rush.'

'Really?'

'Yeah. You should try it sometime.'

'No, thanks. Knowing my luck, the cord would probably break. What did you get up to afterwards?'

He chuckles and shakes his head. 'That's classified information, I'm afraid.'

'What goes on stag night, stays on stag night?' I raise an eyebrow.

'Exactly.' He smirks.

'I hope you didn't take your brother to a strip joint . . .'

'I'm not saying *anything*.' He grins, then stretches his arms above his head and yawns loudly. His T-shirt rides up and shows his tanned abdomen, dark hairs creeping from his navel downwards . . . I do an involuntary shake of my head to bring myself back to my senses.

We've decided to go out for breakfast at a café in Manly. Nathan pulls up a chair opposite me and picks up a menu.

'That blonde last night was into you,' Sam says to him, after a moment. The nausea I instantly feel has nothing to do with the amount of alcohol I consumed last night.

'What blonde?' Molly pries.

Nathan doesn't answer.

'Ah, a pretty little thing who wouldn't leave him alone. You were on fire last night, mate!'

Nathan rolls his eyes and shakes his head.

'Poor Amy,' Molly says.

Poor Lucy, I think dismally, and try to focus on the menu. When I look back up at him he's staring at me. I can't read his expression.

'I'm going to go for bacon and eggs,' Molly decides out loud.

'That sounds good; make that two,' Sam adds. Nathan opts for an omelette and toast.

Molly and I head off to the counter to place our orders. In the end I choose pancakes and maple syrup. I need stodge and I need sugar, I decide, knowing full well that what my body actually needs is a nice banana or something. Bollocks to that. Back at the table I notice Nathan is drawing patterns in salt grains that he's poured onto the wooden surface. I lean over, take a pinch and superstitiously throw the salt back over my left shoulder.

'Oi!' he says. 'You've ruined my design.'

'Your design.' Sam sniggers. 'What are you designing, mate?'

'Could've been my house, you never know.' Nathan grins back at him.

'That'll be the day.' Sam laughs.

Ten minutes or so later, the waitress appears with our food.

'So what did you boys get up to last night?' Molly asks as we tuck in. 'I hope you didn't allow any bony strippers to gyrate on my husband,' she says, turning to Nathan. Both boys laugh, but with guilt or outrage, I'm not sure. 'Actually, I don't want to know.' She looks at me ruefully.

I've gone off my pancakes. But I've eaten one and I'm feeling pretty stuffed. I don't really want to pig out in front of Nathan in any case, so I put my knife and fork together on my plate.

'How's your omelette?' I ask after a while.

'Not bad.'

'Doesn't look as good as the one you made me.'

'Did you hear this?' Molly turns to Sam. 'Nathan made Lucy an *omelette*.'

'Jeez, that's advanced, mate. You'll be doing a Jamie Oliver next.'

'Christ, what do you think I am, completely incompetent?' he replies, jokily exasperated. I do wonder if Nathan gets pissed off with all the stick he gets from them.

'Right, I'm off,' he says after a few more minutes, standing up and reaching into his pocket for his wallet.

'Are you going surfing today?' I ask.

'Yeah, I might go out later,' he answers. 'But right now I'm going home to bed.'

He throws down $10, checking with Molly if it's enough. Sam stands up and gives him a big bear hug.

'Thanks for looking after me last night, mate,' he says.

'Yes, thank you for looking after my fiancé!' Molly looks up at them cheerfully.

'Alright, mop-head, see you later.' He ruffles her hair. 'See ya, Luce.' He glances back at me. And then he's gone, and I feel empty inside.

Chapter 7

'Do you want to come to the shop with me today?' Molly asks.

'No,' I reply. 'I think I'll go into the city.'

It's Monday morning and Sam is making himself breakfast while Molly and I unload the dishwasher.

'Why don't you meet me for lunch?' Sam asks.

'Ah, that'd be nice,' Molly encourages me.

'Okay, that'd be great.' I smile, a little uncertain.

Sam and I used to feel relaxed in each other's company years ago, but we might not be as comfortable these days without Molly around. Maybe it'll be good to spend some time with just him. Build our friendship back up on purely platonic terms.

It's hot and stuffy on board the speedy Jetcat to the city and a baby won't stop crying. I'd give anything to be standing with Nathan on a green and cream ferry looking over the railings at the seals.

I still can't stop thinking about him. This crush, or whatever the hell it is, shows no signs of weakening. It strikes me at that moment that I haven't had a single crush on anyone in three years, and now someone has come along just when I needed a distraction from my fears about my boyfriend. I wonder how many more hours I'll get to spend with Nathan before I leave.

Before I leave. Only six more days left and then I'll be heading home on another dreaded flight. Home to James. Home to our flat. I usually love the thought of going home to our flat. Well, I usually love the thought of going home to my boyfriend, but let's not get into that now. Or maybe we should. I need to get some perspective on things, much nicer though it would be to bury my head in the sand and ignore it all.

James was my first proper boyfriend. Even though we met when I was twenty-two, I really hadn't had a boyfriend before him. Just a couple of flings. I'd lost my virginity to someone called Dave in my first year of university, something I intensely regretted afterwards. I was drunk and it wasn't love. But I had stubbornly resolved to make it work, even though Dave and I had nothing in common. It ended when I saw him snogging another girl in the corner of the student union and I made a right spectacle of myself by throwing his pint of beer over him. I was devastated at the time. He was devastated I'd wasted his pint. To be honest, he was a bit smelly and had terrible dress sense. I probably just needed someone to take my mind off Sam.

Molly wrote more often than Sam. He was never good at writing – only talking. And gardening ... Over the years, my friendship with Molly strengthened while Sam and I drifted further apart. There was nothing I could do. Sam used to confide in me when he and Molly had a bust-up. Now I'd gone, he only had Molly to confide in.

I think it was James who finally cured my Sam obsession.

Because it was an obsession. I remember once going round to Sam's house to find him listening to moody music in his bedroom – the very room I'm staying in now. I asked him if he was okay. I could see he was anything but. He told me that at the school disco the night before he'd seen Molly cosying up to a guy in the year above us. I'd seen it too. At the time, instead of feeling sorry for Sam, I'd been hopeful that maybe she'd find someone else and leave him free and single for me. But I tried to reassure him.

'She does love you, you know.'

'I don't know, Lucy. She's so hard to read sometimes.'

'I could talk to her if you like?'

'No, it's okay. I don't want you brought into this.'

I'm already in on this, I thought. If only I could take myself out of it.

He took my hand and said, 'What a shame you and I aren't into each other, Lucy.' I squeezed his hand tighter, silently screaming: I *am* into you! I'm in love with you! 'But we're too much alike, aren't we?' he continued.

I had to look away to stop him from seeing the pain in my eyes.

I remember now that Nathan's door had been ajar and I peeked in as I walked out of Sam's room. He seemed so young back then, skinny legs sticking out beneath his shorts. He had his hair long then too, in contrast to Sam, who always kept his short. He was sitting strumming on his guitar and I could see his lips moving as he mouthed the words to a song I couldn't hear. He looked up, startled, then shouted at me: 'Close the door, Lucy!'

'I'm not listening!' I shouted back. But he slammed the door in my face.

I held on to my feelings for Sam for years, through all the

letters from Molly telling me about how she was comforting him in the wake of his parents' deaths, right through to just a few years ago when you could sense their relationship had reached a whole new level.

I never told James how I felt about Sam, but I did tell him about our friendship. I think I did a pretty good job of making out how purely platonic it was from both our sides, and then after a year or two I began to believe it as well. Sam was just a high-school crush. I know it's deranged, but I'd enjoyed the teenage angst and feelings of unrequited love, and leaving Australia so suddenly had only served to draw out those feelings for longer.

'Lucy!' Sam exclaims, as he appears down the path in the Royal Botanic Gardens wearing beige shorts and a beige long-sleeved shirt. He has a straw hat on his head, green gloves on his hands, and big black boots on his feet. His legs are much hairier than they used to be. He looks kind of cute. Definitely not fanciable.

'Hi, you,' I reply, as he leans down to give me a kiss.

We walk back the way I've come. 'I hope it's not this windy on Saturday,' he muses.

'I was thinking the same thing.'

A little, red trackless train drives past, pulling three carriages full of people. 'That's what you'll be arriving in on the Big Day.' Sam grins.

'*Really?*'

'Yep.' He laughs. 'Didn't Molly tell you?'

'No, she didn't.'

'I hope I haven't ruined the surprise. Don't tell her I've told you, just in case.'

We walk back out past the Opera House and down the steps to the lower pavement, which is bustling with busy bars.

We choose one and take a table just outside the doors, where we're sheltered from the wind. Sam goes to place our order, waving aside any attempts to force payment on him.

'I want your advice,' he says, once he's seated again. He takes a small red box out of his pocket and pushes it towards me. I open it up carefully.

'Wedding present for Molly,' he tells me. 'You think she'll like it?'

It's a silver bangle, studded with tiny diamonds.

'It's beautiful,' I gasp. 'Are these real?' I point at the diamonds.

'Yep,' he confirms.

'Sam, she's going to love it.'

'Phew. So glad you think so.'

'She told me about your proposal,' I say after a moment.

'Did she?'

'Yes. So romantic in the glasshouse . . .'

'. . . in amongst the Australian tropical rainforest . . .'

'. . . with the city looming overhead.' I smile.

'Did she tell you about my wet trousers?'

'No!' I laugh.

'Goddamn sprinkler system. I knelt down on the platform and got soaked through.'

'Well, at least you knelt down. Good boy! Your mother would have been proud of you.' I immediately take a sharp intake of breath. Should I have said that?

He smiles sadly. 'I wish they could have been here.'

'I know you do. Me too.' I look up into his big brown eyes and see they're filled with tears.

116

'Bloody hell, Luce, look what you've gone and done now.' He laughs, brushing them away.

'I'm so sorry.' Reaching across the table, I squeeze his hand, tears pricking my eyes.

'Thanks,' then a moment later, 'Right! Change of subject, please!'

So we sit there, drinking our drinks and chatting about old times until finally Sam's due back at work. He kisses me goodbye, then embraces me in a big bear hug, rocking me sideways for a few seconds before standing back and holding me by my arms, looking down at me.

'Why don't you move back?' he says. 'We miss you.'

'I miss you guys too.'

'But seriously, why don't you? James can come too!' he suggests chirpily.

'Nah, he can stay put.' I giggle. 'I'll move back and marry your brother instead.'

Sam throws his head back and laughs heartily. 'See ya tonight,' he says, turning away.

Oh, if only he knew . . .

Three hours later, worn out from swerving around the hoards of Japanese tourists, I return to the ferry dock, if not exactly laden down with shopping bags, with at least a few nice purchases. I found a pretty white skirt in Country Road, a funky bead necklace in Witchery and even a couple of silly boxing kangaroo pens for my work colleagues, Chloe and Gemma.

The return Jetcat ride seems quicker than the journey over and soon I'm disembarking onto Manly Wharf. With the sun beating down, the last thing I feel like is a twenty-minute walk up the hill, but the prospect of having the house to myself for an hour and resting out in the garden on a sunlounger with my book, is too tempting. I spot a café and order a small cup of vanilla ice-cream to make the journey pass quicker, and then start the trek back to Sam and Molly's place.

A young mother jogs by in a navy-blue tracksuit, pushing her pram as she goes.

A minute later I hear the footsteps of another jogger behind me and move over to the left of the pavement to let them pass.

'Lucy!'

It's Nathan.

'I thought it was you.' He slows down to join me on the pavement. 'Where have you been?'

'I've just been into the city to see your big brother and do some shopping.' My heart beats faster in my chest as I look up at him. 'I'm not looking forward to the walk home, though.' I motion up the steep hill with my ice-cream spoon.

'Come back to my place if you like and I'll give you a lift.'

'Really?' I feel stupidly ecstatic.

'Of course.'

We turn round and head back into town towards the beach. He walks slowly, laid-back.

'Not surfing today?' God, I fancy him.

'I went out this morning. Good waves. You should've come,' he answers.

'I would've done if you'd asked me.'

'Really?'

'Yes.' How can he not tell?

We cruise along the street in his battered station wagon and up the hill towards Sam and Molly's house. Nathan pulls up outside and turns off the ignition, cutting short the Aussie rock song that was blaring out of the stereo.

'Want to come in for a cuppa?' I ask him hopefully.

'Why not?' He unbuckles his seat belt.

I can barely keep the smile from my face as we go into the kitchen. I put the kettle on, while Nathan gets a couple of mugs out and pours in some milk, before chucking a couple of teabags on top.

'Ew!' I laugh. 'You're supposed to put the milk in afterwards.'

'Try it. It's better this way,' he says confidently.

'But the tea won't brew properly,' I argue.

He reaches over and plucks out one of the teabags before tipping the milk down the sink. 'I'll prove it to you.'

'Okay, you're on.'

The kettle boils and I pour water into both cups.

'That looks disgusting.' I snigger, looking over at his watery, milky concoction.

'You'll eat your words soon, Luce.' He grins, stirring his teaspoon around.

'Good colour,' I observe, a minute later.

'Especially compared to your scummy one,' he says.

Hmm. Mine does look a bit scummy.

'Well?' He eyes me questioningly as I take a sip from both mugs of tea.

In response I pour the contents of mine into the sink.

He smacks his hand down on the counter, victoriously. 'I told you!'

'Yeah, alright, alright, don't be a bad winner.'

He leans across me and flicks the kettle switch back on, chest so close to mine that we're almost touching. I breathe in, then take a step back.

'Right, I give up, I'm going to sit down.' I try to keep an even tone to my voice.

He joins me at the table with a brand-new cup of tea. I offer him a TimTam and we do the routine where we dip our biscuits in and suck out the insides. Mine breaks off and plops into my drink.

'Oh, I hate it when that happens,' I moan. He starts laughing and passes me another one.

After a while the front door opens and Molly appears.

'Hello!' she cries. 'What's so funny? Ah, TimTams,' she says, clocking the packet.

'Want one?'

'Yes, please. I'll be back in a second.'

'I should probably be getting off.' Nathan stands up.

'Okay,' I respond sorrowfully.

'So when do you want to go to Oceanworld?' he asks.

'Seriously?'

'Yeah. What are you up to tomorrow?'

'I can't tomorrow – we've got to go and buy shoes.' Damn.

'For the wedding?'

'Yeah. With Andie.'

'May the force be with you,' he says, grinning.

'Why, is she a nightmare?' I whisper.

'Who's a nightmare?' Molly asks, coming back into the room.

'Er, Lucy's . . . tea!'

I smack him on the stomach.

'Oof!' He clutches himself.

'I'm off, Molly.' He turns to me. 'How about Wednesday?'

'What's happening on Wednesday?' Molly asks nosily.

'Nathan and I were thinking about going to Oceanworld. Are we doing anything then?'

'No, no, I don't think so.'

'Cool. Wednesday it is.'

'You two get on well,' Molly says, when he leaves.

'You think?'

'Oh, yes. You can tell how much he likes you.'

'Really?' I ask hopefully.

'Don't worry, I mean platonically.' She laughs.

'Oh, of course.' I join her in the ridiculousness of it all.

The next day we've got the dreaded shoe-shopping trip, and even though I've been warned, I can't wait to meet Andie.

My excitement is short-lived.

'No, I don't *like* those ones!' Andie is squealing at Molly and throwing down the twelfth pair of children's shoes she's tried on that afternoon. The sales assistant shakes her head in mild disgust.

'I told you, I want to go to the *zoo*!'

'Well, you're not going to the zoo until we've found you some shoes!' Molly replies in utter frustration. She turns to me. 'I am never having kids.'

I grin. 'You say that now . . . Look, these ones are pretty.' I pick up a sparkly pink pair.

'No, they've got to be white or silver, Lucy.'

'I want these ones!' Andie screams.

I look at Molly and mouth 'Sorry.'

'Well, you can't have those ones!' Molly snaps.

'But I want *these* ones!' she cries.

'Oh, for fu— *pity's* sake.'

Fifteen minutes later a jubilant Andie skips out of the shoe shop wearing bright pink sparkly shoes. She has refused to put her old ones on again.

'Zoo!' she screams happily.

'No, we've got to get Lucy's shoes first.'

'Zoo!' she shouts. 'Zoo, zoo, ZOO!'

People on the street are starting to stare. Molly gets out her mobile phone and speed-dials a number.

'Mum, can you come and take her? She's driving me nuts.'

A pause.

'No, we haven't even got Lucy's shoes yet.'

Pause.

'No, I'm not doing this, Mum! She's being a brat!'

Pause.

'She wants to go to the frickin' zoo!'

Pause.

'Frickin' isn't a swear word, Mum. You're getting confused with fuck.'

Ten minutes later Molly's mum turns up and bundles Andie into the back of the car.

'Are you taking me to the zoo, Mummy?' we hear her say through the open window as the car drives off. I start to laugh.

'It's not bloody funny. My mum lets her get away with everything.'

'Come on,' I tell her. 'You need a drink. Hell, *I* need a drink. We'll get my shoes after that.'

Chapter 8

'Did you know that the Giant Cuttlefish has green blood, three hearts, tentacles and the ability to change colour and shape?' I ask Molly and Sam the following evening at dinner. I keep remembering these titbits of information from my day with Nathan at Oceanworld.

'I had no idea,' Sam says, amused. We're eating fresh prawns out on the porch.

The aquarium was phenomenal. A massive circular tank surrounds you as though you're in a bubble, with enormous stingrays hovering above you like spaceships. I didn't even know they grew that big.

There was one dodgy moment when Nathan found a *Wheel Of Fortune*-style wheel and span it to see what the chances of a shark attack were compared to other nasty deaths. It landed on boating accident, narrowly missing out the largest wedge, which was aircraft accident. Luckily a nearby tank of crayfish reminded me of a joke so I told him that to take his mind off it.

'*Listen, I've got a joke for you!*'

'*About bloody time. Bet it won't compete with the quality of my elephant jokes, though.*'

'*Shut up and listen, smartarse. Kevin the crab and Lottie the Lobster Princess were madly in love. And then, one day, Lottie scuttled over to Kevin in tears. "We can't see each other anymore," she sobbed. "Why not?" gasped Kevin. "Daddy says that crabs are too common," she wailed. "He says you're the lowest class of crustacean and that no daughter of his will marry someone who can only walk sideways." Kevin was mortified, and edged away into the darkness to drink himself into a state of aquatic oblivion. That night the great Lobster Ball was taking place. Lobsters came from far and wide, but the Lobster Princess refused to join in with the fun, choosing instead to sit by her father's side, inconsolable. Suddenly the doors burst open, and Kevin the crab strode in. The lobsters all stopped their dancing, the Princess gasped and the King Lobster rose from his throne. Slowly, painstakingly, Kevin the crab made his way across the floor . . . and all could see that he was walking FORWARDS, one claw after another! Step by step he made his approach towards the throne, until eventually he looked the King Lobster in the eye. There was a deadly hush. Finally the crab spoke. "Fuck, I'm pissed."*'

Nathan laughed so much that he slapped the aquarium glass and got told off by a staff member. We left in fits of giggles soon afterwards.

'Only three more days to go,' I turn my attention back to Sam and Molly. 'How are you both feeling?'

'Nervous,' Molly admits.

'There's nothing to be nervous about.' Sam rubs her shoulder.

'You don't have to spend the day looking after my sister.'

'Nah, I'll only have Nathan to worry about.'

'Ah, he'll be alright,' Molly says.

'He's a bit anxious about his speech,' Sam continues. Nathan is Sam's best man. 'Speaking of Nathan,' he adds, 'we've got to get him over here to do something about that guttering.'

I follow Sam's gaze upwards to the roof.

'What does Nathan have to do with the guttering?'

'He's a bit of a handyman,' Sam explains to me. 'He did all the renovations on this place.'

'*Really?*' That boy is full of surprises.

'Yeah. Oh, I know we tease him about building his own place and all that, but he could do it. If he ever gets his arse into gear.'

'And who can tell when that'll be?' Molly says drily. 'Knowing Nathan, he'll pack up and head off up the coast again. I can't see him settling down.'

'Not even with Amy?' I pry.

'Who knows? He's silly not to. With her parents' help they could build the house of their dreams.'

I've no idea why I ask these questions because I rarely like the answers.

'So are her parents well off, then?' I just can't help myself. I remember her going off at the hen night to her parents' house near Circular Quay.

'Very. You know who her dad is?'

'No.'

'Bill Benton.'

I look at Molly blankly.

'Well-known businessman.'

'He owns the Sleeptown hotel chain,' Sam elaborates.

'Oh, right . . . Huh. She doesn't seem as if she comes from a wealthy family . . .'

125

'I know!' Molly exclaims. 'That's one of the things that we like about her. She's just a regular surf chick.'

'I'm telling you, Nathan is nuts.' Sam shakes his head and plonks his beer down on the table in front of him. I feel like picking up the bottle and smashing it over his head. Instead I change the subject.

It's Friday and we're in the garden at Molly's parents' house in Mosman, which is a ten-minute drive from Manly across the Spit Bridge. We're drinking wine and enjoying the peace while Andie is up in her bedroom tearing the limbs off her Barbie dolls (probably). Molly's mum, Sheila, is in the kitchen cooking a lamb roast for dinner. It's been a warm day so neither of us really feels like eating a heavy meal, but Sheila was insistent.

Molly's mum looks like an older, shorter, fatter version of Molly. They even have the exact same head of hair. Molly's dad, Bruce – yes, really – is a university lecturer, while Sheila teaches at Manly Village Public School, where Sam, Molly and I first met, aged five.

'Have you spoken to James recently?' Molly asks me, diamond bracelet glinting in the late afternoon sun. Sam gave it to her in a private moment just before we left. Not surprisingly, she loves it.

'Yeah, he called me last night.'

James rang while I was reading in bed, to wish me good luck with my bridesmaid duties, knowing we probably wouldn't get to chat tonight at Molly's parents' place. He'd just got off the tube on his way into work and was calling from his mobile, but his voice kept cutting out so we didn't speak for long. He jokingly warned me not to step on Molly's train and passed on his best wishes to the bride and groom. I tell her this, now.

'Ah, that's nice.' She smiles. 'Things alright between you?'

I shrug my shoulders and sigh.

'Don't worry, you'll be okay.'

I'm not sure I want us to be okay. She misreads my expression.

'It's probably just the time difference,' she says. 'It must be weird speaking to him when he's getting ready for his day ahead and you've just had a glass of wine with us. You wouldn't be on the same wavelength.'

'Yeah, I suppose so.'

'Have you talked about the whole text message incident again?'

'No, not really. It's just too hard. We're so far apart from each other. To be honest, I've just been getting through the days and I'll deal with it when I get back.'

'That's probably not such a bad idea.'

I glance over at my friend and feel a rush of affection. Why can't I tell her the truth? I'm not lying about James – I really *will* have to sort this out when I get back. But I can't tell her what I'm going through about Nathan. I still think she'd disapprove. Or laugh. Either way, I don't think she'd take me seriously.

And to be honest, I'm not sure who would. My friends in England all think the world of James. He's popular, funny, good-looking, has a fantastic job . . . When you weigh it up on paper, no one in their right mind would understand why I'm falling for a jobless surfer who is two years my junior. It's madness. Yet I can't help the way I feel. And I don't know who I can talk to about it.

Maybe I should tell Molly. Maybe she *would* understand.

No. I can't. She wouldn't.

'Molly! Lucy! Dinner's ready!'

We pick up our glasses and head back inside.

Later that night, after we've successfully managed to turn down second helpings of Sheila's lamb roast without offending her – no mean feat – we leave Molly's parents to their TV viewing and head upstairs for an early night. Molly is sleeping in her old bedroom and I've been given the spare room down the corridor, but after we've brushed our teeth and taken off our make-up, I head into her room and climb onto her small single bed with her.

'I can't believe you're getting married tomorrow.'

'Neither can I.'

'And to Sam!'

She looks at me and smiles. 'It's mental, isn't it? After all these years.'

'It's amazing.' It's been bothering me since the hen night that she might still think I hold a torch for him but I haven't felt comfortable bringing it up again. Now I find myself saying, 'I am over him, you know.'

'I know.' It's evident she means it. 'It's funny,' she adds, 'I always thought you and Sam would end up together.'

'No!'

'Really,' she says, smiling.

'That's mad.'

'Not really. You guys always seemed much better suited to each other than he and I were.'

'Well, opposites obviously attract!'

She laughs. 'It certainly seems that way.'

Again I consider telling her about Nathan. But something holds me back. What would be the point? I'll be gone on Sunday and it will all be over.

Molly goes quiet for a moment and then asks me suddenly, 'Do you remember your last night in Sydney?'

'What, nine years ago?'

'Yes.'

How could I forget? It was Australia Day, 26 January 1998. Princess Diana and Michael Hutchence had died the previous year and the fireworks on the Harbour Bridge paid tribute to them. Red, white and blue, gold, pink, purple and green sparks showered down from the bridge and fired up over the harbour. It was one of the most dazzling displays I'd ever seen. Sam, Molly and I had gone to Circular Quay with the rest of Sydney and had found ourselves a tiny patch of pavement on Fleet Steps, just outside the Botanic Gardens' gates on the other side of the harbour. Actually, in the exact same place where the marquee will be tomorrow, I realise now with surprise. We'd stood together, Molly and I on either side of Sam, and watched the fireworks, getting emotional as we listened to Elton John's 'English Rose' version of 'Candle In The Wind' and INXS's 'Never Tear Us Apart' on the multiple radios people had brought with them. That night Mum and I were staying at a hotel in the Rocks area and Molly and Sam were going back to Manly by ferry. We hugged as if it were the last time we'd ever see each other, all three of us in tears. Then I stood alone and watched them board the ferry and wave to me from the lower deck as the departing boat churned up the wake in the harbour.

Molly pauses, as if contemplating whether to tell me something.

'Why do you ask?' I prompt.

Again she remains silent. I wait patiently for her to speak. Finally she looks at me.

'I think Sam was in love with you.'

'*What?*' I almost fall off the bed.

'I think he realised after you left.' She looks wounded, and I don't know what to say.

'But that doesn't make sense; he was never into me!'

'I think that all changed once he realised he'd lost you.'

I can't believe it. After all those years of gut-wrenchingly painful, unrequited love, he felt the same for me *after* I left?

'Does . . . he . . .' I can't ask the question.

'No, I don't think so.' Relief is apparent on her face.

'Phew,' I say. And find I really and truly mean it.

Molly leans over and wraps her arm around my neck and I thank my lucky stars that it all worked out right in the end. We might so easily have lost our friendship if I'd stayed.

'I'm really pleased you're here. I can't think of anyone else I'd rather have with me tomorrow.' Her voice is muffled.

'I hope you'll do the same for me when I get married,' I struggle to say, my breath being squeezed out of me by her hug.

If I ever get married.

In the morning all hell breaks loose.

'I want to go on the train! I want to go on the train!' Andie is screaming.

'We'll be going on it in a couple of hours,' Molly states with exasperation.

'I want to go NOW!'

'Andie, you're just going to have to behave for Molly today,' Sheila tells her firmly. Andie snatches the hairbrush out of her mum's hands and throws it across the room. It narrowly misses a vase full of flowers.

'Look! I won't let you be my bridesmaid if you don't behave!' Molly shouts. 'I'll just have Lucy. I only need one. Sam's only got his brother.'

'But I'm your *sister*!' Her bottom lip starts to quiver.

'Well, start acting like one!' Molly yells.

'Hush, hush,' Sheila soothes them both as she goes to retrieve the hairbrush.

'Do you want me to do your hair?' I ask Andie sweetly. 'We could plait it?'

'No. I want Mum to do it!' She points at Sheila. Molly and I look at each other, unamused. Then the doorbell rings to announce the arrival of the make-up artist.

Three-quarters of an hour later, after the make-up artist has departed, Molly stands surveying herself in front of the mirror.

'I look like a CLOWN!' she yells.

'Molly, you do not!' Sheila shouts.

'I do! I'm taking it off!' She stomps up the stairs and Sheila gives me a look. I hurry after her. Molly is on the verge of tears in the bathroom. She's right; the make-up artist has gone way overboard. The foundation is too dark and the blusher is too bright. Even the eyeliner looks wrong on Molly's eyes.

I opted to do my own make-up for a very good reason. I've always wondered how someone who's never met you before can know what's right for you on one of the most important days of your life.

'Let me help you,' I offer. 'Shall we take it off and start again?'

Molly nods dolefully.

'Okay. Where's your normal foundation?'

Half an hour later both of our make-up bags have been put to excellent use and Molly now looks like a beautifully – *subtly* – blushing bride. We've opted for a pretty creamy-beige sheen over her lids and dark brown mascara. Light apricot blusher and a rosy shade of lippy complete her look. Nothing too Coco the Clown-like.

Thankfully the hairdresser did a much better job and Molly is thrilled that someone has actually managed to tame her hair. She looks breathtaking in the long white dress which she made in her workshop at home, and as I help her down the front steps of her parents' home, tiny diamanté crystals across her bodice sparkle in the sunlight.

Even Andie looks gorgeous in her silver dress, a smaller version of mine, after finally allowing the hairdresser to do a last-minute tong job on her dead-straight hair. My chestnut hair has been piled up high above my head, a few curls cascading down. It looks a tad too neat for me, but the hairdresser promised that it would loosen up.

We've barely even glanced outside this morning because it's been so manic, but the weather is perfect. A light summery breeze, only a few clouds in the sky. I feel like someone up above is looking out for us.

Nathan called Molly this morning to wish her luck. He had a message for me. 'What did one elephant say to the other? Nothing; elephants can't talk.' Molly didn't find it in the least funny, but it made me smile.

Molly and her dad go in one car up ahead and Sheila, Andie and I follow behind. All of us are quiet; even Andie. Eventually we're crossing the Harbour Bridge and winding our way towards the Royal Botanic Gardens. When we arrive, I get out of the car and go over to attend to Molly.

'You okay?' I ask her quietly.

'Yeah,' she murmurs. 'Very surreal, isn't it?'

I nod my agreement.

The red trackless train is waiting for us at the entrance. I help her into the front carriage, lifting up her dress so it doesn't drape on the ground, then Bruce climbs in next to her. Molly's mum and Andie sit behind them and I step up into the back.

I wonder what it would have been like if James had been here. Would he have been allowed to arrive with the wedding party? Would he be sitting next to me right now, as we wind our way past the hundreds-of-years-old fig trees, while bystanders call out their best wishes?

Finally we see a group of around sixty people up ahead. Molly looks calm – unwaveringly calm – and I feel edgy as hell. She steps down from the little red carriage and links her arm through her mum and dad's – both of them walking with her to the front. Andie and I follow behind, clutching bouquets made entirely of Australian flora: Sam's idea. The crowd parts – there are no chairs – and there, standing underneath a great old gum tree, is Sam. And Nathan. I can't help myself. I start to cry.

The ceremony passes by in an emotional blur. Sam and Molly have written their own vows and they read them to each other, holding hands solemnly. I find the tears won't stop falling, and I don't even have a tissue. Even Sam chokes up, but Molly is calm. I have to keep furtively wiping my eyes every ten or twenty seconds until the first reading when the attention moves away from the five of us and the registrar. Then Nathan is next to me, holding out a Kleenex. He hasn't shaved for the wedding – I wondered if he would – but he looks handsome in a well-fitted charcoal suit and silver tie. I take the tissue from him gratefully, impressed that he's such an organised best man, and he gives me a sympathetic smile. It just makes my tears flow faster and I start to laugh quietly, embarrassed. He rubs his hand on my shoulder and I almost step into his arms, then I wonder if he knows about Sam and me and our history. What if he thinks I'm crying about that? The thought snaps me out of it.

The reading finishes, the registrar wraps it up, we sign the witness papers, my signature directly below Nathan's scrawling one, and my two best friends in the whole world are pronounced husband and wife. Everyone claps as they kiss. Then Andie picks up a basket full of gum leaves and offers them around to people to use as confetti. We throw them as a blissfully happy Molly and Sam pose for photographs.

As we sit down to eat, I notice that Amy is sitting at a table two away from us. She looks pretty in a pink and white spotted chiffon dress. I catch her eye and smile. She smiles a tight little smile back and looks away.

The waiting staff bring out the first course, a light crayfish salad, and top up our glasses with champagne. The whole marquee is buzzing. Molly and Sam to my right keep laughing and kissing each other and Nathan, next to Sam, is engrossed in conversation with his aunt, Katherine. I met her earlier, and she seemed friendly. Her long greying hair is tied up in a loose bun on top of her head. She works in an art gallery in the city and her partner, Simon, looks about fifteen years her junior. At least she approves of toyboys.

At that moment I feel lonely. Again I wonder what it would be like if James was here. How different would this holiday have been? Would I have responded to Nathan in the same way if James had been here? I miss my boyfriend suddenly, fleetingly.

It's time for the speeches. First Bruce stands up and has everyone laughing with his tales of Molly growing up and how he, as a father, much preferred me as Molly's friend rather than Sam, a red-blooded teenage boy. But now he couldn't be happier with her choice. Sam continues in the same vein, keeping it light and fun. Finally it's Nathan's turn. He looks nervous.

'I'm not really one for speeches so you're just going to have to bear with me, I'm afraid. First of all I'd like to thank the brides-maids, Lucy and Andie. Lucy came all the way from England for this and she's been a great support to Molly for the last two weeks, and – how long have you guys known each other?' He pauses, looking down at Sam and Molly.

'Twenty bloody long years!' shouts Sam and everyone laughs.

'When Sam first asked me to be his best man and I realised I'd have to stand up and give a speech, I felt like throwing myself over that wall out there into the harbour. To be honest with you, I still do. But he promised me I could keep this brief so I'm going to take him up on that.' I notice he's not reading from any notes.

'I want to tell you something about Sam. When we were kids he always looked out for me. And when Mum and Dad died, he almost gave up his scholarship so we could both stay in Sydney and get a place together. I had to nick off travelling in order to persuade him to go to uni. But that's just Sam.

'He's the best brother I could ever have. He's the closest family I have. And I know Mum and Dad would have been very proud of him. I'm just sorry they can't be here to see him tie the knot with Molly. They always loved her like she was part of the family and now she really is.'

By the time he's finished there's not a dry eye in the place, Sam, Molly and myself included. I glance across at Nathan after he's sat back down. He seems a little embarrassed with all the attention and my heart goes out to him. He looks over at me and we smile at each other for a moment, before I turn back to my dessert.

Twenty minutes later our plates have all been cleared and the staff are starting to move tables away for the DJ. I look around but I can't see Nathan, then I spot him over by Amy's table; he is crouching down behind her chair and she has swivelled round to talk to him. I feel a white pang of jealousy shoot through me. 'Get away from her!' I want to shout, but I know how ludicrous that is. I have no hold over this man. In less than twenty-four hours I'll be flying home. To my *boyfriend*, for Christ's sake.

I peek back over at Amy and she turns around and looks right at me. I quickly avert my gaze.

I need to get away. I have to clear my head. I check with Molly that she doesn't want anything and then get up and go through the open marquee door, back through the gate into the gardens. It's late afternoon and the wind is just starting to pick up. I have to lift my long silver skirt up slightly as I wind my way back past the old gum tree, past the sculptures, to find myself standing in front of a cluster of bamboo, towering high above me, forty or fifty feet into the air. I look up for a minute and listen to it clacking together and creaking and groaning in the breeze. People have carved their names into the bright yellow and green stalks:

Robin x Helen
Sal hearts Dean

Even some Japanese and Chinese, which I can't decipher. I look at the information plaque:

Bambusa Vulgaris – Common Bamboo

'What do you call a sheep with no legs?'

I spin around and he's there, behind me, unlit cigarette in his hand. He's taken off his suit jacket and loosened his shirt collar and tie.

'Go on.' I smile.

'A cloud.'

'That's funny!'

'Yeah, I'd forgotten that one,' he says, lighting his cigarette. He uses matches, not a lighter, and he has to cup his hands together to stop the breeze from blowing the flame out.

'How's Amy?'

'Not the best.' He scuffs the gravel on the pavement with his shoe.

'What's wrong with her?'

'She wants to know what's going on. She wants to know how I feel.'

'How *do* you feel?'

He takes a long drag on his cigarette before answering. 'I don't think she's the girl for me.' He looks at me suddenly, intensely, then glances away.

'You need to tell her that.'

'I know.'

Am I the girl for him? We're so different. The more I get to know Nathan, the more I realise how little we have in common. Am I too old for him? I've been to university and he barely even finished high school. I have a career and I love it. I *do* love it, I think fiercely. I've got the best job in the world! What would I do if I moved here? Good jobs are much harder to come by.

I don't share with him the thoughts that are rushing through my head. I still don't even really know what he thinks of me.

'Are you looking forward to going back to England tomorrow?' he asks finally.

'Not really,' I answer.

'How do you feel about seeing your boyfriend again?' He is staring at me steadily with those bluey-grey eyes.

'Not good. I just don't know.' I look away because his gaze is too intense. Then I turn back to him, abruptly. 'How can you afford not to work?'

'Well, the house is half mine, you know.'

For some reason I just assumed Molly and Sam owned the house outright now, but of course Nathan would have inherited half.

'Did they buy you out of it?' I ask.

'No,' he swiftly denies it. 'I don't need all that money and they couldn't afford to do that. They pay me rent and give me a share of the B&B money. Who knows, one day we might sell the house, but not yet.'

'Don't you want to have a job, though?' I press. The fact that he doesn't work bothers me.

'I don't really know what I'd do.'

'Isn't anything better than nothing?'

'You've got to be kidding, haven't you?'

'Well . . . I mean . . . Don't you think your parents would have wanted you to do something? Have a career?'

His eyes turn stony. I've pushed it too far.

'I'm sorry, that was harsh.'

But his response surprises me. 'No, you're right. They would be disappointed.'

'I didn't mean they'd be disappointed!' I'm horrified.

'No, they would,' he says flatly. 'They would be so proud of Sam, though. Going to university, getting his qualifications and then scoring this job. All I've done for the last few years is surf, bum around and live off the earnings from their family home. I don't think they'd be proud.' He inhales a last, long deep breath of his cigarette and then drops the butt down and squashes it into the pavement with his not-quite-shiny shoes.

I immediately feel passionately overprotective. 'They *would* be proud. You're amazing. You're a talented musician and an incredible surfer, and you're the kindest, nicest guy I think I've ever met.' I grab his hands. 'It doesn't matter if you haven't quite found your feet yet – you will. There's still lots of time.'

Nathan looks at me for a moment. Then he frees one hand and places it on my face, his thumb rough as he brushes away a single tear that has slowly started to make its way down my cheek. I want to kiss him. I so want to kiss him. I tear my eyes away from his and look at his mouth. He cups my face with both of his hands, smudging away the tears that are falling freely. Just kiss me! I'll cancel my flight, leave James for good, stay here with you!

I will him to place those warm lips on mine. I look into his eyes and never want to look away. We're so close I could just reach up and pull his face down to mine.

But he doesn't. And I don't. And a few moments later I realise my tears have stopped falling and he has no reason to be holding my face, brushing them away. We smile at each other sadly as he strokes my cheeks with his thumbs one last time, before letting go, leaving me cold and damp and bereft without his touch.

'There you are!' Amy cries as she totters down the path in too-high heels towards us. I step back away from him. 'They're going to shut the gates soon, you have to come back.'

I realise with surprise it's almost closing time at the Botanic Gardens. Amy puts her hand out to Nathan. He doesn't take it; just joins her and starts to walk away by her side. I follow on behind them, thinking she looks like a nine-year-old in her mother's heels, as we make our way back down through the gardens and out of the gates. The DJ has the party in full swing when we get back.

'I was wondering where you were!' Molly exclaims when the three of us reappear. 'I'm about to throw the bouquet. Go on, off you go, I'm getting together all the unmarried girls.' As Amy teeters off, Molly grabs my hand and looks at me seriously. My heart stops for a moment as I wonder if she's worked out what's going on. 'Go and stand to the front right – that's where I'll throw it,' she says urgently.

'Okay.' I start to walk off and she pulls me back. What now?

'I mean to *my* right.'

'Okay!' I laugh and follow her instructions. Serious business, this bouquet throwing . . .

Of course it doesn't go anywhere near me. Amy makes a jump for it and almost falls over when she lands back down on her heels, but she doesn't manage to grab it either. In the end it goes to one of Sam and Nathan's young cousins from Western Australia.

The sun is setting outside the marquee now and the guests wander out to stand by the railings and watch it sinking. 'Where's Lucy?' I hear Sam's deep voice asking. He and Molly are side by side, and both grin when they see me. 'Lucy, come here,' Sam says, holding his hand out to me. He wraps his arm around me and we stand there, watching as the harbour is cast in a peachy glow and the lights of the city's business towers grow brighter.

This reminds me of my last evening nine years ago. Only then it was a completely different brother who was filling my head. I feel like I'm going to cry again and have to furiously swallow over and over as I choke back my tears. Then someone shouts 'Look!' and we see the bats take flight, thousands of them – a gigantic black cloud gliding silently away from the gardens and towards the city. It's spectacular.

Molly and Sam turn to each other and I hang back, letting them go. The other guests are dispersing and moving towards the marquee. When I look around for Nathan I see him further down the wall, staring out at the harbour. Amy is by his side.

It's very distracting. Wherever I am over the next couple of hours, I'm wondering where Nathan is. I only have to be in one place for one minute before I find myself peering around to clock his position. I feel like a woman possessed. Right now he and Amy are talking to a group of young guys and girls – I think the people Amy was sitting with earlier. She's laughing and he's look-ing mildly amused. Before I can look away he catches my eye and motions me over. I'm not sure I'll feel at ease around his friends – especially if they're Amy's too – but it would be weird not to go to him. I leave Jenny, Amanda and some of the other hens behind on the dance floor, being careful not to slip over in my high heels. Nathan steps aside and makes room for me in their little circle.

'Guys, this is Lucy.'

'Hey, Lucy!' they all exclaim drunkenly. 'Nice to meet you.'

'You too.'

'You coming tomorrow?' a tall, cute guy with a light brown Afro asks me.

'Nah, she's flying back to England,' Nathan chips in.

'Ah, too bad,' the cute guy says.

I look up at Nathan questioningly. 'It's Barry's birthday,' he explains, nodding at his mate. 'We're having a beach party.'

'Oh, I see.' A pause. 'Are you going?' I ask him.

'Of course.'

'Yeah, mate, you're not going to miss out on a piss-up with your pals, are ya?' Barry says, wrapping his arm around Nathan's neck. 'And Ames'll be there too,' he adds, throwing his other arm around a radiant Amy.

In my daydreams I'd imagined him seeing me off in the morning. Sam and Molly will have left for their honeymoon in Bali and I'll be alone. The realisation makes me unbearably miserable.

'LUCY!' Molly interrupts loudly from the other side of the dance floor.

'Nice to meet you all . . .' I feel sick with disappointment as I excuse myself and go over to her.

'We're setting off to our hotel shortly,' she says tipsily. 'We'll just say our goodbyes to everyone else, but don't you go anywhere.'

I use the opportunity to go and say farewell to Molly's parents and Andie, who's leaning drowsily up against her mum.

'We'll be off soon too, love. So nice that you could come. You look gorgeous!' Sheila gushes. 'Doesn't she, Bruce?'

'Gorgeous!' Bruce agrees wholeheartedly.

'Thank you,' I reply, embarrassed, and bend down to Andie. 'Bye, Andie.'

'Bye.' She smiles sleepily up at me.

'Hope to see you soon.'

She doesn't answer.

'Aah, she's tired, poor little mite,' Sheila says.

'Bye, both of you. Lovely to see you again.'

'You too, Lucy. Good luck with everything.'

After I've said my goodbyes to all the hens I'm not quite sure what to do with myself. I don't feel comfortable walking back to Nathan and Amy's group now so I go and wait by the wall overlooking the harbour and stare at the city lights until Molly and Sam reappear, fifteen minutes later.

'I love you,' Molly says, squeezing me tightly.

She releases me to Sam and he holds me close in his strong arms. I break away after a moment and pull Molly in, in a three-way hug.

'Don't leave it so long, okay?' Her voice is barely audible as she presses her face into my hair.

'I won't. I'll be back before you know it.'

We let go of each other and look over to the other side of the marquee where the little red train has pulled up, on loan from the gardens for the night. Molly and Sam climb onto it and the waiting guests start to clap and cheer as the driver pulls away. Someone has tied cans to the back of the last carriage and they clank together noisily.

But when the laughter from the guests dies, and the train disappears around a corner, taking my best friends in the whole world with it, I'm besieged with an overwhelming sadness. I feel lost. Totally lost.

'Alright, Lucy?' It's Molly's uncle, Ken. 'You ready to go to your hotel now? We'll catch a cab out at the front.'

I'm staying the night in a hotel so as to be well placed for a taxi to the airport in the morning. It's not the same one as Sam and Molly's – that was too pricey – but it's nice enough.

'It's alright, Ken, we'll take her.' Nathan appears by my side, closely followed by Amy, and my heart immediately lifts.

'Are you sure?' Ken asks me.

'Yes.' I nod brightly.

'Well, your suitcase is already there, dear, so you just have to check in.'

I thank him. He was kind enough to drop my luggage off for me at the hotel earlier.

'Okay?' Nathan asks, glancing down at me. If only we didn't have Amy with us, but I'm so glad we're not saying our final good-byes just yet.

'Nathan and I don't have long if we're going to catch the last ferry,' Amy enlightens me. She seems more confident somehow, and I'm not sure why.

Nathan hails a cab and opens the door while Amy and I climb in. She stays seated in the middle, obviously expecting him to go around to the other side, but he leans in and tells her to budge up, so she moves over to the window. I shift along and sit in the middle, between them.

'Harbour Rocks Hotel, please,' I tell the driver. None of us really speaks on the way there. The warmth of Nathan's leg is pressing into mine and I can feel his chest rise and fall with every breath. I'm jittery inside. I so want to reach down and take his hand. He's looking away from me, out of the window. I follow his gaze to the city towering overhead.

Nathan insists on paying the driver and comes back to my door to help me out, even though I'm already stepping onto the pavement. His touch on my bare arm leaves it burning. I wonder if I'll feel like this next time I see him. Will I feel like this about anyone ever again?

All three of us go up to the front desk and they wait with me while I check in, Amy shuffling from foot to high-heeled foot impatiently as Nathan stands beside me.

'You should check out the Gumnut Café round the corner for breakfast. Dad used to take me there.'

'Okay.' I smile up at him.

'We'd better go,' Amy urges Nathan. 'We're going to miss the last ferry.'

He turns to me. 'Are you going to be alright tomorrow?'

'Yeah. It'll be easy to hail a cab from out there.' I motion to the doorway.

'Well, okay, then.'

It's awkward for a moment. Do we hug? Kiss? Instead I turn to Amy.

'Bye, Amy.' She gives me a little hug.

I withdraw and turn to Nathan.

'Bye,' I say, and he leans down to me and I up to him as we hug quickly, unfulfillingly, with Amy standing by. They turn to leave, she looking up at him, he not looking back at me, me watching them push out through the glass doors.

Then suddenly he's back and my heart soars.

'I almost forgot to give you this.' He presses something into my hand. I look down. It's the cassette tape from his car.

'Nathan . . .' I put my hand on his chest. I could ask him to stay. I could ask him to come to my room with me.

'Bye, Luce.' He leans in and kisses me on the corner of my lips. And then he's gone.

I look down at the cassette in my hand, then I lift my silver skirt and make my way upstairs to my bedroom along the corridor, where my suitcase is waiting.

I sit on the bed for a moment, then stand and take off my shoes. I unzip myself mechanically, stepping out of my dress and laying it over a chair. I open my suitcase and pull out my cosmetics case.

I take off my make-up slowly, meticulously, all the while staring at myself in the mirror. I unclip my hair, letting it fall around my shoulders, and then I reach up and unclasp the diamonds from my ears. Dropping them into my jewellery bag I go and sit on the bed. Alone. I bury my face in my hands and start to sob, so silently it almost kills me.

Chapter 9

My eyes are puffy when I wake up and I feel like someone has clawed them out. I manage to doze off again until my phone starts buzzing at 9.45. Nathan? I snatch it up. No, it's the alarm I set last night.

I have to leave at midday for the airport so I shower and pack at a snail's pace. I lug my suitcase down the stairs, one bump by one, and check out. Leaving my case at reception, I wander out of the hotel, looking for the Gumnut Café.

A waiter comes over to hand me a menu as I take a seat outside. This little place is fascinating. Most of the other tables are full. Several backpackers, a few elderly people, a young couple . . . The table bases are made of old-fashioned Singer Sewing Machine treadles and the chairs look as if they were stolen from a primary school fifty years ago. Large white, red and blue umbrellas hang overhead to protect the diners from Sydney's showers. There's no need for that today, though. It's a lovely morning and the sunlight appears dappled through the lime-green trees.

I turn my attention to the menu and decide on a special: French Toast and maple syrup with crispy bacon. I can't bring myself to order an omelette.

The waiter takes my order and returns soon afterwards with a pot of tea in an old silver teapot. I thank him.

'Are you alright, love? You look a bit glum sitting here on your own.'

'No, I'm okay, thank you,' I quickly reply, trying to hold back the inevitable waterworks.

'Alright, I'll leave you to your thoughts, then,' he tells me kindly, and moves off.

My phone starts to buzz and I grab my bag and hurriedly rummage around until I locate it.

'Hello?'

'Lucy!'

It's Molly.

'Hi!' I practically yelp. 'Where are you?'

'At the airport. I just wanted to call and wish you a really good flight home. And to say thank you. Thank you so much for coming over and being here for us. I'm going to miss you!'

'I'm going to miss you too! The wedding was flawless. Have a fantastic honeymoon. Call me when you get back.'

'I will. And good luck with James. I know everything's going to be okay. He's the guy for you. Hang on, Sam wants a word.'

I wait a second until Sam's voice comes on the line.

'Hey.'

'Hi.'

'Thanks again. Stay in touch, won't you? We're going to miss you.'

'Same here.'

'Don't cry, Luce, you'll set me off.'

148

'I'm sorry.' I sniff. It's all too much.

'Will you be okay getting to the airport?'

'Yeah, no problem.' I just wish your bloody brother was here with me!

'Well, we'd better go. Lots of love.'

'Lots of love.'

I rummage for a tissue and wipe my tears away as the waiter comes back over with my food. I don't know why I ordered anything; I can't eat it. I pick up a piece of bacon in my fingers and bite it, crunching for a few seconds. I try to eat some French Toast but don't get very far. The waiter knows better than to ask why I've lost my appetite.

After breakfast I collect my bag from the hotel reception and hail a taxi which takes me on the very same route that I was on exactly two weeks ago. I feel like I've been hit with a stun gun, but that's no bad thing. At least I'm not crying. The airport isn't at all busy, so I'm able to walk straight to the desk and check in. I pull my phone out of my bag for the umpteenth time and scrutinise it. It's switched on and functional. Battery still fine. No text messages. No missed calls. Even if I could bring myself to call Nathan I don't have his number. I still hold out a glimmer of hope that he might call me.

I have to go through Immigration and I can delay it no longer. I've been scouring the airport, in case Nathan turns up at the last minute, but it seems he really has gone to the beach party with his friends. And with Amy. I stand on the concourse, looking back towards the airport terminal entrance, and then step into the Immigration queue. Finally I'm at the front and I hand over my passport. Then I'm through. I glance back one last time and don't see him. He hasn't turned up to try and stop me from leaving. That really does only happen in the movies.

Half an hour later, when I'm stepping onto the plane and finding my seat next to a ginger-haired businessman, I take my phone out of my bag and look at it. Just as before, it's switched on and functional. Battery still fine. No text messages. No missed calls. I press down on the little red button and the light on my phone dims, just as the light does in my heart.

Sydney to London

Sunday: Depart Sydney at 1655
Monday: Arrive London Heathrow at 0525
Duration: 23 hrs 30 mins

The flight isn't even half full, so the ginger guy next to me turns and says with a heavy German accent that he'll make the most of the empty row of seats across the aisle. Wishing me a good flight, he picks up his belongings. I look out of the window at the sunny Sydney afternoon; Nathan will be enjoying his party. And Amy will be enjoying having Nathan to herself.

The tiny TV screen in front of me is playing a cheesy film about Australia. I watch as green wineries appear on screen, followed by images of wild horses running through a field. Tall mountains and waterfalls give way to clear blue oceans and white beaches. Then I see a surfer, crouching and slicing through the water, up and under the curl of the wave before he finally stands fully upright on his board and slowly sinks back down, into the ocean. Just like Nathan did, the first time I saw him surf. Oh, God.

Will he ever tell Amy he's not interested? *Is* he interested? Sam and Molly might convince him he is. They could get married and have children. My heart feels like it could collapse at the thought. And I'm going back to James. I don't want to see him. My mind is too consumed with Nathan and I don't want to give up *any* of that head-space to James. I'm not ready to let go of Nathan yet.

I pull out the cassette tape that he made me and look down at his scratchy handwriting. Rolling Stones' 'Gimme Shelter', Radiohead's 'Talk Show Host' . . . I hold the tape tight to my chest. I'll have to buy a cassette player in Singapore so I can listen to it. I wonder if they even make them any more. James will think I've gone mad. He's a technology junkie.

The plane zooms down the runway, forcing me back into my seat and then we're off the ground and climbing. I look below at the sunlit streets and spot the city's tall towers. The Opera House and the Harbour Bridge look tiny. I see the greenness of the Botanic Gardens and close my eyes, remembering for a moment how Nathan almost kissed me. He *did* almost kiss me. I imagine him taking my face in his hands and roughly bruising my lips with his. I feel light-headed, then weighed down with sadness.

He's gone. It's over. What could have been never was and I'm going home.

In a parallel universe Nathan is sitting on his bed and playing his guitar, lazily looking over at me. I reach across and touch his leg and he puts his guitar on the floor and draws me to him, onto his lap. He's undressing me, pulling my damp T-shirt over my head and unclasping my bikini top. I lean back as he lifts his own faded brown T-shirt over his head and pulls my naked upper half back to him, pressing my body into his. He's kissing me. Kissing my lips, kissing my jaw, kissing my neck. He takes me in his arms and manoeuvres me so I'm underneath him. He hovers above me, hand on my thigh, sliding up my skirt, blue-grey eyes looking intently into mine.

I love him. I love him.

I could leave James, go back. But I don't even know how Nathan feels. Does he feel *anything* for me? Have I got it completely wrong? I dismiss those doubts and go back to my daydream. And it's these images that carry me through the next twenty-four hours until, finally, I'm home again.

London

Chapter 10

It's a clear, dark night as we fly towards Heathrow. Below me little towns group together in the darkness, their lights resembling clusters of bright stars in the Milky Way. I've almost bled the second lot of batteries from my newly-purchased cassette player dry, listening to Nathan's tape incessantly since Singapore. I've barely slept.

I look out of the window again trying to spot the saucepan. I've been searching for it sporadically for the last few hours but now I give up. It must be on the other side of the plane.

We land at around half past five on Monday morning. James might've already left for work by the time I get home.

An hour and a quarter later I'm struggling to haul my suitcase onto the Heathrow Express to Paddington and no one is offering to help. It makes me remember Sam, heaving my bag up onto his truck to lie amongst his plants when I arrived in Sydney. It seems so long ago, but it's only been two weeks.

He and Molly will be on their honeymoon now. It's nearly six o'clock in the evening in Sydney. I wonder what Nathan's doing.

I still haven't changed my watch back to UK time and I'm not sure when I will.

At Paddington Station I drag my suitcase out of the carriage and wheel it back along the platform, lagging behind all the other travellers. The air looks brown because the glass in the domed ceiling above is so dirty but, through a broken pane, a shaft of light floods in. It's a beautiful winter day. Actually, I realise, we're well into March now and it's technically spring.

I lie my suitcase down on the platform for a moment and unzip it, pulling out my black, knee-length woollen winter coat. Then I head away from the hum of engines and the shrieking blow of conductors' whistles in the direction of the taxi rank. We live only a five-minute drive from here and all I want right now is to get home and have a nice cup of tea.

That sense of anticipation is short-lived. There's a long queue of people waiting in line for the black cabs, a disadvantage of arriving in rush hour. Maybe I could walk it? A blue sign up ahead tells me Marylebone is three-quarters of a mile away. Easy. I head past the Hilton with its lanky doorman in top hat and tails, and into a square full of tall trees. My suitcase clunks noisily on the uneven pavement.

The sun up ahead pierces my eyes as it comes into view and I'm practically blinded. I cross the road and a scooter zooms around the corner, just missing me and giving me a fright. It's ironic how I need my sunglasses more here at this time of year than I even did in Sydney last week.

By now my hands are practically purple and I wish I'd packed some gloves. The cold air is painful in my nostrils so I breathe in and out of my mouth instead, producing cloudy puffs of carbon dioxide. I'm starting to think this walk wasn't such a good idea.

I look around for a taxi but can't see one. A plane flies above a red-brick building, climbing up into the sky. I suddenly feel desperate.

I wonder if James will be home. It all depends on whether he's got an early meeting at work. In some ways I hope he will have already left to give me time to gather my thoughts. I'm not sure I'm ready to see him yet. Or speak to him. I should have called to let him know I've landed; as it is, I haven't even switched my phone back on.

It briefly occurs to me that Nathan might have left me a message. I halt on the pavement and take a minute to check, tapping my foot impatiently while the operator tells me I have one voicemail. But it's just James asking me to hurry home so he can see me before he leaves. I put my phone away, feeling dejected.

Finally I'm on Marylebone Road. I wait at the pedestrian crossing until the traffic comes to a standstill, then I cross over and head around the back past old Marylebone Station towards Dorset Square. The square always looks pretty, even in winter, with its naked tree trunks, while in summer it's heavenly: full of leafy trees and hedges, the greenest grass and a few welcome park benches. Unfortunately it's a private square and we don't have a key. A memory comes back to me of last summer and James bringing me here.

We'd just bought our flat and, both of us having rented for years, were so excited to finally own our own home. Even if James's parents helped quite a lot financially and Terry and Mum gave me my deposit, it still felt like it was ours alone. It was only a small, one-bedroom place in a bit of a state when we moved in, but we dreamt about turning it into something special. We completed the sale on a Wednesday and although we weren't properly moving in until the weekend, we decided to take our sleeping bags and stay overnight together. It was damned uncomfortable on the floor as we had no mattress, but we giggled our way through the night, aided by several glasses of red wine.

The weather was perfect that weekend. A clear, sunny Saturday in July with a cool breeze. The flat was full of boxes and we were exhausted from lugging them up three flights of stairs. I suggested to James that he nip down and grab a few things from the local supermarket. He was gone for ages and just as I was starting to feel a bit miffed that he was shirking the work, he called me from his mobile and asked me to come downstairs. He sounded very pleased with himself and I assumed he must've bumped into some friends, but when I got outside and looked around, I couldn't see him. My phone rang again and he told me to come over to the square. There he was, standing inside the black railings with a mischievous grin on his face.

'James! You can't go in there; it's private!'

'It's okay – they let me in,' and he pointed down to the other end of the square where a young family were playing with their baby.

Over on the grass James had set up a picnic. He'd even bought a rug, along with a bottle of sparkling wine.

I look over at the little square now, tiny white snowdrops pushing through the soil, and smile at the memory of James being so romantic. But melancholy seeps back through me like poison and my smile fades.

I don't want to be here. I want to be in the warm heart of Sydney. In the warmth of Nathan's arms. I try to ignore the dull ache in my chest as I cross over the road and into our street.

My hands are now frozen to the bone and I'm exhausted. By the time I reach our flat, I can't bear the thought of trying to drag my suitcase up all those stairs. Then the front door opens.

'Lucy!' James rushes out of the door. 'How lucky is that? I was just leaving.' He engulfs me in a warm hug. 'I didn't know what time you'd be back. Did you not get my message?'

'Yeah . . . I got here as quickly as I could.'

'You're freezing,' he says, rubbing my arms. 'Here, let me take this upstairs for you.'

'I just walked here from Paddington!' I wail, suddenly much in need of sympathy.

'Oh, baby, you must be knackered.' He carries my suitcase in through the communal door and over all the junk mail partially covering the grubby grey carpet. I climb the stairs behind him, looking up at him in his suit and feeling utterly detached.

James unlocks the door and pushes it open with his right shoulder, steps through and holds it for me while I pass, both of us out of breath. Then he takes me in his arms, holding me tightly for several seconds, pulling my body into his, while our breathing starts to slow to a regular pace. It feels oddly like I'm being unfaithful.

James pulls back and surveys me, eyes looking searchingly into mine. He looks smart in his tailored black suit, pristine white shirt and a dark-blue and turquoise striped tie.

'You look different,' I say.

'Haircut.' He flashes me a cheeky grin.

'Oh, yes.' His sandy hair is a bit shorter, I realise. Not quite as floppy.

'Poor thing, you look exhausted,' he says. 'Did you get much sleep on the plane?'

159

I shake my head, surreptitiously remembering that I'd stayed awake during most of the flight from Singapore, listening to Nathan's tape.

'Come and have a look through here . . .'

I follow him through to the living room. It's the same; all black and white.

'Well?' he asks eagerly. I glance from left to right, past the black leather couch he'd insisted on buying, past the cool white acrylic coffee table and matching magazine rack, until my gaze falls on the television. We seem to have acquired a brand-new flatscreen.

'Oh!'

'Do you like it? It's got the *best* sound. I thought it would be ideal for all the DVDs you have to watch for work.'

'Oh, right,' I say.

He looks crestfallen. 'Don't you like it?'

'No, no, I do! It's amazing. I'm just really tired, that's all. I can't really take it in. It's been a long flight.'

That seems to placate him.

'You can show it to me properly tonight, okay?'

He's already picked up the remote control and is pointing it in the direction of the telly, but then he freezes and looks at his watch. 'Yeah, actually, I'd better go.' He plonks the remote control back on the coffee table and kisses me on the lips. 'But I wish I could stay. Shame I've got this bloody meeting or I'd go in late . . .' he adds sexily, and kisses me again, slower this time.

His lips feel wrong. I pull away.

'What's up?'

'I haven't cleaned my teeth yet.'

'Ah, okay.' He leans down and gives me a kiss on the cheek then draws me in for another hug. I force myself to relax because all I feel is tense. His body is warm and I breathe in his aftershave. He starts to feel a little more familiar.

'Okay, gorgeous, better go,' he says, pulling away. He gives me one last peck. 'It's great to have you back.'

After he's gone I go over to the window and peep through the venetian blinds down to the street. When he's turned the corner and is out of sight, I go into the bedroom. Pulling back the duvet in its white Egyptian cotton cover, I study the sheet underneath. I can't see anything suspicious. I lean down and smell it. Recently washed? Or does it always smell like this after two weeks? I examine the pillowcases for rogue strands of female hair, and then feel underneath the mattress for underwear or anything that a lover might've left. Nothing. Lucy, you're being ridiculous.

In the kitchen I put the kettle on and tip a little milk into the bottom of a white mug. Then I drop the teabag on top and pour in freshly boiled water, stirring my teaspoon until the milky water turns tea-coloured. I think of Nathan the whole time. From now on I will always make tea his way.

After a minute I fish out the teabag and then blow on the liquid before taking a tentative sip. I've over-brewed it and it's too strong. All of a sudden I feel depressed.

I've spent so much time crying in the last thirty-six hours that I don't know how I have any tears left, but my eyes still well up. Back in the bedroom, I climb into bed, pulling my carry-on bag with me. I get out the cassette player and lie there, listening to Nathan's tape. I don't want to be here. This feels wrong. So wrong. It should be raining outside. It should be cold, grey and miserable like it usually is when you come back from holiday, not bright and icy and sunny. And I should be on cloud nine at the prospect of seeing my boyfriend-of-three-years tonight, but instead the thought fills me with dread.

Here I am, alone in this flat, alone in this double bed, on the other side of the world, and I would give anything – *anything* – to have my sexy messy-haired surfer here with me.

Not James.

Eventually the sound slows to a drawl and I give up, knowing the batteries are well and truly kaput. I'll have to buy some more later. I'm shattered. I set my alarm for three hours' time, swap my clothes for comfy PJs and climb in between the sheets.

The sound of the home phone ringing wakes me up. I'm so tired I feel like someone has filled my body with sand. I fumble around on the bedside table for a minute, trying to locate the phone.

'Hello?' I answer groggily.

'Hello, baby.' It's James. 'Were you sleeping?'

'Mmm.' I can barely speak, I'm so exhausted.

'Wakey wakey. You won't be able to sleep tonight if you sleep now.'

'Mmm.'

'Listen, I'm going to be a little late – I've got a meeting with my manager at five thirty. I couldn't put him off. So I'll probably be back around eight. Do you want me to pick up something on the way home? Or shall we order takeaway?'

'Oh, I don't know. I'll get something.' It'll be good to get out of the house, even if it's only around the corner.

'Okay, honey, can't *wait* to see you tonight. Don't go back to sleep!'

After he's hung up my alarm goes off – my three hours' sleep time is over.

The flat is freezing. Turning the central heating on, I stumble through to the bathroom and run a bath, pouring bubble bath generously into the hot stream of water. I climb in slowly, letting my limbs take to the warmth until I'm immersed up to my neck. I pull the bubbles up and over my body so I'm completely covered. They glimmer prettily in the overhead lights. I lie there, looking around at our nice, clean bathroom and feel an unexpected wave of contentment. The entire room is white. In fact, the only colour in here comes from the dark green towels that are hanging over the white heated towel rails. I love it. The tidiness clears my head, even if I'm not naturally the neatest person. I remember James this morning, all smart in his tailored suit, and feel a surprising rush of affection. My boyfriend. I can't believe he's gone and bought a flatscreen TV. For my DVDs! We barely do any DVD PR. But it'll be nice to watch my chick flicks on there.

After a while, when I'm so hot I feel like I need a cool shower, I squeeze a generous amount of exfoliating scrub onto my palm and apply it all over my arms and legs. It scratches coarsely against my skin and the smell of citrus fruits wafts up my nose. I dip my arms, legs and shoulders back under the water and rinse myself off, then unplug the bath and stand up, wiping my hands over my body to get rid of the sticking bubbles. I step down onto the dark green bathmat and dry myself off, feeling fresh and clean. I turn back to survey the empty bath. There goes my tan, I think dismally. The base of the bath is dirty and scummy. I switch on the shower-head and wash my tan down the plughole.

I call my mum to let her know I'm home safely. She wants to hear all about my trip, how much Manly has changed and what it was like going back 'home' again, but I'm still feeling weary so I fob her off with the promise to ring her later for a proper gossip. I spend the rest of the afternoon unpacking and doing laundry. Eventually I grab my coat, scarf and gloves and go downstairs out onto the street. A pigeon skids around in front of me as I walk to the supermarket, trying to evade my steps without going to the effort of flapping his wings. At the checkout I spot some batteries and, feeling naughty, buy them anyway.

Back at the flat, unlocking the door, I feel quite different to how I felt this morning. Our black and white living room is neat and tidy and I have a sudden urge to lie down on the sofa and watch telly.

The new remote control isn't too tricky to work out so I make myself comfy amongst all the fluffy white cushions and flick through the channels on our Sky+ box. Remembering my conversation with James at Sydney airport, I search for UK Gold. I smile with relief when I come across it.

Later, I swap the dead batteries in my cassette player for the brand-new ones and open the wardrobe in the bedroom, looking to the back where my shoe rack is. I take the cassette player and the empty cassette case with Nathan's scrawling handwriting on it, and hide both right at the back underneath my heels. I don't really want to deal with James's questions about my new purchase.

As I close the cupboard door, I come face to face with my reflection. I look pale and sneaky, and my eyes are still puffy from crying. Then I hear James's keys in the lock.

'Hi!' I call, coming out of the bedroom into the living room.

'Hi.' He looks weary as he shuts the door behind him and comes to give me a kiss on the lips.

'Good meeting?' I ask. 'You're back early.'

'Oh, it was alright. Derek wanted me to bring him up to date on the contract situation with the Brigadellis. They're investment bankers based just around the corner from here, and they still haven't filled out their paper . . . Sorry, this is really boring.' He smiles and stops himself. 'What's cooking?'

'Lasagne.'

'Cool.' He unbuttons his suit jacket and loosens his tie.

Back in the kitchen I peer into the oven. The cheesy top is just starting to brown.

He appears a minute later. 'What are we drinking? Red?'

'Sure.'

I set the table in the living room and he emerges with two full glasses of wine. 'Candles?' he asks.

'Sure,' I say again. He grabs a couple of tea-lights from a drawer and lights them using electric-blue-tipped matches from a funky matchbox.

'Where did you get those?' I ask him.

'Just a bar around the corner from work. New,' he answers, by way of explanation. I nod my head but don't say anything.

I wish I didn't feel uncomfortable at the thought of him going out drinking without me.

When I bring the lasagne back through, James is sitting at the table with the remote control, flicking through the TV channels. I put our plates down and go to sit but he grabs me by my wrist. 'Come here, baby,' he pulls me onto his lap. 'Do you like your present?' he asks me chirpily. 'Isn't it brilliant? Listen, check out the sound.' He turns the volume right up. And up.

'James, you'll piss off the neighbours.' He keeps going. 'James!' I shout.

'Listen to how loud it goes!' he yells.

'James, turn it down!'

He does so, grinning defiantly. 'Bloody fantastic, isn't it?'

'Mmm,' I agree, getting up off his lap and going to take my seat. 'Shall we turn it off while we eat?'

'Spoilsport.' He smiles, but switches it to mute. That's a compromise as far as I'm concerned, even if he has left yesterday's recorded rugby game on.

'Cheers,' he says, and leans over to chink my glass. Then he tucks in. 'So how was your flight? God, how was the wedding?'

'Um, it was good,' I reply unenthusiastically. I don't really want to talk about it in any detail. Not to James anyway.

'Just, "Um, it was good"?' He laughs and reaches across to stroke my hand. I recoil. I can't help it.

'Lucy! What's wrong with you?' He's concerned now. 'Baby, what's wrong?' he asks, coming over to crouch in front of my chair. I can't look at him. There's a scrum or something going on between the guys in black and the guys in white on the telly. Or are they wearing dark green? I can't tell.

'Lucy?'

I drag my attention back to my boyfriend, who is studying me from his kneeling position. He's changed out of his suit into his cream Reiss jumper and dark blue Levis.

'What's wrong?' My eyes fill up with tears. 'Lucy, please tell me? Are you still worried about that text?'

'No,' I tell him.

'Good,' he replies hurriedly, 'because there's nothing to worry about. What is it, then?' He reaches up to stroke my face. I resist the impulse to draw away.

'Was it hard going back to Sydney?'

I nod.

'I was worried you were going to feel homesick for Australia now you're back.'

'Were you?' I ask, surprised through my tears. I didn't expect him to understand.

'Of course. It was your home for most of your life. It was bound to be difficult going back after such a long time and then leaving again so quickly.'

I nod as he picks up a napkin and dabs at my damp cheeks.

'Sorry,' I murmur. I can't help but think of Nathan and his rough hands, standing there by the bamboo cluster at the wedding. I focus my attention back to James and the tears slowly come to a standstill. His eyes look at me kindly. They're the same colour as his jeans.

'I'm so pleased to have you back, honey. Here, have some wine.' He picks up my glass and puts it in my hand. 'Don't let the food go cold.'

So he takes his seat again and makes a concerted effort to pay me more attention. I realise after dinner that I'm exhausted. It's getting on for nine in the morning where I've just come from. James seems fine with the idea of watching the rest of the rugby so I go to bed alone. I'm relieved. I'm not ready to make love to him again yet. I don't know when I will be but definitely not yet.

I've barely spoken to James since I've returned and I know I'm going to have to force myself back to normality with him, but right now I just want to be left alone with my thoughts.

Soon I'm back in Nathan's bedroom with him in our parallel universe. I fall asleep willing myself to dream of him. But, to my dismay, I don't dream at all.

Chapter 11

The next morning I wake up early enough to watch the sunrise. I grab my dressing gown and creep quietly out of the bedroom away from my sleeping boyfriend and into the living room where I pull up the venetian blinds. I look directly down the road at the glow of the rising sun across the distant rooftops – it's not so bright that it hurts but it still leaves dozens of tiny imprints on my eyes when I close them. Long thin clouds – or vapour trails from forgotten aeroplanes – are lit from below. They look like orange streaks of lightning.

I walk into the bedroom where James is still fast asleep. He looks peaceful and I feel a wave of love for him. I didn't even wake up when he came into the bedroom last night – I must've been out cold.

'James.' I rub his arm gently.

'Huh?' he opens his eyes and looks at me sleepily.

'It's quarter past seven,' I tell him.

'Oh, shit. I have to go.' He leaps out of bed and stumbles through to the bathroom. I don't start work until 9.30 so I've got

168

loads of time. In fact, it's such a nice, bright day outside that I might just walk. Even though it does look cold out there.

I work off Soho Square, just south of Oxford Street. It's a lovely walk in the summer – it takes a good half an hour – but in the winter and in the evenings I usually tube it the three stops.

I pack my bag for work, remembering Chloe and Gemma's boxing kangaroo pens along with some high-heeled boots. I'll walk to work in trainers and change when I get there. At this rate I'll be half an hour early so that will give me time to check my backlog of emails.

I step down onto the street and cross the road close to the square. A man in a green woollen hat rollerblades past me with a large black dog in tow and we wish each other a good morning. My trainers grate over the grit that's been put down to stop people slipping over on the ice. It's uncommon to have a frost at this time of the year. I recall the sand in Nathan's car and feel morose as I walk down to Marylebone Road and take a left past the West City Council building. Two stone lions sit on their haunches on either side of the steps, guarding the pillared entrance. The steps of the register office are peppered with confetti. There must have been a wedding on Saturday. Much as Sam and Molly's gum leaves were a nice idea and wholly appropriate, I do like good old multicoloured tacky stuff.

Imagine if James proposed? At the moment that thought terrifies me. What would I say? Lucy Smithson is a bit of a tongue twister. I prefer the sound of Lucy Wilson, I think, not for the first time. I used to repeat that to myself as a teenager. Of course, back then it was Sam I dreamt of marrying. Now the name Lucy Wilson makes me think of his brother.

What an idiot. Anyway James is not likely to ask me to marry him anytime soon. We've only just bought this place together and I'm only twenty-five. But then so are Molly and Sam. I don't know, twenty-five just seems so much younger in London. But then, James is twenty-seven. All I know is I'm sure as hell not ready for that sort of commitment yet. Not with James anyway. Surely not with anyone.

Marylebone High Street is a hub of activity. People wearing fleeces and big winter coats queue outside the door of coffee shops and on another day I'd join them to grab a latte and a pastry, but I drank a coffee just fifteen minutes ago and I don't feel like another one.

I adore Marylebone High Street with its little boutiques, funky design shops, restaurants and bars. The number of evenings last summer that James and I wandered over here and sat outside on the pavement, drinking wine and nibbling on olives . . . This place has such a continental feel about it – you feel like you're on holiday even when you're not. In a way it reminds me of Sydney. I wish Nathan could see this part of London, where I live. I think he could feel at home here.

I take a left and wander through the wide back roads. A few black cabs lumber past but apart from that, it's not busy.

Eventually I cross over Oxford Street into Soho Square and I'm almost at work. Our office hours are fairly flexible. I've even worked from home on a few occasions. Again I feel lucky. An image of Nathan floats back into my mind but I force myself back to the present. I can't think of you now, I tell him silently. You're not here and I'm not there.

I'm here. With James. And I want to be happy like I was before. Before Sydney. Before you came into my life.

'Lucy!' Mandy, my boss, calls, as soon as I push through the wooden door into our large, modern open-plan office. 'How are you?' She swivels her chair round to talk to me.

Mandy is in her late thirties, five foot five and super-slim, with cropped blonde highlighted hair. The only other thing that we know about our elusive boss, aside from her appearance, is that she's been married twice, and now lives with a man in west London. And we know that only because we read it in a press article about Mandy Nim PR six months ago. None of us have met Mandy's partner. She clearly doesn't believe in mixing business with pleasure.

'Great, thanks.' I smile.

'Not planning on moving back there, are you?' she pries.

'Er . . . No?'

'Good! Well, we must catch up later. Got some exciting things coming up.'

'Excellent. Look forward to hearing about them.'

She can come across as intimidating, but Mandy doesn't phase me normally. I'm not on top form now but I'm sure I'll perk up by the time we have our next one-to-one. I don't know if that will be this afternoon or later on in the week. No doubt she'll pencil me into her diary before the morning's out.

It's weird to be back. So much has happened in two weeks, but for everyone else it's probably just been business as usual.

Mandy has a team of fifteen young, friendly staff, including people in accounts and admin.

I make my way over to my desk. It's far neater than I left it. Bless the work experience girl – or workie, as we call the hoards of them that pass through the office.

I switch on my computer then go to the kitchen to make a

fresh pot of filter coffee. Gemma arrives as I return to my desk. 'Lucy! Welcome back.'

'Lucy!' Another cry from the doorway as Chloe bustles in with two plastic bags. She has a brand-new Hermès Birkin bag which she got as a freebie so I have no idea why she still needs plastic bags. She cracks me up.

We all do similar jobs, although I've been here the longest and tend to get the bigger accounts, but there's no jealousy between us.

'How was your holiday?' Chloe gushes as she plonks her Birkin and plastic bags down next to each other. Gemma wheels her chair over. Chloe is twenty-five and my height at five foot six, slim and pretty with long blonde hair and Gemma is a couple of inches taller than us, attractive and curvy with a choppy dark medium-length bob. She's twenty-three and has been here for six months, while Chloe joined Mandy Nim a year ago.

'Incredible. I didn't want to come home.'

'I bet you didn't. Where in Australia did you go again? Sydney?' Chloe asks.

I nod.

'I loved Sydney!' Gemma went travelling for a year after university, before she joined Mandy Nim. 'That's where you're from, isn't it?' she asks.

'Yeah; I used to live in Manly.'

'Manly – phwoar, the surfers on that beach . . .'

I blush at the thought of one surfer in particular and busy myself looking in my bag for their presents to distract them from noticing.

'I can't wait to go to Australia,' Chloe pipes up.

'When are you going?' I look up, interested.

'I don't know. One day!'

When I hand over their kangaroo pens, they both squeal and proceed to have a mini boxing match, thumbing the tiny mechanism to make the boxing-gloved kangaroos punch at each other. It keeps them entertained for a minute before they turn back to me, laughing.

'So what did you do in Sydney?' Gemma asks.

I fill them in briefly on my trip and the wedding, leaving out details about James. And any mention of Nathan, of course.

'Have you any photos?' Chloe is desperate to see Molly's dress.

'No.' I'd realised this on the plane. It pains me but I don't have a single picture of the wedding – or of Nathan.

My first day passes by in a blur. Jet-lag hits me at about 4 p.m. and Mandy sends me home early. I'm grateful.

I decide to catch the tube back, which comes as quite a shock after two weeks of living a laid-back holiday lifestyle. I could have just walked home but it's freezing and I'm tired. Very tired, now. Three stops later and feeling faint from stupidly wearing my winter coat on the tube, I make my way to the exit. Within a couple of minutes I'm back out in front of the terraced five-storey cream stucco house that we call home. The trains from the nearby station are noisy but we're used to it now. It's part of the reason why this road isn't crazily expensive. Terry often says we'll have to move further out and buy a bigger place when we have kids, and I remind him that I'm only twenty-five, for crying out loud. I just want to stay here in our little one-bed flat for as long as possible. I'm certainly not thinking about having children anytime soon.

I make my way wearily up the three flights of stairs and unlock the front door.

'Lucy!' James says, surprised. He's standing in our living room in his suit and has his mobile phone in his hand. He snaps it shut.

'Hi,' I say.

'You're home early.' He comes over and gives me a kiss.

'Mandy sent me home. I'm knackered.' I eye his phone suspiciously. 'What's your excuse?'

'I had a meeting on Baker Street with some clients – you know, the ones I told you about. It wasn't worth going back to the office. I'd just finished speaking to Derek when you came in. Do you want a drink?' he asks, looking back over his shoulder at me as he goes into the kitchen.

'Sure,' I tell him. His phone starts to ring.

'Oh, bugger off, will you?' He flips it open.

'James here. No, it was fine. Yes. Yes, that's right.' He keeps talking as he walks into the bedroom. I hover by the kitchen door, listening. I can barely hear him so I go out into the living room and strain to take in what he's saying.

'Yep, he just wants to clarify a couple of points in his contract before we sign. That's right . . .'

Okay, so it is only work. I'm becoming paranoid. I go back through to the kitchen and lift a couple of glasses down. A minute later he joins me. 'How was your first day back?'

'Yeah, good. Gemma and Chloe seemed really pleased to see me.'

'Where are your earrings?' he asks suddenly.

My hands immediately go up to my ears. 'I took them off to go su-swimming,' I tell him, altering my first lie halfway through to form another one. I haven't even told him I went surfing in Sydney. He'd only feel threatened because he doesn't know how to do it himself. And I'm certainly not about to admit I removed my earrings before I left because I couldn't get the guy I went surfing *with* out of my mind.

'Where did you go swimming?' he asks.

'Manly beach, a few days ago. I forgot to put them back on,' I explain.

'Oh,' he says, looking upset. 'Didn't you wear them at the wedding?'

'Um, oh, yes, I did actually,' I stutter. 'Sorry, I'm getting confused. I put them back on but took them off again for the flight because it's uncomfortable enough on the plane without having bits of metal digging into the back of your ears . . .' I realise I'm rambling and no doubt making him suspicious, so I quickly tell him I'll go and find them now. Feeling guilty, I head to the bathroom to discover the earrings floating around loose in my jewellery bag. They seem heavy on my ears.

Back in the kitchen and keen to divert the attention away from me, I decide that now is as good a time as any to broach the subject I haven't been able to stop obsessing about.

'James,' I say.

'Yes?'

'Did you ever find out who sent that text?'

'No, Lucy, I told you, it wasn't worth causing a fuss,' he responds.

'What if I *wanted* you to cause a fuss?'

'What do you mean?'

'What if I said to you that if you didn't find out who sent that text, I would check it out myself?'

He looks at me in surprise, then lets out a sharp laugh.

'Seriously, though,' my voice is brittle, 'if I said to you that our relationship was over unless you gave me the names of the culprits who ruined *at least* twenty-four hours of my life, what would you do?'

He stares at me gravely now. 'I'd find out, of course.'

'Would you?' I ask him hopefully.

'Of course I bloody would,' he insists. 'I'm not going to lose you over some little tossers from my work, am I?'

'Go on, then.' I call his bluff.

'What?'

'Call and find out.'

'Are you serious?'

'Yes. I am.' I look him dead in the eye.

'You want me to ring around this evening?'

'Yes. Or I will.'

'Okay, then.' He raises his eyebrows and gets out his phone. 'I'll call Jeremy now and see if he can shed any light on it. But it's going to make me look like a right twat.' He scrolls through the names in his contacts list, then presses the green button and puts his phone up to his ear.

'Wait!' I say.

He looks over at me.

'Hang up!'

'Are you sure?'

'Hang up,' I tell him.

He flips his phone shut.

'I'd do it if you wanted me to,' he says.

'No. It's okay. It's okay.'

I go to bed early again that night but this time James comes with me, holding me in his arms as I fall asleep. I'm sure he'd like to have sex with me, but he doesn't try it on, and if I wasn't so tired I might ask him why.

The next morning when I wake up again just in time to catch the sunrise, I allow myself half an hour of thinking about Nathan, wondering what he's doing, what could have been. I'm lost in my sad thoughts as the sun grows bigger and brighter in the sky, but when James appears from the bedroom I tell myself that's it for the day. I try to keep my daydreaming to a minimum on the way to work, and the next morning, I allow myself just ten minutes of feeling lonely and depressed before I force myself to buck up. As the first week passes, James and I settle back into our easygoing routine. I stop playing segments of my stay in Sydney over and over in my head like a film on repeat. And when I do start to drift back into thoughts of nights out under the stars, cool, damp beaches and that tall, messy-haired surfer, it all seems a touch surreal and I drag myself back to the all-too-real present.

'Hello . . .' James says sleepily when he wakes up to find I'm still in bed with him at eight o'clock on Saturday morning.

I look down at him, his blue eyes struggling to open.

'Hi.' I smile. 'I was just thinking about breakfast in bed. Do you want some?'

'No.' He yawns, pulling me back down. 'Not yet.'

He grins at me sexily as he guides my hand to his boxer shorts. We haven't made love since before I went away to Australia but now, feeling how turned on he is, I suddenly crave it. I smile naughtily at him as I slide out of my pyjama bottoms and he hovers above me and starts to kiss me passionately. I ease his boxers down and run my hands over his broad chest as he unbuttons my top.

'I love you,' he murmurs as he turns his attention to my nipples. When he eventually enters me I gasp. It feels raw. Different. As his pace picks up I can't help it; I start to think of Nathan. What would he have been like in bed? Suddenly it's Nathan's chest, Nathan's bum, Nathan's eyes looking into mine. We climax at the same time and Nathan pushes deeper, harder into me. Then he pulls out and rolls over and I look at James. I start to sob.

'What's wrong?' he asks me, sitting up in alarm.

'I'm sorry . . .'

'Lucy, what is it?'

I've never cried after sex before.

'That was just so . . . intense.' I wipe my eyes.

'Baby, come here.' He laughs with relief, pulling me back into his arms. 'I love you,' he tells me again. I lie there silently for a moment, thinking of Nathan and wanting to cry more. I breathe in deeply and James holds me tighter. I've got to let go, I silently tell myself, which makes me weep again – my breath coming out in raggedy gulps. James pulls me away from him and gazes full of concern into my teary eyes. I look back into his blue ones and see a flicker of Nathan looking back at me. I turn away. 'What is it?'

'Nothing. I'm just feeling a little overwhelmed with it all.'

'With all of what?' he asks me.

'Oh, God.' I sit up in bed. 'It's just been too much these last few weeks,' I try to explain. 'Going back home after all these years, seeing my oldest friends – I don't have that sort of history with anyone over here. And then Molly and Sam's wedding . . .

I felt heartbroken when I had to leave them again. I wanted to stay.'

'Weren't you even looking forward to seeing me again?' he asks sadly.

'Yes, of course,' I lie awkwardly. Then I come clean. 'Actually, no. I'm sorry, James, but I wasn't.'

What? Where did that honesty come from?

He looks at me with surprise and hurt. But I feel oddly indifferent towards his pain.

'I'm sorry.' I try to mean it. What's wrong with me? 'It's just that . . . I felt like I was in another world over there. You were so far away and that text really screwed my head up for a while. I had such a good time with my friends and it was summer, the sun was shining . . . I felt . . . I *wanted* to be . . . single.'

'Great!' he exclaims.

Why am I telling him this? Am I trying to punish him for having sex with me? All of a sudden, compassion flows through me.

'God, I'm sorry, James. I shouldn't have said anything.' I reach over and squeeze his hand. It remains limp in my grasp. 'James, please. I didn't mean it to sound as harsh as that. I just need to settle back in. I don't know why I'm acting like this.'

He lies there, eyes staring straight ahead.

'James, *talk* to me.'

Silence.

'I should have kept my bloody mouth shut!' My anger hits me out of the blue and instantly shatters his chilly demeanour.

'No, it's okay.' He meets my eyes at last. 'I'd rather you were honest with me.'

'I don't mean to upset you. Please bear with me. I'm just a bit freaked out, okay? It will be alright.'

'I know.' He reaches over to rub my shoulder.

I brush away the last of my tears, and, feeling like a traitor towards my boyfriend, glance longingly at the cupboard where Nathan's tape is hidden and buried.

Chapter 12

It's the following weekend. Mandy has kept me on my toes at work all week. She's won a new account – the launch of a brand-new bar in Soho, which is in the process of being bought by famous Italian footballer Gianluca Luigi and his American fashion designer wife, Eliza. Mandy wants me to oversee the whole shebang, which means a trip to Milan next month to meet with the clients, and organising a kick-ass star-studded party. It's a major deal for me – I've PR-ed bar launches before, but nothing this big – and she's promised me a nice bonus if I pull it off. Plus I get to meet the Luigis and all the girls in the office fancy Gianluca.

Chloe and Gemma are very envious. Chloe keeps asking me to try to wangle another place for her to join me in Milan. It would certainly be a lot more fun if she did. The thought of it is daunting at the moment.

Almost every night this week, James has put pressure on me to have sex with him. I feel like he's testing me after my recent outburst. I've been using the old jet-lag excuse, but I know it's wearing thin. It does at least seem he's now forgiven me for telling him I didn't want to leave Sydney.

The only other run-in we've had was the other morning when I came into the bedroom to find him changing the dial back to UK time on my watch. I shouted in dismay, startling him with my reaction. He offered to put the time back to how it was but I despondently told him it was too late; the damage was done and now it just wouldn't be the same. The poor love couldn't understand my disappointment at all. He was only trying to help, I guess.

As for Nathan, I'm still trying hard not to think about him.

On Saturday morning I remember that Sam and Molly return from their honeymoon the next day so I call up Interflora and order a big bunch of flowers to be delivered to their home. James comes into the kitchen just as I'm telling the girl on the other end of the phone what the card should say.

'I think something along the lines of . . . Okay, how about . . . Um. "Welcome home, guys! Hope you had a great honeymoon" – no, make that "an *amazing* honeymoon. All my love, Lucy".'

'AND James,' James interrupts as he gets a glass down from the cupboard and fills it up with orange juice.

'Oh, yes, can you make that, "Lots of love, Lucy and James". And can you do a couple of kisses too, please.'

'Charming,' he says, when I get off the phone.

'Sorry.' I smile. 'It's only because you weren't there for the wedding.'

He takes his juice through to the living room and plonks himself down in front of the telly.

'Let's go for a walk,' I suggest. We've just had ten days of wind and rain. Today's the first sunny day for ages.

'Oh, I was going to watch the rugby.'

'James . . . It's such a lovely day. Come on, it'd be nice to do something together.'

'It's just that I've been really looking forward to this.'

'Don't you want to spend time with your girlfriend?'

'Oh, Lucy, please don't start.' He moodily takes a sip from his glass and puts his feet up on the coffee table.

'Fine.' I get my coat. There's no point in arguing with him once his mind is made up. So much for the flatscreen television being a present for me. Bloody thing.

Outside on the pavement I realise just how warm it is. It's almost April and the weather has well and truly picked up. I wind my way through the back streets until I hit the south side of Regent's Park. Bright yellow daffodils spring up from grassy banks and the trees are bursting with blossom. It makes me forget my mood with James and feel cheerful.

'Lucy!'

I turn around to see James jogging towards me down the path.

'Hello!' I'm delighted. He stops in front of me and bends over, trying to catch his breath.

'Decided to come and join you, after all.' He grins up at me.

'Ah, that's nice.'

'Christ, it really is warm, isn't it?' he says, taking off his grey Gap jacket.

We wander down the path, alongside the pond and stop to watch as children feed the ducks.

'Can you believe those monkeys escaped from the zoo last year and were roaming around the park?' James says, smiling.

'What monkeys?' I ask.

'You know – the squirrel monkeys. A whole gang of them

escaped by climbing up the trees in their enclosure. Where were you when that happened?'

'I don't know.' I'm confused. 'I can't believe I haven't heard about it.'

'Well, it's true, Lucy,' he says wryly.

'Are you sure it's not just another of your tall tales?' I smile up at him.

'No, it's not!' he replies, annoyed.

Whatever.

'So I haven't really told you about my work this week, have I?' I change the subject.

'No.' He turns to look at me expectantly. I fill him in on the Luigi account and my forthcoming trip to Milan.

'That's a shame,' he says, before qualifying it. 'I mean, it's good for you, but you've only just come back. I don't want you to go away again.'

'James,' I reproach gently, 'it's only for a weekend.'

'I know,' he says. 'Just make sure that Gianluca twat keeps his hands off.'

'He's hardly going to go after *me*, is he?' I laugh.

'Bloody better not, or I'll 'ave him,' he responds good-naturedly.

Gianluca *is* rumoured to be a ladies' man – even though he's been married to Eliza for six years – but I'm quite sure I'll be safe.

'The other thing I need to talk to you about is Easter,' I press on.

'Right . . .'

'It's just that I know I said I'd come back to your parents' house, but I'm really missing Mum,' I add. 'After the visit back to Sydney, I kind of need to be with her right now. Does that make any sense?'

184

He nods but he's evidently disappointed.

'Would you come with me?' I ask hesitantly.

'I can't. You know I promised Mum I'd go and have Easter Sunday at home with Gran. She's getting old and it might be her last ever Easter. It'd mean a lot to them if I was there.'

'Okay, I understand.' There's not really a lot I can say about that. 'I promise I'll come home with you at Christmas, though,' I offer.

'That'd be great.' He leans down and kisses me on my forehead.

I do wish he'd come with me – he hasn't been to Somerset for ages – but it will be good to spend a few days with my family. I have a sudden craving for a pint of bright orange cider at our local pub. And a cream tea! Mmm. I'd better go for another walk tomorrow.

The next morning the home phone starts ringing at half past seven.

'Who the hell is that?' James moans.

'I'll get it.' I jump out of bed and take the ear-piercingly loud phone through to the living room before answering it.

'Hello?' I say groggily.

'Shit! What time is it?' Molly's voice comes shouting down the line.

'Seven thirty.' I laugh.

'Oh, bloody hell. Sam, it's seven thirty!' she yells down the earpiece.

'Ow!'

'Whoops, sorry, Lucy.'

'Anyway, how *are* you?' I ask.

'We're brilliant! Thank you soooo much for the flowers! That's why I was calling. It was so thoughtful of you.'

She fills me in on their trip to Bali. Five minutes later: 'Then this great big bloody elephant stepped backwards and we were like, whoa!'

I laugh at her story, thinking of Nathan. I wonder if elephants will always remind me of him.

'So how about you? What's it been like being back there?'

'Not too bad.'

'Work okay?'

'Yeah, work's good actually.' I tell her about the Luigis. She doesn't keep up with European football and didn't even bother to watch Australia in the recent World Cup so she has no idea who I'm talking about. 'Tell Sam, he'll know.'

I want so badly to ask about Nathan but the words just won't come.

'How's James?' she enquires.

'He's good. Sleeping. Well, trying to.'

'I'm sorry. I just can never remember the time over there.'

'Don't worry.'

'You sound a little down, Lucy. How are things *with* James? Are you two okay?'

'Pretty much,' I tell her. 'It's been a bit weird coming back after having such a nice time with you guys. I felt quite heartbroken leaving, if I'm honest, but it's not so bad now.'

Eventually I give in to my urge. 'How are Nathan and Amy?' I ask, settling for a compromise.

'They're really good actually. They were over here earlier.'

I can't bear the thought of them together.

'Were they? Are they back on again?' I ask tentatively.

'Who knows? They were here when your flowers arrived actually. They said to say hi.'

186

'Did they?' I feel pleased, even though she said 'they'. I want to know more but I'm perfectly aware I shouldn't be thinking about him at all. Anyway I assume he will have seen the card from 'Lucy *and* James'.

'Yeah. Oh, Nathan said to tell you something.'

'Really?' I hold my breath.

'Damn, I can't remember what it was.'

I wait for her, willing her to remember.

'Was it a joke?' I ask.

'Hey? Oh, no, I don't think so. Sorry, it's gone. I'm sure it wasn't very exciting.'

I'm so disappointed I can barely breathe.

'Well, I guess I'd better go.' She wraps it up. 'We should talk more,' she says, and I agree. We really don't speak very often at all – once every few months if we're lucky.

'Say hi to Sam for me. And Nathan,' I slip in sneakily. 'And Amy,' I add as an afterthought.

James calls me back through to the bedroom. 'Was that Molly?' he asks. 'Why can't she get the time right?'

'Oh, James, give her a break.'

He humphs. 'Come back to bed.' He holds his hand out to me.

'I might go and get us some breakfast from the café.'

'No. Come back to bed.'

I walk over to his side of the bed, hesitantly. He takes my hands and pulls me down.

'I'm hungry,' I moan.

'Lucy . . .' he says sternly, and starts to kiss my neck. He's not going to give up, so in the end I give in.

I don't cry this time.

Chapter 13

It's the Thursday night before Easter and I'm on a packed train on my way to Dunster in Somerset to stay with Mum and Terry. Even Tom and Nick are coming home for the weekend. Tom is bringing his new girlfriend, Meg, and threatening a gruesome murder if we embarrass him too much. This is going to be hilarious! I can't imagine him with a serious girlfriend.

This evening I passed up after-work drinks with Gemma and Chloe. I keep meaning to go out with them and I'm sure they'll stop inviting me if I'm not careful but I genuinely couldn't help it this time as I'd already booked my train ticket. The great thing is, Mandy's agreed to let Chloe come on the Milan trip with me next week. She is dying of excitement, whereas poor Gemma is dying of jealousy.

It's dark by the time I arrive at the station so I can't wait to wake up tomorrow morning and see the countryside. Mum and Terry are standing on the platform and they smother me, one after the other. I love Terry dearly now – he's like a father to me. Certainly more of a father than I ever had, that's for sure.

'So your mum was telling me about this Lugee account, Lucy?' Terry says from behind the wheel. Mum's insisted that I take the front seat beside him.

'Luigi,' Mum butts in. 'You know the Luigis, Terry!' she reprimands.

'Oh, yes, dear, I just keep forgetting. Memory not quite what it used to be, you know . . .'

Terry is twenty years older than Mum which makes him sixty-five. But he's an old sixty-five.

Mum was only nineteen when she fell pregnant with me. I'm sure I was an accident. My dad was a bit of a hopeless case. Probably still is. I haven't seen him in years, but the last I heard he'd left his home town of Dublin and was living in a crummy flat in Manchester. Mum left him when I was just a baby. I suspect that under the influence of alcohol he could be quite violent. And he was under the influence of alcohol practically all the time. That I know, at least. Although Mum rarely talks of him.

'So come on, love, when do you go to Milan?' Terry asks. I fill them in on my forthcoming trip and by the time I'm done we're home. Mum puts her arm around me and hugs me tightly as we follow Terry up the path to the front door. It's a chilly evening, so she goes straight into the kitchen and puts the kettle on top of the Aga.

I love this house. It's incredibly cosy despite its size. Five bedrooms, three floors; I'm on the top along with Nick and Tom, Mum and Terry are on the first floor with the living room and the spare bedroom, and on the ground floor is a dining room, which we rarely eat in, preferring instead the large country kitchen.

'I was thinking we'd have a nice brandy,' Terry suggests. 'Would you rather a brandy, Lucy?' he asks me.

'Actually I wouldn't mind a Baileys . . .'

'Oh, you two.' Mum smiles. 'Well, I'm still having a cuppa.'

Nick is down the pub with some friends. When I hear him stumbling in at midnight, I'm tempted to get out of bed and go and say hi to my little stepbrother. Well, not so little, actually. He's eighteen now and tall, with very, very short dark hair. A bit of a stud with the ladies, so I hear from Mum.

Meg, Tom's girlfriend, is beautiful. Medium-length, light blonde bob and dark brown eyes. She's a trendy city girl from the looks of her, in skinny jeans and a funky top which I recognise from All Saints. Tom is tall and gangly, with shortish, light brown hair. He's skinnier than his younger brother, who I suspect has been doing a few weights in his bedroom because he looks more grown-up and manly every time I see him.

'Alright, bro?' Nick mumbles from the breakfast table. He seems very hung-over.

Meg stands shyly next to Tom in the doorway. They've just arrived from the station. Nick holds his hand out to her and introduces himself. She steps forward and takes it timidly.

'Right!' Tom says, quickly putting his arm around Meg's shoulder. 'Shall I show Meg up to her room?'

'I've made up your bedroom for the two of you – is that okay?' my mum asks. Bless my mum. And bless Tom for not simply expecting to be allowed to sleep in the same room. Even though that's plainly what they've been doing for the last four months.

'Brilliant. Thanks, Diane,' he says, leaning in and giving my mum a kiss.

She blushes and hurries him away. 'Off you go!'

'Big bro's done alright for himself,' Nick drawls after they've left the room.

'Oi, you, keep your hands off!' Terry admonishes him.

'As if I would,' he objects.

'Ah, I'm only joking, kiddo.' Terry laughs, reaching down to pat his younger son on one of his broad shoulders.

Terry and his wife, Patricia, had a messy divorce a year before he met Mum. To have a break from it all, he took the accountancy job in Australia, but a couple of years away from his boys took its toll on him, which is the reason we moved back to England. Tom and Nick have ended up spending more time with their dad, while Patricia moved to Cornwall with her new husband. Tom and Nick don't like him very much, and I think that's probably why their mum doesn't mind them staying with their dad.

That night after we've all finished arguing over why Terry shouldn't let Nick off the £6,000 rent for landing on his Park Lane Monopoly hotels, I head upstairs to my bedroom.

This was my bedroom for only a couple of years before I went away to university. Mum and Terry have since done it up so the walls are the palest pink and the curtains are blue and white Laura Ashley. Hardly 'me' but at least I've got a double bed.

I try calling James. He doesn't answer his phone and it goes straight to voicemail. I try again. Voicemail. That's odd. I could have sworn he said he was having a night in tonight. I nervously press redial one more time. Still voicemail.

I go to the bathroom to get ready for bed, then try him again. And again, just as I'm dozing off.

Eventually I give up and fall into a troubled sleep, where I dream about my mum telling me she has cancer and Terry draining the blood from her sick, white body. I wake up sobbing at around six in the morning. My heart is pounding and I can't get back to sleep so eventually I go downstairs in my dressing gown.

I look out of the kitchen window. Spring is well and truly here. The pear tree in the front garden is bursting with pinky-white blossom and there's a misty haze over the pale blue sky. I can hear a blackbird trilling away somewhere and I have a sudden desire to go outside. I step into Mum's wellies; our feet are almost the same size. Then I pull on her warm Barbour jacket and unlock the back door, walking off down the garden path. Tilly and Tonker, our brown and white goats, bleat at me as I approach. 'Hello, boys.' I hold out my hand and Tilly, the brown one, comes over to nuzzle his face against it. I open the door to the chicken coop and let the hens out. Smiling, I watch them as they make their way out into the garden. How I love it here.

Back in the house, Mum is already dressed and in the kitchen. She looks up, startled, when I walk in through the door.

'Lucy, you frightened me! What are you doing outside at this time?'

'Couldn't sleep. Bad dream.' I don't elaborate.

'Oh, that's no good. Do you want a cup of tea?'

I resist the urge to show her how to do it Nathan's way. She's too much of a purist.

After a little while, Smokey, our grey cat, comes in through the cat flap with a dead field mouse and plonks it at Mum's feet.

'Smokey!' she berates.

'Ew.' I leave her to it. I head back upstairs and try James again. His phone just rings and rings. I feel sick. Where is he? What is he doing? I distract myself by taking a shower but as soon as I'm finished, I call him again. He answers, finally.

'James! Why haven't you been answering your phone?'

'Shit, have you been trying to call?'

'Only about twenty bloody times!'

'Sorry. I left it here last night,' he moans.

'What do you mean, you left it? Where are you?'

'I'm at home now. But I went out last night. Bit of a late one.'

'I thought you were having an early night.'

'Lucy, please keep it down, my head hurts.'

I take a deep breath before speaking again. 'Where did you go?'

'Some of the guys from work dragged me to a party,' he answers.

'Kicking and screaming, I bet.'

'Hey?' He sounds confused. 'Lucy . . .' Now he's weary. 'What's the problem? If you were here, you could've come too. What's the big deal?'

I don't *want* to nag him but I can't help myself. 'Why didn't you answer your phone?'

'I left it here by accident.'

'I was ringing at midnight,' I say.

'Yeah, and I was out until one,' he answers reasonably.

'Oh. I called this morning too.'

'Christ, was that you? I thought I was dreaming. I am *knackered*!' He sighs.

'Okay, well, now I know you're alright, I'll let you go back to sleep.'

'Thanks, baby,' he says sleepily down the receiver.

193

I'm not happy about this at all. Why does he always have to go out with his sodding mates? I can't stand them!

Mum and Terry's tea shop is a cosy place with red and white chequered tablecloths, wooden chairs and a few knick-knacks on shelves around the walls.

'I'll be with you in a minute,' Mum calls out to me when I go to see her in the afternoon. A few minutes later she re-emerges with tea and sandwiches for the lunchtime stragglers.

It's 2.30 and we've probably got half an hour to an hour before the afternoon tea brigade turns up. It's Easter weekend and Dunster, with its medieval castle and picturesque high street, is predictably busy. Mum brings me over a pot of tea and two bone-china cups, plus a couple of currant scones with jam and clotted cream.

'Aw, thanks, Mum.'

'Freshly baked this morning by Terry.' She smiles. 'So how are you, Lucy? You don't seem quite yourself.'

'Don't I?' My mum knows me better than anyone else.

'No,' she shakes her head, 'you don't. So what's up? Is everything okay with James?'

'Erm . . .'

She waits patiently, gazing at me intently over her teacup. Suddenly I find myself telling her everything.

Everything.

'Do you love him?' she asks, when I've finished. She's talking about Nathan.

'I don't know,' I answer truthfully. 'I don't think so, but when I was leaving, I felt like I did. Maybe it was just another one of my obsessive crushes.' She knows all about my love-triangle past.

'Well, at least you're over Sam . . .'

'Yeah, I know. I mean, honestly, what is it with these bloody Wilson brothers?'

She smiles, then becomes serious again. 'And you're still in love with James?'

'Yes.'

'Have you told James how you feel about Nathan?'

'No, Mum, are you mad? I could never do that, he'd hit the roof!'

'Well, Lucy, you're going to have to figure out what you want, my darling, because you shouldn't be stringing either of these men along if they're not the ones for you.' She looks at me pointedly.

'I'm hardly stringing Nathan along, am I?' I'm frustrated. She says it like she sees it, my mum.

'Maybe not Nathan, but what about James?'

'But, Mum, what if he *has* cheated on me?' I ask.

'And what if he hasn't? What evidence do you have, apart from the text?' She eyes me questioningly. I don't answer. I'm beginning to regret telling her anything, but I usually appreciate her honesty once I've had a chance to think about it.

'Lucy,' she says gently. 'How would you feel if James was having the thoughts about another girl that you've been having about Nathan?'

I pause for a moment and think. Nausea sweeps through me as I put myself in his position.

'Don't you believe *thinking* about cheating is almost as bad as *doing* it?' she persists.

I know she's right. But I don't know what to do. Apart from the uneasy feeling I sometimes get about James when he goes out with his friends, Mum's right: I don't have a lot to go on. And I do have a tendency towards paranoia. At least I do with James. And I haven't had another proper boyfriend who I can draw experience from.

'Just have a think about it,' she tells me. 'You'll know what to do when the time is right.'

'I hope so, Mum. I really hope so.'

Chapter 14

'I can't believe we swung this trip to Italy together!' Chloe laughs, as we perch on stools at a trendy bar in the Porta Ticinese area of Milan and order a couple of vodka sours with passionfruit – or vodka sour *alla maracuja*, as they soon become known to us. Italian barmen show off their cocktail-mixing skills in front of us. We want to ignore their posing but they are quite pretty to look at.

It's a sunny, late Saturday afternoon and Chloe and I arrived in Milan this morning. We've been wandering around the cathedral and the Galleria for a few hours and have just been at our hotel getting ready. We're going for the full works tonight. I'm wearing a knee-length, dark green dress which skims my curves and Chloe is in tight black trousers and a sparkly silver top. We're both wearing kitten heels. My hair is curling loosely just below my shoulders and Chloe has partially tied her long blonde hair back with a couple of clips. We look pretty hot, even if we do say so ourselves. And judging by the looks and wolf whistles these Italian men are giving us, we can't be too far off the mark.

'Thank you for asking Mandy.' Chloe beams.

'You're very welcome,' I reply. 'It wouldn't have been any fun on my own and I've been meaning to come out with you and Gemma after work for ages.'

'Have you really?' She looks pleased.

'Yes, truly. I'm sorry, I just never seem to get round to it.'

'Too busy going home to your lovely boyfriend.' She grins.

'Mmm.'

Actually, it was odd with James last week. He seemed a little distracted after Easter and wouldn't open up to me about it. To be honest, I'd been feeling preoccupied since my chat with Mum, so I didn't really want to press him. He did say his dad – a lawyer too – is trying to persuade him to retrain as a criminal lawyer. I hate the idea of him defending rapists and murderers and the like.

'More likely petty thieves,' James said, but I didn't feel at all reassured. I hope he tells his dad to piss off, interfering old sod.

Two drinks later, Chloe and I are still at the first bar, and haven't yet set off to meet the Luigis.

'Shall we bother with dinner?' I ask. We had planned to go for pasta but we've been too busy stuffing ourselves with the free *aperitivi*.

'Nah. Let's just try to score another plate of these mini pizza thingies,' Chloe replies, turning to work her charms on the barman.

By the time we arrive at Gianluca's bar – named simply Eliza, after his wife – we're both feeling decidedly tipsy. We're ushered through the main room to the VIP area, which is dark and sumptuous, with low-level lighting and a dark grey and silver bar. We spot Gianluca immediately, over in a black velvet booth, surrounded by stunning women. One petite dark-haired girl in a slinky dress drapes her leg seductively over his thigh. Eliza is nowhere to be seen.

'What shall we do?' Chloe whispers. 'Should we go over and introduce ourselves?'

'I don't know.' I pull a face. Eventually we head to the bar and '*due vodka sour alla maracuja*' trips off my tongue.

The barman gets to work – another olive-skinned Italian. He leans in close as he pours the drink, dark eyes looking deep into Chloe's green ones. The light in here is dim but I can still see her blushing.

'*Scusi*,' I interrupt, and he turns his hot-blooded attention to me.

'*Si*,' he drawls sexily.

That's where my Italian ends.

'We're here to see Gianluca,' I tell him.

'You're not the only ones,' he replies in heavily-accented English, nodding over to Gianluca and his gaggle of girls.

'Yeah.' I manage to restrain myself from rolling my eyes. 'But *we're* here for a business meeting.'

'Aah. Mandy . . .'

'. . . Nim PR,' I finish off helpfully.

He nods, coming out from behind the bar. 'Gian!' he calls. They speak in Italian briefly while Gianluca looks over to us. He pats the woman's leg abruptly and she sulkily disengages herself and moves away. I assume he's going to get up and come over, but instead he rubs his hand on the recently vacated black velvet seat.

'*Ragazze*! Girls!' he cries. 'Come and join me!' The other women are forced to make room for us as we take our place on either side of him. He pours us champagne.

He is devastatingly good-looking, I think, as he ogles my breasts. Shame he's such a smarmy bastard.

'So, *signorine*,' he says, reluctantly tearing his black-coffee-coloured eyes away from my cleavage. 'How do you like my bar?'

'It's very nice,' I answer, and he smiles smugly and nods his head. 'It would be good to see the rest of it . . .' I add.

'*Certo*. Of course.'

We follow him as he takes us through the VIP area, back into the main bar. Trendy party-goers make a concerted effort to act normal. Gianluca seems oblivious to all the attention, but he's no doubt lapping it up. The bar is dark out here too. It would be nice to see some colour.

Back in the VIP room, Gian, as he insists on being called, keeps topping up our glasses with champagne. I'm slowing down now but Chloe is a couple of glasses ahead. I hope she knows what she's doing.

'So,' Gian says as he turns to me, 'do you have a boyfriend?'

'Yes.'

'*Peccato*!' he exclaims in disappointment, before turning to Chloe. 'And you? Do you have a boyfriend?'

'No,' she replies uncertainly.

'*Eccellente* . . .' He tops up her glass a little more.

'Er, where's your wife?' I ask him.

'Oh, she cannot come out tonight.' He dismissively waves his hand.

What the hell are we doing here? I find myself thinking. I'm not really complaining, because this has been a fun trip so far and this randy bugger is paying for it, but don't we have to do *any* work?

'So, what do you want from us? Mandy Nim PR,' I clarify quickly.

'I want a big party. Lots of celebrities.'

'Have you decided on a name for the bar yet?' I've heard 'Luigi's' and 'Milano' flagged up. I really hope they don't choose either – they sound like dodgy Italian restaurants to me and I've said as much to Mandy.

'No, no. But let's not talk about work. Let's drink!' Gian turns his attention back to Chloe and I wonder how we can get out of this. I wonder if she even *wants* to get out of this.

My phone beeps to announce a text message. It's from James:

IS HE BEHAVING?

I smile, then type back:

WITH ME BUT NOT CHLOE

WANT ME 2 COME SORT HIM OUT?

I snigger and Gian glances over at me. Chloe catches my eye, looking a tad panicked. That's all the incentive I need. I determinedly flip my phone shut and stand up.

'I'm ever so sorry, Mr Luigi, but we have to leave now.'

'Oh, no. No, no, no, no, no!' he says, taking Chloe's hand. She gently but firmly extricates herself. He stands up, looking heartbroken. 'Well, if you must,' he says, leaning in and kissing me slowly on both cheeks before turning and doing the same to Chloe.

'He slipped me his card, the dirty bastard,' she exclaims as soon as we're outside.

'Bloody hell,' I say. 'His poor wife.'

'I don't like her very much anyway,' Chloe answers. 'She pouts at the paps like a pro one minute and disses them the next. But he was a tosser. They're well suited!'

We giggle all the way back to the hotel.

'I can't believe he came on to you!' Gemma gasps in the office the following Monday.

'He was a wanker, Gemma, you didn't miss much,' Chloe says.

'But I can't believe I didn't go,' she moans.

It is a shame. I've definitely bonded with Chloe now and it would have been fun to get to know Gemma better too. I wonder how she would have reacted to Gian's sleazy affections.

Mandy rolls her eyes when we tell her about the trip but she isn't too bothered, because at least we haven't wasted company time. Now it's full steam ahead with the party. After several PR lunches and dozens more bottles of champagne, I've lined up the Beckhams, Elton and David and a few other biggies who should guarantee us the gossip columns the following day. Provided they turn up, of course. They all purport to be friends with Gian and Eliza but you never can tell. It's a fickle business.

That week at work one of my friends from university texts me. I made two good friends while I was there, but I haven't seen either of them since last November. Karen lives in Charlton, south London, and Reena lives west, in Fulham. We used to catch up much more regularly but as we're so busy with work and boyfriends, we've all just let it slip. It's quite hard to get the three of us together nowadays.

Anyway, Reena and Karen have booked tickets to see the West End production of *The Sound of Music* on a Saturday at the end of May. They have a ticket for me on the off chance I can go. I tell James.

'Oh, we've been invited down to Henley that weekend,' is his response.

'What do you mean? Since when? Who with?'

'Edward and Susannah. Edward's parents have a house on the river and they're abroad. He asked me at work this afternoon. I said we'd go.'

Edward is James's colleague and he's pretty full of himself. I don't particularly like him and I barely know his wife, Susannah.

'Well, I wouldn't mind seeing Reena and Karen. I haven't seen them for months.'

'They don't want me to go, do they?' he asks.

'No, I think it's more of a girl thing.'

'Thank God for that. I'll go to Henley alone, then.'

'What's *wrong* with you?' I ask. He's been in a bad mood all week.

'Nothing's wrong with me,' he retorts.

'Why don't you talk to me about it?'

'Because there's nothing to talk about.' Then his voice softens. 'It's nothing. I'm sorry, I'm just having a shit week at work and my dad is still going on about this criminal law training and all this other crap.'

'You've got to tell him no!' I insist.

'It's not that easy. You know my dad, for fuck's sake, when have you ever heard anyone tell him no?' James sighs and turns back to the telly. 'Sorry, I just want to switch off, if that's okay.'

I leave him to it, going back through to the bedroom. It's at times like this I crave listening to Nathan's tape. I've taken it out a few times in the last six or seven weeks, just to look at his messy handwriting. I've resisted listening to it, but every time one of his songs comes on the radio or on the TV, I retreat into myself. I can't help it.

One Friday evening in mid May, on my way back in from work, I empty our post box in the communal hallway and recognise Molly's curvy handwriting on a package. James isn't back yet when I get upstairs and I'm grateful for the peace and quiet while I see what Molly's sent me. I rip open the envelope and pull out some photographs, along with a letter. They're wedding pictures.

The first is of Molly, Andie and me standing under the big gum tree in our white and silver dresses. The next one is of Sam and Molly, clinking champagne glasses with a view of the Opera House and the Harbour Bridge behind them. They're laughing as they look at each other. The third and final picture is one of the wedding party: Molly, Sam, Andie, Nathan and me. I sink down onto the sofa.

He looks gorgeous, dark hair falling messily, just below his chin. He hasn't loosened his tie yet in this picture. I peer closely at it. At him. At last I have a picture of Nathan – something to have and to hold. I look down at his image and feel a dull ache inside. I miss him so much.

I pick up Molly's letter and begin to read.

Hi you!
I thought you might appreciate some wedding pics. Sorry it's taken so long; I just haven't been able to get my arse into gear since the honeymoon.
I am LOVING being married! It's strange – it's the same as it always was but subtly different. We know we're in this

together now, for life. It does change things a little. Sorry if
that sounds a bit pretentious, but it's weird.

  Sam's work is going well . . .

I scan the letter, looking for Nathan's name. Ah, there it is.

Nathan and Amy have well and truly called it quits . . .

What?

She was putting pressure on him and he was having none of it
so he had to move out. It was all a bit of a drama, actually.
He came and stayed with us for a while but she kept calling,
day and night, and turning up on the doorstep unannounced.
Eventually she realised she had to let him go. After all this,
we're not so sure she was right for him anyway. You know
what Nathan's like. Doesn't want to make a fuss of things.
Now he's put an offer in on a run-down little place a few
minutes from the beach. We remortgaged the house to help him
with his deposit, but the B&B business has been doing
brilliantly so it's all good. Anyway it was about time he saw
some of his parents' inheritance. Sam's just thrilled he's using it
wisely. The place he's bought is in a bit of a state but he
reckons he can do it up on the weekends. Oh, because that's
the other thing – he's even got himself a full-time job on a
building site!

I put the letter down. Stunned is not the word. I read the rest of
it but that's pretty much the gist of it. Nathan gets a big chunk so
Molly really must be consumed by what's going on with him.

He's got a job? Set Amy straight? Bought himself a place of his own? Surely that's too much of a coincidence after all this time. Does it have anything to do with me, I wonder meekly. On the one hand I can't believe it would but, on the other, it is possible. I suddenly have an urgent desire to call Molly and talk to her about it. Not about my feelings for Nathan; I just want her to take me through her letter. I calculate the time. Now the clocks have gone forward that makes it a nine-hour time difference. Which means . . . five o'clock in the morning. Bugger.

My phone beeps. It's a text from James:

GOING FOR A FEW. BACK SOON XX

Great. There go our dinner plans. He was going to take me out this evening. But actually, right now, I need some time alone. I turn my attention back to the photos.

Nathan. He appears overpoweringly familiar. I wonder if he ever thinks of me. He must do. Surely he must do.

I go into the bedroom and get his cassette player out from the back of the cupboard, putting the headphones in my ears. The Killers' 'When We Were Young' comes hammering out. A lump forms in my throat as I read Molly's letter again.

At about midnight I get another text from James. He's sent me a couple during the evening, keeping me posted. This one says:

CARSHING AT JEZZAS

I assume he means 'crashing'. And I assume he means 'Jeremy's' – a twatty mate of his from work. I also assume he's drunk. He never calls Jeremy 'Jezza' unless he's out of his face. Fabulous.

Funnily enough, though, I'm not particularly bothered. I take the cassette player, photos and letter with me to bed and lie there listening and reliving the time I spent with that sexy surfer. If James were to come home and find me here, he'd want to know about my cassette player. But I'm listening to it, no matter what the consequences are. I can finally see Nathan clearly again.

Chapter 15

I wake up early. It's 6.45 in the morning. Still no James. The photos, letter and cassette player are next to me on the bedside table and I reach over for the photos. I study the picture with Nathan in it and feel jittery again.

I can't stop wondering what would have happened if I'd kissed him. If he'd stayed with me that night, my last night in Sydney. What would have become of us? And of James and me?

After a while I go and take a shower. Back in the bedroom, in the cold light of day, I know I should put the cassette player away, but I'm keeping the photos out. When will James come home? It's weird that he stayed at Jeremy's last night; he'd usually just catch a taxi. Maybe he couldn't find one at that time. A few doubts niggle at me, but I just have to look over at Molly's letter and it somehow settles me. I'll call her now. It's 5 p.m. on Saturday there so she might be at work but it's worth a go. I head through to the living room and pick up the phone, taking it to the sofa. I know her number by heart, even though I hardly call it. But as I'm about to dial, it starts to ring, painfully loud, in my hand.

'Hello?' I ask hesitantly, wondering if it's her. Or James?

A deep voice answers me: 'How do you stop a herd of elephants from charging?' My heart fills with joy as it continues, 'Take away their credit cards.'

I'm so delighted I squeal with laughter.

'How *are* you?' I ask, when I calm down.

'Not bad, thanks.' Nathan chuckles. 'How about you?'

'It's so good to hear your voice!'

'Aah,' he says gently. Neither of us speaks for a few seconds.

'I got a letter from Molly last night, telling me how you're doing,' I say.

'Really?'

'Yes, I know all about your house and the job. And Amy . . .'

'Yeah, that was a tough one.' He pauses, and I wait for him to go on. 'But she's alright now.'

'Is she?' I ask hopefully. I want her to be alright. Just not alright with him.

'Yeah, she's doing fine. Got herself a job in her dad's office.'

'Wow,' I say. 'She'll be climbing up the ranks in no time.'

'Yep, she probably will.' I know he's smiling.

'But what about you? Tell me about your house!'

'Well, it's got four walls, a roof . . .'

'Oi! Stop joking. Are you doing it up, then?'

So he fills me in on his work on the house, how much he's enjoying stripping it back to its bones and fixing it back up again. From the sounds of it he'll probably have it finished in a few weeks.

'And then what will you do?' I ask.

'Then I plan to put it on the market. Get started on the next one.'

'Wow.' I'm so impressed I can barely speak.

'So what's happening in your life?' he asks.

I tell him about my work and have him laughing at the Gian Luigi story.

'What about your boyfriend?' he asks when I've finished.

'Oh, he's okay,' I say. 'He stayed over at a mate's last night actually, so I'm here alone.'

'Oh,' he says. 'Does he often do that?' I know what he's thinking.

'No, not really.' I smile. 'But anyway let's not talk about him. I want to hear more about you. Have you *really* got a job?'

Twenty-five minutes later I've heard all about the boutique hotel he's helping to build on the waterfront and he's assured me I'm right to palm off Susannah and Edward in Henley and go to the theatre instead with my friends. I'd been feeling bad about it.

'Why would you want to spend a weekend with people you hardly know or like when you could be catching up with mates you haven't seen in ages?'

'Such a wise head for such young shoulders.'

'Stop taking the mick.' He laughs, and I think: I wasn't actually. But he speaks again. 'Want to hear a joke?'

'Have you got one?'

'Yep, the *Sound of Music* debate reminded me. Two nuns are driving their car through Transylvania when suddenly Count Dracula lands on the bonnet, snarling at them through the windscreen. "Quick, show him your cross!" screams one of the nuns. The second nun leans out of the window and yells, "Oi! Get off the fucking car!"'

I'm still giggling when James's key turns in the lock and he comes in, looking bedraggled.

'It's been so good to talk to you,' I say warmly, wrapping up our conversation as James takes off his coat. I don't want to tell

Nathan that James is back. I'd rather not plant the thought of my boyfriend back in his mind.

'You too,' Nathan says.

James is looking a little surprised. I suspect he was anticipating a shed-load of grief from me for coming in at this hour, but after my conversation with Nathan, I don't really give a toss.

James heads off in the direction of the bathroom.

'Will you call me again?' I ask Nathan hopefully.

'Definitely. Next time I think of a joke. And you can always call me. Although I've only got a mobile at the moment so it's not the cheapest.'

'Shit, have you been talking to me all this time on your mobile?' I gasp.

He laughs. 'Don't worry about it.'

We ring off and I'm so ecstatic I can hardly contain myself. When James wanders back through with a towel wrapped around his waist a few minutes later, I have a big grin on my face.

'How was your night?' I ask him merrily.

'Good, thanks,' he replies, still freaked out by my good mood. He comes over and gives me a kiss on the top of my head. 'I'm just going to get dressed,' he says.

I sit there for a moment looking down at the receiver.

'Who was that?' James asks, when he reappears a few minutes later.

'Sam's younger brother, Nathan,' I tell him truthfully, but slip the 'younger' in so it seems less threatening.

'Oh, I didn't know he had a brother,' he responds.

'Yeah.' I hand him the wedding photos. He flicks through the first two, quickly, then pauses on the one of the wedding party.

'That's him there.' I point.

'You'd think he could brush his hair.' He grins. I poke him in the ribs, good-humouredly.

'Give 'em here.'

James hands the pictures over.

'Want to hear a joke?' I ask.

'Yeah, okay.'

I tell him the nun joke.

'I don't get it,' he says.

'You know, "show him your cross" . . . your *Jesus* cross, and the other one takes it to mean "show him you're mad" . . .'

James shrugs his shoulders at me.

'Never mind.'

It's a Saturday evening a couple of weeks later and I'm meeting Karen and Reena outside Strada in Piccadilly. James has gone to Henley on his own. He seemed fine about it.

'I'm so glad you could come.' Reena gives me a big hug. 'You look gorgeous,' she says, pulling away.

'So do you!' I exclaim. She's dazzling anyway. Her parents are from Bombay (well, Mumbai, now) but she grew up in Buckinghamshire. She has the smoothest caramel-coloured skin, dead-straight dark chin-length hair and her eyes are a striking green. Everywhere we go, men – and women – stare at her. Karen and I always told her she should be a model in her spare time but she wanted to concentrate on her studies. She's a doctor now. Beautiful *and* smart. I would be jealous if she wasn't so bloody nice. It's so good to see her again.

We go inside, take a seat and have a quick catch up about life, love and work, until, ten minutes later, Karen arrives in a flurry of perfume and shopping bags.

'Sorry, sorry,' she says, in her broad Yorkshire accent. She's from Hull, up north. 'I just couldn't resist,' she says, plonking bags from French Connection, Oasis and Zara down at our feet. Then she leans in and gives us both big kisses, making loud smacking noises as she pulls away.

Karen was always the boisterous one in our group and it used to drive us nuts when we'd go out to a quiet restaurant only to have her draw attention to us with her deafening voice. But now it just makes us smile.

'How are you?' Karen asks as she pulls up a chair. 'No, I'll just nick some of their rosé, thank you,' she says to the hovering waiter. 'Is that alright?' She turns back to Reena and me.

'Of course,' we both insist. Karen grabs the bottle and pours wine into her waiting glass and then tops up both of ours. 'Let's order olives!' she says, suddenly.

'Go for it.' I laugh. She'll come back to us in a minute. She's always like this; can rarely concentrate on anything for more than a few seconds.

'How's Paul?'

Paul is Reena's boyfriend. He's also a doctor.

'Good, thanks,' Reena answers. 'Busy.'

'Well, he bloody would be, being a doctor.' Karen laughs. 'And what about the gorgeous James?' She turns her attention to me.

'He's cool.'

'How's his work?'

'Busy too.'

'You girls and your busy men . . . Thank goodness Alan is a builder. Nine to five! Always got my man at home.'

Karen is a hairdresser in Greenwich, south London, ten min-utes' drive away from where she and Alan live in Charlton. She

213

and I did media studies together, until she decided it wasn't for her and retrained as a hairdresser.

'I like your new hairdo . . .' I always feel obliged to say it, although actually I'm not *overly* keen on this one. She's dyed it the blackest black and has spiky hot-pink highlights sprouting out everywhere. But it doesn't matter if I like it or not; if her past behaviour is anything to go by she'll change it in a matter of weeks. And she wouldn't give a crap what I thought anyway. What it must be like to have her confidence . . .

After the musical, our voices hoarse from singing along, we head for a quick drink in a nearby pub. Karen goes to the bar while Reena and I spot a couple of people leaving a table.

'That was brilliant, wasn't it?' Reena says.

'We should go to *Dirty Dancing* next!' I suggest.

'Yes! Why don't we?'

Karen comes over to the table with three vodka-lemonade-and-limes. 'Do you fancy coming to see *Dirty Dancing?*' I ask her.

'God yeah!' she exclaims. '*Really?* After all this bloody time trying to pin you down, are we really going to get another date in the diary?'

I look at her, a little taken aback. I know she doesn't mean anything malicious by it, but it still hurts a bit.

'Yes,' I say, meekly.

'Well, that would be bloody brilliant.' She grins, and Reena smiles too, a tad embarrassed on my behalf.

Karen has a point. These two catch up with each other practically every month and I'm usually snowed under with work or with James. He tends to socialise at City bars with his colleagues during the week while I'm out at launches or wining and dining clients, and occasionally we go out for dinner or clubbing with his mates from work on Saturday nights. But I'm never that comfortable around guys like Edward or Jeremy. Although Edward doesn't say an awful lot, he always makes me feel like he's judging me with his dark eyes and humourless face, and Jeremy, well, Jeremy is just a slimy git. They don't feel like my friends, and they're not: they're James's.

I decide right there and then that I'm going to insist that James and I make an effort to go out with Reena, Karen and their boyfriends next time they're planning a big night out.

It's good to see them again. I don't have many friends in the UK, after coming here at the age of sixteen. I didn't really bond with anyone at college in Somerset, where I did my A Levels, so Reena and Karen are my closest friends here. I think of Gemma and Chloe again and remember what fun Chloe and I had in Milan. I am definitely, definitely going to go out with those two next Friday after work.

Chapter 16

'Hang on, hang on, I've got one for you. How many mice does it take to screw in a light bulb? Two. The hard part is getting them in the light bulb.' I hear Nathan chuckle at my joke. We've been on the phone for twenty minutes. I'm in the bedroom because James is in the living room, watching the cricket. The rugby and football season is over and now we're onto tennis and cricket. Whoopie-doo.

To say I've been preoccupied wondering when Nathan would call me again is an understatement. I totally forgot to ask him for his mobile number when he rang me the first time so it was a huge relief to hear his voice when I picked up the phone this morning. It's Saturday evening in Australia and he's at home – the renovations are finished now, and he's had a few estate agents in to value the house today. He'll be sad to leave it, he says, but he's already put an offer in on the next one, a couple of streets away.

It's the weekend after my theatre trip and Nathan is pleased to hear I went.

'Did your boyfriend go to Henley with Edward and whatsher-name?' he asks.

'Susannah? Yes.'

James came home late on Sunday afternoon, looking tired and hung-over. They'd all been up drinking red wine until the early hours.

'Give me your number this time,' I say after a while.

'Shit, sorry, we forgot last time,' Nathan says.

'I know. I'm glad you called again. Where *did* you get my home number, by the way?'

'Molly's address book again. It's handy that, I now have a plumber, an electrician *and* a hairdresser!'

I laugh. 'You're not going to cut your hair too much, are you?'

'Nah. But it does need a trim now that Amy's off the scene. She used to cut it for me,' he explains, and my heart sinks slightly. I do still wonder what went on between them. Was it more or less than either of them made out? Not that it's relevant anymore, apart from satisfying my warped curiosity.

'Does Molly know you've called me?' I ask.

'Nah, she'd only give me stick.'

'Do you think so?'

'Well, don't you?' He turns the tables.

'Erm, maybe. I don't know.' I didn't mention it either when I called her a couple of weeks ago to thank her for the photos.

'So,' he says, breaking the slightly uncomfortable silence, 'do you have a pen handy?'

'Was that that bloke again?' James asks, when I walk back into the living room.

'Sam's brother? Yes.'

'That's a bit odd, isn't it? Him calling you all the time?'

'It's hardly all the time,' I retort. 'He's only called me once before. And anyway, he's a friend.'

'I thought Sam and Molly were your friends,' he grumbles.

'They are,' I say firmly. 'But they've just got married and they're bound to be more caught up with each other. Besides now I'm friends with Nathan too. Do you want a cup of tea?' I head into the kitchen.

'Er, no, thanks. I think I'll have a beer in a minute.'

It's only 11.30 in the morning. I switch the kettle on and take down a mug, smiling as I make tea Nathan's way.

I'm thrilled that we're back in touch, but waiting for his call over the last three weeks has been driving me stir-crazy. I almost cracked and rang Molly to get his number last Sunday, but managed to control myself.

I hate to admit it to myself but, deep down, I know this thing with Nathan is going to kill me all over again.

'So tell me more about this holiday, then?'

James has booked five days off to go to Malaga in Spain with a bunch of friends from work and is flying out next Friday – back Sunday night, just over a week later.

'You know I want you to come too,' he's saying.

'How can I?' I frown. 'Mandy won't give me a week off at the drop of a hat. And we've got the Luigi bar launch on Friday.'

'Shit, that totally slipped my mind.'

'I thought you were going to come with me?' My tone is sulky.

'Lucy, sorry, I was, but this is just too good an opportunity to pass up. You know I haven't been on holiday for ages and Jeremy's got this flash pad through one of his clients so it just works out. Come down for a long weekend,' he suggests.

'Alright, I'll ask Mandy on Monday. I just don't understand, though, how you managed to get a week off like this at the last minute when you couldn't even come to Sam and Molly's wedding, with several months' notice.'

'Lucy,' he turns to me, infuriated, 'you know that was because I'd just been promoted. Don't you think I work hard enough that I deserve a holiday?'

'Of course you do.' I relax slightly.

'And I'd really like you to come,' he says, looking at me sincerely with his deep blue eyes.

'Okay.' I smile. 'I'll try.'

'I'll look on the internet this afternoon and see what flights are available. Then at least you'll have an idea.'

'Okay, that'd be good.'

Eugh. I go through to the bedroom and start sorting through laundry. So much for me insisting we go out with *my* friends. Now, here I am, agreeing to spend a whole weekend with James's work colleagues. But weighing up the crappy company against the prospect of a weekend in the sun with my boyfriend, *plus* there's the free accommodation to consider . . . I may as well.

Who did he say was going? Edward and Snooty Susannah, Jeremy and his latest shag. James also mentioned another couple of guys who he thinks I might've met before. The names Terence and Hector ring a bell but I can't put faces to them. And another girl from work called Zoe.

'Isn't Zoe the girl I met at your Christmas party?' I ask, coming back through to the living room.

'Jeez, you've got a good memory.' He looks impressed.

Well, I can also remember wondering if it was she who sent the text.

219

'What?' he asks, seeing my unamused expression.

'Nothing,' I tell him.

'Don't worry, she's got a boyfriend.' He grins. 'Come here, baby. You're such a funny thing!'

I'm walking to work every day at the moment. The rhododendrons in Dorset Square are blooming with pinks and purples and the wisteria hanging out at the front of our building is bursting with colour. The trees are full of new green leaves and the warm smell of freshly mown grass in London's many squares screams out summer. In contrast, the tubes are so hot and stuffy that I barely take them anymore and the exercise is doing wonders for my thighs. The only thing missing from my journey is Nathan's tape. James still doesn't know about it and he'd definitely suspect something was up if he found it. Of course, I could download all of Nathan's songs from iTunes and put them on my iPod but it just wouldn't be the same.

It's Friday, the night of the Luigi launch, and the office is buzzing when I arrive.

'They don't do bar reviews!' Gemma is berating the workie.

'Who doesn't do bar reviews?' I ask. I assume our workie – Kelly – has been doing the ring-round of journalists to see who's coming to the party and has mistakenly rung someone inappropriate.

'*heat* magazine,' Gemma answers.

Journalists hate it when you ring up and try to PR something that has nothing to do with their publication. Sod 'em. We can't read everything, especially not the poor workie who's putting in enough hours for free as it is.

'Oh, I wouldn't worry,' I say, trying to reassure her. 'As long as someone from Girls Aloud falls over drunk or Paris flashes her knickers, we should still make "Week In Pictures".'

I've just come from a morning meeting with the clients at the venue. It's almost ready – they're adding the finishing touches. They went for 'The White Lounge' as the name in the end, which I don't mind. Design-wise, they've gone for the polar opposite to the bar in Milan. This one is all white: white velvet booths, white tables, white and silver bar . . . In fact, it reminds me of the ice bar in Sydney. It looks spectacular but I wonder how long it will be before someone spills red wine over the seats. Oh, well, their problem, not mine anymore.

Eliza is just as Chloe and I had imagined her: aloof, bitchy and very up herself. Her husband, Gian, is as lecherous as ever. The only time he keeps his hands to himself is when his wife's around. And that isn't very often, so it's a lose-lose situation as far as we're concerned. But she'll be there tonight. She always turns up when the snappers are out.

Even Kelly is coming tonight and she's beside herself with excitement. At first Mandy didn't want anyone with spiky purple hair and a nose stud representing her company, but I managed to persuade her. I gave Kelly James's ticket because he flies out to Spain this evening.

He managed to find me a flight at two o'clock tomorrow. I'm returning on Monday night as I don't want to push my luck with Mandy at this late notice. I still have my bonus to consider.

We finish work early so we have time to get ready. I have to be there at five o'clock to oversee the guest list. We've called all the picture agencies, we have a host of photographers coming to the venue and we've rolled out white carpet for the stars to walk down. Thank goodness it's not raining, otherwise it'd be grey within minutes. Chloe and I managed to persuade Gian to make vodka sour *alla maracuja* the cocktail of the night. We have to be on our best behaviour until 9 p.m. and after that we're allowed to let our hair down.

Apart from Gemma throwing up in the toilets at midnight and Chloe and me having to call her boyfriend to get him to come and collect her, the party goes off without a hitch. Seventy-five per cent of the celebrities that we'd invited turn up, which is a good success rate. The Beckhams don't deign to join us, probably because Gian slagged David off recently and said he was more famous for his haircuts than his football. He's just jealous because Becks is better paid. And better looking.

I'm on top of the world, until I wake up the next morning with the mother of all hangovers. I meant to pack on Thursday night, really I did, but I thought I'd have enough time this morning. I climb gingerly out of bed and swallow Ibuprofen for my stonking headache.

The plane eventually departs around three hours late so by the time I arrive in Malaga it's after nine o'clock with the time difference. James texts to say they're already down the main street, five minutes' walk from the villa. They'll be pissed by the time I get there, I bet, and I'm going to feel really out of it. The last thing I want to do right now is drink. I'm tempted to go to the villa and sleep. I text him back to ask him to meet me there in half an hour, which is how long my journey will take, according to the taxi driver.

He's not there when I arrive so I sit on the steps by the gate and wait for him. Five minutes later, I text him again.

'Sorry, sorry,' he calls, as he runs up the path. He grabs me by the hand and leads the way into the villa and through to our bed-room. The living room is littered with empty beer cans and fag ends.

'Party last night?'

'Yeah.' He grins. 'Bit of a mental one.'

Our room is all white walls and white wicker furniture. We've got a double bed too.

'Do you want to get changed?' he asks.

I exhale noisily and collapse on the bed. 'Can't we just stay here? I'm knackered.'

'Come on, Lucy,' he says buoyantly. 'It's fun down the street. Everyone's in the party mood. Let's go and have a few drinks!'

'I'd give anything to just curl up with you and spend some time alone . . .' I reach over and take his hand.

'No, you wouldn't.' He grins good-naturedly and tugs on my hand to pull me up. 'Come on, baby. You get to see me all the time. The others will think we're losers.'

'I don't give a shit,' I tell him, then realise that sounds a bit harsh considering they've given us this free holiday. 'Okay.' I sigh. 'But I need to have a shower first.'

He rolls his eyes and flops down on the bed, wiping his brow. It's hot outside and he's sweaty, probably from running up the street to meet me.

Five minutes later I'm back in the bedroom, pulling my red and white summer dress from Warehouse out of my bag.

'Erm . . .' he says, looking at it.

'What?'

'Don't you have anything more . . . sexy?' he asks tentatively. 'It's just that the other girls are all dolled up and you might feel a little out of it in that.'

'Oh, bloody hell.' I sit back down on the bed. I didn't bring much with me.

I empty the contents of my bag out and he picks up a black vest top with lace trim. 'This and your jeans would look good,' he says.

I'm a bit hot in my jeans but he reassures me that the bar is air-conditioned. I pull on the vest top and accessorise it with a chunky silver necklace and strappy red heels and then I turn to my make-up. I decide to vamp it up with dark silvery-grey eyeshadow and two coats of mascara. I forgo the lippy and stick with sheer lipgloss instead. I leave my hair down.

'Perfect!' James grins, pulling me down to lie on top of him. He puts his hands on my waist. 'Mmm, very slim . . .'

'All that walking,' I answer.

'Maybe we *should* stay here,' he says, raising one sandy eyebrow. He kisses me on the lips, slowly, languidly. I can taste the alcohol on his breath but it's not unpleasant. That's one thing about James; he is a *very* good kisser.

'Hey, you, you're going to ruin my lipgloss,' I chastise gently.

'So put some more on,' he says, flipping me over so that he's on top. He kisses me again and moves against my leg, then he moans, gets up, and drags his hand through his hair.

'Come on.' He sighs. 'We should get back down there.'

I climb off the bed, disappointed, and touch up my lipgloss in the mirror. I powder my nose again too, because my face is flushed.

The air is warm, and colourful pink and orange bougainvillea hangs over whitewashed walls as we make our way back down the path to the hub of the action. James holds my hand as he helps me negotiate the cobbles in high heels.

It feels like the whole of Spain is out tonight. Bars overflow onto the pavements and loud banging music comes out of every venue. People are shouting and laughing. I'm suddenly feeling more up for it. We go to the bar and James orders us a jug of Long Island Ice Tea. The table is already full of half-empty jugs of variously-coloured cocktails.

'Lucy!' Jeremy shouts, standing up. He leans across the table and gives me a sweaty kiss on my cheek. I turn and say hi to everyone else.

'Hello, Lucy,' Edward says drily from next to Jeremy, dark hair flopping over his eyes. Susannah, his prissy-looking wife, smiles snootily at me. She's in her early thirties and her auburn hair is quaffed expensively atop her head. We have nothing in common, I'm absolutely certain of that. God knows why James thought I'd like to go and stay in Henley with them for a weekend. Is he barmy?

There are eight people around the table: Jeremy and his latest squeeze, a slender blonde called Lila, Edward and Susannah, Zoe, the brunette from the Christmas party, her boyfriend, Jim, and Terence and Hector, the two guys I vaguely recall from another office do. They seem to be on the pull from the way they're eyeing up the girls at the bar.

As I survey James's mates I wonder if one of these blokes sent that text. I bet they'd all shit themselves if I brought it up now.

I grin, inwardly. I'm tempted.

Jeremy rushes off to find another chair. His hair is slicked back with gel and it looks hard and crispy to the touch. Everyone shifts around so I can squeeze in between James and Jim. James grabs the jug and pours me a cocktail.

'We're all having Sex On The Beach again tonight, Lucy, if you want to join in.' Jeremy leers.

'You're so funny,' I reply, straight-faced. 'I think I'll stick to Long Island Ice Tea.'

James touches me on my leg and warns in my ear, 'Be nice.'

Apart from James in a dark blue T-shirt, all the men are wearing shirts. They seem to have left their ties at the office, at least.

'So what do you do?' Jim asks, from beside me. His blue shirt is unbuttoned casually and I can just see a few hairs on his chest. I give him a brief overview of my job.

'And you?' I ask. 'Are you a lawyer too?'

'Oh, no.' He shakes his head a little too quickly and it makes me smile. 'I work in IT.' He seems nice. Slim, with short strawberry-blond hair and just a hint of freckles.

'How long have you and Zoe been together?' At the sound of her name, Zoe's ears prick up and she turns to join in the conversation.

'Must be about,' Jim looks at her for confirmation, 'eight months now?'

'About that,' she says blandly.

'Zoe, do you want a top-up?' Edward interrupts, jug in his hand.

Hector, who's very tall and skinny, and Terence, who's chubby and a bit shorter than James, arrive back at the table sniggering. They've spent the last ten minutes up at the bar with a couple of platinum-blonde girls who look like they could be Swedish.

'We've scored!' They giggle. At first I think they mean they've pulled and I'm surprised because, compared to them, the girls are supermodels, but then I see the tiny packet Hector is waving in his hand.

'Yes!' Jeremy shouts, getting up and rubbing his hands together in glee. 'You coming, James?' he asks, then his eyes immediately dart towards me.

'No, thanks,' James answers, leaning back and putting his arm around my shoulder. He rubs my back.

'Save some for me!' Lila calls desperately, as her boyfriend heads off in the direction of the men's toilets, leaving the rest of us at the table.

I turn to James, feeling sick. 'I hope you don't . . .'

'Don't be stupid, Lucy,' he replies heatedly.

'Then why did Jeremy ask?'

He takes his arm away from my shoulders in exasperation. 'He's only being polite!' The others are watching us with amusement. I'm not about to cause a scene so I drop it.

I don't enjoy the rest of the night at all. Half of the group are on a completely different wavelength but I feel separated from all of them, as they've been here drinking for hours and I'm never going to catch up. I really want to go back to the villa and fall into bed. I say this to James.

'Shall I come back with you?' he asks. Well, yes, that would be nice, I think.

'I will come back with you,' he says, with certainty in his voice before I even answer.

To much 'booing' from the others we say our goodbyes and head out of the door.

'That was a bit awkward,' James says, as we walk back up the busy street.

'You could have stayed if you'd wanted to,' I snap.

'I'm hardly going to leave you to go back on your own, am I?' he snaps back.

Paige Toon

'Just go!' I tell him fiercely, storming off ahead, which isn't easy in my strappy heels. I've suddenly had enough of the day, of the evening, and of James.

'Lucy, wait,' he calls, running after me.

'No, seriously, James, just go back and get shit-faced with your so-called mates!' I'm angry now.

'Hey! That's not fair. They invited us and I don't want to get shit-faced.'

I give him a look.

'Oh, fuck off, Lucy.'

'Maybe I will,' I tell him meaningfully, before storming off again.

'Do you want the key?' he calls after me, spitefully. I stop in my tracks. Shit! He walks up the hill towards me in no great hurry. I suddenly want to cry. I suddenly want to speak to Nathan.

'Lucy, come on,' James says softly when he sees the tears in my eyes. 'I'm sorry.'

I follow him as he unlocks the garden gate and leads me past the swimming pool to the front door.

'You can go back if you want,' I say reasonably.

'I don't want,' he answers.

At 3 a.m. I wake and James isn't in bed next to me. I sit up, brushing the sheets because I can still feel sand in the bed from his beach trip the day before. I get up and pad quietly over to the door. I can hear the others out in the living room. They're quiet, obviously chilling out now after the mayhem down the main street. James must've gone back out there to join them. I climb back into bed, feeling unsettled.

I doze in and out of sleep but an hour later he still hasn't returned. I start to feel anxious. I get up again and go over to the door. It's quiet outside. Where the hell is he? I really, *really* don't want to go out there and look like I'm nagging him in front of his mates so I get back into bed. I can't fall asleep.

At 5 a.m. I can stand it no longer. I pull on the jeans and vest I was wearing earlier and open the door. The light is still on in the living room. I walk silently down the corridor and listen. Nothing. I stick my head out and see that the living room is empty, beer cans and fag ends still covering every surface. Straining to listen, I can just hear voices coming from outside. I peek out through the sliding doors that lead from the living room to the garden. James, Jeremy and Zoe are sitting on the steps, talking quietly. They seem to be alone. I don't feel comfortable going out there. Jeremy is a twat and Zoe is aloof. I go back to bed, feeling nauseous.

I wish I had Nathan's cassette player here with me. I get out of bed and find my phone. It must be about 2 p.m. in Sydney. Sunday afternoon. He's probably surfing. I type out a text:

> IN SPAIN WITH JAMES N SHITTY LAWYER MATES. FEEL
> OUT OF IT

I go to press send then reconsider. I return to the message and type *Miss u* at the end. Then I press send, my heart aflutter. I stare at the phone and wait. He's probably surfing, he's probably surfing, I chant internally. A minute later my phone buzzes. I snatch it up.

> WHAT DO U CALL 10000 LAWYERS AT BOTTOM OF SEA?
> A GOOD START. MISS U 2

My heart swells with happiness as I type back:

HA HA. FUNNY. U NOT SURFING?

His reply comes back almost immediately:

NO. WORKING

NEW HOUSE ALREADY?

YES. SIGNED FRI

WOW. IMPRESSIVE. LET U GET BACK TO IT

OK. DON'T WORRY. B OK. CALL WHEN U GET BACK?

WILL DO

After I type this I go back and add a few kisses, then press send.

Feeling happier and calmer I manage to doze off again and when I wake up at 8 a.m., James is sleeping next to me.

'Oi.' I prod him.

'Huh?' he murmurs.

'Where did you go last night?'

'Shush . . . Sleeping.'

I sigh and roll over but I'm wide awake now. I grab my phone, go into the ensuite bathroom and lock the door. Then I reread Nathan's text messages from last night.

MISS U 2

He misses me. I hold the phone against my chest as though it will somehow, stupidly, bring me closer to him. Then I read through each message again, and press delete, my heart sinking a little more as each one disappears from my inbox. I do the same with my sent messages.

An image of my mum's face regarding me over her teacup comes back to me. I shouldn't be doing this. I have to be careful. I know it's wrong, what I'm feeling. But I can't stop. I can't help it. I'm falling for Nathan all over again. But he's on the other side of the world and I'm here, with James.

I think again, not for the first time, about leaving James. But what then? Where on earth would I go? What would I do? I do love him. He made an effort to bring me over here to be with him this weekend and I know he loves me too. I adore our flat. My job is brilliant. I remember how warm Mandy was with me on Friday night, congratulating me on a spectacular launch. And if I did leave England now I'd really miss my friends. Karen, Reena and I are going to the theatre again next month and Chloe, Gemma and I have decided to make Thursday or Friday a regular drinks night. I'm excited about making some more girlfriends. And what about Somerset? I love going home to Mum, Terry, Tom and Nick. I had such a good time with them over the Easter weekend. My stepbrothers and I went down to the pub on Saturday night and had a few pints together. And Meg was great; she definitely fits in with our family.

I look down at my phone again. But I miss you, I think. And I miss Sam and Molly, my oldest friends. And Sydney with its crystalline waters, jagged skyline and sunsets so beautiful that they make your heart sing.

I've never felt so torn.

Chapter 17

'I haven't brought it,' I say dully, the contents of my carry-on bag strewn across the bed. I've forgotten my sodding swimming costume.

'Maybe one of the girls has a spare one,' James suggests.

'I don't want to wear one of their spare ones!'

'I'm only trying to help, Lucy. Anyway, why not?'

'They probably wouldn't fit. Lila and Zoe are like bloody giants!'

'Alright, calm down. Why don't you go for a wander down the street and buy another one?'

'Do you *know* how difficult it is to find a decent swimming costume? I tried on millions before I settled on my green bikini!'

'Now you're just being difficult.'

'No, I'm not!' Well, yes, I am.

'You can still come to the beach, can't you?'

'I suppose so,' I respond sullenly.

'Oh, dear,' Susannah coos later, 'what a shame you won't be able to go swimming. It's lovely in the water.'

'Just come and stand up to your knees,' Lila suggests.

'If I had some Big Feet I'd be alright, wouldn't I, James?'

He gives me a look.

'What are Big Feet?' Lila asks.

James laughs and brushes her off. 'Nothing, Lucy's only being silly.'

I feel a bit mean.

They all head off to the water, leaving me sitting on the sand with James.

'Stop being so moody,' he scolds. 'It's not their fault you forgot your bikini.'

'And my sunglasses.'

'And your sunglasses.'

I know, but I just can't help it. I don't like them. Any of them. Well, that Jim's alright but he's a bit quiet.

'James! Come in!' Jeremy shouts from the water. James looks at me.

'Come on, then,' I say, walking over to the water and wading through the waves up to my knees. Susannah's right; the water is lovely. James goes a bit further out and Edward jumps on him from behind, pulling him underwater. I wince, as I wait for one of them to splash me. Susannah wades over.

'It's wonderful, isn't it?' she says.

'Yeah, nice,' I agree and make an effort to smile at her. 'Sorry I couldn't make it to Henley the other weekend,' I say.

'Henley?' she asks, looking confused. 'Oh, *Henley*!' she exclaims. 'Oh, no, don't worry about it. We'll have to go back there another time.'

The uneasy feeling swirls back into the pit of my stomach. That was a bit odd. How can she not know what I was talking about? I glance over at James suspiciously as he tries unsuccessfully to float on his back and comes back up spluttering with water.

'I might go and get an ice-cream,' Susannah says to me brightly. 'Anyone want an ice-cream?' she calls out to the crowd in the water.

She leaves me standing in the shallow water on my own and I watch as the others bob with the gentle lift of the waves. James looks over to me and smiles. I half smile back. This doesn't feel right at all.

'Did you *go* to Henley with Susannah and Edward a few weeks ago?' I ask James later.

'Hey?' he responds, confused. 'You know I did. What are you on about?'

'Susannah didn't seem to know what I was talking about when I mentioned it to her earlier,' I explain.

'Really? She's a weird one, isn't she?' He shakes his head in bemusement.

'I can't disagree with you there.' I decide to drop it.

Back in London I have almost a whole week in the flat on my own before James is due to return the following Sunday. Strangely, I don't feel too lonely. Nathan texts me on Wednesday to ask if I had any success increasing the number of lawyers at the bottom of the sea. We text back and forth a few times but it's too hard to talk to him properly during the week with the time difference and both of us being at work. On Thursday night I go out with Gemma and Chloe and we're all hopelessly hung-over the next day at work. That evening I invite them back to our place for a pizza and a DVD. Gemma has plans with her boyfriend but

Chloe joins me and it feels good, sitting there, watching *The Devil Wears Prada* with someone who is fast becoming a proper friend.

'Are you missing James?' she asks me.

'Um, it's weird, but I'm kind of enjoying having the flat to myself,' I answer truthfully.

She tuts. 'I'd *kill* to have a boyfriend like James or Martin.' Martin is Gemma's boyfriend. 'But you guys aren't having problems, are you?'

'Erm . . .' I don't really want to shatter her rose-tinted view of my boyfriend because it's lovely – and reassuring – to have people's envy, but I suddenly find myself wanting to open up to her.

'You know when I went to Australia . . .'

I tell her about the flight and the text.

'Yeah, but that all sounds perfectly reasonable, what he's saying,' she comforts me.

'It's just a feeling I have.'

And then I tell her about Nathan.

'Well, no wonder you're confused about James,' she says when I've finished. 'Your heart is elsewhere.'

'Is it, though? Is it really? Nathan's on the other side of the world. I don't know when or if I'll ever see him again. Maybe I'm just feeling like this because it's safe. He's like a fantasy boyfriend; very few flaws. When I think about him I don't have to deal with reality.'

'That's conceivable,' she muses. 'But why can't you talk to James?'

'About Nathan?'

'No, about how you feel about him. The text. The fact that you still worry about it.'

'Perhaps.'

'Why are you so reluctant?'

Because I don't believe he'd tell me the truth. I don't say this to Chloe. No one likes to admit they don't trust their boyfriend. Instead I answer, 'I'm not reluctant. I've just got a lot to think about, that's all.'

We're friends, Chloe and I, but we're not close enough that I feel I can tell her absolutely anything. I don't have that closeness with anyone. Not even Molly. The realisation makes me feel very isolated.

I ring Nathan the next morning and he answers immediately.

'Hello, you, I was just finishing work on the house for the day.' His voice travels warmly down the line. 'So, tell me about Spain. I want all the gory details.'

'It was a disaster.' I fill him in on the trip and he listens carefully.

'And when does James get back?'

'Tomorrow,' I answer. 'The launch party went well, though, and my boss has given me a nice bonus, so it's not all bad. What about you? What have you been up to this week?'

'Well, it was my birthday on Thursday . . .'

'*Really?* Oh, happy birthday! I wish I'd known. I'd have sent a card.'

'That's alright.' He laughs. 'You don't even know my address.'

That makes him a Gemini, I'm thinking. Good match for a Libra like me.

'What did you do for it?'

'Guys from work took me out for a few drinks and after that I just went round to Sam and Molly's.'

'How are they doing?' I ask.

'Really good. Busy with the B&B, though. Molly's had to cut down her hours at the shop. So what about you? What are you up to today?'

'I might go to Regent's Park for a wander. Maybe head down Marylebone High Street and do some shopping.'

'Sounds nice.'

'It is.' I smile. 'When are you coming over, so you can see for yourself?'

He laughs softly and I realise I'm holding my breath, waiting for his answer. 'Not anytime soon, I'm afraid. Got to get this house finished and it's tougher than the last one. Plus, work's really busy.'

'Fair enough,' I reply sadly. 'Have you got any jokes for me?'

'Funny you should say that . . .'

'Go on,' I urge.

'Okay. An Englishman goes to the doctor and says, "Doctor, doctor, I really want to become Irish!" and the doctor says, "Okay, well that's quite a simple procedure; all we have to do is remove twenty-five per cent of your brain."'

'Eesh,' I interrupt. 'My dad's Irish.'

'Bear with me,' he says. 'So he has the operation and afterwards the doctor comes in and says, "Oh, no! There's been a terrible mistake! Instead of removing twenty-five per cent of your brain, we've removed seventy-five per cent!" The man looks up at him and grins. "No worries, she'll be right, mate."'

I crack up laughing.

'So what *is* the deal with your dad?' he says suddenly. 'Molly says that you never talk about him.'

'When were you talking to Molly about my father?' I ask, taken aback.

'Sorry, I wasn't being nosy. Well, actually I was.'

'What do you want to know?'

'Where is he now?' he asks and I realise I don't mind his prying. Molly's right. I never talk about him. Not to her, James or anyone.

'He was in Manchester, last I heard. My grandmother – his mother – used to send me birthday and Christmas cards until she died a couple of years ago, and she'd tell me what he was up to. Because he never bothered . . .'

It was when Mum dragged me back to England that I first tracked down my dad. Growing up, I always wondered about him and started to ask questions, which I know my mum found difficult to answer. It was especially tough because after years of living alone with me she had finally found happiness with Terry and she had no desire to go back and relive her painful past. That's when I found out about my father being an alcoholic. But I still wanted to meet him. My mum finally put me in touch with my dad's mother in Dublin. My grandmother and father were the only relatives I had left on that side of the family. She was overjoyed to hear from me and together we planned for me to stay with her in Ireland. We decided to surprise my father, who lived on the next street.

It was a disaster. My dad was off his face on booze, and the moment we walked into his house he shouted and threw a book at us. His place smelt of urine and was a complete tip. When I called my mum later in floods of tears, she barely knew what to say. She'd warned me but I hadn't listened. There was little she could say to comfort me.

My gran took me back there the next day, promising he was better in the mornings, and he was. But not much better. He didn't want to know about me and what I was doing. He didn't ask after Mum. He mumbled into his whisky and shifted uncomfortably in his seat. I resolved never to see him again.

My grandmother stayed in touch. But I hadn't felt comfortable in her house, either. She was very pernickety and obviously not used to having people around. I didn't know where to sit or how to behave. I was only seventeen at the time and it was all a bit much. We wrote to each other for a couple of years but soon even those letters dried up and we just sent the odd card instead. When she died I didn't go to her funeral. The last thing I wanted was to see my father again. I wish now I'd gone. I still feel terribly guilty about it.

I never really spoke to Molly about any of this. Sam's parents had just died when I went to Dublin, and I didn't want to add to their burden.

'I'm sorry, Lucy,' Nathan says softly, when I finish telling him.

'Thanks.'

'Have you ever thought about . . . No, I don't suppose you'd want to,' he says.

'No, I don't.' I really don't want to see my dad again. If he's still a drunk like he was back then, then I've got no time for him.

'Did he ever remarry?' Nathan asks.

'Not that I know of, no. I don't think I've got any half-brothers or half-sisters.'

'I was just wondering about that,' he says.

'Tell me another joke!' I insist suddenly. I don't want to talk about this any longer.

'I don't know any more,' comes his sorrowful reply.

'Really?' I ask. 'Are you all dried up?'

'I'm afraid so. Do you realise, everywhere I go, everyone I meet, I pester them for crappy jokes?'

'Do you?' I squeal. 'Me too!'

He laughs.

'So, what now?' I giggle. 'Is this the end of our relationship?'

'Is that what this is? A relationship?' he asks.

'Yes.' I smile. 'A relationship of sorts.'

He chuckles, then says, 'I'll give you a week to come up with another joke. And it had better be a good one. Otherwise, it's over, honey.'

That week at work, Mandy calls me into the meeting room. She's just signed a new client, and wants me to handle the account.

'Ooh, how exciting. What is it this time?' I'm thinking make-up . . . handbags . . . shoes . . .

'Have you heard of the "Mockah Chockah" song?'

'Er, no.'

'Not even when you went to Spain?'

'I'm afraid not,' I admit, feeling inadequate.

She slides a CD and a DVD across the desk to me. I pick up the DVD. The picture on the front cover is of two girls who appear to be in their early twenties – one blonde, one brunette – both with short and spiky haircuts, flanking a camp-looking blond guy in a tight purple T-shirt and bright orange shorts. The girls are wearing pink leotards, purple leg warmers and orange wristbands. We're talking cheese of Parmesan proportions.

I look up at Mandy inquisitively.

'Titteesh. A new Russian boy–girl group. Their "Mockah Chockah" song has been sweeping the nightclubs in Europe since early May and now it's being released here. I want you to do the PR for it. We're looking for a Number One.'

'Right . . .' I answer, still confused. 'Titteesh? That's the name of the band?'

'Yes,' Mandy replies, a hint of a smile forming at the corner of her neatly lip-lined lips. I fight back the urge to dissolve into hysterical laughter.

'Have a listen, watch the DVD, learn the dance—'

'Dance?' I can't help but interrupt.

'Yes. It's a *novelty* song, Lucy. They always have a dance.'

Ten minutes later I'm in the small back office watching the television screen through my fingers. Holy shit, this song stinks! And I've never seen a dance so ridiculous. I do vaguely remember the tune from Spain, now. I press a button on the DVD remote control and watch it over again, scarcely feeling any better, even as a PR plan starts to evolve in my mind.

> *We like a Mockah Chockah*
> *Show us with your hands*
> *We like the way you look*
> *And we love the way you dance*
>
> *We like a Mockah Chockah*
> *Like the way you move*
> *Like the way you kiss*
> *And we love the way you groove*
>
> *Mockah Chockah hot!*
> *Mockah Chockah slow*
> *Mockah Chockah now!*
> *Go! Go! Go!*

And so on.

I peep my head out of the door and look over at Gemma and

Chloe. I really want them to see this and share my pain but Mandy is at her desk in full view.

'You okay, Lucy?' Mandy calls, eagle eyes never leaving the computer screen in front of her.

'Yes, fine, thanks!' I turn back to eject the DVD.

'Any ideas?' She swivels to look at me as I make my way back to my desk.

'A few,' I respond.

'Good.' She nods abruptly, before swivelling round again to her computer. I swear she's trying to keep a straight face.

Titteesh – I can't believe that's their name – are arriving in the UK on Monday for almost two weeks of solid PR. It's Wednesday now, so I don't have long if I'm going to formulate a plan that will propel this godawful group and their crappy, crappy song to the top of the charts in just over a fortnight. I hope mankind will forgive me.

Chloe and Gemma naturally think it's the funniest thing ever. I can practically hear them thanking their lucky stars that they weren't chosen to run this campaign. They're not so jubilant, however, when Mandy calls a team meeting that afternoon and tells them they have to assist me in any way I see fit. I smirk at them across the table with a twinkle in my eye. Maybe this won't be so torturous after all.

'James, I have to use the DVD player,' I tell him that night.

'Aw, Lucy, the tennis is on,' he moans.

I don't mind the tennis, actually; it's better than the cricket any day.

'Sorry, but I must. I have to learn this stupid dance routine.'

'What stupid dance routine?'

'Give me a sec and I'll show you.'

A short while afterwards, James is beside himself on the sofa as I swing my arms and kick my legs like a baton-wielding maniac. Without a baton, unfortunately.

'Stop laughing, you little shit!' I pant as I attempt a twirl before jumping to my right to repeat the routine.

'I can't . . . I can't . . . I can't . . . *believe* you're going to do this around London,' he manages to spit out, tears streaming down his face.

'I'm glad you find it so funny,' I snap, but I'm smiling really.

My plan is to get the group to perform their novelty dance in front of iconic London landmarks on Monday and post the video on the infamous internet site YouTube the following day. The week after next, the single is released and the television and radio promotion will start, so this week I'm going to drag Titteesh around various magazine and newspaper offices and get them to teach willing journalists the dance. Well, when I say *I*, I mean *we*. I'm buggered if I'm going to let Chloe and Gemma get off lightly.

By Saturday morning, though, I'm starting to feel panicky. Titteesh are arriving on Monday and I still haven't properly sourced the locations where we're going to shoot the video. I tell James of my concerns as he's buttering toast in the kitchen.

'Well, you'll just do Trafalgar Square, Downing Street, Piccadilly Circus, that sort of thing, won't you?' he suggests.

'Yeah, but I'm not sure where to go first or if you can even film in those locations.'

'Just wing it, Lucy. You'll be fine.'

But I'm still worried.

'How about we go and check out some locations today? Would that put your mind at rest?'

'Would you do that with me?' I ask him hopefully.

'Sure.'

'Ah, that's so sweet! Thank you!'

I realise as we're walking out of the door that I haven't called Nathan yet and I was supposed to do that today. I peer down at my watch. It'll be too late to call him when we get back. I'll just have to wait until tomorrow. For once, work has to come first.

The next day is Sunday and James is watching Wimbledon.

'I'm just going to make a phone call,' I tell him, wandering through to the bedroom.

'You're not ringing that bloke again, are you?' he asks.

'Nathan? Yes.'

'Lucy, you speak to him more than me . . .'

'James, I do not,' I respond calmly. 'If you want to switch the tennis off we could go and do something instead?' I know full well that he won't. Yesterday's location sourcing took a lot longer than we thought and we were both shattered by the end of it. Missing one full day's tennis was hard enough for James.

'Forget it,' he grumbles, turning back to the match.

Nathan answers on the second ring.

'And there's me thinking it was all over,' he sighs.

'You said I had a week!'

'It's been eight days, Lucy, I was going out of my mind.'

Is he flirting with me?

'What have you got for me? I hope it's a good one . . .' he says.

'You tell me. Two goldfish in a tank. One says to the other, "Are you driving this thing or am I?"'

'That sucks.' I can hear him trying not to laugh. 'That's just not funny. I'm afraid we might have to call it a day.'

'Wait! I have another one.' In between all the 'Mockah Chockah' madness this week I've still managed to pester people

244

for jokes I haven't heard before. A guy from accounts and one of the receptionists came up trumps.

'This one will get you. Right, a duck walks into a bar and asks, "Got any bread?" And the barman replies, "No." And the duck asks again, "Got any bread?" And again the barman says, "No!" "Got any bread?" "I said, no! N. O. NO!" "Got any bread?" "Oh, for crying out loud . . . N-O spells NO and I mean NO!" "Got any bread?" "NO NO NO NO NO NO NO!" "Got any bread?" "Look, if you ask me one more time if I've got any bread, I'm going to nail your fucking beak to the fucking bar! WE HAVE NO BREAD!" "Got any nails?" "No!" "Got any bread?"'

Nathan laughs. 'Okay, you got me. Consider us back on. So,' he says, 'when are you coming back to Australia to see me?'

'I don't know.' I smile, collapsing back onto the bed. I'm pleased that he said 'me' and not 'us'.

'Because I'm not really into long-distance relationships,' he continues.

He is *definitely* flirting with me.

'Well, you might just have to come and see me . . .'

'Alright, then.'

'When?' I grin. As *if*!

'How does the end of September grab you?'

I sit bolt upright.

'Are you joking?'

'No,' he says.

'You're serious?' I'm flabbergasted.

'Yep.'

'*Really?*'

'If you ask me that one more time I'm going to nail your fucking beak to the fucking bar!'

245

It turns out that one of the guys from Nathan's work has just returned from London where he's been helping to build the new Wembley Stadium. The building company running the job is Australian and they've been looking for more Aussie builders to work over here. As simple as that.

'How long are you coming for?' I ask, almost lost for words.

'If it all goes to plan, and it might not yet, we'll see, but if it does, they're trying to line us up with three-month working visas. So we should be there until early January.'

By we, he means his friend Richard from work who also wants to come to England.

'Where will you stay?' I want to tell him he can stay here but of course that's ridiculous. Even if we did have a spare room, James would never allow it. And anyway that would just be asking for trouble. It was bad enough having him sleep in the room next door to me at Sam and Molly's house.

'I haven't figured that part out yet. Somewhere in north London, I reckon, judging by what the guy from work said.'

After we hang up I sit on the bed for a moment feeling shell-shocked. Then I go through to the living room.

'James?'

'Yes?'

'You know Nathan, Sam's little brother?'

'Yeah . . .' he says, eyes still fixed on the telly. Suddenly he yells, 'That was in, you moron!'

I carry on. 'Well, he might be coming over here in three months' time.'

That gets his attention.

'So you'll be able to meet him!' I add cheerfully.

'*Great!*' Oh, the sarcasm.

'James, don't be mean.' I keep my tone playful. 'He's a nice guy; you'd get along well with him.'

He looks up at me from the sofa, blue eyes staring intently at me and I avert my gaze to the tennis on the telly. 'Who's winning?' I ask.

'Lucy, come here,' he says and reaches up for my hand.

'James, careful!' I squeal as I start to lose my balance. He doesn't let go, just pulls me firmly down onto his lap so I'm kneeling above him.

'Do you fancy him?' he asks, looking searchingly into my eyes.

'No!' I laugh.

'Really?'

'James, stop being silly.'

He reaches up and rubs his thumb over my nipple, through my T-shirt. Then he takes my face in his hands and starts to kiss me, slowly at first, then harder, like the expert kisser he is. I respond to him more passionately as he reaches down and unbuckles his belt.

But when we've finished I feel dirty.

Chapter 18

'Are you *serious*?' Chloe squeals on Monday at work.

'Shh! It might not happen yet. He's still in the process of sorting it out.'

'Lucy, what time are you going to collect the clients?' Mandy calls from her desk, interrupting our gossiping.

'I've got a car coming in twenty minutes,' I call back.

Titteesh are flying in direct from Portugal where they've been on a promotional tour around the Algarve's bars and nightclubs. Chloe comes with me to collect them from the airport because we're launching straight into 'the operation'. We don't have long if we're going to get this video up onto the internet tomorrow.

Two hours later we're standing in front of the Millennium Wheel on London's South Bank and Chloe is trying to hold a camera steady while attempting not to laugh as the three members of Titteesh whirl and twirl in front of her. I'm blasting their song out of a portable stereo player and wishing the ground would swallow me up as the crowd of people in front of us grows.

Suddenly two girls aged about nine or ten begin to join in with the dance routine. Alexei, the male member of the band, gasps in animated delight and encourages them to form a twirling circle.

> *Mockah Chockah hot!*
> *Mockah Chockah slow*
> *Mockah Chockah now!*
> *Go! Go! Go!*

They chant as more kids run to join in, followed by a few laughing students. The girl band members, Regina and Varvara, join Alexei in enthusiastically welcoming every single newcomer. Regina, the blonde one, pulls me into the circle. I put on a brave face and embrace the madness as the crowd just keeps growing.

It's the same at Buckingham Palace, only this time there are guards trying not to look, which makes it even more hilarious.

By the time the day is over, Chloe and I can't get the bloody song out of our heads. I'm still singing it that night as I try to fall asleep, *and* in the morning when I wake up. In the shower I actually sing it out loud.

'Lucy, shut UP!' James shouts from the bedroom.

> *We like a Mockah Chockah*
> *Like the way you move . . .*

'I'm not joking,' he calls.

But I can't stop. I've got to hand it to them; this is catchy shit.

*

'You didn't just call *Q* magazine?' I gasp in horror on Tuesday morning, as Gemma hangs up the phone. How embarrassing. 'What did they say?'

'No, thank you.'

'Now there's a surprise.'

It's quite possibly the most surreal week of my life. In between accompanying what is surely the campest, cheesiest band on the face of the earth, to every magazine and newspaper office that will allow us through the doors, I also keep remembering that Nathan might be coming to the UK. Nerves sweep through me every time I think of him, but I'm trying not to obsess about it too much. It might never happen.

On Thursday, Chloe and I accompany Alexei, Varvara and Regina to begin a four-day tour of the clubs in Manchester, Birmingham, Glasgow and Cardiff. We watch in amazement as they manage to get entire dance floors joining in with their insane dance routine.

Back in London on Sunday night, we're both exhausted, and we haven't even started on the television and radio promotion yet. The single comes out the following morning.

That next week is the same, passing by in a promotional blur. We've had over 150,000 hits on the YouTube website and the momentum is really picking up pace. Mandy calls me over to her desk on Tuesday morning. She can't keep the smile from her face.

'Check it out,' she says, pointing to her screen. The midweek single results have come in. Titteesh and their 'Mockah Chockah' song are heading straight into the top spot. They're 30,000 copies ahead of their nearest competition, which is sensational.

'I think it might be time to crack open the champagne, don't you, Lucy?' She grins up at me.

'I don't know.' I smile. 'We don't want to jinx it . . .'

But the single just keeps flying off the shelves, and download sales are sky-high. Radio DJs moan and groan every time they play it, but they have to because it's on every station's playlist. The whole of the United Kingdom seems to have gone 'Mockah Chockah' crazy.

On Friday, Mandy announces there's no way a few glasses of champagne can jinx anything; nothing is going to keep this single from the Number One spot on Sunday. She cracks open a bottle and even cracks a smile as it fizzes all over the carpet.

'To Lucy,' she says, raising her glass at me. 'If anyone could do it, I knew you could. And to Chloe and Gemma, as well. You girls have *all* done an outstanding job. Truly. Outstanding.'

By the time I catch up with Karen and Reena after work that night, I can't stop buzzing from all the champagne and praise coursing through my veins. We're off to see *Dirty Dancing* and we meet outside the theatre at 7.15, just before the show starts. The interval is short and sweet, so it's not until later, when we're safely ensconced in a dark corner of a Soho bar, that we can talk properly.

'Nobody puts Baby in a corner!' Karen shouts, as she arrives back from the bar with three Seabreezes. Reena and I cringe and peek at the other punters with embarrassment.

'What have you been up to this week, then, girlies?' Karen grins. She's changed her hair again. Now she's got blonde extensions underneath her dyed-black real locks. I'm still not keen.

'Well, you know the "Mockah Chockah" song?' I say, sipping my vodka, cranberry and grapefruit cocktail.

'I hate that song!' Karen throws her hands up in the air.

'What song?' Reena interrupts.

'You know the one.' Karen groans. 'Whatcha! Whatcha gotta? Gotcha! Mockah Chockah! Know you! Like a lotta! Mockah! Mockah Chockah!'

'Very good.' I laugh.

Reena nods her head in recognition. 'I know the one you mean . . .'

'It's so shit. What about it?' Karen turns to me.

'I'm sorry,' I say, giggling.

'What do you mean?'

'I've been doing the PR for it. It's going to Number One on Sunday.'

'Please, God, no! I can no longer call you my friend!' she cries, getting a few sidelong glances from the people nearby.

'Oh, it's not that bad.' Reena laughs. 'It's pretty catchy. I quite like it.'

Karen looks at her with contempt.

'No, no, it's okay, Reena, you don't have to be nice about it,' I say. 'I know it's one of the worst songs ever written in the history of mankind.'

'*One* of the?' Karen responds. '*The*, more like. What are they like? What are their names? Vagina and Vulva or something?'

'The guy is called Alexei—'

'Guy? Are you *sure*?' Karen interrupts.

'And the girls are called Regina and Varvara.' I laugh.

'I prefer the names I gave them,' Karen continues. 'If you said them in a Russian accent you could almost get away with it. 'Ello. My name is Vulvarsh. And thees is my friend, Vageen . . . We come from the planet Titteesh.'

Reena and I are in hysterics.

'Anyway what else is new?' Karen asks when we've regained our composure. 'What's up with you and James? All good?'

I immediately waver between wanting to tell them about Nathan and knowing it's not a good idea. Suddenly, on an impulse, I find I can't stop myself.

'So he's going to be here in two and a half months?' Karen asks eventually. She's kept a remarkable attention span throughout my entire story, not interrupting, not giving anything away. It's been a bit off-putting, to be honest.

'Yes,' I reply.

'Lucy, what the hell are you doing? You're playing with fire and it's not bloody smart.'

Bollocks. I should have listened to my intuition.

'I don't condone cheating,' Karen carries on.

'I'm not cheating; he's just a friend!' This was a mistake. I should have kept my mouth shut. I was hoping for empathy, not grief.

'Yeah, right . . .' She gives me a rueful look. 'Just make sure it stays that way. If it gets physical, I don't want anything to do with it.'

'Chill out, for crying out loud. I would *not* cheat on James!' Would I? 'I'm just really bloody confused.'

Reena steps in. 'Karen, calm down. Lucy seems to know what she's doing.'

'Alright, alright!' Karen puts her palms up. 'I just don't want her to get hurt, that's all.'

It's then I suddenly remember Karen's first boyfriend cheated on her when she left him behind in Hull to come down to university in London. I wonder if that's why she's reacting so strongly.

'You're one of my best friends, you know that, right?' she says in her warm Yorkshire accent, grabbing my hands. I look into her brown eyes. 'It's your bloody star sign, that's the problem.' She drops my hands and sits back in her seat.

'Hey?'

'Libra. Same as me. Always weighing up the scales. Indecision, indecision.'

'You're not unsure about Alan, though, are you?'

'No, he's *lovely*. But you remember what I was like about media studies and hairdressing.'

'True.' I soften. 'What do you think?' I turn to Reena, tentatively. I still haven't heard her verdict yet.

'Lucy, you've always been a smart girl,' she says, and from her it doesn't sound patronising. 'I know you'll do the right thing.'

Suddenly the 'Mockah Chockah' song comes blasting out of the sound system.

'Come on, let's do the dance!' I jump up as Karen moans. But she makes an effort to twirl her arms and spin around as the rest of the bar descends into chaos.

The next day is Saturday and, apart from one television appearance in the morning, Titteesh are no longer my concern. I should be enjoying my freedom but I can't get Karen's negativity out of my mind. It's the same on Sunday. I don't even feel like calling Nathan and telling him about my mad couple of weeks. I know he'd find it funny, but something holds me back.

That evening, when 'Mockah Chockah' is confirmed as the UK's Number One single, James gives me a gorgeous bunch of pink, purple and orange gerberas.

'To match the group's costumes.' He laughs. 'Well done, baby. What a result.'

'Thank you.'

'What's wrong? You don't seem very pleased?' he queries.

'No, I am. But I'm exhausted after all that.'

'It's been a tough PR job. But Mandy must be well chuffed with you. You'll get a promotion and a whopping great pay rise in no time. Soon you'll be nipping at my heels,' he jokes.

I find myself wondering if he would mind me earning more than him. He's always been the main breadwinner and that's never really bothered me. In fact, it's been quite reassuring knowing I'd have the security in the (distant) future if I wanted to cut back on my hours and have kids. I can't bear the notion of putting my career on hold yet, though.

How would I feel if *I* were the main breadwinner? That's probably how it would be with Nathan, and I'm not sure I'm entirely comfortable with that thought.

Oh, God. What's it going to be like if he comes over here? I know everything between us will change if he's in England, and that terrifies me. It's all very well getting to know someone on holiday, but when they suddenly materialise on your doorstep, in your world . . .

It's plain from the last time Nathan and I spoke, that James is starting to feel funny about our conversations. What will he be like when Nathan is here in person?

And how will Nathan feel when he meets James? That's perhaps even more worrying to me, and I'm not proud of it. James has never been anything more than a name to Nathan but once he comes, literally, face to face with the reality that is my long-term boyfriend, it could scare him off completely.

There's also the little matter of how *I'll* feel when I see Nathan again. It's as I explained to Chloe some time ago: at the moment he's safe. He's on the other side of the world. He's not real. He's not flawed. I've been carrying around this fantasy image of a sexy surfer and I'm worried that, in actuality, Nathan won't live up to it.

And then of course there's the worry that he will.

Chapter 19

It's early August and Gemma has invited us for a barbeque on Primrose Hill.

'What a pain in the arse,' James is moaning as we make our convoluted way by tube. 'It probably would have been quicker to walk.'

'Cheer up, we're nearly there now,' I say, reaching over to squeeze his hand. He's carrying the rucksack with all our things. We've packed the rug he bought last summer for our picnic in Dorset Square, plus a whole host of other goodies like Moroccan couscous, potato salad, crisps, raspberries and strawberries. We'll never be able to eat it all.

Primrose Hill is busy all year round, but right now, in August, it's positively heaving. People stand at the top of the hill like soldiers, looking down over the city. We find Gemma, her boyfriend, Martin, Chloe and a few other guys and girls we don't know, halfway up the hill, under a tree. They've already got the portable barbeque set up and smoking. Gemma told me definitely *not* to bring anything for the barbeque because Martin had gone way overboard with sausages and beefburgers. She wasn't lying.

'Hey,' she calls, as we approach. James met Gemma and Chloe at a bar launch we PR-ed last November and he kisses them hello now. Gemma introduces us to Martin and her friends. Martin is tall, skinny and has short black hair. The last time I saw him he was collecting a very drunk Gemma from the Luigi party. He looks a lot happier now.

After lunch, when the others have gone off to play Frisbee, Chloe turns to me and asks about Nathan.

'Has he booked his flight yet?'

'Not yet, but I got a text from him last week and it appears his visa application is going through so it should all be happening. I haven't spoken to him for a few weeks, though.' Nor have I listened to his tape. I even have a joke for him but I can't bring myself to call him, and it has nothing to do with the fact that the last phone bill came in at a whopping £80 and I had to hide it from James.

'Really?' She's surprised at my downbeat manner. 'You haven't gone off him, have you?'

'I'm not a teenager,' I joke. Then I sigh. 'You know what? In all honesty, I am a bit freaked out. I know I sound fickle, but I felt so at ease, chatting to him on the phone before. Now he might be coming here . . . I don't even know if I'll still be attracted to him in London.'

'Yeah, I know that feeling,' she says. 'I once had a holiday romance with a guy called Franz in Germany. When he turned up unannounced in London a couple of months later I almost died! I didn't fancy him at all. He looked totally out of place on my turf.'

Moments later James comes back and flops down on the rug next to us. He pulls me back so I'm leaning up against him; his T-shirt is damp from his sweat. Frisky business, this Frisbee lark.

'What are you girls talking about?' He's slightly out of breath.

'Oh, men,' Chloe answers casually and I look over at her in alarm.

'Yeah? What about them?'

'I need one!'

'Do you?' he asks her, leaning up on one elbow now and flashing his trademark cheeky grin. I sit back up.

'Yes,' she says. 'Know any nice single men?'

'Actually,' he replies, 'I do know a couple of guys from work.'

'I hope you're not talking about Hector and Terence,' I say, sternly.

He laughs. 'No, they're not good enough for you.' He grins at Chloe and she blushes.

Looks like Charming James has come out to play.

'Set me up on a double date, then.' She smiles.

Soon afterwards, Gemma and the others appear back up the hill, followed by the Frisbee brigade.

'We were thinking we might wander down to the zoo a little later. Want to come?' she asks.

I look over at James. 'Probably not. We went last year, didn't we, hon?'

'Hey,' Martin says, 'did you hear about the escaping monkeys last summer?'

I look up at him sharply.

'That's right.' Gemma laughs. 'Squirrel monkeys. One of them – I think her name might've been Betty – was roaming around Regent's Park for ages!'

'See, Lucy?' James says smugly. 'I told you.'

'Yeah, okay.' I smile, graciously allowing him to revel in his victory. 'Sorry.'

The following Monday at work I realise that Chloe is serious about this double-date malarkey.

'Honestly, Chloe, this is a bad idea. James's colleagues are all tossers.'

'They can't be that bad, Lucy, if he's friends with them.'

'No, they are. They're all twats.'

'Oh.' She sounds dejected. I feel mean. Maybe it wouldn't hurt. Maybe I'd have a better time going out with them if I had a friend of mine with me. I say this to her and her face immediately lights up.

'When shall we go?' she asks.

'Next Friday?'

'Yeah, that would work.'

'Nice!' Gemma chips in. 'Cancelling our weekly drinks? What a bloody cheek!'

I didn't realise she was listening. 'Sorry, Gem, do you want to come too?'

'Nah, it's alright. I've been meaning to gatecrash Martin's Friday-night work drinks for some time so I'll probably do that.'

Next Friday, Chloe and I nip off to the toilets at six o'clock to start getting ready.

We catch a cab to the City, where James's offices are, and the closer we get, the more suits we see.

'Are you *sure* you want to date a "suit"?' I ask Chloe, smiling.

'Well, you do and he's a bit of alright.' She checks her reflection in her compact mirror, before snapping it shut. 'Anyway all I'm interested in is what the guy looks like *out* of the bloody thing.'

We arrive at the bar to find it heaving with City boys and girls. Chloe and I make our way through the throng, keeping an eye out for my sandy-haired boyfriend and his wanker mates.

I spot Jeremy first.

'Lucy!' He waves at me.

'Ooh, who's he?' Chloe asks as we weave our way towards him.

'Why, you don't fancy him, do you?' I look back at her in surprise. 'He's a right idiot.'

She laughs. 'I don't mind him.'

Oh dear. I'd better lighten up if this is the way it's going to go.

Jeremy engulfs me in a hug and plants a wet kiss on my face with his big red lips.

'Hi.' He beams at Chloe. I introduce them.

'Hello,' Chloe says chirpily, and Jeremy gives her a kiss too, before going off to order us vodka cranberries at the bar.

James is sitting with a group of City slickers round a booth table. He stands up immediately and squeezes past his pals to greet us. I recognise a couple of the guys from the Spanish holiday, and Zoe, who nods a curt hello and gives Chloe the once-over. She's glowing, and has obviously been topping up her tan in the park since she arrived back. That or she's a fan of spray-ons . . . She looks infuriatingly good, in any case. Edward, Susannah and Lila aren't here, though, and hmm, let me think. Nope. I don't miss their company at all.

'Hello.' James kisses me on the lips, followed by a kiss on the cheek for Chloe. He's taken off his suit jacket, removed his tie and unbuttoned his shirt a touch. He looks good, and I can just make out his smooth, toned chest.

'So, who's who?' Chloe shouts above the music.

'Right,' James shouts back, glancing furtively at his mates around the table. 'Don't make it too obvious you're looking at them . . . That tall, lanky one on the end is Hector. Stop, you're being too obvious!' He prods her arm. Chloe turns her head quickly. 'The chubby one next to him is Terence—'

'They're the ones you want to avoid,' I interrupt, loudly.

'Yeah, don't worry about that.' Chloe laughs. 'They're safe with me. Not my type.' She gives a mock shudder.

'Oh, they're not that bad,' James defends them. 'Anyway that's Zoe, who obviously isn't of interest . . .'

'Pretty,' Chloe muses, and we can just hear her above the music.

'Not my type,' James bats back. 'And next to her is where it gets interesting.' I sneak a peek. That one in the dark grey shirt is pretty cute. 'He's new,' James explains, clocking Chloe's interest. 'His name's William.'

'Single?' Chloe asks, eyes lighting up.

'Yep.' James grins.

'Gay?' she asks, wryly.

'No!' He laughs. 'Split up with his girlfriend a few months ago. Bit shy, though.'

'Okay . . .' she says.

'Next to William is Tim—'

'Nah, don't fancy him,' Chloe interrupts so James moves on.

'And then we have Bryce. Canadian,' he explains.

'Not bad.' Chloe nods. Yeah, he's not bad actually. I've met him once before.

'And that's John and Nicholas. Both got girlfriends,' James shouts, as Jeremy comes back from the bar with our drinks.

'Here you go, ladies,' he yells, and we thank him. He starts to nod his head to the music. I like The Chemical Brothers, so even I'm feeling more in the mood for this. I take a sip of my vodka cranberry. Strong. It'll be doubles.

'So what do you do?' Jeremy shouts at Chloe, and I turn to James and smile happily.

'It's nice having you here,' he shouts in my ear.

'Ouch!' I reply.

'Sorry,' he says, giving me a kiss. He taps Chloe on the shoulder. 'Come and meet the others,' he yells, taking her hand and leading her over to the table. Jeremy looks disappointed. I follow them and smile at everyone as he introduces 'Lucy! My girlfriend!' and 'Chloe! Her friend!' to all the people she or I don't know.

'How's Lila?' I turn to Jeremy, referring to the leggy blonde he was shagging in Spain.

'Fuck knows,' he shouts back. I look at him reproachfully and turn away, but he pulls me back and shouts in my ear, 'I haven't seen her since June.'

Zoe passes me on her way back from the loo and I motion to her.

'Where's Jim?' I shout.

'Atasttasar!' she answers.

'Sorry?'

'AT. ANOTHER. BAR,' she shouts, louder this time. 'GOING. TO. MEET. HIM. SOON.'

'WHY. DOESN'T. HE. COME. HERE?' I shout back, just as loud, and she shrugs at me, before heading back to her seat. Bugger off, then. I turn back to Chloe. She's talking to Bryce, who's stood up to join us. William is still sitting at the booth, though. He glances up at me and I smile. Come and talk to me and I'll set you up with my friend, I tell him telepathically, but he doesn't move. James must be right about him being shy. I attempt to join in Chloe and Bryce's conversation but I can barely hear them, so I decide to go to the ladies' room instead.

When I come back, Zoe is standing up with her coat and

briefcase and appears to be saying goodbye to James and Jeremy. She walks out through the bar as I approach and I clock Jeremy raising his eyebrows at James.

'What's up?' I ask.

'She's being a moody bitch at the moment,' Jeremy shouts back.

Lovely, I think, and James pulls me to him and gives me a kiss on the lips. He grins at me, then leans in to kiss me for longer this time.

'Cut it out, you two!' Jeremy yells in our faces.

It's actually a really fun night. The music is great, the drinks keep flowing, and Chloe seems to be having the time of her life. It's hilarious seeing the guys fawn over her. She's been single for over a year since splitting up with her man and she deserves some attention. It was a complicated break-up. They shared a flat together – although they didn't own it, thank goodness – but they had to continue living together for six weeks after they ended it because they couldn't terminate their contract and neither of them could afford the rent on their own. At least the split was mutual; a case of growing apart. But it was still traumatic towards the end for Chloe when Chris, her ex, started seeing someone else.

James is on top form. Funny, witty, sexy, and I'm proud to be there with him. I notice a few girls at the bar checking him out, but he's the perfect boyfriend, paying me lots of attention. Jeremy drags us to a club and we all go, minus John and Nicholas, who head home to their girlfriends.

We secure a spot at the back and pile our coats and bags up on the velvet bench seats.

At about 2 a.m., James and I collapse down on the bench after half an hour on the dance floor. He's not a bad dancer, especially when he's had a few. Now he draws me to him for a passionate snog. When we pull away, Jeremy is coming back to the table, grinning at us, dirtily.

James leans back in again and nibbles my earlobe, then growls in my ear, 'Let's get out of here.'

Chloe is sitting further down the bench, laughing and talking intimately to Bryce. William seems to have left already. We offer to call her a cab but she's having far too much fun to leave, so we say our goodbyes.

My gorgeous boyfriend and I, meanwhile, will go home and have mind-blowing sex.

Chapter 20

The phone rings at nine o'clock the next morning and I snatch it from the bedside table.

'Hello?' I ask sleepily.

'Oh, bloody hell, have I done it again?' Molly gasps. 'What time is it?'

Laughing, I tell her.

'Ah, that's alright. Get up, you lazy sod!'

I glance over as James groans and pulls his pillow over his head, then I grab my dressing gown and go through to the living room. My head is pounding.

'Urgh,' I say to Molly. 'Sorry about that. Just had to get out of the bedroom. Big night last night.'

'Really?'

'Yeah, but how are you?' I ask groggily.

'Really good, thanks,' she answers, then says excitedly, 'I've got some news.'

My God, is she pregnant?

'Oh, you're not . . .' I almost start screaming down the phone.

'I'm not what?' She's confused.

'Sorry,' I reply. 'Go on.'

'Nathan's going to London!' she bleats.

'Oh, I know that.' I laugh, and immediately realise my mistake. Molly and Sam don't know that Nathan and I have been chatting.

'You *know*?' she asks, taken aback. Okay, the truth is out, and I'm just going to have to deal with it.

'Yes,' I answer. 'He called me a couple of weeks ago and told me.'

Now, this is a tricky one. Do I tell her the full extent of our chats and chance her getting suspicious or do I water it down and risk her asking him about it? Oh, the web of lies you're weaving, Lucy McCarthy . . .

'He didn't tell me that!' She's disappointed at not being the one to break the news.

'Oh, you know, obviously just thought he'd better . . .' I trail off. 'Anyway! Isn't it exciting!'

'Yes, although Sam and I are desperately jealous. We *will* make it over there one of these days.'

'You'd better! It would be about bloody time . . .'

'So,' she continues, 'if he gets there on the last Saturday in September, you might even be able to go to the airport and meet him?'

My heart skips a beat. 'Has he actually booked his ticket, then?'

'I thought you said you knew!'

'No, I mean, I knew he was thinking about coming . . . But . . . Wow. So he's really coming, then?'

The last Saturday in September, I think, as we ring off. I feel jumpy. Literally sick with anticipation. I am *definitely* going to see him again. Hang on, why didn't he call me himself to let me know he'd booked his ticket? I feel hurt. It occurs to me then, for the first time, that maybe he's also feeling weird about seeing *me* again.

I consider calling him. But no. I still feel uncomfortable at the thought of having a conversation. I decide to text instead.

FLIGHT BOOKED THEN? MOLLY TOLD ME

YES. SHE KNOW WE SPEAK?

YES. SORRY. LET SLIP

HA HA. DON'T WORRY

I pause for a moment and then type out:

WHAT'S GREEN AND TURNS RED AT FLICK OF A SWITCH?

???

A FROG IN A BLENDER

TERRIBLE, LUCE, TERRIBLE

Relief sweeps over me and I suddenly regret not calling him and hearing his voice.

HOW'S HOUSE COMING ALONG?

GOOD. ALMOST DONE

YOU'LL BE TURNING INTO UR DAD NEXT. REAL PROPERTY
DEVELOPER

A few months ago I would have been utterly on edge mentioning
his late parents, but we seem past all that now.

THAT'S THE PLAN

Halfway through September, Mum comes to London for a shopping trip. She meets me at the flat.

'Hello, Diane,' James greets her warmly. He's not coming out
with us for lunch. It's good to have some time to catch up with
Mum alone as I haven't been back to Somerset since Easter and
it's rare for her to be able to get away from the tea shop.

'So, have you been counting down the days?' she asks me drily,
as soon as the waiter brings our drinks. We've managed to get a
seat on the pavement outside a chic restaurant on Marylebone
High Street and it's a lovely sunny Saturday with a welcome cool
breeze. August has been stifling.

'No, Mum.' I frown. I told her about Nathan coming here in
a brief conversation a couple of weeks ago. We haven't had a
heart-to-heart about it, though. Often when we speak, James is in
the room or near by, but I genuinely haven't felt like discussing
it and I'm finding it annoying that people keep asking.

I know it's my fault for telling them in the first place. I keep kicking myself. I wish I hadn't told anyone. Reena called me up the
other day and was full of concern, which I didn't want or need, and
Karen called a few weeks ago to give me another lecture. My friends
seem to be enjoying the drama of it and that just irritates me.

'When does he arrive?' Mum asks.

'Two weeks' time.'

'Gosh,' she says. 'Not long.'

I still don't want to talk about it, but the weight of her stare pressures me into opening up.

'James and I have been getting on really well,' I say. 'So it's a bit weird.'

Mum nods. 'Well, that's good.'

'Mmm.'

There's silence as she sips on her glass of white wine.

'Oh, Mum, I don't know. I haven't even spoken to Nathan since I found out he might be coming. I'm really weirded out. I don't know whether I'll still feel the same about him. In a way I think I'm scared of *not* feeling the same about him. And I know that's crazy. But now I'm not sure if it was real love in Sydney or just a stupid crush.'

'Well, Lucy,' she finally speaks, 'I hope for your sake it *is* the latter. Otherwise it could get messy. But you'll soon find out, either way. Are you going to meet him off the plane?'

'I don't know. I've thought about it. If I do I'll have some time with him alone. Because there's no way James will get up at five o'clock in the morning . . . But I haven't made up my mind yet.'

'On the contrary, Lucy, I think you *have* made up your mind. Just be careful,' she cautions.

'I'm going to go and meet Nathan at the airport,' I tell James.

'Are you?' he asks, surprised.

'Yeah,' I answer. 'I think it would be nice. Molly and Sam did the same for me.'

He sighs with disapproval and turns back to the telly.

'It's not a big deal, James.'

'If you say so,' he says, but I can tell he's not over the moon. I go over to the couch and climb onto his lap.

'Oof,' he says, as I squash his stomach. It's full of the leftovers from our Thursday night Indian, if the smell from the kitchen is anything to go by.

'Sorry.' I grin. 'Anyway you don't mind, do you?'

'Suppose not.'

He wriggles uncomfortably, so I climb off him again and go back through to the bedroom to text Nathan my intentions. He texts me straight back with his flight details.

I wonder if Nathan senses my discomfort. I wonder if that's why he's also sticking to short texts rather than proper conversations.

But it's not like he's coming here for me, I keep telling myself; he's coming because he wants to experience working in London. Here's me arrogantly thinking I might have something to do with it, when for all I know he could already have another 'Amy' on the scene back in Australia. Maybe that's why he hasn't called. Maybe it's because he's overwrought with sadness and remorse about leaving her to come to the other side of the world for three months. Actually, that thought makes me feel off-colour. I hope it's not that . . .

The nerves properly set in the week before he arrives.

'Are you going to the airport?' Chloe whispers to me, when Gemma disappears from her desk on Friday.

'Yes,' I whisper back, and she opens her eyes wide.

'It's not like that,' I tell her tetchily. 'I just don't want him to land here and feel out of it.'

'I thought he had a friend coming too?' she asks.

271

'Richard, yes,' I confirm. 'He arrived a couple of weeks ago and was doing a bit of backpacking around Europe. Nathan had to finish his house.'

'What house?' she asks, and I fill her in quickly before Gemma comes back. Just telling her about it makes me feel proud of him, though, and a few butterflies swarm through me. I clip their wings. I keep hearing Mum's warnings:

It could get messy . . . Be careful . . .

I don't go out that Friday night. Nathan's flight arrives the next day at the ungodly time of 6 a.m., and I need to get to Heathrow for 6.30 at the very latest. I'm in bed when James gets home late. I can hear him stumbling around in the darkness, cursing as he stubs his toe on the end of the bed. I don't stir. I can't fall asleep, but I'm stubbornly trying to. My alarm will wake me up at 5 a.m., to give me time to get dressed, catch a cab to Paddington and jump on the Heathrow Express. As it is, I'm out of bed at 4.30 after about only two hours' sleep, and spend the extra time work-ing the concealer on the bags under my eyes. I creep around getting ready, so as not to disturb James, but he's out cold.

I decided the night before what I was going to wear: dark blue jeans and a fitted greeny-bronze jumper, which brings out the amber flecks in my eyes.

Nathan's flight has already landed when I arrive at the airport at 6.20. I wait behind the ropes, watching as incoming passengers emerge into the arrivals hall. After a couple of minutes I feel rest-less and decide to go and get myself a hot chocolate. There's a queue and I shift from foot to foot as I keep an eye on the sliding doors. I'm anxious. I take my drink back to the ropes and wait again, alongside the minicab drivers holding their white signs. Just as I'm starting to worry I might've missed him, the doors open and he's there.

He looks different, unfamiliar. I watch him intently as he searches the crowd for me. He's wearing a faded green hooded top and beige-coloured cords and his black guitar case is slung over his shoulder as he wheels a large suitcase. Finally he spots me and grins. My stomach starts to catapult.

I'd forgotten how tall he was. I immediately feel myself blushing. He still has stubble and his dark hair is a little longer than it was before, falling messily to a couple of inches below his chin.

'Hello, you.' He smiles, bending down to kiss me on the cheek. Then he lets go of his suitcase and guitar and says warmly, 'Come here.' He wraps his arms around me in a tight hug and holds me for several seconds as I breathe him in. Memories come flooding back. He smells familiar, and it's not his aftershave because he's not wearing any; he just smells of Nathan. Suddenly I don't want to let go. I squeeze my eyes shut as all the resistance and resilience I've been building up vanish in a nano-second. He releases me, gently.

'How was your flight?'

'Long,' he answers. He looks exhausted.

'Come on, it's this way.' I lead him out towards the trains, praying my legs will hold me up.

Nathan is staying in a flatshare in Archway, north London, with Richard and three other antipodeans. It must be a big place to fit five of them in. Either that or it's going to be a squeeze.

On the train we grab two seats by the window, facing each other.

We've barely spoken on the walk here and I've felt shy and awkward. Now, sitting here facing him, I force myself to lighten up and soon we relax back into each other's company. He tells me about the two houses he's done up and promises to show me the pictures when he unpacks his suitcase. We talk about work – my job and his new one, which he starts on Monday. And we chat about Sam and Molly and have a laugh about her ringing me up a few weeks ago and me thinking she was pregnant.

We don't talk about James.

'I'm glad you're with me,' Nathan says as we change trains. 'These tubes would have freaked me out.'

'You'll soon get used to them. They're easy,' I tell him.

It's still early on a Saturday morning so the carriages are practically empty, and we sit, side by side, swaying with the movement. I glance down at his left hand, steadying his guitar case between his long, slim legs. God, I fancy him. I shake my head quickly. Not this again. Please, not this again. But even as I'm silently saying it I don't mean it. I like this feeling.

I think of James stubbing his toe last night in the darkness and feel a rush of affection. Immediately feeling deceitful towards my boyfriend, I look away from Nathan and down to the other end of the carriage.

The house where Nathan's staying in Archway is a tall, three-storey terrace, halfway up the hill towards Highgate Village.

'Highgate's supposed to be nice,' I say, thinking that Archway is a bit of a dump. He hasn't seen 'nice' England at all yet and this is certainly a change from Sydney.

He hauls his suitcase up the front steps, exhausted from wheeling it up the steep hill, and presses the doorbell. Eventually we hear movement and a tall, slim, attractive blonde with a pixie-cut hairdo opens the door.

'Nathan?' she queries, in a sleepy Aussie accent. She's wearing pale pink pyjamas.

'Yeah.' He grins. Uh-oh, I think.

She opens the door wide and lets us pass. I introduce myself and discover that her name is Ally.

'Your room's up here,' she says to Nathan, leading the way up two flights of stairs, and pointing out the bathroom on the way.

'The kitchen and living room are on the ground floor. Help yourself to milk or anything and I'll show you which shelf is yours later for when you go to the supermarket. Now, if you don't mind, I'm going to go back to bed.'

Nathan's room is a box room with a single bed, small wardrobe and bedside table. There's barely enough room to lie his suitcase on the floor so he leaves it standing up and props his guitar case against the wall.

We catch each other's eyes and grin. I squeeze past him and go over to the window. It looks out over the overgrown back garden; at least he's not facing the busy main road. A large barbeque sits to one side of the long grass. The Aussies would have made good use of that this summer.

I turn back and look at him. He's watching me, smiling.

'Let's go and get some breakfast,' I suggest.

Thank goodness. Highgate *is* lovely. Fruit and flowers spill out onto the pavement of the old grocer's and quaint village shops line the rest of the high street. We take a left and go into Café Rouge for a continental breakfast. It's not quite nine in the morning.

Neither of us have proper appetites yet, so we order lattes and a basket of French bread, pastries and conserves. Nathan leans back in his chair and surveys me.

'You look different,' he tells me.

'Really?'

'Yeah. Can't work it out.'

Probably a bit slimmer, I'm thinking, but I don't really want to point that out.

'When does Richard arrive?' I ask.

'Tomorrow, I think.'

'So, who else are you sharing with? Do you know anything about them?'

'No, not really. Rich sorted the pad out. I think there are two girls and a guy.'

So Ally has a friend. I hope she's not a stunner too.

'Have you got anything planned today?' I ask, as our bread, pastries and lattes arrive.

'Sleep, I reckon,' he says.

'Poor thing, you must be knackered.'

He nods.

I resist a sudden impulse to reach over and touch his face. Even though his bluey-grey eyes are tinged with redness from the twenty-four-hour flight, I'd still happily sit here for hours and stare into them. Then I think of James waking up alone at home this morning. He claimed he'd forgotten I was going to the airport and was hoping we could do something together today. I don't believe he forgot for a minute but, knowing Nathan would probably be jet-lagged, I promised him I wouldn't be away too long.

'Are you warm enough?' I ask Nathan, as he puts his hands in the pockets of his hooded top and scrunches up his shoulders.

We're heading back through the park we spotted on our way here.

'Yeah, I'll be alright,' he tells me bravely.

We walk side by side, close to each other so we're occasionally touching, and head past the tennis courts and down the path. We take a left and wind our way across to the other side of the hill, then suddenly there's a break in the leafy green trees and we have the most dazzling view of London.

'Wow!' he says, and even I'm amazed. This view easily rivals the one you get from Primrose Hill.

'What's that thing?' he asks, pointing at a tall, cylindrical building in the City.

'That's the Gherkin,' I tell him, remembering he's interested in architecture. 'And the Millennium Wheel is over there. We should go on it sometime.'

'That'd be cool.'

'Shall we sit down?' I ask, and we take a seat on one of the many benches which have been dedicated to loved ones who've passed away.

'Wouldn't it be nice if you could buy a bench while you were alive and had time to enjoy it?' Nathan muses.

'Yeah,' I say. 'This bench is dedicated to Lucy McCarthy and Nathan Wilson, who love this park and will be mightily pissed off if they come here and find you sitting in their seats.'

He chuckles and I turn to him. 'I haven't heard a joke from you in a while?'

'Mmm, we haven't really spoken much recently, have we?' he says.

'No,' I agree. I don't *think* that there's another 'Amy' on the scene back in Australia. But I don't know for sure.

'So, do you or don't you want to know what Henry the VIII and Kermit the Frog have in common?' he asks, looking at me sideways.

'Go on.'

'Same middle name.'

After a while we wander through the park to the other side and down the hill to his house.

'Do you have to get back?' he asks. 'Or will you come in for a cuppa?'

'No, I can come in,' I reply. We still haven't mentioned James.

The house is silent; the antipodeans must've had one hell of a night. We hunt out the kettle, milk and teabags in the kitchen, but can't find any clean mugs so I wash up a couple in the crowded sink. The kitchen is a complete tip, every available surface overflowing with dirty dishes and food crumbs. I feel bad that I didn't think to take Nathan to the supermarket in Highgate so he could stock up on a few necessities. I'm feeling protective of him, here on the other side of the world. I want to look after him.

I also want to run him a nice hot bath and strip him naked but, hmm, maybe we should stick to grocery shopping.

'I still make tea your way, you know,' I say, trying to stamp out the dirty thoughts zooming round my head.

'Ah, good, another convert.' He smiles. I wonder who else he's converted.

'How's Amy?' I ask and immediately want to kick myself.

'She's fine, last I heard,' he answers. 'I think she might have a boyfriend.'

'That's good. So, you . . . Do you . . .' Stop it, Lucy! Don't ask if he's got a new girlfriend!

278

'Nah.' He grins, and I feel my face heating up. I should have gone with my instincts.

We take a look at the living room, but it's such a mess that we go back up to his room.

'You haven't had a cigarette since you've arrived?' I look back at him as he follows me up the stairs.

'Trying to give up.'

'*Really*? How long's it been?'

'Only a few weeks, so I might still relapse,' he says. 'Especially if this lot are heavy smokers.'

'Be strong!' I tell him in a faux American accent as we go into his room and close the door.

'When are you going to unpack?' I ask, sitting at the end of his bed.

His flatmates have made it up, not too neatly, with orange and yellow checked sheets.

'Later.' He lazes back into the corner, leaning up against the wall. It reminds me of being in his bedroom in Manly and I shiver as I recall the fantasy that I created on the plane journey to London.

'What time have you got to get back?' he asks me.

I check my watch: it's 10.30. 'I'm not in any hurry,' I lie. 'Although I'm pretty shattered. I only had about two hours' sleep last night.'

'So excited about seeing me.' He grins, and I smile back but don't answer. He puts his empty mug on his bedside table and props up the pillows, sliding down further on the bed. He looks exhausted.

'I should let you sleep,' I say.

'Don't go yet.' He holds his right hand out to me, sleepily. I take it, then, not knowing what overcomes me, I lean back against him, so his arm wraps around me from behind. He murmurs into my hair and pulls me in tighter. After a while, his breathing begins to slow and he falls asleep, and not long afterwards I do the same.

My beeping mobile phone wakes me. I climb up, away from sleeping Nathan and rummage around in my bag for my phone. Shit! It's 2 p.m.! James is asking where I am. I text him back hurriedly, telling him I'm on my way home and turn back to look at Nathan.

Using the back of the Café Rouge receipt, I scribble him a note to say I'll call him later, signing it, *Love, Lucy xxx*. I feel like a teenager writing Christmas cards, choosing between 'From', 'Lots of love', and the most telling of them all, 'Love' alone.

Nathan is still sleeping peacefully, messy hair falling across his eyes. I gently push it off his face and then kiss him softly on the cheek. My heart is so full of him and for a moment everything that I felt for him in Sydney comes back in force. Sorry, Mum, but this is not just a crush.

My phone beeps again, snapping me out of it, and Nathan stirs, rolling over onto his back. I step quietly out of his room and close the door behind me.

Back downstairs I can hear the television on in the living room and I consider sneaking past without saying hello, but realise that would be rude. I pop my head around the door to see Ally, a grungy dark-haired guy in his early twenties and another girl, a spiky-haired brunette with multiple earrings in her ears. She looks to be fairly short from where I'm standing, but it's hard to tell. They're all smoking; it reeks in here.

'Hi,' I say. 'I'm Lucy, Nathan's friend. He's upstairs sleeping.' I smile. 'Would you wake him up in an hour or two?' Introducing themselves as Ned and Billie, they nod their assent.

I check my phone as I'm walking out of the door and back down the hill to Archway. James's message says simply:

YOU'VE BEEN AGES!

I don't reply.

Chapter 21

'Where the hell have you been?' James asks me crossly from the living-room sofa, as I open the door.

'I told you,' I snap. 'I went to get Nathan from the airport, then I took him back to his place in Archway to help him get settled.'

'I didn't realise you were going to be all bloody day.'

'I've hardly been all day, have I, James? It's only three o'clock.'

'I thought we were going to do something together. What have you been doing all this time?' he rants.

Blimey, I didn't think he'd give me this much grief.

'We went for breakfast and a bit of a walk and then fell asleep,' I answer.

'You fell *asleep*?' he asks me incredulously.

'Yes . . .' I reluctantly reply.

'How the fuck did you manage to do that?'

'James, don't speak to me like that! I haven't done anything wrong. I was exhausted from waking up at four thirty. I couldn't get to sleep again after *you* woke me up at midnight when you

282

stumbled in out of your face!' I turn the tables on him, like only a professional girlfriend can.

'Don't you bloody turn the tables on me,' he growls. Bollocks.

'Look, it's not a big deal,' I tell him. 'I fell asleep because I was knackered and he was jet-lagged. That's all!'

'Sounds a bit fucking dodgy to me.'

'Stop swearing at me!' I raise my voice and he appears to calm down slightly. I walk off to the kitchen to get a glass of water. When I turn around he's there, behind me, watching me. I jump. 'You frightened me.'

He looks straight into my eyes. 'You do fancy him, don't you?' he asks calmly, but there's a deadly tone to his voice.

'Of course I don't!'

'You do.' He says it steadily and I don't know what to say.

I look up into his deep blue eyes and find myself shrugging helplessly.

'No, I don't,' I feebly persist, but it's no use. He can see right through me. Guilt must be riddled across my features. He shakes his head at me in disgust.

'What's going on, Lucy?' His mouth is stretched into a tight, thin line.

'I don't know,' I tell him honestly.

'You do fancy him,' he says flatly.

I can't answer.

'Fuck!' he exclaims, and runs his hand through his hair, angrily.

'James . . .' I put my hand on his arm. He shakes me off and stalks back into the living room. I follow and perch on the sofa beside him. His expression is pained, distraught, and I suddenly feel overwhelmingly sorry for him.

'I love you,' I tell him gently. He doesn't answer. 'I love you,' I say again.

'Do you love him?' he asks, head shooting round to look at me, eyes widening a touch. 'Is that why you didn't want to leave Sydney and come back to me?'

'No!' I vehemently deny, but he stares at me with disbelief.

'James, I love *you*,' I try again, and put my hand on his bicep. He doesn't shrug me off this time.

'You can't see him again,' he says suddenly, resolutely.

'James—'

'No, Lucy,' he interrupts, looking at me. 'You can't see him again.'

'I can't just ignore him. He's here alone! He's the brother of one of my best friends!' James shakes his head, looking away from me. 'Don't be like this. Don't be unreasonable.'

'*Unreasonable?*' He looks at me in amazement, and lets out an indignant laugh. 'Un-fucking-reasonable? You've got to be bloody joking.'

I look away from him, defensively. This is hopeless. I go through to the bedroom and strip the sheets, then start putting away all the items of clothing that have been piling up on the chair over the last few days. He turns the sound up on the TV.

This can't be happening, this can't be happening, I repeat to myself as I complete menial household chores. I *will* see Nathan. I can't not see him. I *won't* not see him. There has to be a way round this. I keep myself busy while James continues to ignore me from the living room. After a while his dark shadow appears at the door.

'Are you going to see him again?' he asks me listlessly.

'James . . . I can't not . . .'

'I'm going out.' He turns away.

'James! Don't!' I follow him in dismay. He's putting on his jacket by the front door and his face is drawn, white.

'Please don't go.' I take hold of his arm but he shakes me off, slamming the door behind him.

Have I just lost my boyfriend? I ask myself wildly. How the hell did that happen? I sit on the sofa in disbelief. After ten minutes I try calling James but his mobile diverts to voicemail. Where has he gone? Maybe he's on the tube.

When his phone does eventually ring, he doesn't answer it and after a while he switches it off. Either that, or he's on the tube again. I pray it's the latter; that he'll be home soon. But at 11 p.m., after an evening of confusion and anguish, he texts me to say he'll see me tomorrow. I immediately dial his number to call him back but he diverts me, and the next time I try he's switched his phone off again.

He doesn't come home that night, and I feel sick to my stomach. It's awful; on a par only with the flight to Sydney when I thought he'd cheated on me. I briefly consider calling Nathan but I can't talk to him about this. I can't talk to anyone – they'd only say I brought it on myself. In the end I cry myself to sleep.

At about ten o'clock the next morning, Nathan calls me himself, merrily saying hi until he hears my voice.

'What's wrong?' His concern sends me over the edge and I start to cry again.

'James . . . James left.'

'Why?' he asks. 'What happened?'

'We . . . had . . . an argument,' I stammer, trying to breathe. 'He didn't come home last night.'

Nathan listens as I continue to cry quietly down the phone, neither of us speaking. I can't let on that we were arguing over him. That's the last thing I can do, which just makes me feel worse. As I calm down, I realise he hasn't spoken for a good couple of minutes. God, he must think I'm a total wreck. I *am* a total wreck.

'Nathan?' I ask. Is he even still there?

'Yeah. I'm here.' I understand then that the poor guy just doesn't know what to say. What *can* he say?

'Are you okay?' I ask him. 'Did you get plenty of sleep?'

'Yeah, yes, I'm fine,' he says, brushing me off.

'Is Richard there?' I ask banally.

'Er, no, he should be getting here around midday, I reckon.' He's evidently uncomfortable and I suddenly feel horribly ashamed that I sobbed down the phone to him. The silence is deafening. What must he be thinking? If anything was going to slam home the reality of my boyfriend, this perhaps is it.

'What are you doing today?' I ask, trying hard to act normal, but it comes out sounding weak, pitiful.

'Um, I don't know. Just getting ready for work tomorrow, I guess.'

'Are you looking forward to it?' I ask awkwardly.

'Yeah, I suppose so,' he answers. 'Look, Luce . . .' His voice trails off and I hold my breath, wondering what he's going to say. 'Why don't I call you next weekend, hey? I've got a busy week at work and . . .' My heart sinks with every word. '. . . you know, give you time to sort things out with . . . James, you know?'

'Okay,' I answer monotonously. 'Okay.'

I wish him good luck at work and we hang up.

After that, I curl up into a ball and sob.

Well done, Lucy, you've probably lost your boyfriend of almost four years and now you've scared off Nathan as well.

I don't want to lose James, though. Not yet. I don't know about 'not ever', but definitely 'not yet'.

When he walks in looking dishevelled and unshaven at two o'clock that afternoon, I rush out to greet him.

'I'm so glad you're home!' I wrap my arms around him. He gently but firmly detaches me and heads towards the bathroom, shuts the door in my face and locks it. I gravely wipe the tears from my eyes and go through to the kitchen. I must pull myself together. We must stop this. We must sort this out.

When James comes through after ten minutes, I say that to him, firmly. He doesn't answer.

'Where did you go?' I demand.

'You don't get to ask me questions like that.' He speaks to me like I'm a stranger.

'Can we talk about this?' I plead.

'Do you know what?' He turns to me and eyes me malevolently. 'I'm fed up with talking about it. Let's just call it a day, hey?'

'What do you mean?' I ask, alarmed. 'You don't mean . . . split up?'

'No.' He laughs, and for a second I see a flash of my gorgeous boyfriend, but his laugh turns sour. 'I just mean, let's not talk about it anymore. I'm sick of talking.'

Thank God. 'Please, can we . . .' I go over to him, wanting him to wrap his strong arms around me and hold me tightly. He touches my arm with his hand.

'It's alright, Lucy,' he says, and wipes the tears creeping down my face. 'It's going to be okay.' He takes me in his arms and squeezes me so tightly I can barely breathe. I bury my head against his neck. After a moment, he pulls away. I'm expecting him to lead me to the bedroom but he doesn't. 'Let's go and see what's on the telly,' he suggests instead.

We spend the rest of the afternoon in a strange, surreal silence, trying our best to forget the painful last twenty-four hours.

The next morning I don't want to go to work. My eyes are still puffy and my face is blotchy from all the crying I did over the weekend. I consider calling in sick, but James is heading into the office as normal so I force myself to perk up.

'What's wrong with you?' Chloe asks, wide-eyed, the second I arrive at my desk. I'm twenty minutes late. I shake my head at her, and don't answer. A few minutes later, when my computer has warmed up, I receive an email from her.

WHAT'S UP? NATHAN OK?

I don't want to talk about this now. I type back:

TELL YOU LATER

I avoid her gaze throughout the day and do my best to be as normal as possible. On my way back to my desk at one point I see Chloe and Gemma whispering; they break away as soon as they see me. I ignore them.

Towards the end of the day I send Nathan a text:

SORRY BOUT YESTERDAY. HOPE FIRST DAY OK?

A torturous half an hour later he writes back with:

YEAH GOOD

He doesn't mention our phone call. It makes me feel queasy.

'Did you call him today?' James regards me later, over dinner.

'No,' I answer truthfully. I look up at him, cautiously. 'I did text him to say I hope he had a good first day, though.'

'Oh, for fuck's sake, Lucy.' He slams down his knife and fork and pushes his chair out from the table.

'I had to!' I exclaim. 'He doesn't know what's going on; it would have been weird not to acknowledge him in some way.'

James gets up, leaving his half-empty plate. He slouches down on the sofa and switches on the flatscreen, turning the sound up loudly. I watch him in dismay. That bloody TV. I can't finish my meal, so in the end I clear the table and wash up the dishes. He doesn't broach the subject again, and we sit and watch a wildlife documentary in silence. Eventually I go to bed and he follows me soon afterwards. The space between us is vast. I fall asleep feeling utterly miserable.

Tuesday isn't much of an improvement. I don't contact Nathan again and he doesn't contact me. I don't know what's going to happen here; it's a bloody disaster. Again I curse myself for revealing to James how I feel about Nathan. But there was nothing I could do. I shouldn't have bloody well fallen asleep in his room! Why did I do that?

But this was going to happen sooner or later. You knew that, didn't you, Lucy?

The girls try to get me to go out with them on Tuesday for lunch but I'm so busy with work that I do have a proper excuse. Chloe pesters me again by email, wanting to know if it's about Nathan, but I deflect her questions. I'm going to have to tell her sometime, but I really, really don't want to talk about it now.

By Wednesday, I'm feeling a bit better. James and I have settled into a slightly uneasy truce. He asked me if I called Nathan yesterday and I could deny it, honestly.

The girls try again to take me out for lunch but I fob them off with work excuses. That evening when I leave the office at 6.30, Chloe runs after me.

'Lucy! Wait up,' she calls. I pause. 'What's going on? Why are you so unhappy?' she pants, when she's caught up. 'Is it Nathan? Or James?' she persists.

'It's both,' I answer.

'Will you come for a drink?' she asks and I waver. 'Come on,' she encourages.

In the dark, gloomy pub we take our Pinots to a table and I fill her in. She listens patiently.

'Bloody hell,' she says, when I've finished. 'What a nightmare.'

'Mmm.'

'What are you going to do?' she asks. 'Will you still see Nathan?'

I shrug my shoulders, weakly. 'I just don't know.'

'Lucy! Talk to me! Stop clamming up,' she demands. 'What's going through your mind?'

'What's going through my mind is that I'm completely and utterly fucked!' Here we go; I'm off on one, now. 'I've fallen for a twenty-three-year-old, sorry, twenty-*four*-year-old surfer, builder, whatever the hell he is, who may as well be from another fucking planet! I don't trust my bloody boyfriend and I don't know why. And that's just *fabulously* ironic, isn't it? Because *I'm* the one who's thinking about CHEATING!'

'Jesus,' she says, backing off with wide eyes.

I take a deep breath and look at her woefully, my head collapsing onto my right hand.

'Hey.' She reaches across the table to give my other hand a reassuring pat. 'It will be alright.'

I don't respond. She hesitates.

'You're not really thinking about cheating on James, are you?'

'No.' Yes. Maybe.

'Good. Because that will only make matters worse, I assure you.'

'I know.' Of course I know. But I also know that if Nathan had kissed me in Sydney, I sure as hell would have kissed him back. Acknowledging that fact doesn't make me like myself very much.

On Thursday, Gemma and Chloe defiantly drag me out through the door to take me to lunch. I keep telling them I'm too busy but they insist. We sit in a café and order our sandwiches from a waitress. Finally they turn to me, with odd expressions on their faces. I suddenly sense something's wrong.

'What is it?' I'm nervous.

They glance at each other, sideways.

'*What?*'

'Um . . . Does James have a sister?' Gemma asks me.

'No, he's an only child. Why?'

'It's just that . . .'

'What? *Tell* me!'

Chloe speaks. 'I'm sorry, I should have said something last night, but I just couldn't. Gemma saw James on Primrose Hill on Sunday morning with a tall, dark-haired girl. They looked kind of . . . together.'

'What do you mean?'

'He had . . .' Gemma starts, and I nod hastily, encouraging her to go on. 'He had his arm around her. They were on a bench . . .'

I feel like someone has punched me in the stomach. 'What did she look like?'

'Tall, slim, long dark hair . . .' She fills me in, hesitantly.

'I kind of thought . . .' Chloe speaks.

'Yes?'

'I thought it sounded a bit like the girl at his office drinks that time?'

'Zoe? But she's got a boyfriend!'

'That's what I thought!' Chloe slaps her palm down on the table. 'It's probably nothing. It's probably nothing to worry about,' she adds. 'But I – *we* – just thought you should know, with all that, you know, all that's going on.'

'Does Gemma know about Nathan?' I ask Chloe.

'Um . . .' she shifts uncomfortably.

'It's okay.' I smile at them both, tightly. 'Thank you for telling me.' I know it's no fun being the bearer of bad news.

That afternoon drags by like no afternoon at work ever has. I don't want to call James; I want to see his face when he explains what's going on, and then at least I might have a better idea about whether he's lying his bloody arse off.

At half past four I can stand it no longer and ask Mandy if I can leave as I'm not feeling well. She's not too pleased because we're very busy at the moment launching a new PR campaign for a hot young jewellery designer and I shouldn't even have taken a lunch hour, but she doesn't try to stop me.

I can't handle the tube or the walk at the moment, so I catch a cab, spending money I don't really have and adding to the guilt I already feel over leaving work early. Brilliant.

When I arrive home I text James and ask him to come home as quickly as possible because we need to talk. He texts back:

WHY?

292

I don't reply.

He walks through the door at seven o'clock with an odd look on his face.

'What's up?'

'Where were you on Saturday night?' I ask him, trying to read his expression. He laughs uncomfortably. 'Answer the question.'

'I told you, you don't get to ask—'

'Answer. The. Fucking. Question.'

He walks past me to the kitchen. 'James!' I am hot on his heels. 'Who the hell is she? The brunette? *Primrose Hill?*'

He turns to face me. 'Zoe,' he answers tonelessly, and I look at him, wild-eyed. I expected him to deny everything.

'What do you mean? Why Zoe? Is she the one who sent me that text?' My voice increases in urgency and volume with every question.

'No, she's not!' he denies forcefully. 'I *told* you that was the blokes at work. Zoe's just a friend.'

'I didn't know you were friends with her?' I push, confused.

'Yeah, of course we're friends. I work with her, don't I?'

'Did you stay with her on Saturday night?'

'I crashed over there, yes,' he replies, a touch defensively.

'Where was Jim?' I ask, and I just know what's coming.

'They broke up.'

Surprise, surprise.

I laugh at him, bitterly. 'You are full of BULLSHIT!'

'Lucy, calm down!'

'Don't you *dare* tell me to calm down! My friend *saw* you! You had your arm around her! Don't tell me she's just a friend because I DON'T BELIEVE YOU!'

'She is just a friend,' he tells me steadily, but keeps his distance.

'Liar!'

'Lucy, calm down.' He comes towards me, his face contorted with frustration. 'She is Just. A. Friend,' he insists. 'I was comforting her because her boyfriend, you know, the one you thought was *such a nice guy* in Spain, fucking CHEATED on her!' His voice becomes angrier with every word that comes out of his mouth. He runs his hand through his hair and turns to me, coldly. 'Do you realise how lucky you are?' he asks. 'Do you? I had to sit there at Zoe's house on Saturday night while she bawled her eyes out because Jim is a lying, cheating son-of-a-bitch. The poor girl was beside herself. So, do you, Lucy? Do you realise how bloody lucky you are that I wouldn't do that to you?'

I look at him, unable to work out if he's lying or not. I want to believe him. I do want to believe him. But he doesn't try to convince me. He's waiting to see what I say.

'I don't want you seeing her anymore,' is what I come back with.

'*What?*' he asks, confused.

'I don't want you seeing her anymore,' I repeat determinedly.

'Lucy, that's ridiculous.' He laughs hollowly. 'I work with her. We're friends. I'm not going to *not* see her.'

'Do you fancy her?' I ask him.

'No!' he exclaims.

'I don't believe you.'

'I don't!' he insists. 'This is about Nathan, isn't it?' he asks, and I look at him meaningfully, but don't answer. 'Oh, for fuck's sake,' he says.

'He's just a friend,' I tell him bluntly. 'Just like Zoe. He hasn't done anything wrong.'

'It's not the same.'

'Yes, it is,' I respond firmly, and he doesn't speak for a while. I add, 'Maybe the four of us should go out sometime, just *as friends* and see how we get on?' He's clearly not keen on that idea. 'Seriously,' I continue, 'I think you should meet Nathan. You'd get on with him. And he *is* my friend, James,' I say, my voice softening. 'I really do want to be friends with him. *Just* friends.'

'Okay,' he speaks finally. 'But if he ever tries anything on with you I'm going to knock his fucking block off.'

Chapter 22

The girls try to persuade me to join them for Friday-night drinks, but I'm determined to have a quiet night in. I attempt to explain James's behaviour on Primrose Hill with Zoe but, even as I'm saying it, I know it sounds lame. Although they probably don't believe his excuse, they make a reasonable show of pretending to. While I don't like the fact that Chloe and Gemma doubt him, there's nothing I can do.

James goes out for a big night with his work, even though I ask him not to stay out too late. When, at about 10 p.m., I text him to ask where he is and he doesn't reply immediately, I call him. There's no answer so I call him again. And again. Eventually he picks up and the noise from the crowded bar he's in is deafening. I shout down the phone but he can't hear me. I shout as loudly as I can, worrying about the neighbours, and ask him to go outside so we can talk. He shouts back that he's leaving soon. And that, unfortunately, is that.

An hour and a half later he comes home, by which time I'm in bed, trying to sleep. I sit up and ask him groggily if she was there.

'Was who where?' he answers, trying to sound less pissed than he obviously is.

'You know who I mean,' I snap. 'ZOE!'

'Shush, Lucy, ow!' He stumbles, putting his hand to his ear.

'Don't shush me,' I loudly reply, and he groans, slumping down on the end of the bed.

'Thought we were past all this,' he moans sadly, and I immediately feel sorry. Yes, I'm annoyed with him for staying out so late and no, I'm not comfortable with the whole Zoe thing, especially now that my work friends have become involved, but I want to see Nathan. And if that means James seeing Zoe, well . . .

'Alright,' I say graciously, and slide back down underneath the duvet. 'Let's just forget it.'

I call Nathan the next day, making a point of doing it in front of James. This is no big deal, my sign language is screaming, we can all be friends here.

'Hey,' he answers. 'I was just thinking about you.' I'm dying to know what exactly he's been thinking, but I can't ask in front of James. Instead I ask him how his first week at work has been, willing us to return to normality.

'Good, thanks. Bit of a culture shock.' He's working on a large hotel near Wembley Stadium and is finding his new boss to be a ball-breaker in comparison to the guy he worked for on the boutique hotel in Manly. It's a much larger workforce here, and a lot less responsibility. In other words, less challenging and not more fun. I suspect he misses his home-renovation work too.

'Have you done any sightseeing?' I ask, not wanting him to dwell on the downsides of his job. The last thing I want is for him to start missing home and looking forward to leaving.

'No, nothing. Still feeling a bit jet-lagged, but we might go into town later.'

'You should. Hey, maybe we could meet you for a drink tonight?' I glance down at James, who rolls his eyes.

'Yeah, that'd be great,' Nathan replies. I try to keep a relatively straight face. I don't want James to pick up my excitement.

'Why don't you call me when you're setting off and we'll make plans?' I suggest.

'Cool. I need to go and get a new mobile because this one is costing me a fortune.'

'Sorry . . .' I say, but he laughs.

'No, I didn't mean you.'

'Okay, well, speak later.'

We ring off and I turn to James. 'That's alright, isn't it, hon? It'd be good for you to meet him.' We've got to make this less of a big deal. Nathan is only here for three months and then he'll be buggering off home again.

Ouch. The thought gives me a nasty little shock. Is that really the first time I've fully comprehended the three-month thing? That's not long. At all. I turn away from James, not wanting him to see my troubled face.

Well, I think eventually, I don't know why we've all been getting our knickers in such a twist over it. Nathan will be gone soon. Zoe, on the other hand, is here to stay. And I don't like that thought, not one iota.

Nathan calls to say that he and the others are going to be at the Walkabout pub on Charing Cross Road from about 7 p.m.

What a cliché, I think. James says it out loud and we grin at each other.

I'm on edge as we walk into the packed bar, not quite

believing I'm about to introduce my boyfriend to the guy I haven't been able to stop thinking about for months on end. James seems fairly relaxed. He's wearing a dark green long-sleeved T-shirt and grey cargo pants and looks pretty sexy. Nathan is taller than James by about two or three inches, but James is broader, more manly. He's also four years older. They look very different.

I try to steel myself against Nathan as I scour the crowds, giving James's hand a quick squeeze before letting go. I'm here with my boyfriend. My *boyfriend*.

I spot Ally and the dark-haired girl from the flat – I can't remember her name – and another tall bloke with short brown hair who I'm guessing could be Richard. James takes my hand again and we make our way through the crowd towards them.

Suddenly I see Nathan, heading back to his flatmates with four beer bottles. I stall for a split second, resisting the urge to drop James's hand, but I keep walking. I don't think James notices.

It's odd seeing Nathan greet James. Very odd indeed. There don't appear to be any uncomfortable undercurrents between them, though, and I'm relieved, realising I was holding my breath for the duration of their introduction. I force myself to concentrate as Nathan introduces his flatmates. Billie, I remember, when it's the turn of the girl with multiple piercings. I was right about her; she is short.

Ally looks even better out of her PJs. She's wearing hardly any make-up and has the clearest skin. When she and Billie go off in search of the toilets, James turns to Nathan and Richard.

'Is she single?' he asks them.

'Sure is,' Richard answers.

'There you go, mate,' James says, nudging Nathan good-humouredly. 'You could be in there.' Nathan grins, but doesn't say anything. A sharp pain shoots through me.

I can't catch Nathan's eye, and it's driving me slightly barmy. Why won't he look at me? I have every intention of being a good girlfriend tonight, paying James lots of attention, but right now I'm distracted. James and Richard are having an animated conversation about rugby which is boring me to tears and Nathan doesn't seem to be interested, either. Eventually he turns away from them and stares at the big screen where there's a football match playing. I can't take it anymore. I leave James's side – he's so caught up in his conversation about scrums and who knows what else that he doesn't even notice.

'I didn't know you liked football,' I ask Nathan, for want of something to say.

'I don't mind it. Better than rugby,' he says, giving me a side-long glance as the corner of his mouth curls up in a half smile. 'You alright?' he asks.

'Yes, thanks.' I move around to stand in front of him, forcing him to turn his attention away from the football and onto me. I manage to restrain myself from prodding him in the stomach. He looks down at me, amused, as if reading my thoughts.

'Isn't he the guy you did that bar launch for?' he asks, nodding back up to the football. I turn round to the big screen to see Gian Luigi take a penalty. He misses.

'Yeah, that's him. Well done for remembering.'

Nathan doesn't reply, just carries on watching.

I rack my brain for one of the many jokes I heard weeks ago but never called him about. One comes back to me.

'Hey,' I say. 'Two biscuits in a tin. One of them says, "Where do you live, then?" And the other replies, "I'm not going to tell you, because you'll come and steal my washing."'

'You are such an idiot.' He chuckles and my heart lifts. I peek over his right shoulder at James. He's still caught up in his conversation with Richard. I return my gaze to Nathan, whose bluey-grey eyes are watching me, steadily.

'You don't really fancy Ally, do you?' I screw up my nose, as though fancying Ally is the last thing anyone on this green earth would ever want to do. He laughs in what seems remarkably like disbelief, and for a worrying moment I think he's going to refuse to answer my question, but he just shakes his head.

'No, Luce, I don't fancy— Ah, where have you two been?'

Eek! That was close. Ally and Billie return after a twenty-minute hiatus.

'On the pull,' Ally exclaims. 'No fit men in here.'

'On that note, I think I'll leave you girls to it,' Nathan dismisses himself and rejoins James and Richard. My heart sinks as I watch him leave. I shake myself and try to focus on my earlier intentions to be a good girlfriend.

'Where's Ned?' I ask the girls, impressed that I remembered his name, at least.

'Gone out with his girlfriend,' Billie replies.

'So James is your boyfriend, then?' Ally asks.

'Yes,' I say, and she gives me a funny look. What does that mean? Does she fancy him? 'We thought Nathan was,' she says discreetly, and looks at me meaningfully. Oh . . . It clicks. They must've assumed that when I came downstairs from his bedroom last Saturday. I hope they don't say as much to James.

'No, we're just friends from Sydney,' I tell her, straight-faced, and ignore the mischievous look she gives me.

'So what do you do?' I turn to Billie.

I don't get another chance to speak to Nathan alone. All I want is to go away to a dark corner with him but it's just not going to happen this evening.

Though I do my best to be attentive to James, I can't help but tense up when he wraps his arm around me and pulls me back into him on a few occasions. Each time my eyes dart towards Nathan to clock his reaction, but he seems to be steadfastly evading me.

James gives me the nod just before eleven so we leave them to it. He shakes the boys' hands again while I stand there awkwardly and smile my goodbyes. Nathan meets my eyes for a split second but then takes a swig of his beer and heads back to the bar. I try to mask my disappointment at the apparent demise of our familiarity. I should just be feeling enormous relief that James appears to be over his jealousy.

'That was okay, wasn't it?' James says, looking across at me from inside the cab I persuaded him to get.

'Do you like him?' I ask casually.

'Yeah, he's alright.' He grins.

'What?'

'You don't really have the hots for him, do you?' he asks, with a mix of surprise and mild distaste. 'If it was Richard, I could understand; he was a good laugh, but Nathan is a bit of a weird one. He doesn't say much, does he?'

I force myself to laugh. 'No, he doesn't really.'

At least James doesn't think to ask about our long phone conversations. Because Nathan does open up. He opens up to me.

But it's okay. James doesn't need to like Nathan loads. In fact, it's probably better that he doesn't.

*

'So, how did it go?' Chloe asks excitedly the minute I arrive at work on Monday morning. Gemma manoeuvres her seat over and is all ears.

'It was fine,' I respond.

'Fine?' Chloe's voice is disappointed. 'What, no fist fights, broken bottles, nothing?'

'Stop it!' I laugh. 'No, it was fine. They got on fine.'

It *was* fine. It probably was a good thing that Nathan was a bit detached with me. I have to start thinking of him in a platonic sense. This is the reality of my situation now.

'Boring!' Chloe yawns.

'Oi!' I snap playfully.

'Sorry, I'm just fed up with my own tedious existence. When are we going out with James for Friday-night drinks again?' she asks.

'Do you still want to?' I grin. She's obviously over her Bryce snub; the silly Canadian who snogged her but never called.

'Yeah, I wouldn't mind getting to know William a bit better.' She smiles.

'That's the spirit, girl.' I laugh. Now *that* was a fun night. I promise her I'll arrange another one.

Karen and Reena both call me that week too, wanting to know how it's going. I'd expect nothing less, but naturally I get completely different reactions from both. I speak to Reena first, who seems happy to accept that I've turned a corner and am determined to consider Nathan a mere friend. Karen, on the other hand, tells me I sound like a children's TV presenter and thinks I'm away with the fairies.

'Oh, bugger off,' I laugh irritably.

'Come on, Lucy. When you saw him again for the first time, did you or did you not want to get into his pants?'

303

'Shut up!' I'm outraged. I'm sitting in Soho Square on my lunchbreak. Karen's husky Yorkshire voice laughs down the line, then she grows serious. 'I don't know why I'm teasing you; you know I don't approve of all this.'

'Well, then, you should be encouraging me to think about Nathan platonically instead of accusing me of being in La-la land.'

'Yeah, yeah, whatever. So when am I going to meet this surfer dude?'

'Well, it might be sooner than you think . . .'

Friday is my twenty-sixth birthday. Karen and Alan, Reena and Paul, Chloe, Gemma and Martin, are all coming to Marylebone for the evening. Yesterday James even suggested himself that I invite Richard and Nathan along, which of course I'd done already.

While my friends are desperate to meet Nathan at last, I'm mortified by the idea. I hope they don't give anything away. I'm trying to keep my anticipation in check about seeing him again, reminding myself that he'll be different with me in public to how he is when it's just the two of us. What if he's detached and distant to the point that my friends wonder what all the fuss is about? I shouldn't care, especially as I'm trying to get over him, but I do. Of course I do.

The girls spoil me rotten all day at work and Mandy buys me cakes in the afternoon. James sends a massive bunch of flowers to the office, which sends Chloe bonkers with jealousy. But that's nothing compared to the look on her face when I show her the necklace he gave me this morning. It's a white-gold chain, with a large diamond solitaire to match my earrings.

It's beautiful. I love it. And I also hate it with a passion because every time I look at it I feel like a duplicitous bitch.

We're well into October now, the nights are getting longer and colder and I'm starting to travel by tube again. I want to go home first and get ready, instead of going out straight from work. And I've invited Richard and Nathan for a quick drink at the flat. We're meeting the others in a bar on the High Street later.

I soon regret my tube decision. People pile in behind me and we're like sardines, packed in tightly.

Just as I'm thinking about getting off at the next station and walking rather than suffer this unbearable squash, the train comes to a halt in the tunnel. There's a fire in the next station, apparently, and it's being evacuated. The woman next to me feels faint, and I have to shout at people to move further down the carriage to try to give her some air. A nightmarish half an hour later, the train finally starts up and moves off.

I always do my make-up in front of the wardrobe mirror, sitting cross-legged on the floor. I dig out a black headband and drag it over my forehead, pulling my fringe away from my eyes. Then I fish out my tinted moisturiser and squeeze a tiny amount onto my palm.

The doorbell rings. Oh, bollocks, they're here and I'm not ready. I look around the room: unmade bed, half-covered with clothes, make-up spilling over the floor . . . I won't be showing Nathan the bedroom, then. I listen to James's welcoming voice as they come up the stairs. He'll sort them out with beers until I get out there. Done with my foundation I quickly hunt out my green Shu Uemura eyeshadow and rub my finger over it, smudging it across one eyelid. I do the same on the other eye. Then I rummage around in my bag for my mascara. There's a knock at the door. Shit! 'Come in?' I pray it'll be James.

'Hi,' Nathan says as he peers in. 'Happy birthday.'

'Thanks. Sorry, I'm still getting ready.'

He opens the door further and comes in. I desperately want to pull the headband off my head.

'This place is amazing,' he says, talking about our flat. He towers above me and then sits down on the floor behind me, beer in hand. I swivel around to face him, my feet almost grazing his leg.

'Did you find us okay?'

'Yeah, no problem. Good directions.' He takes a swig from the bottle.

'I was running a bit late; got stuck on the tube,' I explain, turning back to the mirror and picking up my mascara wand. It doesn't look like he's going anywhere so I may as well get on with it and try to ignore the mess.

'Oh, really? Which line?'

'Listen to you, which line. You sound like a Londoner already.'

He chuckles and I tell him about my journey, while I finish my make-up. Finally I tug off my headband and fluff out my fringe.

'Okay, done,' I say. He pushes himself up and holds his hand down to help me up. I squeeze by him, palm still ablaze from his touch, and lead the way out towards the kitchen. Damn it, damn it, damn it!

James and Richard are watching the rugby. 'No!' James shouts, as one team – I think it's pretty safe to assume the opposition – scores a try. Nathan follows me into the kitchen and leans against the counter while I open the cupboard, searching for some honey-coated peanuts and cashews.

'Nut?' I offer him, trying to sound normal.

'Thanks.'

'Do you need another beer?'

'Nah, it's okay. Still going.' He's wearing a black jumper and dark blue jeans. They look new. I pour myself a glass of white wine and we look at each other sideways, locking eyes until it starts to feel uncomfortable.

'Where are we off to tonight?' he says finally.

'Just down Marylebone High Street,' I reply, and turn my attention to finding a cashew amongst the peanuts.

My stomach seems to be hosting a birthday party of its own.

Chloe and Gemma are already at the bar when we arrive, brimming with anticipation. They don't know which one is Nathan and they look quite comical, eyes darting from guy to guy, waiting to be introduced.

'Hello, you two.' James smiles and kisses them.

'Chloe, Gemma, this is Richard and this is Nathan . . .'

'Phwoar!' Chloe exclaims in my ear as soon as the boys move aside to queue at the bar. I urge her to keep her voice down, but naturally I'm delighted with her reaction.

'That Richard's a bit of alright, too.' She giggles.

'Single,' I tell her and the look on her face makes me want to laugh. She's unstoppable.

Reena and Karen arrive together with Paul and Alan and shower me with kisses and presents. It's Karen's birthday next week so I wish her a good one in advance and hand over her gift, a leather washbag from The White Company. Definitely not a freebie.

'Is that him?' she whispers in my ear, looking at Richard and barely acknowledging the parcel in her hand.

'No,' I whisper back. 'He's at the bar.'

'Which one?'

'Stop looking. Here he comes now.'

'He *is* gorgeous,' she concedes and my heart fills with joy for a split second before she continues. 'But that's no excuse to fuck James around.'

'Oh, Karen, please don't start.'

'Alright. I'll let you off. Seeing as it's your birthday and all.'

She chinks my glass and I take a large gulp of wine before looking around for Reena.

Towards the end of the evening I spot Nathan coming back from the bar and I break away from the group.

'Having a good time?' He smiles down at me.

'Really nice,' I reply happily.

He seems different, more chilled out to last weekend at the Walkabout pub. We haven't had a chance to talk, just the two of us, but at least he hasn't been avoiding my eyes all evening.

Karen was right, of course. I have been away with the fairies this week, pretending I'd turned a corner and had started thinking of Nathan as a mere friend. I hated how detached he was with me last time. *Hated* it!

'Your friends are great,' he says.

'They are, aren't they? I still wish Sam and Molly could be here, though.'

'I know you do.' He smiles. 'Hey, I'm sorry I didn't get you a present. You didn't give me enough notice about your birthday.'

'That's okay, I wasn't expecting anything.' I laugh.

'What are you up to tomorrow?' he asks.

'Nothing.'

'I was wondering if you'd like to go to Windsor Castle? James too, obviously,' he adds quickly.

'That'd be lovely!' Another place I've never visited.

'Cool. What time shall I pick you up in the morning?'

*

When he said 'pick you up', I assumed Nathan meant he'd meet us on foot at the flat so I'm surprised to see him standing out in front of a Saab 900i. Richard is waiting in the front seat, so James and I pile in the back.

The upholstery is ripped and the creamy-brown paintwork has faded, but the car suits Nathan. He bought it for £500 to use while he's here. As we pull out onto Marylebone Road in the direction of Windsor, he turns the sound up on the radio. I notice he's got a cassette player and wonder if he misses his tapes.

Walking up to the castle, Richard and Nathan ahead of us, James takes my hand. I scold myself and grip James's hand more tightly as I study Nathan's back profile, hoping he doesn't turn around.

Inside the stone walls we head first to the State Rooms. James and Richard are blown away by all the guns, but my interest peaks when we get to Queen Mary's Dolls' House. James fidgets impatiently and he and Richard go to wait outside. But I refuse to rush. I had to endure the weapons, for pity's sake.

Nathan stays by my side as I peer closely through the glass at the tiny replicas.

'Incredible, isn't it?' I whisper. I feel like we're in a library, it's so quiet in here.

'Yeah,' he whispers back, and I drag my eyes away from the dolls' house to look up at him. The room is so dimly lit that I can barely see his expression, but my heart flutters as he meets my eyes in the darkness. I want to kiss him.

Lucy! Your boyfriend is metres away! Cut it out! I bring myself to my senses, just as a small girl turns the corner and starts to tell her mother petulantly that she really needs a dolls' house like this because hers isn't anywhere near big enough.

Nathan and I grin at each other and head towards the door.

'That reminds me of shopping for Andie's shoes.'

'I don't know how you're still sane,' he says.

'Sane? Well, I don't know about that . . .'

In St George's Chapel, Nathan stands quietly and looks up at the ceiling, while I follow James and Richard to the altar. I know I have to be careful not to seem too attached to Nathan, so I link my arm through James's as we wander past the impressive choir stalls. After a few minutes he and Richard again lose interest, so I offer to retrieve Nathan and meet them outside.

I find him still gazing upwards in amazement.

'That is mental,' he says. I look up and take in the beautiful intricate stonework. When I turn back to him he's still shaking his head in wonder.

Afterwards, Nathan drives us to Eton for afternoon tea.

'It would be nice to have a car, wouldn't it?' I turn to James. He nods. 'Maybe we could buy this off Nathan when he leaves?' I suggest.

James shakes his head, reaching out to flick at the ripped upholstery in the back of Nathan's seat. The music is playing loudly so Nathan can't hear, thankfully. I turn away and look out of the window. *I* like this car.

As we wander along the streets of Eton, I stop for a moment outside a quaint antique shop to look at the tiny silver charms in the window.

'That Concorde one is cool,' Nathan says from beside me.

'Yeah. Hey, James, I'm just nipping in here,' I call. He and Richard are looking in the window of a model car shop a couple of doors away. Nathan follows me into the shop and I ask to see the box of charms. The sales assistant notices me fingering the Concorde one.

'Flew its last flight right over our heads,' she tells me.

'Would you like it?' Nathan asks.

'Yes, I think I would.' I smile.

'I'll get it for you . . .'

'No, it's okay!'

'I want to. Birthday present.'

'Ah, thank you. Every time I see Concorde, I'll think of you.'

'Cheers,' he laughs, sarcastically. 'That'll be often, then?'

'Look.' I show James, later.

'Mmm,' he says, barely interested.

I put the charm in my purse, and feel oddly more attached to it than to the expensive diamond necklace hanging around my neck.

Chapter 23

It's November and we're all going to Gemma and Martin's flat in Primrose Hill for fireworks night. The leaves on the trees have finally turned. It seems like only a week ago that they were green, but now they drop from the branches in varying shades of red, orange and yellow.

The smell of chestnuts cooking on the street corners in town has been making me crave Christmas already. I love this time of year here. It's just not the same in Australia, where the sun is beating down and everyone walks around in shorts and T-shirts instead of hats, scarves and woolly winter coats. No amount of tacky tinsel and the sound of 'Jingle Bells' blaring out of shop doorways Down Under can compete with England's dark nights, fairy lights and warm log fires.

We all gather at Gemma and Martin's for mulled wine before the fireworks display, then head off up the hill with rugs and flasks of milky, sugary coffee. Nathan is here, with Richard too, and Chloe has joined us for the evening. We lay our rugs down on the grass and chatter happily as we wait for the fireworks to start.

'Did you guys make it to Harrods last weekend?' I ask Richard and Nathan.

'Yeah. What a sight that shop is.' Richard laughs. 'I've never seen anything so gaudy. Got a couple of tea towels to take back for my granny, though.'

I'm sitting between James and Chloe. Gemma and Martin are to my right, and Richard is next to Chloe on my left with Nathan at the end, so I have to lean forward to see his face. He's nodding at Richard in agreement.

'What do you guys think of Old Blighty?' Chloe asks.

'Ah, it's great,' Richard enthuses. 'I definitely want to come back.'

Chloe nudges me gleefully.

'What about you, Nathan?' she asks. 'You coming back?'

'I don't know.' He smiles at her. 'We'll see.'

Downcast, I hear James exhale from beside me and turn to look at him sharply, but he's not listening to our conversation. Instead he's typing a text.

'What's wrong?' I ask him.

'Oh, it's Zoe. She's upset.'

'About Jim?' I ask, feeling uncomfortable.

'Yeah,' he answers, distracted as he continues to type, then presses send.

Moments later a text comes back.

'Oh, for God's sake,' he snaps, reading it before starting to write another one.

'What's she saying?' I ask evenly.

'She wants me to go and see her.' I frown and look away. 'Don't worry,' he assures me hurriedly. 'I'm telling her I'm busy.'

Good, I think. He sends that text and wraps his arm around

me, drawing me close and keeping me warm. It's freezing tonight. I'm still slightly on edge, wondering if another text is about to come in. But instead his phone starts to ring.

'Sorry, sorry,' he mutters, and stands up, flipping his phone open. He wanders away from us and I immediately feel cold again.

'James alright?' Chloe asks.

'Zoe playing up,' I say.

'Who's Zoe?' Richard asks.

'Just some girl from James's work,' Chloe chips in.

'She's a friend,' I explain. 'Her boyfriend cheated on her.'

'Oh, right.' Richard pulls a face.

I glance across at Nathan. He's staring off down the hill and, even though he's close by, I suddenly miss him. Really miss him. I wish we could have some time alone to talk properly. It's impossible to speak to him with all these people around. Moments later James comes back.

'Is she alright?' I ask coolly.

'No, not really.'

'Oh.' I feel a little sorry for her. 'Why don't you go and see her?' I suggest magnanimously.

'Would you mind?' He looks at me, relieved. 'I won't be long, I'll just go and check she's okay.'

He bends down to give me a kiss on the lips but I turn my face so he catches my cheek instead. I watch as he ambles off down the hill towards Zoe's place, only a five-minute walk away. My spirits lift as I turn back to my friends. 'When are these bloody fireworks going to kick off, then?'

Nathan opens one of the flasks to offer me coffee.

'I'll share that flask with you, then?' I get up and go to sit beside him. Gemma and Martin close the gap next to Chloe.

'Sure.' He smiles at me as he hands it over.

Something unpleasant is niggling away at me. I shouldn't have encouraged James to go and see Zoe just so I can spend more time with Nathan. That was manipulative.

But James made the decision to leave, didn't he? In fact, he chose Zoe over me! His girlfriend! How dare he? Right, no more niggling thoughts, thank you . . .

It's a clear, dark night, and we can see the lights of London ahead of us. I lie back on the rug and Nathan does the same. The stars are bright overhead.

'There's the saucepan,' I point, and he grins.

'Not as bright as Down Under, though, are they?'

'No. Hey, I've been practising this one for ages.' I edge closer to him on the rug, trying to get warm. 'I'll probably still forget how it goes. Sherlock Holmes and Dr Watson go on a camping trip. After a good dinner and a bottle of wine, they retire for the night, and go to sleep. Some hours later, Holmes wakes up and nudges his faithful friend. "Watson, look up at the sky and tell me what you see." "I see millions and millions of stars, Holmes," replies Watson. "And what do you deduce from that?" Watson ponders for a minute. "Well, astronomically, it tells me that there are millions of galaxies and potentially billions of planets. Astrologically, I observe that Saturn is in Leo. Horologically, I deduce that the time is approximately a quarter to four. Meteorologically, I suspect that we will have a beautiful day tomorrow. Theologically, I can see that God is all powerful, and that we are a small and insignificant part of the universe. What does it tell you, Holmes?" "Watson, you idiot!" he exclaims. "Someone has stolen our tent!"'

I squeal with laughter at my own joke and startle Chloe and Richard. I can't believe I remembered it right.

'Sorry,' Nathan apologises to them. 'Lucy's cracking herself up.'

I smile across at him in the darkness and feel jittery.

We're silent for a moment, then he speaks. 'James alright?'

'Yeah . . .' I brush him off. 'How are *you*? I feel like I haven't had a proper conversation with you for ages! How's your job going? Is your boss being nicer to you now?'

'He's alright,' he says.

'Still busting your balls?'

'Not really.' He laughs. 'But, well . . .'

'What?'

'I guess I'm still feeling out of it.' I nod, encouraging him to open up. 'It's just that the other guys there are all older than me. Even Rich is three years older, and I don't think my boss takes me very seriously, you know? I don't exactly look like your typical burly builder.'

'Thank goodness. Sorry, I mean, no offence to burly builders, but I just . . . like you the way you are.'

'Aw, Luce.' He smiles. 'It's fine. I kind of miss my renovation work but I'll be getting back to it in a couple of months.'

My face falls and I picture my heart thudding more dully in my chest. 'Do you have another house lined up?'

'Not yet. A couple of estate agents are on the case, though.'

An almighty bang scares the living daylights out of me and I jump. Nathan laughs as we both sit up to watch the fireworks, me desperately trying to forget his forthcoming departure so I can enjoy having him here while I can.

The display is spectacular.

'They're not as good as the ones in Sydney Harbour, though, are they, boys?' I look across at Nathan and Richard.

'It's a close call,' Richard says.

But they still provoke plenty of oohs and aahs. Off in the distance, dozens of smaller shop-bought sparks are going off. Richard points them out. 'Why do people bother with the crappy small ones when they can see crazy big displays like this?'

'I know!' Chloe agrees. 'And little shits will still be setting them off for weeks to come at all hours of the bloody night.'

I think of my stepbrothers back in Somerset.

'What are you smiling at?' Nathan whispers.

'Just thinking that Rich is right,' I reply, 'but there's also nothing like the thrill of setting off your own. I know that from watching my stepbrothers, Tom and Nick, in the back garden at home.'

'That's so true. Sam and I would have such a laugh with Dad. Used to drive poor Mum nuts. She was always worried we were going to blast someone's eye out.'

I snuggle even closer to him, pulling the rug over our legs to keep the cold out.

'I'd like to meet your stepbrothers,' he says to me.

'I wish you could. Shame you can't come to Somerset for a weekend while you're here.'

He doesn't say anything. It would of course be perfectly possible for him to visit Somerset but it's hardly likely to happen. James and I are going there at the beginning of December and I doubt I'll get a chance to go home before then. I couldn't invite Nathan home without James, and I would never dare ask James if Nathan could gatecrash our December weekend.

After a while, James reappears. The only space next to him on the rug is at the other end beside Martin and Gemma, and he doesn't look too pleased. I squeeze Nathan's arm regretfully and stand up to join James, the cold air immediately making me shiver.

'How was she?' I ask him.

'Not the best.'

'You missed the fireworks,' I point out annoyingly.

'It's okay, we saw a few from her balcony.'

Suddenly I'm the one feeling annoyed. 'Oh, nice, so you watched the fireworks with her, then.'

'Lucy, please,' he grumbles, running his hand through his hair and turning to look back down the hill. 'Why are women so . . . *draining?*'

'Charming!' I snap.

'Sorry, sorry,' he soothes me. 'Jesus, it's cold.'

'I'm bloody freezing,' I agree, glancing back woefully at the blanket still covering Nathan's legs. He's not looking at me so I can't catch his eye and smile. I turn back to James, who's examining my face.

'*What?*'

'Nothing,' he says, pulling me to him and vigorously rubbing my arms to try to warm me up. 'Do you mind if we go soon?' he asks. 'I'm knackered.'

Later, when we're sitting on the tube on our way home, James turns to me. 'I didn't like coming back up the hill and seeing you sitting so close to Nathan.'

'Well, you buggered off to see Zoe!' I snipe, outraged.

He sighs. 'It's alright, it's no big deal. But I'm just saying I didn't like it. I felt a bit . . . jealous,' he adds.

'There's no need for that.' I pat him on his leg.

'I'd just rather you didn't spend too much time alone with him.'

'Look, don't worry,' I say. 'There's really no reason why I would. We're busy during the week at work and on the weekends we can all go sightseeing together. You and I keep meaning to get out more and now we've got a proper excuse, haven't we?'

'Yeah, I suppose so.' He smiles uncomfortably.

'You're different with Nathan than with James, you know,' Chloe says the following Monday at work.

'Hey?' I shift, embarrassed.

'No, you are,' she tells me. 'Isn't she, Gemma? It's something about the way you talk to each other. You laugh more!'

'I laugh with James,' I respond defensively.

'Of course you do,' she mollifies me. 'But it's different. Oh, never mind,' she says when she sees my expression. 'Forget I said anything.'

But I can't get her comment out of my head. It's true. I do chatter more around Nathan. James and I don't really have the same sort of relaxed banter. Am I more myself with Nathan, though? Or does he just bring out a different part of my character? I think I like myself more when I'm around him. And that, in itself, is confusing.

Over the next few weeks, James does join Nathan and me on several sightseeing trips. We go on the Millennium Wheel, to museums, even the Tower of London. Richard is always in tow, and even Ally too on a couple of occasions. The two of them seem to get along well, which is both comforting and disappointing in equal measure. I feel bad for Chloe, who is rather smitten with Richard, but relieved that Ally hasn't set her sights on Nathan.

But, while I spend my weekdays looking forward to the weekend when I'll see Nathan, when I do see him it's always a let-down. I find I can't relax around him at all – mainly because

James is there. How ironic, considering Chloe's comments. I'm trying to be as normal and cheerful as possible with both of them but, to be honest, I don't really feel myself around anyone at the moment.

This weekend, James and I are going home to Somerset. Every year, in early December, the people in the town switch off all the street lights and use only candles in their front windows. As it's my turn to spend the festive season with James and his family in Kent this year, he promised he'd join me and mine for the 'Dunster by Candlelight' weekend.

We arrive in Dunster on Friday afternoon, in the nick of time to see the candlelight procession begin. My stepbrothers and Meg are already there and the five of us rug up warm and make our way down the village lanes. There are hoards of people lining the main street; everyone is buzzing. A flame juggler wows the crowds as we head across the road to the tea shop. Mum is closing early for the day so she and Terry can join in with the proceedings, and they're just lighting the candles in the front window.

James insists on buying everyone hotdogs from the Tithe Barn restoration stall, and then we stand and watch as a man and a woman on stilts in Victorian costume totter down the street, hooking dozens of lit lanterns onto tall posts.

The fire roars in the corner of the pub we end up in later. Tom turns to Meg and gives her a kiss on the lips and James does the same to me. 'Eugh, would you lot cut it out?' Nick grumbles, and we all laugh. He still doesn't have a girlfriend. I wonder how many poor girls' hearts he's broken in the three months since he started university in Nottingham.

The next day it is *pouring* with rain. It's coming down so heavily that it looks like there's a giant sprinkler system in the heavens, chugging out water in bursts that carry sideways in the wind. Normally on a grey day like today all the lights would be on in the house, but we're sticking to the theme of the weekend and using just candles. It's too wet even to venture out of the house to the pub so in the late afternoon we decide to play Trivial Pursuit instead.

James is my partner and he's excellent at these questions. How good would Nathan be, I wonder, remembering that he left school at sixteen? I smile proudly as James scores another piece of Trivial Pursuit 'cheese' for us.

Tom and Meg form another team, while Mum, Terry and Nick make up a third. I look around at my family and am filled with love. Tom kisses Meg as she gets a question right. They're so right together. So uncomplicated and content. Why can't James and I be like that? Why on earth did I have to go and mess things up by falling for Nathan? I watch Mum and Terry as Terry pours another glass of brandy and chortles happily. They've been together for, how long has it been? Over ten years? But they look like newly-weds.

Nick grabs the bottle from Terry and decants some into his own glass. My adorable stepbrother. He's so handsome. But I do wonder if he ever gets lonely.

And then I look at James, 'my' James, as he reads out another question to Mum's team and nudges Nick away as he tries to sneak a peek at the answer. It's good to have him here at home with me again. It feels safe. It's been so long since he's seen my stepbrothers but, apart from the odd roll of Nick's eyes, they seem to be getting along well.

James and I make love by candlelight later that night in my bedroom. And afterwards, lying in his arms as he falls asleep, I realise I haven't thought of Nathan too often this weekend. My heart aches as I realise it'll be another week before I see him, and I'm immediately infuriated with myself. Why can't I let this be? Why can't I be more like my older stepbrother, with his wonderful, straightforward relationship? It'll be easier when Nathan goes home to Australia, I tell myself, but another sharp pang shoots through me at the thought. Will I ever stop obsessing about him? Is this Sam all over again?

My mind ticking over ten to the dozen, I eventually get out of bed and quietly search my bag for my purse before creeping down the corridor to the bathroom. Inside, I lock the door and take out Nathan's silver Concorde charm.

When we were at university, Karen was a firm believer in the idea of a pros and cons list to help her make up her mind about big decisions. I'm not about to go and find a piece of paper and a pen at this hour, but I silently make a list in my head.

Nathan pros: *obviously* I'm attracted to him; he's sexy and funny. But above all, he 'gets' me. He understands me. And I feel like I could talk to him for hours, weeks, months – God, *years* . . .

Nathan cons: lives on the other side of the bloody world, two years' younger than me, left school at sixteen, might be getting his act together now with his career but from what Sam and Molly have said in the past, he may very well chuck it in to go travelling again at the drop of a hat. He's a headstrong, independent guy – why would he even want a long-term girlfriend? Look at what happened with Amy.

What about James? Pros: we've been together for four years now. We have a history together. I remember when we first fell in love and we couldn't get enough of each other. We lived together practically from day one and now we have our own amazing place. He has a great job, which bodes well for the future. He's intelligent, mature, also sexy, *and* a bloody good kisser. Very good in bed too.

Hmm, I wonder how good Nathan is in bed. What if we don't click between the sheets?

James cons: don't trust him. Never have.

Why not? Do I trust Nathan? Yes, I do.

Does James have anymore cons? He watches a lot of sport. But hey, if I lived in Australia with Nathan he'd be going off surfing at all hours of the day. That could drive me bananas.

Anyway now I'm just being picky. I dread to think what someone would come up with if they did a pros and cons list about me . . .

The upshot, though, is that James does love me. He looks after me and cares for me.

There's one clear winner but, I think desolately as I look down at the charm in my hand, it's not the winner I wanted.

Chapter 24

'You will never guess who I met last night!' Chloe gasps. It's Friday morning, four days since we got back from Somerset, and Gemma and I are just getting started on some envelope stuffing because the workie called in sick. Chloe has been for an early morning meeting with a cosmetics client.

'Who?' I ask, as she dumps her bag and coat and reaches for a stack of envelopes.

'William!'

'Who's William?' Gemma chips in.

Turns out Chloe bumped into James's colleague at a bar and they got chatting. He's asked her out on a date tomorrow.

'So, not so shy, after all?' Chloe says, looking like the cat that got the cream.

'Tell her to watch out,' James says later.

'Why?'

'He's a bit of a liar, that one. You should see the things he gets away with.'

'What do you mean?' I ask with concern, although warning

bells are going off in my head because I know the same could be said of James.

'Confidential business stuff. I shouldn't say. Just make sure she's careful.'

It's Saturday and Nathan is taking me to Highgate Cemetery. James wasn't keen; he might meet Zoe for lunch instead. Which is fine by me. I can't quite believe I'm having a day alone with Nathan.

Ally answers the door to me. 'Come in. Nate's upstairs.'

Nate? When did my Nathan become Nate?

I can hear him playing his guitar behind the closed door. I pause for a moment, then imagine Ally or someone walking by, so I knock. He stops playing abruptly and calls me in.

'Hello, *Nate*.' I grin at him cheekily. He grins back and starts to put his guitar down. 'No, don't stop playing,' I plead, but he shakes his head, embarrassed. I sit on the bed and look at him sorrowfully. He laughs. God, he's sexy, sitting there with his long leg tucked up on the bed, in position from cradling his guitar.

'Is Richard coming today?' I ask him, hoping he'll say no.

'Nah, he's going out with Ally.' Nathan gives me a knowing look.

'Oh, *really*?' I'm thrilled that his housemates have other plans. 'Are those two finally on together, then?'

'Yep.' He laughs. 'Come on, let's go.'

The cemetery is fascinating. Decrepit tombs line stony paths and ivy seems to cling to every surface. We peer through the dank trees and can make out countless gravestones that haven't been preserved. It's eerie.

Nathan's hand brushes against mine as we climb the steep paths and I have to concentrate on not grabbing hold of it. If Richard and James were here, I'd be okay. But here, now, alone, I'm finding it hard.

'You alright?' he asks me. 'You seem quiet.'

'Yeah,' I murmur, and try to focus on the tour guide's story about the large stone lion resting atop one of the tombs.

Afterwards we make our way back up the hill into Highgate with the intention of finding somewhere for lunch. I switch my phone on to find a voicemail waiting. It'll be James. But no, it's Mum, asking me to call her urgently.

She answers on the first ring. 'Lucy . . .'

'What's up?'

'I've got some bad news.'

'What?' I'm hesitant.

'Lucy . . . your father's dead.'

'Not Terry?' I gasp, and Nathan looks across at me, sharply.

'No,' she says quickly. 'Terry's fine. Your *real* father.'

'What happened?' I sink down onto a park bench.

My father *was* still in Manchester; he lived and died an alcoholic. The neighbours alerted the police when the flat started to reek of his decaying body. He'd been dead over a week before they broke in and found him. The police didn't know who to call as dad had no immediate family left. In the end they traced his wife from over twenty years ago. My mum.

It's the weirdest sensation. I don't feel sad. I don't want to cry. I feel oddly detached. I sit there looking down the hill at one of the almost-bare trees and find myself wondering how long it will be before the next leaf falls off. Five seconds . . . Twelve seconds . . . That one took a whopping thirty-two seconds.

'Lucy . . .' Nathan says tentatively. He reaches down and takes my hand and I let him hold it.

Twenty-two seconds . . .

'Lucy,' he tries again. 'Talk to me.'

I can't look at him. I just keep staring down at the trees. I picture my father dead and buried in one of the tombs that we've just been looking at:

Joe McCarthy . . . Father of one . . .

I didn't want to see my dad again. Not now, maybe not ever. But that was *my* choice. Now that choice has been taken away from me, and the realisation is shocking.

'I must go to the funeral,' I say tonelessly.

'Of course,' Nathan says. 'Of course.'

'I should call James.' He lets go of my hand and I dial James's mobile. He doesn't pick up. I hang up and try again. Voicemail. It's then that I start to cry.

Nathan takes me in his arms and holds me tight, while I sob into his warm shoulder. I shift, trying to get closer to him, but I can't, side by side on this bench. It's so frustrating.

'Come on,' Nathan says gently. 'I'll take you home.'

I don't want him to let me go, but he does.

He finds a place to park outside our terraced-lined street and unbuckles his seat belt. I stay seated.

'Lucy?' He comes around to the passenger door, opening it and taking my hand to help me out. He holds it the whole way up three flights of stairs. At the top he takes my handbag from me and finds my keys, then unlocks the door.

The flat is silent. James must still be with Zoe.

I sit there, while Nathan makes me tea, wondering why my copy of *Bridget Jones's Diary* has been put back on the DVD shelf upside down, and notice that there's a ring on the coffee table where James or I must have forgotten to use a coaster.

Nathan puts a mug of tea in front of me. He sits down and takes my hand again.

'Lucy, I'm worried about you,' he says. 'Let me try James again?' I nod slowly. He gets my phone out of my bag and presses redial. After a while he hangs up and tries again.

'Don't worry,' I tell him. 'It's okay. He'll be back when he's back.'

Nathan looks at me, relieved to hear me talking. 'When's the funeral?' he asks.

'Tuesday.'

'Wow, that's quick.'

'He died three weeks ago. They've been trying to trace his family.' My voice sounds vacant.

'Is it in Manchester? Will James go with you?' he asks.

I nod to both questions.

'Good. But if he can't,' he says, 'for whatever reason, let me know and I'll drive you.'

'Thank you. That's really kind.' I turn to look at him for the first time since Mum's phone call and my eyes well up again.

'It's okay,' he soothes. 'It's okay.'

I lie down and rest my head across his lap and he strokes my hair while my breathing slows.

'What the hell's going on here?' At the sound of James's voice, Nathan and I jolt awake. We must've fallen asleep again. Oh, Christ.

James is looking down at us accusingly. Nathan gets up but James doesn't move back to make room for him and for a split second it appears James is going to square up to him.

'My dad died!'

'What?' James pushes past Nathan to get to me.

'My dad died,' I tell him again.

'Baby,' he says, taking me in his arms.

'I couldn't get hold of you!' I cry.

'I'm sorry, baby, I'm sorry.'

I pull away and look over at Nathan, standing awkwardly by the coffee table.

James follows my gaze. 'Thanks for looking after her, mate,' he says.

'No worries,' Nathan answers, and motions towards the door. I nod at him. 'Give me a call if you need anything, okay?' he tells me.

'I will.'

After he's gone I feel lost for a moment. Nathan was so sweet to me today, and James was just so awful to him. I'm utterly despondent. I try to focus on relaying to James what Mum told me.

'Baby, you *don't* have to,' he says, when I tell him I'm going to the funeral. 'You shouldn't put yourself through this.'

'I'm going, James. Will you come with me?'

'Honey,' his face falls, 'I don't know how I can. We've got this conference on Tuesday and Wednesday and it's really important that I attend. Lucy, you don't really want to go, do you?'

'No, I don't want to, James. But I'm going to.'

'Will your Mum go?'

'I don't know. I'll ask her.' I turn away from him.

My mum doesn't want to and I don't push her. She feels terrible but, after all these years, with the hurt he's caused her, she just can't bring herself to go. She doesn't want me to either, but she understands why I have to. I want to make up in some way for not attending my grandmother's funeral. At the time I really didn't want to see my dad. I'll never have that concern again.

'Will James go with you?' she asks.

'Yes,' I lie.

Nathan picks me up at seven o'clock on Tuesday morning.

When we've wound our way north of London and finally reach the motorway amid rush-hour traffic, I take his tape out of my bag and put it in the player.

'You've still got it?' he asks me.

'Of course I do.'

It takes us a long three and a half hours to get to Manchester, thanks to the traffic. I fall asleep and Nathan keeps driving. The funeral isn't until midday, so we find the cemetery then go to a greasy café nearby.

'Thank you for coming with me,' I say to him, once we're seated. 'I don't know what I would have done . . .'

'James would have come if you'd told him how much you wanted him to,' he says.

'Maybe.'

Nathan doesn't answer. The waitress comes over with our food.

My father is being cremated because it's cheaper than a burial. The vicar is surprised to see me; he didn't know my father had any relatives. A few people are seated, including a couple of old codgers. I don't know who they are and I don't want to know. When the vicar asks me if I'd like to do a reading, I decline. The service is short, perfunctory, soulless.

Afterwards a plain-clothes policewoman introduces herself to me. She has some of my dad's belongings in her car and wants to know if I'd like them.

'I thought my mum said to give everything to charity?' I ask, unsettled.

'We have,' she tells me. 'These are personal items. Only a small box.'

Back in the car with the box on my lap, I'm filled with dread at the thought of what's inside.

'You don't have to do this now,' Nathan says.

'I want to. Before we get out of here. Do you mind?'

Rain is beating down heavily on the windscreen and the afternoon sky is dark and stormy. It'll be completely dark in a couple of hours and we still have to drive back down to London. Nathan switches on the overhead light and I open the lid.

There's a weird smell. Musty, decaying . . . as if the scent of my dad's dead body is clinging to his belongings. I have an overpowering urge to get out of the car and stand in the rain, or at the very least open a window and let the elements come in. But I restrain myself, acutely aware of how much Nathan has done for me already. I don't want to freak him out completely, however claustrophobic I'm feeling.

Inside the box there are twelve books, including the Bible, seven vinyl records by Irish artists I don't recognise, a cheap-looking metal watch, a gold wedding ring, and a few envelopes.

I spot my mum's handwriting immediately.

I open the door of the car and retch. The rain is pouring down as I continue to retch but nothing comes up.

'Lucy!' Nathan pulls me back and I close the door. 'You don't have to read these now!'

But I can't stop myself. That's how I am. Last page of a book . . .

Searching through sales racks . . . I remember Molly pointing all this out when I refused to delete James's text back in her workshop in Sydney.

One of the envelopes is thicker, firmer, so I start with that. In there is a letter and a photograph of a little girl, standing on a balcony of an apartment block, grinning up at the camera, brown hair cut in a childish bob.

Lucy, age 5, my mum has written on the back. Bracing myself, I open the letter and start to read . . .

> *Joe,*
> *This is your daughter. I thought you'd like to see what she looks like because you're not going to see her in person anytime soon.*
> *I'm not coming back, so don't try to contact me. After what you've done, I never want to see you again. You're pathetic. Evil. You don't deserve this picture of Lucy but I'm rising above that. One day, if you ever manage to sort your fucking life out, I might let you see her. But until then . . .*
> *Diane*

It doesn't sound like Mum. She never sounds like that. I don't understand. I pass the letter to Nathan and reach for the next envelope. The water from my wet hair is trickling down my neck but I barely notice.

> *Joe,*
> *Tell your mother to stop writing to me. The new tenants are sick of forwarding her letters.*
> *Diane*

I'm bewildered. I don't get any of this. The rest of the envelopes contain letters to my father from my grandmother. There doesn't seem to be anything significant in them, just what she's been doing in the garden and news about the neighbours, that sort of thing. After a while I give up reading them.

Why was he in Manchester? Why would he have left his home in Dublin? I don't know. And now I'll never know.

It occurs to me that I'm the only blood relative of Joe McCarthy left in the world. The sole tie I have with my so-called father is his surname.

'You okay?' Nathan asks me, pushing my wet fringe off my forehead, like he did that time on the beach in Manly. My heart flips just looking at him. I reach out and put my hand on his face. His stubble is softer than I would have thought and it surprises me. Then he kisses my wrist and I'm leaning towards him, loving him, wanting him. He catches my eye and holds it. He must know how I feel. He must. He takes my hand from his face and gently puts it down.

'I'm sorry . . .' he says. 'I'm sorry.'

And the moment is broken. I sit back in my seat. It's as if he's slapped me. He reaches across to touch my cheek and I flinch away. I can't look at him, but I can feel his stare. I can sense his hurt.

'Please,' I say. 'Take me home.'

I feel empty, flat. I can't look at James when I get back that evening, telling him I just want to watch the telly and not talk about any of it. I leave the box with my dad's things by the sofa, and James eyes it warily, but I ignore him. I can't take in anything on the television screen in front of me. I feel like everything is happening in slow motion.

The home phone and my mobile have been ringing, but I refuse to answer either. When James keeps trying to, I warn him to leave them. I don't want to speak to anyone. My life is a mess. I'm in love with James. I'm in love with Nathan. Nathan is leaving. My dad is dead.

Eventually James's phone rings and he flips it open, leaving me in the living room and going through to the bedroom. He comes back a few minutes later.

'That was your mum. She's worried about you.'

I don't answer.

I don't go to work the next day, even though we're busy; I still can't face anyone. I lie on the sofa, ignoring the phone. The sound of the shrill ringing is strangely therapeutic, but in the evening, when James comes home, he snaps at me. I let him take the phone off the hook and the ringing stops.

I wonder if Nathan has been trying to reach me.

By Thursday morning I've made a decision to go to Somerset for the weekend. I need to see my mum. I book myself a train ticket and then ring her to let her know my intentions. I leave a note for James, telling him I've gone home. He's never seen me like this and he doesn't know how to deal with me.

Mum comes alone to the station to collect me. She hugs me tightly but I don't return her embrace.

'Lucy, darling . . .'

We drive home in silence.

With Tom at work in London now, and Nick at university, it'll just be mum, Terry and me this weekend. Terry smiles at me sympathetically when I arrive and tells me he's sorry about my dad.

'You'll be okay, kiddo,' he says, giving me a comforting hug.

This must be difficult for him too. He's sensitive enough to know this weekend is about Mum and me, though, and it's a relief to be able to break away and go up to my bedroom without worrying about offending him.

Mum knocks on my door a little later. I'm lying on my bed staring up at the ceiling.

'Lucy, please talk to me.' She perches on the bed with a cup of tea for me. 'Tell me about the funeral. Did James go with you?'

I force myself to sit up. 'No, Nathan did,' I say, daring her to give me a look. She doesn't. 'I found your letter,' I tell her. She looks confused. 'You know, with a photo of me when I was five . . .' Recognition registers and pain flickers across her face. 'Tell me what it was like, Mum. Please. I need to know.'

My father was an alcoholic, abusive bully who cheated on my mother time and time again. Once she came home to find him with two hookers in his bed. When she tried to leave, he grabbed her by the hair and smashed her against the wardrobe, knocking her out. She was pregnant with me at the time.

The abuse continued. When he wasn't screwing other women, he would screw my mum, with, but mostly without, her consent. One time his mother – my grandmother – found her sobbing uncontrollably and bleeding because he had bitten her neck in a violent rage. She still has the scar. But my grandmother did nothing.

When I was born my mother decided we had to escape, but one of the neighbours, who saw her packing a suitcase, ran to get my dad from down the pub. He threatened to throw me at the wall and told Mum he would kill us both if she ever left.

But she did leave eventually. Because she knew he would kill us if we stayed. She escaped with me to a women's shelter in London and with their help, managed to find us a tiny studio flat. She got a job as a secretary and over the next couple of years, life settled down.

One day my grandmother turned up on her doorstep. She'd hired a private investigator to track us both down and was desperate for a reconciliation. She tried to persuade Mum to go back to Dublin to meet with my dad, swearing that he had changed, but my mum never wanted to set eyes on the bastard again. Over the next year my grandmother continued to write and send money. Eventually Mum had enough cash for a one-way ticket to Australia. It wasn't the outcome my grandmother had ever anticipated.

Mum tells me now that my dad did write many times, asking her to come back. He wanted to meet me. But she wrote to him only three times. Once to send him a photo of me because she was feeling generous, another to get him to tell his mother to stop writing, and finally to request a divorce.

'Where are their letters now?' I ask.

'I burnt them. I'm sorry,' she tells me.

Nathan calls me that night, as I'm climbing into bed. I've had eighteen missed calls since Tuesday night, so this time I answer the phone.

'Lucy! You're there!' He was obviously expecting voicemail again. 'Where are you?'

'Dunster.'

'Where?'

'Somerset. It's where I live. Where my mum lives,' I correct myself.

'Yes, of course.'

I say nothing, waiting for him to speak.

'Lucy . . .'

'What?' I snap.

Silence.

'Nathan, if you've got something to say to me, just say it! Why can't you say it?'

'What do you expect me to say?' he asks.

My heart is pounding so hard, I don't answer him.

'Lucy . . . Luce. About the other day . . .'

I wait.

'God, do you have to make this so hard for me?' he asks. 'When are you coming back? When can we talk?'

'Now is a good time.' I don't know why I'm being so mean. I can't help it.

'I . . . don't know what you expected me to do? In the car . . .'

'Please don't. Don't mention it again.'

He sighs. 'I'm leaving in three weeks.'

'Maybe we shouldn't see each other anymore, then.'

'I don't want that!' he exclaims, frustrated now.

'Well, what *do* you want?'

'I think it's *you* who has to decide what she wants, don't you?' he responds, angrily. 'Look, please, let's talk when you come back, okay? Lucy? I do know something about what you're going through, you know,' he adds, and my heart breaks at the sound of his sad voice.

'I know you do.' I'm more gentle now. 'But, Nathan, really, what's the point? Next week I'll have only a few days in London and then James and I are going to his parents for Christmas. By the time I get back, I might see you only once or twice before you go home.'

'We can't leave it like this, though, Luce,' he says sadly. 'We have to say goodbye. Please. Will you call me?'

I tell him I will, but I'm not sure either of us believes it.

Chapter 25

I arrive back at our empty flat on Monday, not caring that I've missed another day of work. James has left a pile of post for me on my bedside table, and I recognise Molly's handwriting on the top envelope. I open it up to find a card telling me how sorry she is about my dad and that she hopes I'm coping. She and Sam miss me more than ever. There are cards from Gemma and Chloe, Reena and Paul and Karen and Alan too. I feel loved, and it makes me happy and sad at the same time.

James has moved the box of my dad's things from by the sofa. I spend ten minutes frantically looking for it and eventually find it in a storage cupboard near the boiler in the kitchen. I leave it there. I'm angry with him for hiding it away but, at the same time, I accept it's better that the box isn't still by the sofa where I'd just stare at it morbidly.

Nathan calls me on Tuesday morning when I'm back at work. I divert him to voicemail. My heart wanted me to pick up, but my head won that round. Things would surely have been a lot less painful if I'd listened to the latter a bit more over the past year.

Mandy, Chloe and Gemma have been very sweet to me since I went back to work. Chloe and Gemma haven't said much, but their sympathetic looks and tea-making capacity speak volumes. I'm relieved that it's nearly Christmas and the office is winding down, although I still feel bad about how much time I've had to take off. Chloe tries to distract me by telling me about her date with William.

'Oh, she won't stop going on about him,' Gemma interrupts.

'Is that right?' I smile.

Chloe grins happily. 'Yes. He is *divine!*'

'Seriously? Did it go well?'

'That date, and the next one, and the next one,' Gemma chips in again.

'Are you two a proper item, then?' I enquire, and Chloe nods.

'Yep, he is just lovely. In fact, he's invited me to their Christmas work drinks on Friday night – you should come too! It would be such a laugh . . .'

Our office closes that lunchtime for our Christmas break.

'That'd be great.'

'So, you see?' she adds merrily. 'James was wrong about him being shy.'

I suddenly remember James's private warning to me a couple of weeks ago. What did he say again?

'Tell her to watch out . . . He's a bit of a liar, that one.'

But I can't bring myself to destroy Chloe's mood. Not just yet anyway. Not before Christmas.

Nathan calls me on Wednesday morning but once more my head wins the battle. Then, that evening, I arrive home to find him leaning up against his Saab, smoking a cigarette. He spots me at the same time as I spot him, and I freeze momentarily. He drops his cigarette butt onto the pavement and squashes it out as I approach.

'I thought you quit?' I ask him, unsmiling.

'Relapse,' he says.

'Have you been here long?'

'Half an hour, forty minutes . . .'

'Come in, you must be freezing.'

He locks his car and follows me up the stairs.

Inside the flat I put the kettle on and offer him beer, wine or coffee before deciding on a glass of wine for myself. He opts for coffee because he's driving.

When I go back through to the living room he's leaning forward on the sofa with his head in his hands. I sit at the other end, tucking my feet up and facing him. I sip my wine and wait, watching him. His messy hair falls sexily to just above his chin. When did he get a haircut, I wonder . . .

Finally I can bear it no longer.

'What are you doing here, Nathan?'

He sighs and leans back. 'I don't know.' He turns to look at me, his eyes filled with anguish. He holds his hand out to me for a second, then lets it fall on the sofa when I don't take it.

I do want to be close to him. I want to take his hand and snuggle up against his chest and let him hold me tight. I want to kiss him. I want to make love to him.

I want him not to be going home in just over two weeks.

'Your coffee's getting cold,' I say.

'I don't care.'

'You would if I'd made you a tea.'

He smiles for a fleeting moment and I can't help but smile back.

'Lucy, please, come here.' He holds out his hand to me again. I edge closer to him on the sofa and let him take my hand. He looks at me sadly. 'I don't know what's going on,' he says. 'I don't know what to do. I see you here, in this amazing flat with this great job and lovely friends—'

'And let's not forget James,' I say, before I can stop myself.

'As if I could.'

We fall silent for a moment.

Eventually I speak. 'What about you? You're going back to Sydney in two and a half weeks. Surely you wouldn't *consider* staying on?'

'Even if I could delay my flight for a bit, where would that leave us? I'd still want to go back home eventually. I miss the beaches. I miss the surfing. I miss my brother – he's the closest family I have.'

'My mum is the closest family I have,' I reply quietly.

'I know! And I'm sorry. It's a bloody nightmare.'

'I don't even know how you feel about me.'

'Yes, you do.' He holds my gaze. 'Yes, you do.'

My heart pounds in my chest. 'James will be back from work soon,' I say finally.

'I should be going, then.' He stands up, while I stay seated. Oh, God, I don't want to let him leave. But I *have* to.

'What are you doing for Christmas?' I blurt as he reaches the door, trying to delay his departure. Is this it? The moment I let him walk out of my life for good?

'Just spending it with Richard and Ally and everyone at the house. None of us has any family over here, so, you know . . .'

'Well, I hope you have a good one,' is all I can muster. Please don't leave. Please.

'You too.' He smiles sadly. 'Maybe we'll catch up when you get back? Before I fly home?'

'Maybe.' Let him go, Lucy. Let him go.

He opens the door and pauses for a moment to look back at me. Oh, God, no! He starts to walk through, then stops suddenly, and gets something out of his pocket.

'You forgot your tape . . . after the funeral,' he says, placing it on a shelf.

And then he's gone.

'Nathan! Wait!' I run towards the door, open it and pull him back inside. And then he's kissing me, up against the wall, pressing his lips to mine, and I never, ever want him to stop.

Finally he tears himself away, rough hands still holding my face. He bends down and kisses me again, slower this time, touching his lips to my jaw, my neck and back to my mouth again. I slide my hands up inside his jumper and feel his taut, toned stomach. I know I have to stop. It takes all the willpower in me to pull gently away. I lean back on the wall and he rests against the door, watching me, breathing heavily.

'What now?' he asks and we both smile guiltily.

'Whoops,' I say.

'Bugger,' he replies.

Then we become serious.

'Oh, God,' I say. 'This has just become a whole lot more complicated.' I try to curse my head for letting my heart get one over it.

He pulls me to him and wraps his arms around me, holding me tightly for a minute.

'I'm sorry this is such a mess,' he says into my hair. 'But I don't want to lose you.'

Paige Toon

'No, *I'm* the one who's sorry.' I pull away. 'It's over with James. I'll speak to him tonight. It will be okay.' I will myself to believe it.

But as soon as he's gone I realise more profoundly than ever what a complete and utter fuck-up I've got myself into.

When James comes home half an hour later, I'm sitting on the sofa, absent-mindedly fingering Nathan's Concorde charm, totally caught up in my thoughts.

'Hi!' He grins at me as he takes off his jacket. 'Changed your mind?' he asks, noticing both the full mug of cold coffee on the table and the glass of wine in my hand.

'Mmm,' I nod.

'What's up?' he says when he sees my expression.

'We need to talk,' I say sadly, and his face freezes in fear as he sits down on the sofa.

'I can't do this anymore, James. I'm sorry.'

'Lucy, what are you saying?' he asks nervously, eyeing the silver charm in my hand.

I've made up my mind. Nathan understands me, he 'gets' me, he *loves* me. I know it will be a rocky road for us; he's going home soon and that thought fills me with sickness and dread, but I can't let him leave without giving us a try. I want to be with him. In *every* sense of the word.

'It's Nathan,' I tell James.

'What about him?'

'I love him.' I have to be honest. No more secrets. No more lies.

'What? *What?*'

'I'm sorry,' I say again.

'Lucy, what the hell—? I . . . No!' He tries to take my hand, but I scrunch it up into a fist. 'Lucy, no! Don't do this . . .' he pleads.

344

'I'm sorry, James.'

'Stop saying you're fucking sorry!' He's shouting now.

But I remain unwaveringly calm.

'Lucy, I love you. I *love* you! You can't just give up on us, not after all these years. Please! We can work this out!'

'No, James,' I shake my head, 'we can't. You know it as much as I do. If we were meant to be together you wouldn't be . . . shagging Zoe.'

'*What?*' He looks at me as though I've just suggested he chop off his hand and use it as a doorstop.

'I know, James, I think I've always known. I just haven't wanted to admit it to myself.'

'Lucy, you're fucking nuts, do you know that? I AM NOT SHAGGING ZOE!'

'You can deny it all you like,' I respond, still calm. 'I know it's true.'

He grabs his hair with his hands and pulls it so hard I'm terrified for a moment it might come out.

'James, please stop,' I beg him sadly. 'It's okay. It's okay.'

'No, it's not bloody okay, Lucy! I love you, for fuck's sake! I'm not shagging some silly bitch from work. I would never do that to you!' he yells, in total exasperation.

On another day I might just believe him.

He flips open his phone.

'What are you doing?' I ask.

'I'm calling Jeremy,' he answers.

'Why?'

'I want him to tell us who sent that text.'

'James, it's okay, there's no need.'

'No, it's not . . . Hi, Jeremy, it's James. Look, buddy, I've got a bit of a problem. Yeah . . . Yeah. You know back in February when Lucy went to Australia? Well, someone sent her a text from my phone. It's okay, it's no big deal; I just need to know who it was.'

I wait patiently while he wheedles it out of Jeremy. Finally he hands the phone to me. I wave his hand away – I don't want to speak to Jeremy – but James insists.

'Hello?'

Jeremy explains that he barely remembers it now but one of the guys did indeed text me from James's phone when he went to the bar to get a round in. They all had a great laugh about it, and the following week had a whale of a time MSN messaging each other about why James had never said anything. Maybe they'd sent it to the wrong Lucy? Tee bloody hee.

When he's done telling me, I hang up and look at James's expectant face.

'It doesn't mean anything.'

'How can you say that?' he demands.

'You could've lined Jeremy up to do that just in case I ever asked. He would do that for you.'

'That's ridiculous! Is this about Zoe? Because I'll call her too.'

'Yeah, right, as though she's going to admit to anything,' I say sardonically.

His shoulders hunch as he looks at me, bewildered.

'Lucy, you've just lost your dad, you've been confused since you got back from Sydney, you're not yourself at the moment. And that bloody dickhead sticking his oar in hasn't helped!' he adds heatedly, then laughs cynically. '*Has* he stuck his oar in?'

'No,' I tell him truthfully.

'Well, at least that's something.' He smiles wryly. 'Baby, please. You don't have to do this. We can't just throw away four years.

That . . . *idiot* will be gone soon and then what will you have? Nothing, Lucy, nothing. You will regret this, so much. Don't do it, honey. Because once you go with him, I won't take you back. I won't!' he insists fiercely.

'And what about Zoe?'

'What about her? Baby, you don't really believe I'd do that to you, do you?'

'Yes.'

'What, so you think I've been going there and shagging her for weeks and you've just let me, have you?' he asks sarcastically, throwing his hands up in the air. 'Honey, that's ludicrous. Why would you do that?'

'Because it was the only way you'd let me see Nathan,' I say simply.

He looks at me like I've just slapped him hard across the face. Then he gets up, puts his coat on, and leaves. I don't try to stop him.

At some point in the middle of the night I wake up sleepily to find James's arm around me. It feels nice, comforting, and I wriggle back against him without thinking. In the morning we're still intertwined and I gently extricate myself. He opens his eyes and looks at me, blearily.

'Baby,' he pleads, trying to tenderly draw me back. His eyes are puffy and he looks like he's been crying.

'James, I can't,' I reply softly, and get out of bed. I go and wait in the living room in my dressing gown as he gets ready for work. I'm not going into Mandy Nim today.

James comes through half an hour later with his briefcase, looking smart in his suit. He kneels down in front of me, forcing me to look into his eyes and come face to face with the pain I've inflicted.

'I haven't given up on you,' he tells me, reaching out to touch my cheek. I resist the urge to recoil. 'I know you're confused at the moment but don't do anything silly. I love you, baby. And it's going to be okay.' He leans forward and kisses me lovingly on my forehead and then, tears welling up in his eyes, he walks out.

I stay sitting on the sofa in my dressing gown for over two hours. It's my mum who eventually snaps me out of it.

'Lucy,' she says down the phone, 'they said you were ill at the office. What's wrong?'

'It's all such a mess, Mum.'

She listens while I fill her in, begging her not to say, 'I told you so.'

'So what's your plan, now?' she asks eventually. 'You've almost got rid of your boyfriend, next it'll be your flat and after that your job, the way you're going. That'll make it easier for you to go back to Australia and leave everything behind, won't it? Because you won't have much to leave if you carry on the way you're going!'

'Mum!' I exclaim, but she's unrelenting.

'Look, I just want you to be realistic. It's a major thing to leave your whole life behind and start again from scratch in another country. I know that from bitter experience.'

'But, Mum, this is not about you,' I say sadly.

'Oh, Lucy. Of *course* it's about me. It's about *us*, our *family*. We don't want you to leave England! I know you're confused but you mustn't make a decision like this too hastily. Just, please, buck yourself up and get back to work. Don't get yourself fired as well.'

What am I doing? I'm so used to my mum being the voice of reason; am I really making a huge mistake?

I take a shower, turning the hot water to cool after a minute to try to blast my senses back into action. Then I phone the office to say I'm coming in at lunchtime. Mum's right; I have been taking the piss at work recently. Mandy demands such high standards and doesn't approve of her staff's personal lives coming between them and their performance at work. She's given me so many incredible opportunities and recently I've been throwing her job back in her face. Fair enough that I've had time off for my father's funeral, but she wouldn't consider my behaviour regarding Nathan and James to be acceptable.

Before I leave, I go to my bedside table and pull the drawer open, my eyes falling on the black velvet box with my diamond necklace inside. I open it up and look at the glittering solitaire.

Oh, James . . . Do I really believe he's been sleeping with Zoe? I remember the hurt on his face last night and this morning. He's been my love for four years and I'm just going to walk away from him like this? Nathan's going home in little over a fortnight. What *am* I going to do then?

The memory of Nathan kissing me up against the wall slams into my mind and I feel dizzy. Would I really choose two and a half blissful weeks with him over a potential lifetime with James?

In a heartbeat.

Chapter 26

'Hey!' Chloe and Gemma smile as I approach my desk. 'What's up with you?' Gemma asks.

'Last night I snogged Nathan and broke up with James.'

'NO!' they both scream.

'*Shhh!*' I warn, looking around to check Mandy's not in earshot.

'Tell us what happened!' Chloe insists. I fill them in while they listen, flabbergasted.

'Shit,' Gemma gasps.

'Have you really finished with James? Really, *really?*' Chloe asks, wide-eyed.

'Look,' I say matter-of-factly, 'I haven't been able to stop thinking about Nathan since I went to Sydney earlier this year. I love him. I have to be with him. Whatever the cost.'

They sit there for a quiet moment, then Chloe speaks gently. 'But, Lucy, James does have a point, don't you think? Once you've shagged Nathan you can never reverse it. I know that's what you want right now, but soon he'll be gone and then you'll be well and truly screwed. James is a great guy and, for what it's worth, I don't believe he's cheating on you with Zoe.'

'Don't you?' I ask surprised. I thought she and Gemma were swayed by the time Gemma saw him with Zoe on Primrose Hill. And again when he went to her house on fireworks' night.

'No, I don't,' she insists.

Great. Now I'm even more confused, and I didn't think that was possible.

'Lucy, have you got a minute?' Mandy calls to me. I'm tense as I follow her through to the meeting room and she closes the door behind me.

'Is everything alright with you? You haven't been yourself at work recently,' she says, once we're seated.

'My dad . . .' I stutter.

She eyes me searchingly. She's not stupid. She knows there's something else.

'I'm sorry,' I say. 'I know I've been distracted for some time now.'

'Do you want to talk about it?'

I shake my head, then change my mind. I'm so confused. Will one more opinion really make a difference? I do respect my boss enormously. She's a strong, independent, successful woman; someone I look up to. Bugger it! I'd really value her advice.

'It's personal. I know you don't like that stuff being brought into the office . . .'

'Don't worry about that,' she encourages me to go on.

'I'm in love with two men.' There. I've said it. It's out in the open.

'Aah . . .' She nods. 'Complicated.' She pushes her chair out from the table and stands up. I remain seated as she goes over to the window and folds her arms, looking down the road towards Soho Square.

'You're not alone in this sort of dilemma, you know, Lucy.'

I look at her in surprise. We all know from the PR article we read about her last year that Mandy has been married twice and now lives with a man in west London, but she never talks about her personal life. She looks back at me, wryly.

'You might very well make the wrong decision and fuck everything up . . .' I've never heard Mandy swear before. 'But I've always been one for following my gut instincts.'

I'm all ears. This is a side to my boss I've never seen. She continues.

'You could stay within your comfort zone and speculate about whether the grass would have been greener for the rest of your life. Or you could say bollocks to it, and go with what's here . . .' She presses her hand to her chest and looks at me intently. 'And it may not seem like the obvious decision to everyone else, and it may be traumatic and complex and utterly terrifying, but you're not one to play it safe, Lucy. I don't think so, anyway. That's why you're my Number One PR girl.'

Mandy's candour and her unexpected compliment make me feel more at ease with her at this moment than I've felt at any time in the four years I've worked here. Funny how the best advice I've received so far has come from such an unlikely source.

'So, did you make the right decision?' I ask her directly.

'I still don't know.' She smiles. 'But hey, I'm optimistic.'

I get home that night to find James already there.

'Have you seen him?' he asks wretchedly, coming over to me at the door the moment I walk in.

'No,' I tell him.

'Thank God. I feel so sick, Lucy. I had to come home early. Please don't see him. Please.' He tries to draw me to him but I step back. Then he starts to cry and it's heart-wrenching.

'James, don't cry!' I plead. He wraps his arms around me and his whole body shakes. I hate myself.

Eventually he pulls away.

'Look, Lucy, all I'm asking is that you come home with me for Christmas so we can have some time together and talk this through,' he implores. 'I love you,' he tells me forcefully.

'I love you too,' I reply sorrowfully, and feel tormented by the look of hope in his eyes when I say it, because I go on to add, 'but I don't think it's enough.'

'It *is* enough, baby. We'll make it work. Just come home with me for Christmas.'

Mum, Chloe, Gemma . . . They all think I'm making a mistake not giving us this one last chance. What about Mandy? What about me playing it safe?

But she doesn't know all the details. She doesn't know about Nathan going back to Australia, or what the future could possibly hold for us. In fact, it's ironic that she unknowingly risked losing her 'Number One PR girl' to a country on the other side of the world.

But I can't leave England for Australia. Not yet, anyway. I'm not ready to give up my job, my friends, my flat. *Our* flat. I *will* have to give it up if I leave James.

Maybe Mum and my friends are right. Maybe I *am* rushing things.

The thought of Christmas at Nathan's dirty house in Archway with his chain-smoking flatmates actually makes me feel a little

353

depressed. But all the trains to Somerset will be full by now so I won't be able to get home to my family. James and I booked our train tickets to Maidstone in Kent to see his parents weeks ago.

I look at James's hopeful face. 'Okay,' I agree, and he crushes the breath out of me as he squeezes me tightly.

'Thank you. Thank you,' he sniffs into my hair.

I feel sick.

Later that night I tell James I'm going out for a walk. I want to call Nathan and I can't do that from the house. But James guesses what I'm up to and begs me not to go. He looks so distraught and I can't bear to see his anguish so I stay with him, accepting I'll have to call Nathan the next day from work. In the end I busy myself packing a bag to take to James's parents for Christmas, but I can't shake the uneasiness I feel.

James tries to make love to me that night. I tell him no, so he holds me tightly as we fall asleep instead. It's suffocating.

'Will you come and meet me later?' he asks the following morning. It's the Friday before Christmas and he's having his work drinks that night. 'I don't have to go, though,' he says. 'If you don't want me to, I won't.'

'No, it's okay.' I smile, uncomfortable with how accommodating he's being. 'I'll come and meet you later with Chloe.'

He pulls me in for another hug and I feel utterly helpless and out of control.

I decide to walk to work and as soon as I cross over busy Marylebone Road and get onto the quieter streets, I'm dialling Nathan's mobile.

'Hi,' he says warmly.

I can't believe I'm doing this. 'Nathan . . .' I start.

'You're not breaking up with him, are you?' he asks sadly. My eyes fill with tears and I try to choke back the golf ball that seems to have lodged itself in my throat. I make my way into Paddington Green Gardens, past the white statue of a little boy looking lost and forlorn, and take a seat on one of the benches.

'I . . . don't know . . .' I dig around in my coat pocket for a tissue.

'Lucy, it's okay,' he says. 'I understand.'

'Do you?' I ask. 'Because I don't. I don't know *what* I'm doing!' A woman in a business suit walks past and eyes me cautiously.

'Yes,' he says. 'I do.'

Neither of us speaks for a moment and I just sit there with the phone to my ear as tears silently track mascara down my face.

'Molly's pregnant,' he says quietly after a while.

'Is she?' I gasp. 'That's brilliant!' I'm suddenly elated.

'You can't tell her you know, yet. She's not quite twelve weeks gone, but Sam couldn't keep it to himself. You'll have to act surprised when she calls. Sorry if that makes it awkward for you.'

'It's okay. I'm so happy for them!'

'Yeah.' He pauses. 'But it's another reason why I have to go back.'

Something inside me dies as I realise this is it. I've lost him. Even though I told James I would go home with him for Christmas, I didn't really believe that was my fate. Now reality sinks in.

James is my future. His parents will one day be my in-laws, and I see years and years of Christmases spanning out ahead of us, juggling our affections between Kent and Somerset and, finally, *our* home when we have a family of our own. Oh, God. I don't know if I can bear it.

'Will you stay in touch?' I ask eventually, still trying to swallow the lump in my throat that seems to have doubled in size.

'Of course.'

Both of us know we can never have what we had. And that wasn't much, but it was enough. I know I'll always have him in my life, through Molly and Sam, but the thought of the future, hearing about him settling down with another girl, getting married and having children with her . . . I start to sob soundlessly.

'Lucy,' Nathan says. 'I'll always care about you.' His voice breaks and it makes me cry harder. 'Call me if you ever need anything, okay?' He's fighting back tears and I know I have to let him go. I want to tell him I love him but the words won't come. My breathing slows and becomes more regular.

'Okay,' I answer. 'Speak soon.'

'Speak soon,' he replies.

Neither of us can bring ourselves to say the word 'goodbye'. I listen with despair as the line goes dead.

I stay there, sitting on the park bench dedicated to My Beloved Wife Jane, and realise that I'll never again be able to listen to a joke, sit on a park bench, hear any number of songs, without thinking of Nathan. Surfing, Sydney, sharks, dolphins . . . Nathan. Molly, Sam . . . Nathan. I'm going to be unhappy for the rest of my life, I think, and don't care how melodramatic or selfish it sounds.

But I will be okay. I'll pick myself up, move on. My future is with James. My one-day husband and father of my children, probably. And Nathan will hear news of *me* from Sam and Molly and feel heartbroken over what *he's* lost. The thought calms me, oddly, and I wipe my face, pick up my bag, and walk the rest of the journey to work in a daze.

'I'm sorry I'm late,' I tell Mandy, the moment I walk in the door. She studies my red eyes and waves me away.

'It's okay.'

'I promise I'll be back to normal in the New Year,' I add, and she peers up at me and says kindly, 'I know you will, Lucy. Don't worry.'

Gemma and Chloe eye me cagily as I go to sit down. None of us can speak openly because Mandy's at her desk, so this conversation will have to wait until lunchtime.

There's a white envelope resting on my keyboard and I open it to find a lovely letter from Mandy telling me what a fantastic year I've had and giving me a large Christmas bonus. I'm gob-smacked and glance over at her. She senses my look and smiles as she continues to type on her computer. It cheers me up somewhat and I try to put Nathan to the back of my mind.

We all head out to lunch at a posh Thai restaurant in Soho – there are fifteen of us in total – and I take a seat at the end of the table next to Chloe and Gemma.

'Don't be too nice to me,' I caution, knowing it would only set me off again. As the waiter tops up our glasses with champagne, I start to fill them in. I mistake their expressions for sympathy at first but I soon sense something's not right.

'What is it?' I ask guardedly. Gemma looks at Chloe, as though willing her to say something. Eventually Chloe does.

'I didn't know whether or not to . . .'

'Go on . . .' I press.

'It's . . . something William said.'

'Tell me,' I say, remembering James's warning about William.

'Well, it's just that, I know you're making a decision about James and Nathan at the moment and I thought you should . . .'

'Just spit it out, Chloe, please,' I ask, not unkindly.

'Er, apparently James has a bit of a reputation,' she says. 'At work.'

'Mmmhmm,' I prompt, thinking: So does William. My straightforward attitude seems to unsettle her. 'What sort of reputation?'

'He, er, is said to, um, screw around a bit.' She grimaces at the sound of the words on her tongue.

'What do you mean? With Zoe?'

'Er, not just her from what it sounds like.'

'Right . . .' I try to keep my feelings in check. 'James also told me something about William.'

'What?' She's wary. I don't want to do this to her, but I have to.

'He told me he's a liar. That you should be careful. I'm sorry,' I add, seeing the look on her face. 'I wanted to tell you earlier but you seemed so cheerful.'

Chloe glances at Gemma and they both fall silent.

'What, you don't believe me?' I ask.

'I don't know what to believe,' Chloe answers. 'But it's just that, well, William's such a nice guy. I don't think he'd lie about something like this.'

Gemma nods in agreement.

'Have you met him?' I ask Gemma, surprised.

'Yes,' she answers. 'Martin and I went out for a drink with them last night.'

'So you were there when he said this?' I'm feeling ever more nauseous at the thought of my friends having a good old gossip about poor little Lucy and her nasty dilemma. Gemma nods, embarrassed. I know I shouldn't shoot the messengers but I suddenly feel angry. I don't need this!

'He just asked after you, that was all,' Chloe explains. 'And I told him,' she adds feebly.

'Well,' I try to keep the coldness from my voice, 'I guess we'll find out the truth later, when we go to meet them.' Then I excuse myself from the table and go to the bathroom.

The person staring back at me is frightening, diamonds glinting dangerously in her ears. I splash cold water on my white face and take several deep breaths, willing myself to calm down.

The mood when I get back is sombre, uncomfortable. We try to lighten up our conversation but it's stifled. Eventually I turn and make conversation with one of the girls from accounts, who is sitting next to me.

James texts me at 4 p.m.

YOU STILL COMING? I MISS U

I write back with a simple 'yes' and feel ill as I press send.

After lunch, Chloe and I kiss Gemma goodbye for the holidays and walk outside to catch a cab. Gemma's going home to her parents' place in Berkshire with Martin tonight.

'I'm sorry if you think I was being out of order,' Chloe says, once we're in a cab.

'It's okay,' I tell her. 'I'm sorry if you think I was.'

She reaches across and touches my leg. 'I'm sure it will all work out.' She smiles. I can't return it.

When we arrive at the bar, James's work party is already in full swing. Jeremy spots us first and comes over to gyrate against me to the music. He's pissed out of his face.

I push past him and we make our way through to the others. William immediately comes over and gives Chloe a big kiss on the lips. She smiles up at him awkwardly.

'Hi, Lucy.'

'Hi.' I regard him suspiciously, but intuitively I just don't get a bad feeling about him. I walk away from them, feeling hazy as I look for James. At least I haven't had too much to drink today; I need to keep my senses. Eventually I spot my boyfriend in a dark booth at the back. He's talking to Zoe and I feel faint as the mini hurricane swirls around in my stomach.

I don't have to be here. I could turn around and leave them to it. But fight always wins out over flight for me. I make my way over to them.

I can't see Zoe's expression but James is frowning. As soon as he sees me his face lights up and he nudges Zoe to get up so he can shift out and get to me.

'Hi, you,' he slurs happily. He pulls me in for a kiss, followed by a long hug, during which he sways me drunkenly from side to side. When he pulls away I see Zoe standing to the side, eyeing us coldly.

'Hello, Zoe.'

'Hi,' she replies, unsmiling. 'I'm going to go to the bar. Want anything?' she asks as she turns to James.

'Lucy, what're you having?'

'It's a free bar,' Zoe tells me, her mouth curling up unpleasantly as she sees me reaching for my purse. I didn't want her to buy me a drink.

'Oh, okay. Vodka and cranberry, then.'

'James?' she asks.

'I'll have another whisky, thanks ba— er, Zoe.'

'No, I mean, are you going to give me a hand? I can't manage three drinks on my own.'

I look at him, daring him to go.

'Don't be silly, Zoze, you can manage five drinks on your own. I've seen you with my very own eyes!' he says jovially. She raises her eyebrows at him and stalks off. He turns back to me and rolls his eyes, but I just stare at him calmly.

'What?' he asks.

'You are so full of bullshit.'

'*What?*'

'James, for fuck's sake.' I laugh bitterly. 'It's so *obvious*!'

'Lucy, cut it out.' He's irate now.

I can't be arsed with all this. It's a bloody joke. I look around for William and Chloe and spot them over by the wall, laughing and talking. James clocks my look.

'Has *he* said anything?' he demands to know about William. 'Because if he has, he's a fucking liar. He shags anything with two legs!'

'*Right* . . .' I narrow my eyes at him.

'That son of a bitch,' James says and I'm fearful he's going to storm over to William right now and knock his lights out.

'What's going on?' Zoe reappears suddenly.

James is breathing heavily and eyeing William with a disturbing look. She puts her hand warningly on James's arm. He shrugs her off. 'Haven't you caused enough trouble?' he asks her nastily. My heart is thumping like crazy in my chest.

'Don't you blame this on me,' she responds angrily.

'Shhh,' he soothes, calmer all of a sudden. He rubs her arm briefly then steps away and puts his arm around my waist.

'I don't think so . . .' I try to detach him.

'Lucy, for God's sake, cut it out!' he snaps. 'I don't need this!'

'Neither do I,' I respond, attempting to wrench myself away, but he just draws me in tighter.

'James!' I raise my voice. 'Let me go! What the hell are you doing?'

'Yeah, James,' Zoe says coldly. 'What the hell are you doing?'

'Why don't you just piss off?' I turn to her, furiously, still trying to wriggle free of James.

'What's going on? Lucy, are you alright?' William says from beside me. Chloe joins us, anxiously eyeing the scene.

'Yes, of course she's alright,' James answers snidely.

'James, let me go!' I snap again.

'Let her go,' William tells James.

'What are you going to do, make me?' he asks viciously.

Then suddenly Jeremy arrives to join in the party. I'm expecting him to face up to William but he doesn't. Instead he goes over to Zoe. 'Zoe, come on.' He struggles to be serious with all the alcohol he's consumed.

'No, Jeremy.' She shakes him off. 'I've had enough of this!'

'Calm down.' He shushes her, rubbing her on her back.

James is still holding me tightly around my waist and glaring at William. I glance over at Chloe; her face is tense.

'James, let me go.' This time I'm deadly calm.

'Yeah, James, let her go,' Zoe bitches.

'Would you shut up!' he hisses at her, and again Jeremy tries to pull her away.

'No, I WILL NOT!' she shouts.

I'd probably pity her if I didn't think she'd been shagging my boyfriend.

'Why don't you calm down?' I turn to her, my voice firm.

'*Don't* tell me to calm down!' She's hysterical now.

'ZOE!' James lets go of me and turns to Zoe, but she violently pushes past him towards me.

'You don't know how lucky you are with your bloody boyfriend and your fancy flat! You don't know what it's like for me!'

'You don't know me at all.' I face up to her, even though she towers above me by several inches. 'You don't know anything about me so don't you *dare* tell me how lucky I am!'

Zoe laughs cruelly then visibly appears to compose herself. 'You *are* lucky,' she says calmly with an evil glint in her eyes. 'In fact, the only thing I don't envy about you is your flannel sheets.'

She may as well have punched me in the stomach as the memory of that text comes back to me, word for word.

HI LUCY! JUST SHAGGED JAMES IN UR BED. THOUGHT U SHOULD KNOW. 4 TIMES THIS MONTH. NICE SHEETS! XXX

'Lucy,' James interjects. I slap him hard, right across the face. Then I do it again. He stumbles backwards into William who pushes him off.

James turns around and shoves him hard in the chest before raising his fist ready to punch. Jeremy drags James back as William squares up to him. I leave them to it. I don't have a minute to waste. I'm dialling Nathan's number as I push through the throng and out onto the pavement.

'Lucy!' Chloe runs outside a minute later. 'Are you okay?'

'Yes,' I tell her. 'I'm just glad I found out now. Before it's too late.' I hold up my phone. 'Nathan's coming for me.'

'Thank goodness.' She puts her arms around me and we huddle in a dark doorway a little further down the road. After a while we sit down on the step.

'Christ, it's cold out here,' she says suddenly.

'Where's William?' I ask.

'He's inside. It's okay, I think he'll calm things down.'

'He was squaring up to James last time I looked . . .'

363

'Don't worry, he's not the type to be violent,' she insists.

Five minutes later James bursts out through the door.

'Lucy!' he shouts. 'LUCY!'

Chloe pulls me back further into the dark doorway and squeezes me tighter. 'Just let him be,' she whispers.

'*LUCY!*' he screams, sounding more panicked.

William follows and tries to settle James. The bouncers will be here next. This is a nightmare. What's going to happen when Nathan turns up?

I don't have to wait long to find out. I see his Saab turn the corner and he pulls up and gets out. James immediately rushes over to him.

'This is all your fault!' he yells, as I break away from Chloe.

'Lucy . . .' James breathes with relief when he sees me, but I run to Nathan.

'Get away from her, *mate*,' James says, maliciously.

'Lucy, get in the car,' Nathan tells me calmly.

'Don't you fucking tell her what to do!' James shouts, shoving Nathan in the chest. William steps in but James turns to push him away too, then he spins around and swings at Nathan, hitting his temple with an almighty thud. Nathan stumbles backwards.

'You're a fucking whore!' James screams at me.

Nathan gathers his senses and punches James hard in the face. Blood trickles down from James's nose as he staggers and touches his fingers to it with surprise.

'I think you just broke my nose,' he says, shocked. Then two burly bouncers spill out onto the pavement and drag James back. I quickly climb in the car and yell for Nathan to do the same.

'I'll call you!' I shout at Chloe as Nathan starts up the car and drives away.

'Pull over,' I tell him when we've gone half a mile down the road. He flicks his indicator on and slows down until he comes to a standstill on a single yellow line.

'Are you okay?' he asks me.

'I was going to ask you the same question.' I reach out to touch his temple gently. He's going to have a nasty bruise in the morning. He flinches.

'I'm sorry,' I say. 'I'm so sorry.'

'You don't have to be sorry,' he tells me softly as he unbuckles our seat belts. He leans over and puts his arms around me. 'You're shivering,' he says, and turns the heating right up, before relaxing back in his seat. He looks across at me.

'What now?'

'Well, I don't think I'm going home with James to his parents' place tomorrow.' I laugh hollowly.

'Do you want to come back to mine?'

'Actually, what I'd really love is to go home to my family.'

'Okay,' he answers, trying to mask his disappointment.

'But I won't be able to get a train ticket . . .' I add.

'Can I drive you?' he asks, hope filling his eyes.

'Would you?' I question, tears filling mine.

'Lucy, of course. Will that be okay with your mum and Terry?'

'I'll call her,' I tell him. 'But can we go back to mine quickly and pick up my bag?' Thankfully I packed last night.

Nathan pulls up outside our flat and comes upstairs with me. He takes my suitcase and I grab a few more things, including the velvet box with James's necklace in it. I bring it through to the living room.

'Come on, Lucy,' he urges, 'we should go.'

'Hang on,' I tell him. He stands and watches me gravely as I remove the diamond earrings from my ears and place them in the box next to the necklace. I leave it open on the coffee table. There's no need to write a note. That sight will speak volumes.

Nathan drives north to Archway while I call my mum. I fill her in briefly.

'Nathan's bringing me home,' I say finally. 'Can he stay with us for Christmas?' I feel awkward as Nathan can hear everything I'm saying.

'Of course he can, love. Of course he can.'

'Thanks, Mum.' My eyes well up again.

'Do you want me to make up the spare room for him?' she asks drily. 'Or will he sleep in yours?'

'Er,' I peek across at Nathan. 'Maybe the spare for now, thanks . . .'

He grins at me cheekily and the butterflies awake in my stomach.

I switch off my phone in case James calls and then wait in the car while Nathan runs into his flatshare to pack a bag.

'Were your flatmates okay about you not being around for Christmas?' I ask when he gets back.

'Yeah.' He laughs self-consciously.

'What?'

'Richard told me he'll be happy not to see my miserable mug around. I've been destroying his and Ally's festive cheer, apparently.'

I concentrate on navigating until we hit the motorway along with thousands of other Londoners heading to the country for Christmas.

'Do you want to tell me what happened?' Nathan asks finally, as I put the map down; we'll be on the motorway for a while now.

I look across at him in the darkness and can barely believe he's coming home with me for Christmas. I remember he's going home himself soon and my stomach freefalls. But I can't think of that now. We have two weeks left together; I want to make them last.

'Lucy?' he asks me gently, and I realise I haven't answered his question.

'Yes, sorry,' I reply, and fill him in on the night's events.

He shakes his head in dismay when I've finished. 'Are you okay?' he glances across at me.

'I am. I feel surprisingly okay.'

James and I would have broken up sooner or later, I know that now. Surely it was only a matter of time before I found out the truth about him . . . I should feel worse about what he's done to me, but I don't. Oh, I know it will get messy. We're going to have to sort out the flat and that will be a nightmare, but it can wait. Right now I refuse to waste a single minute with my sexy, messy-haired surfer.

Chapter 27

We arrive in Dunster close to midnight after almost five hours of Christmas traffic. I dozed off on the way here but poor Nathan looks shattered. The house is dark, and as I search for my set of keys in my bag, Mum opens the door in her dressing gown.

'Lucy.' She gives me a tight hug before turning to Nathan. 'Diane,' she introduces herself.

'We've met.' He smiles. 'Once or twice before. When we were kids,' he explains.

'Oh, have we? I'm sorry.'

'Don't worry, Mum.' I grin. 'He's changed quite a bit since then.'

Mum offers to get us something to drink, but we just want to crash out so she leads the way to Nathan's room on the first floor and goes back into her bedroom across the landing.

'Will you be okay?' I ask Nathan from the doorway.

'Yeah, of course. I'll see you in the morning, yeah?'

'Bright and early.'

'How early? Will you knock on my door? I don't want to sleep in and make a bad impression.' He nods towards Mum and Terry's bedroom.

Ah, bless him. I assure him I will, before closing the door gently behind me and going upstairs to my room.

I wake up at 7.30 the next morning and my excitement about Nathan sleeping on the floor below cancels out for the moment the bad feeling I have about James. I have a shower, then attempt to cover up the bags under my eyes with make-up. I opt for dark blue Diesel jeans and a fitted black jumper and pull my hair back up into a high ponytail. Then I change my mind and take my hair down again. When I'm ready, I go down one flight of stairs and knock on Nathan's door.

'I'm awake,' he calls from inside. 'I'll be out in a minute.'

'I'll see you in the kitchen!' I whisper loudly.

Mum, Terry, Tom and Meg are already sitting around the table. Meg's parents are abroad and she was going to be in the UK alone for Christmas. Tom's overjoyed that she's joining us.

'Hey,' Tom says affectionately and gets up to give me a hug, as does Terry. Meg smiles sympathetically from the table. I'm guessing Mum filled everyone in last night, which is fine by me. I don't want to go through it all again.

'Where's Nick?' I ask.

'Still in bed. Big night down the local,' Tom explains.

I pull up a chair. Moments later Nathan comes down the stairs and I jump back up again. Oh, my God, he's here with my family!

'Hello, Nathan.' My mum smiles. 'Did you sleep well?'

'Yeah, good thanks,' he replies, a touch nervously.

I introduce everyone and they're all welcoming and friendly. No one mentions the bruise on Nathan's temple.

'Would you like a tea or coffee, dear?' my mum asks, and we sit down and help ourselves to local farm-shop bacon, and eggs courtesy of our hens in the back garden.

After a while, Nick stumbles down the stairs. Nathan stands up to shake his hand as I introduce them.

'Fucking hell, mate,' Nick says when he clocks Nathan's bruise.

'Nick, don't use that sort of language in this house, please!' Terry admonishes.

'Chill out, Dad,' Nick replies and turns back to Nathan's bruise. 'That looks bad. Aren't you going to say, "You should see the other guy"?'

'The "other guy" is my boyfriend,' I say mock-prudely, before adding, 'well, *ex* boyfriend. And I think Nathan broke his nose.'

'Shit!' Nick exclaims. 'Way to go, mate.' He grabs Nathan's hand again and starts shaking it. Nathan looks uncomfortable.

'Nick!' Mum exclaims. 'Don't be so tasteless.'

'Sorry, Diane, but if I'd been there I would have done a fuckload more than break his nose.'

'*NICK!*' Terry shouts, but Nick just grins as his dad raises his eyes to the heavens in despair.

Later that morning, after Mum and Terry have left for work and Nathan is showered and ready, I take him outside to see the goats.

'You haven't had a cigarette since you've been here, have you?' I comment.

'Nah. I really will give up this time. This place is awesome,' he says as he gazes around at the green hills and over at the castle amid the trees.

'We'll have to go for a drive to Exmoor National Park sometime,' I suggest. 'Maybe tomorrow? You haven't been out to the country much since you arrived, have you?'

'No, not really. I haven't done anywhere near as much as I meant to. Had all these plans to go for weekend trips to Europe but it just never panned out that way.'

'Why not?'

'Wanted to see you, Luce,' he says, eyes meeting mine.

'Is that your car?' Nick interrupts, walking down the path towards us.

'The Saab? Yeah,' Nathan answers.

'Cool car, man.'

'It's for sale; I'm going back to Australia in a couple of weeks.'

'I want it!' I interject, before Nick can say anything.

'Hey?' Nathan laughs.

'I want it,' I repeat. 'I'll buy it from you.'

'I'm not going to sell it to you, am I?' He grins, touching his hand to my cheek. I swear my heart skips a beat.

'Why not?' I ask.

'You can have it, Luce. If you want it.'

'No, I'll buy it!' I insist.

'No way.' He laughs. 'It's yours.'

'Whatever . . .' Nick mutters and heads off back down the path.

Nathan and I haven't kissed yet. In fact we've barely touched. Not since last Wednesday, up against the wall of the flat. We both know it's inevitable but we just need the right time without any interruptions. The anticipation is making me nervous.

'Meg, Nick and I are off down the High Street if you guys want to come?' Tom calls from the front door.

'Sure . . .'

As we walk down the lane to join them I realise I should text Chloe, tell her I'm alright. But as I type a message my phone starts to beep and buzz, alerting me to various messages that have come in since I switched it off last night. Nathan and I look at each other, edgily.

'I don't want to speak to him,' I say. 'I'm deleting them all.' I actually mean it.

We wander along the street and around the village shops until eventually we end up in a pub. The five of us pull up chairs in front of the log fire.

Just as I sit down, my phone starts to ring. I press divert. Seconds later it rings again. I'm about to switch it off when Tom pipes up: 'You're going to have to talk to him sometime, Lucy.'

'Oh, for God's sake!' I shout at my phone.

'What do you want?' I ask coldly down the receiver.

'Lucy! At last! Where are you?'

'I don't want to talk to you, James. Don't call me again.'

'Hang on! Baby, please!'

'Don't "baby" me, you tosser.'

'Lucy, come on, this is all a big mix-up.'

'Ha!' I can't believe he has the cheek to say it. 'I mean it, James. We're finished. You'll be hearing from my lawyer about the flat.' I look over at Meg, who's trying to keep a straight face. I don't actually have a lawyer. Well, not anymore anyway.

'Lucy, wait!' He's desperate. 'There really has been a mistake. Zoe was a nutcase. She's been obsessed with me for ages!'

'Oh, give the man an Oscar, for crying out loud.' A thought suddenly occurs to me. 'Were you shagging her on holiday?' I ask. 'In Spain? Is that why Jeremy said you'd all been having Sex On The Beach?'

'What?'

'Was that his pathetic little in-jokey way of implying what you'd been up to? Shit, was that why there was *sand* in the bed?'

'Don't be ridiculous, Lucy.'

'Don't you bloody tell me not to be ridiculous. Were you shagging her when her *boyfriend* was there? Did he even cheat on her? You sick bastard!'

'I haven't been shagging her, for Christ's sake!'

I let out a brittle, hollow laugh. 'It's over, James, it's over. You are an astoundingly good liar, but I have NEVER trusted you. And there's a reason for that. The least you can do now is be honest with me so I can still have a grain of respect for you.'

'I am being honest with you!'

'Bull*shit*! If you don't respect me enough to tell me the truth – *right now* – then I never want to speak to you again. Ever!' I wait, giving him a moment.

'Lucy, I *am* telling you the tru—' I slam the phone shut. Then I open the battery compartment and pull out the SIM card, Nathan, Nick, Tom and Meg watching every step of the way. Taking the tiny piece of plastic between my thumb and middle finger, I aim and flick it onto the fire.

No point in wasting a phone, but if I never want to speak to the wanker again, I'm sure as hell going to need a new phone number.

I turn and look at the faces around the table.

'Fuck me, sis, way to go!' Nick high-fives me. 'Sorry, but I always thought he was a twat.'

'I told you they never forgave him for the Big Feet debacle,' I say to Nathan wryly.

Nick laughs. 'Nah, it wasn't just that. I didn't trust him. He was a bullshitter.'

373

'I can go and pick up some things from your flat when I'm back in London, if that will help?' Tom offers kindly.

'Yeah, me too,' Nick agrees.

'Thank you.' I smile at my lovely stepbrothers.

'I think I need a joke after that,' I say, turning to Nathan.

'I've got one!' Nick interjects.

'Oh, here we go . . .' I groan.

'What's the last thing that goes through a fly's mind before it splats on your windscreen?' Nick asks, before continuing. 'Its arsehole!'

'Eww!' I laugh.

'How do you make a hotdog stand?' Meg shouts. 'Steal his chair!'

'What do you call a deer with no eyes?' Tom yells. 'No idea!'

Nathan nudges me. 'We're in good company.'

After the pub I take Nathan for a walk around the castle grounds. The others sense we want to be left alone and don't attempt to join us.

'Those guys are great,' he chuckles.

'They like you too.' And it's true. My stepbrothers seem to click far better with Nathan than they ever did with James.

We climb up the hill towards the castle and are both huffing and puffing after a couple of minutes.

'And you thought the hills in Manly were steep,' I pant.

'Yeah,' Nathan agrees. 'At least you got a view of the ocean from the top.'

'What do you call that?' I point over to my left.

'Shit! Is that the . . .'

'Ocean, yes.' I laugh. It's such a dark day that you can barely make it out, yet there it is, a bluey-grey expanse, stretching out from some of the greenest fields I think I've ever seen.

'Wow.' He takes in the view.

We wander around the castle and then slowly begin to make our way back down the tiny paths, too narrow to walk side by side. The sound of the river thunders up from down below as we head towards it, me treading gingerly in front of Nathan so as to avoid slipping on the wet leaves under our feet.

At the bottom of the path is a bridge leading to a pretty green pasture. Behind us the castle towers above at the top of the hill. I lean over to the right of the stone arch and watch the water quietly rush towards the bridge before going to the other side where it churns and tumbles over the rocks below. I look up and Nathan is leaning against the arch with his hands in his pockets, regarding me with amusement.

'What?' I walk over to stand in front of him.

'Are you okay?' he asks, his face growing serious. 'You seem it. But are you really?'

'I'm fine,' I tell him, folding my arms across my chest. I take in his bruise and suddenly feel emotional. I look away and swallow quickly. Then I turn back to him.

'I'm so sorry. I'm sorry he hit you. I'm sorry you had to get involved.' I shake my head angrily to try to stop the oncoming tears. It's easier if I don't look at him.

'Hey, it's alright,' he says, taking his hands out of his pockets and hooking them through my belt loops. He pulls me towards him, but not so close that we're touching. 'I'm sorry about what he did to you. I can't *believe* what he did to you.'

I take a deep breath, willing myself to calm down. I'm fine, I'm fine, I tell myself. It's all okay.

Oh, who am I kidding? I'm obviously in denial. It kills me that I'll never know the extent to which James lied to me, or the extent to which he cheated on me with Zoe – and others if what William said about his reputation is true. We were together for four years and I now realise I didn't know him at all. At least I can take some comfort from the fact that I never really trusted him. Next time I'll listen to my instincts. But I can evaluate my feelings later, when Nathan's gone. I refuse to spoil the here and now.

I meet his eyes. He's so close, leaning there against the stone arch in his beige cords and black coat, unbuttoned to reveal a hooded grey top underneath.

'I've still got your note, you know,' he says.

'What note?' I'm confused.

'The one you wrote for me on the first day I got here.'

He gets his wallet out of his back pocket and pulls out the Café Rouge receipt. It's signed '*Love, Lucy xxx*'. I can't believe he's kept it all this time.

'It's the only thing I have with your handwriting,' he explains shyly. 'Do you know how relieved I was to finally see those wedding photos?'

'Me too!' I exclaim. 'I was so distraught when I realised I didn't have a single picture of you.' He puts his wallet back into his pocket and smiles at me.

My gaze falls on the dark stubble grazing his jaw, and then to his sexy mouth and those lips. God, those lips . . . I look up into his eyes as he puts his hands on my waist and draws me to him.

He kisses me, slowly at first, then more passionately. I slide my hands up inside his jumper and he takes a sharp intake of breath at my cold fingers. I don't think I've ever wanted anything as much as I want him, right now.

'I love you,' he gasps, tearing his lips away.

'What did you say?' I ask. I heard him, of course. I just want to hear him say it again.

'I love you,' he repeats, kissing my lips softly.

'I love you too,' I respond, as my heart bubbles over with happiness and I begin to laugh.

'What?' He laughs back at me.

'I just love you, so much. And I can't believe you love me.'

'Well, I do.' He chuckles, and pulls me back to him. He cups my face and kisses me again, but I have to stop because I can't stop laughing.

'You remind me of my mum, you know.'

'Sorry?' I'm completely taken aback.

'Your laugh. You have the same laugh. The same sense of humour.'

I look at him in awe. It's easily the best compliment anyone has ever paid me.

'Hey, is that bamboo?' he says suddenly.

I follow his gaze to the cluster by the riverbank. It's not like the bamboo in Sydney, at the wedding; this is much smaller and more densely packed. A tiny dark pathway leads us underneath it and we stand there, surrounded by the shoots in the darkness.

'Do you remember that day?' I ask him. 'In the Botanic Gardens?'

'How could I forget?'

'I wanted you to kiss me so much . . .'

'I wanted to kiss you,' he replies. 'But I couldn't. I couldn't be the other guy.'

'I know.' I put my arms back around his waist. 'But you're not the other guy anymore.'

'No. Now I'm *the* guy,' he says jokily, and I start to laugh until he kisses me again. It's so dark down here and so secluded. I feel like no one would ever find us. Suddenly I catch something out of the corner of my eye.

'Look,' I whisper.

'Is that . . . *snow?*' he asks in wonder.

This is ridiculous; it's just too idyllic. He leads me back up the path towards the bridge and gazes upwards as big heavy snowflakes fall down onto his face.

'I've never seen the snow!' he gasps and I'm overwhelmed with love for him. His expression is adorable.

I laugh. 'Come on, let's get home and have a hot chocolate by the window.'

That night my entire family congregates in the living room in front of the fire to play Pictionary. And hilariously, Nathan and I wipe the floor with the competition. My stepbrothers think we must be cheating because I can't draw to save my life, but some-how Nathan seems to know when a round blob with lines coming out of it is meant to be a horse. He, on the other hand, turns out to be a bit of an artist. I can't help but feel smug thinking that general knowledge, and all those Trivial Pursuit questions that James got right, can be learnt, but raw talent? Well, you've either got it or you haven't.

Eventually the others head off to bed. 'Mum, will you wake us up in the morning?' I ask. 'We want to get up and go for a drive if the snow's not too deep.'

'Sure,' she answers, closing the door behind her and leaving Nathan and me alone together on the sofa. The fire has burnt down to its embers, but there's still a warm orange glow emitting from the fireplace and the lights glimmer prettily on the Christmas tree. Nathan kisses the top of my head and I snuggle into his chest. I can't get close enough to him. I don't know if I'll ever be able to get close enough.

'You're a wriggly thing.' He chuckles, and I pull away to look up at him. He holds my face and kisses me.

Our kiss deepens as I climb onto his lap and he runs his hands up my top. I reach down to touch him.

This is it. I'm going to make love to him tonight.

'Wait,' he whispers urgently. 'We can't do this with your parents next door.'

'Shall we go to my room?' I don't have to ask twice.

In the darkness of my bedroom he lifts my jumper over my head and unclasps my bra, while I turn my attention to his belt buckle. He doesn't stop kissing me and I know now that he's better than James, a million times better. I'm so turned on I feel giddy.

'I love you, Lucy,' he says, running his hands over my naked body.

'I love you too. I *want* you. Don't make me wait any longer.'

He gently eases me back onto the bed so he's above me and kisses my lips, passionately. I pull him into me, gasping and arching my back as he does so.

This is as close to him as I'm ever going to get, I think. And it's perfect.

Afterwards I cry, and he holds me tight, understanding that my tears are nothing for him to worry about. When they've stopped falling he kisses me again. I want to make love to him for the rest of my life.

The following morning we wake up together and lie there for a few minutes just staring into each other's eyes.

'Will you play your guitar for me one day?' I ask eventually.

'I don't know about that.'

'Please . . .'

'Alright. I suppose I might do.' He smiles.

'Thank you,' I say happily. 'Hey, we should go to Newquay one day. Take you surfing.'

'That'd be cool,' he agrees.

It's Christmas morning and we're all in the living room, drinking hot chocolate and looking at our presents. We can barely see the carpet, it's so covered with wrapping paper. Yesterday the snow had finally thawed enough for our drive around Exmoor. And then this morning Nathan took me outside and showed me his car. Well, *my* car. He'd tied red ribbons to the tiny wipers on the front headlights. But that wasn't my only Christmas present; he also bought me a silver bracelet from the local jeweller's so I can wear my Concorde charm.

As for what I got him . . .

Over the last couple of days I've been sneaking away to use Tom's laptop and type up all the jokes that Nathan and I have told each other – as best as I can remember them. I presented *Elephant Jokes and Other Stories* to him this morning and he seemed genuinely touched. We'll add all the crappy Christmas cracker jokes to it later.

But I'm not a total cheapskate. I also managed to find us a couple of last-minute flights to Venice and that is where we'll be for New Year's Eve.

Nathan's phone rings. 'Sorry, I've got to take this,' he says to my family. 'It'll be my brother.'

'He's been waiting for him to call,' I explain as Nathan heads into his room across the landing.

After ten minutes or so, he reappears and calls to me from the doorway. 'Lucy? It's Molly. She wants to talk to you.'

Oh, my goodness, this is it. I take the phone from him nervously and head upstairs to my bedroom.

'Hello?'

'Lucy! What's going on? I tried to call your phone and it's dead and then Nathan says he's with you but he wouldn't tell me anything else!' Molly squeaks down the line. Cheers for that, Nathan, I grin. Leave me to do your dirty work.

'Lucy!'

'I'm here,' I say.

'What's going on?' Molly demands.

'Okay.' I take a deep breath and then calmly speak. 'Nathan and I, well, we're together.'

'*What?*' she exclaims.

'Molly, please, don't say anything. Don't laugh, don't snort, don't make any funny jokes. I'm in love with Nathan and I have been for ages. I fell in love with him in Sydney.'

Silence.

'Molly?'

'Bloody *hell*!' she erupts. 'Why didn't you tell me before?'

'I couldn't. I thought you'd laugh. I thought you wouldn't approve. I didn't think you'd understand.'

'Lucy, of course I would have understood. Well, maybe not at first,' she concedes. 'But you're my best friend. You could have made me understand.'

'I know. But . . . Oh, I don't know, Molly. It's been very confusing, that's all.'

'What happened to James?' she asks.

'Well . . .' I fill her in, as succinctly as I can. We can talk in

381

more detail some other time, but right now she's ringing Nathan's mobile.

Finally she says, 'Shit! If you marry Nathan we'll practically be sisters!'

I squeal with laughter at the thought.

'We'll have the same surname,' she cries. 'It'll be like one big triumphant Wilson family.' I'm still laughing, loving the idea.

'Speaking of family . . .' she says, and tells me what I already know about her pregnancy. I feign surprise, which isn't hard because I'm still over the moon. She's had her twelve-week scan now and all the signs are good; the baby appears healthy.

'I'm so pleased for you two.' I smile.

'Well, you'd better come back for the birth,' she insists. 'If not before . . .' It's a loaded comment and I don't feel like I can ignore it.

'I don't know what I'm going to do yet, Molly. But if I do decide to come back to Australia in the near future, you'll be the first to know.'

That night, up in my bedroom, after we've all returned home from a Christmas pint down the pub, Nathan helps me out of my coat before turning his attention to my jumper, followed by my jeans and T-shirt.

'You've got so many layers on,' he groans. 'This would be so much easier in Sydney.'

'Was that the case when you were with Amy?' Oh, shit, did I just say that out loud? I don't want him to think I'm a bunny boiler.

'Ah, Luce . . . Does the thing with Amy still bother you?' I never told him it bothered me in the first place, but he just seems to sense these things. 'Because you can ask me anything you want and I'll tell you honestly,' he says.

Just him saying that suddenly makes me feel like I don't need to. Oh, I might take him up on it one of these days but, right now, he's said the very thing to reassure me. It's secrets and silence that I can't stand.

'It's okay.' I smile. 'But thank you.'

'Right! Let's get these last layers off, then.' He grins.

Afterwards, lying in the crook of his arm, I stare up at the ceiling feeling a confusing mix of emotions. I've never felt so euphoric. Having him here, in Somerset, with my family . . . But we're going to lose all this and that devastates me. A few tears silently make their way down my cheeks.

'Hey,' he says softly, and bends down to kiss them away. I turn to face him.

'I want you to see England in the spring, in the summer. If you stay, we could come here whenever we want. We could go surfing in Cornwall. We could get a flat together and travel to Europe on weekends.'

'But if you come home with me,' he counters, 'we could buy a house by the ocean and do it up. We could go surfing every day. And we'll be close enough to see our niece or nephew grow up.'

'Oh, God, I can't bear it! I don't want to lose you. I don't want you to leave. It's too soon! But I love my job, and moving to Australia right now . . .'

He looks at me sadly. 'If I stayed, it wouldn't be forever, Luce.'

'But if you stayed, even for six months, I might be ready then. I can't bear the thought of you going in just over a week.' Tears spill down my face and he wipes them away.

'I love you, Lucy. I really, really love you. You and I are meant to be together, no matter what. I know it. But I'm worried about you. If you come back to Australia with me, you'll never be truly happy. A part of you will always be in England, and likewise if you stay, I think a piece of you will always be in Sydney. Your heart will always be torn between two countries, two sets of friends and family . . .'

Suddenly a sense of calm settles over me and I feel I can see clearly for the very first time.

'My heart is here, with you,' I say, resting my hand on his beautiful chest. 'As long as I'm with you, everything else will fall into place.'

Lucy in the Sky

Epilogue

The sky and the long bank of clouds melt into one another, blue into paler blue. To my left, Nathan sleeps beside me, his head turned towards mine, mouth slightly open. I can almost hear his breathing as I watch the gentle rise and fall of his chest. I take his right hand with my left and he stirs, turning away. The bright morning sunlight hits the aeroplane wing and it bounces off, sending a white shaft piercing through my window. The ring on my finger sparkles, like a star in a midnight sky, a wave on a sunlit ocean, a diamond solitaire.

A diamond.

And this time, I smile to myself, I know it's real.

Acknowledgements

First and foremost I would like to thank my editor, Suzanne Baboneau. I never thought I'd enjoy the *whole* writing process as much as I have and that's to a large extent down to you. Thanks to Julie Wright for her brilliantly crap jokes and to everyone at Simon & Schuster for their tireless efforts and enthusiasm. Above all, thank you to Nigel Stoneman, friend first and now my publicist, and without whom this book may never have happened. You are such a Hornbag.

Thank you to all my friends and colleagues at *heat*, but especially Mark Frith: officially the Best Boss Ever. Thank you to Giulia Cassini for her help with all things Italian (and, to some extent, Russian . . .), and to Lauren Libin for inspiring the 'Mockah Chockah' madness and who still insists we could make it a hit. (No, Lauren, no.) And thank you so much to Freya North and Clare Pollock for their invaluable advice regarding all things publishing.

Thank you to all my friends and family on both sides of the world, but especially Bridie Tonkin, whose love and encouragement since childhood literally blows me away. Thank you to my brother, Kerrin Schuppan, who I've always known was a genius, not least when he came up with the title and some great ideas for my book. Love you, mate. Thank you to my mum, Jenny Schuppan – a friend as much as a parent – for everything, including driving me around Sydney while we worked out where Lucy and her pals lived and partied! And thank you to my dad, Vern Schuppan. I wrote a whole book without getting writer's block and now I simply cannot find the words that will do justice to your and Mum's love, support and encouragement over the years. You're my inspiration and I'm so proud of you both.

Last but not least, thank you to my husband, Greg Toon. I can't believe you actually *read* a chick lit book for me, let alone gave me such incredibly helpful advice. You know your opinion means more to me than anyone's. Love you, MC.